JOINED UP

JOINED UP

DAMIEN MOSLEY

Indie Novella

First published in Great Britain in 2021 by Indie Novella Ltd.

INDIE NOVELLA www.indienovella.co.uk

A CIP catalogue record for this title is available from the British Library

Paperback ISBN 978 1 739 95990 6

Printed and bound by Clays Ltd in the United Kingdom.

Indie Novella is committed to a sustainable future for our readers and the world in which we live. All paper used are natural, renewable and sustainable products.

For Jess

CHAPTER 1

CHOCOLATE

I started seeing Camille six months ago when she replied to an email initially intended for Anthony. The email was more of an enquiring nature: a 'top-up' and to catch up with Anthony five years after our last session. As I wrote it, I told myself I didn't need therapy again; it was more a one-off because I could do with the advice and for someone I trusted to reassure me. However, by the time Camille and I sat opposite each other, I had known nothing like it. Halfway through our first session, she handed me a question-naire. The last question asked if I had considered harming myself or ending my life. My answer, 'Yes, most days,' triggered the start of a beautiful friendship.

The thing about depression is that it is a little bit depressing. In a corporate presentation, my friend Jeff once confidently used the immortal closing line, 'in the end, people are people.' The clients loved it but we, his closest friends, would use that line to rib him for the next three and a half years. Jeff 'People Are People' Martin now lives in Seattle and still receives emails from former colleagues asking, 'how's work, buddy, how are the people, are they still people?' The point I make is that to anyone else depression must seem a cop-out – a made-up thing that can be fixed by giving someone a bag of Minstrels and telling them to cheer up. And that can work to an extent. But when you're looking for hemlock online or writing suicide notes to your dead father, then there is probably something deeper going on.

It was Camille who suggested that I meet with Ellie face to face. Before, I would have hidden away and hoped we could brush the situation under the carpet like we had done with every other problem in our family life. I arrived at the café an hour early, partly to mentally prepare and partly because I could not keep my mind on anything else all morning. I had woken up at five. I had tried lying in bed with my eyes closed. I tried reading, meditating, even counting sheep. I ended up going downstairs to make a cup of tea, tiptoeing on our creaky wooden floorboards not to disturb my flat-mate. And long before there was any sign of life, I was out the door, unable to bear another torturous second of waiting.

No one should feel that nervous about meeting their sibling for coffee. Nervous, guilty, and if I was completely honest, more than a little bit resentful. Your older sister finds out you've been contemplating killing yourself, and instead of 'Oh my God, Scott, what's wrong?' she destroys your most treasured possession and calls you a selfish prick. 'Thanks, Ellie,' I wanted to say with cutting sarcasm. But I reverted to the fourteen-year-old boy who had become overawed by the whirlwind of rebellion and anger that was his seventeen-year-old sister and said exactly what I would have said back then – absolutely nothing. Even when she walked out, all I could mumble was 'don't call me a prick.'

The café was on Exmouth Market, or what used to be Exmouth Market before it succumbed to gentrification. Rather than a café, I was in one of the numerous bar-slash-restaurants serving coffee, cocktails, and overpriced 'artisan dishes' which could neither be considered a meal nor a snack. Menus were divided into *Salads and*

Grains, *Small Plates*, *Large Plates*, and included modern classics such as *London halloumi* and *Dingley Dell Farm pork schnitzel*. Did being inside the M25 improve the taste and texture of cheese, or did above average diesel emissions and lack of space enhance the quality of dairy farming? Was ordering schnitzel more satisfying if you were forced to know the origin of the pig whom you had caused to be slaughtered? This might make me sound pedantic, but sometimes I think less is more when it comes to knowing where my food comes from. And perhaps about modern human existence in general.

I chose that specific café because when Ellie would visit me in London ten years ago, it used to be one of our favourite hangouts. Al's Bar, it used to be called, and served lager in plastic glasses at two in the morning and had a tiny basement with an absolutely rammed dancefloor. Now it had a strict policy that a parent or guardian must accompany all twentysomethings and when I popped downstairs to the toilets, I found a giant wood-burning Aga had replaced our dancefloor.

I sat on a long white leather booth with an immaculate, dazzling white table in front of me, surrounded by healthy-looking, presentable, middle-class people in their thirties or forties. Okay, my gripes against gentrification and the middle-class are more than a tad hypocritical. My sister and I grew up in a large detached house in the North London suburbs, and both of us went to a fee-paying, private school. We were probably the first generation to start spending close to five pounds on Starbucks coffee, and years of sheltering from life's problems meant we grew up comparatively healthy looking too. However, what I was not, was presentable. I looked down at myself, and compared to other men around me, all sporting incredibly well-groomed beards and the smart-casual-Sunday-shirt-and-pullover-combos, I genuinely looked scruffy. There was nothing designer about my five-day-old stubble (I was rationing my Gillette Mach 3 as was loath to spend ten pounds on four new blades), and I was still wearing my torn and tattered ten-year-old coat because the jumper I was wearing had some of Tuesday night's curry down the front.

There was another big difference between me and those men with the well-groomed beards and the winter tans, which I imagined resulted from a recent visit to a European ski resort. At that moment in time, in that café on a Sunday morning, none of them were alone. Sitting in the corner with an airy and sunbathed room in front of me, I could see groups of men and women sitting around their tables, all engaged in conversations, laughing, smiling, gesturing, apparently content and unashamedly proud of their place in the universe. And that's where Big Sis should have come in. Stop me looking like a loser in front of the cool kids.

I had brought with me a copy of *The Great Gatsby*. More as a conversation starter than me rereading it. And when I say conversation starter, I mean an elaborate ploy on my part to start us off on a united front and talk about Dad. Obviously, naming me after the author, he was a fan, but Dad also wrote his doctoral thesis on Fitzgerald, and many of his literary review papers centred on the great American novelist who only wrote four novels – to paraphrase a quote from Ellie to Dad from my wonderfully tension-filled teenage years. I then realised that perhaps the book was a bad idea. Our childhoods were privileged. Dad provided us with a big house, good educations, intellectual stimulus, and love and attention. But his one mistake was having Mum leave him and unfortunately, that was something Ellie would not forgive or let him forget. She was a kid, she was angry, but she was deliberately and relentlessly hurtful, and though it might sound trivial, continuous little digs at the great American author were her way of getting back at Dad.

I left *Gatsby* in front of me with my glass of hot chocolate next to it. An ashtray of sugar cubes sat behind them both. I've never claimed to have very adult tastes, and there is probably nothing sadder than a thirty-five-year-old man drinking a child's drink, but it soothes me. The sugar rush and serotonin were comforting, and let's face it, being addicted to sugar and chocolate is a lot less of an issue than me relapsing on gin for breakfast and cocaine as my powder of choice. Well, unless I suffered from type 1 diabetes.

And during my time waiting for Ellie, I had made it to my third hot chocolate – three was too much of a sweet hit even for me so I let the last go cold – and *did* end up rereading half of *Gatsby*.

We were due to meet at eleven, and it was noon by the time I finally got my phone out to text her.

Are you coming? I wrote. I was cradling the phone in front of me, staring at the screen, trying to avoid the fact I could see a rather sheepish, downcast face reflecting off the glass back at me. Immediately, I saw a text bubble appear and the dots of a response being composed.

No.

I waited a few seconds to see if there would be another text bubble. There wasn't.

Where are you? I sent back.

Brighton. Back home.

Thanks for telling me, was my reply.

I like to think I leaned back on the leather booth and rolled my eyes at her distant reply, but I'm guessing I didn't. I do remember that with the sunlight directly flowing into the café and the heating on to combat the cold November day, it had started to feel stuffy, and my face began to feel warm and flushed. I then received another text.

Scott, I really don't care.

It was probably no more than half a minute that I was staring at my phone when I decided I should probably go home too – not much point drinking cold hot chocolate waiting for someone who was in a different county. So I called for the bill. Or at least I tried. When I tried to catch the waitress's eye, I felt my own quickly swell with tears. I looked down and tried to hide my face, pretending to be fixated by *Gatsby*. I could hear people around me continuing to chatter, cups knocking on saucers, and a coffee machine powerfully exhaling steam. But all I could feel were tears involuntarily streaming down my face and a lump developing in my throat. I had not had either sensation in about twenty-five years and had no idea how to stop them. Keeping one hand covering my face, I fumbled for any cash to cover the bill. I then pulled up my jumper to wipe it on the inside and made a rush for the door.

But I didn't make it.

Halfway through my run, I tripped over the leg of a chair and fell crashing to the floor, face first. The next thing I knew, three of the men with well-groomed beards were helping me to my feet and asking me if I was okay. Someone else had passed me a tissue to stop my nose bleeding – at least that was one positive, blood being so less embarrassing than tears. I heard the waitress also say she would get some ice for my lip.

'Thank you. It's okay. You're all very kind,' I repeatedly said before finally managing to back out of the café and walk briskly away with none of my dignity intact and my sister nowhere to be seen.

I didn't realise how much I needed Ellie until then. To be frank, I don't think I even liked her that much, and feel I'm the one with ample grounds for calling *her* a prick for the shit she's done over the years. She was the world's worst sister. Vicky, my ex-fiancée, despised her. She said she was volatile, selfish, and had a pathological need to hate me. Ironically, Vicky had primarily known Ellie when she and I were probably at our closest – those Exmouth

Market days of late nights and bar-hopping, when I was twenty-six. It was perhaps the best year of my life. I was engaged to the girl I had loved since sixth form, and my super-cool, music-journalist older sister, finally wanted to hang out with me.

When I was fourteen, she couldn't wait to be away from us – me, Dad, and our house in Wood Green, North London. Ellie had been offered places to study music at the Royal College of Music, the Royal Academy of Music, and Guildhall School of Music, and she turned them all down to leave London for the West Country and Bristol. At that age, I hadn't fully understood the implications of this shunning. I had thought her university choices in keeping with her subversive nature and anything elitist she would duly turn her back on. That was why, on the day she left, when she was packing up her room, I had quietly hoped that she would be back at weekends and tell me about all her new adventures. But as her younger brother, I thought it was my duty to mask any acknowledgement of missing her with nonchalance and inane banter.

I remember the moment well. I was standing awkwardly in the doorway of her room, staring at all the crates and boxes, surprised that Ellie was taking absolutely everything and leaving a shell behind – no evidence of her whatsoever. She had her back to me, standing at her bookshelves, taking down her biographies of Cobain and Dylan. 'You know, I think I might turn this into a games room when you're gone.' In my head, I thought it a way to break the ice. Ellie would laugh, sit me down on the stripped bed, and give me an inspiring, heartfelt pep talk – she would tell me that she would miss me and that I would be alright, like in an American teen drama. Instead, Ellie kept packing up her books.

'If it makes up for the fact you're never going to lose your virginity. Sure.'

With the pep talk pretty much over, I went back to my room and sat on my bed. On it, I had placed a newly made wooden box –

by me in woodwork class – with a sliding lid and 'Ellie' engraved on it. I knew it was lame but I had spent the previous four weeks trying to craft it. It was for her to carry her pencils and pens for when she would compose music. I just sat there staring at it, thinking how stupid I had been to make it for her. Then I heard the front door slam. I got up and ran to the window seeing Ellie getting into the movers' van. I ran out of my room into hers. All the boxes were gone. I ran downstairs, opening the front door, but the van was pulling away with Ellie in the passenger seat. Our eyes met. She then looked away and put her hand to cover the side of her face. I was fourteen years old. The next time I saw Ellie, I was seventeen. So much for weekend visits.

In hindsight, Ellie might have had a point about never losing my virginity. When I had suggested a games room, I wasn't talking about a pool table, table football, or even multi-player shoot 'em up video games. I was talking about Orcs, Druids, Dwarfs, and Elfin Warriors, all hand-painted miniature models, laid out across a board on the floor that my dad had helped me paint so it resembled Middle-Earth. Yes, in my early teens, I was heavily into Games Workshop and fantasy-adventure strategy games. I like to think I've grown as a person since and developed some less 'introverted' and more outdoorsy pastimes. I'd also like to think that my and Ellie's relationship has also evolved over time, perhaps taking longer than it should have, to the point that now in our thirties, I am godfather to both her children, Millie and Ed. Though the honour is a slightly dubious one seeing that both Ellie and her husband, Mike are agnostic and, as Ellie put it, 'we only took part in the façade as Dad said he'd pay for the do and Millie would get some less shit presents than the crap we can afford.'

The do was lovely, to be fair, both for Millie and then for Ed two and a half years later. Millie is now four and what I remember most was Ellie arriving at Dad's in a mood after a drive in heavy traffic, trying to force the pram and Millie's stuff through the door single-handedly while virtually kicking off Mike's attempts to help. She then walked into the living room, saw all the balloons, cake, and the piled-up immaculately wrapped gifts, and burst into tears. I think that was the second of only three times I had seen her cry. I guess that was one of the few things we had in common. The Roberts kids – Ellie and Scott Roberts – waiting until their mid-thirties before letting out a show of emotion.

And perhaps Ellie also had a point about not showing up to the café. The last year had not been the easiest for either of us. As I left the café on Exmouth Market, I felt my feet moving faster and faster, not just taking me away from the scene of my lost dignity but breaking into a run and running away from... the past? Myself? Ellie? I honestly did not know. And that was extremely frustrating since I was hoping that these were the types of questions I would find myself answering after six months of therapy. But whatever animosity I held for my sister and what grudges she held for me, were not merely a case of suppressed resentment from our formative years. Obviously, that was a contributing factor, but the roots of our current difficulties resided in the events of the last twelve months.

Where my feet did find themselves running to that day, at least eventually, was Stockwell allotments in South London, where I was late for my first day of work.

The Joneses were there already, Mr Jones – Ronnie – out with his fork digging up the turf.

'There you are!' he called over to me as his wife, Judith, looked up with a string of weeds in her hand. 'I thought you'd stood us up!' They chuckled to themselves as I tried to smile apologetically.

'Sorry, got stuck at something north of the river.'

'Where? North of what? Never heard of it!'

I had met the Joneses during that summer, just down the road at Ruskin Park Community Gardens. After a lifetime living in the part of the world which Mr Jones had claimed never to have heard of, I had found myself living for the first time in South London. I shared a flat with a flatmate I hardly knew, and who seemed quite happy to maintain that set of circumstances, and as already alluded to, I was not in the healthiest of mindsets. I found myself spending a lot of my free time wandering Ruskin Park. I would while away the evenings and weekends sitting on a bench in front of a hidden set of gardens, carefully secluded by hedgerow, so I could be alone. Until one day, I wasn't alone. A dozen or so people of my parents' generation had gathered out among the flowers and shrubs, with gardening gloves on and trowels in hand.

'Might never happen,' shouted a voice from among the plants. A man with short white hair and tanned, muscular arms stood mopping his brow, looking over at me. I looked to my left and right to see who else he could be addressing.

'Kind of already has.' I tried to smile back politely.

'Don't tell me. Lad your age, must be girl trouble.'

And he was right. Though my relationship with my sister was not exactly rosy back then either, my descent from depressed into *depression* was triggered by an affair of the heart. Her name was Sarah. And not only had she broken my heart, but she managed to flip a switch in my brain that I could not seem to un-switch.

I say *she* broke my heart, and *she* flipped the switch. In reality, one person rarely holds that power over another. And I can't even say she was the love of my life, considering I was engaged eight years earlier to the *real* love of my life.

The entirety of our physical relationship consisted of one kiss.

'Nice garden,' I called back. 'Is this...' I was just trying to make polite conversation and avoid his question. 'Is this all *your* work?'

'Friends of Ruskin Park. Community Gardens. These, and the veg and herb ones round the back. Giving these a tidy today.'

'I like the hibiscus shrubs.' I nodded to a small bush of yellow flowers by his feet.

'Good eye, lad. Planted those myself. You much of a gardener, then?'

I would not say it was from altruistic motives I took Ronnie up on his offer of putting on a pair of gloves and giving the Friends of Ruskin Park a hand that day – I felt too socially awkward to say no. And when Ronnie asked if I wanted to come along the next day I started showing up every day, even skipping out on work early to do so, largely because it also meant avoiding Sarah.

'So, it's pretty much gone to pot,' said Ronnie, resting his foot on his fork and looking around at the large patch of allotment. 'We really should have been able to do both this and Ruskin, but refurbing the community gardens got a bit out of hand – saying that, I'm not complaining about the result.'

'I bloody am, Ronnie. This should have been us unwinding in your retirement, not you working yourself up into another heart attack!' Judith stood up.

'Oh, you do exaggerate.'

'Scott, what my husband and I would like is if you took the reins here over the winter. Ronnie can keep Chair of the Committee at Ruskin and lay down the law there, but I don't want him coming back here till at least the spring. There's beds needing building, soil needs replacing, weeding, pretty much everything, and I don't want this one sneaking back here. Three afternoons a week, and we're paying you the going rate. No charity needed here, thank you very much.'

Judith was not one to argue with, and Ronnie stood there, grinning like a schoolboy.

'I guess we've been told, lad.'

The first thing the Jones showed me was the shed. Anyone who spent their childhood watching old VHSs of *Dr Who* would be familiar with the acronym TARDIS: *Time And Relative Dimension In Space*. But as there are fewer and fewer of us who admit to being old school *Whovians*, let's just say their shed was surprisingly bigger on the inside than it looked on the outside. As well as containing every form of gardening implement imaginable, there was also a kettle, two armchairs, and what looked like a home brewing kit in the corner.

'Also, Scott, feel free to borrow anything you need to take around with you. If you're to get your business off the ground, you're going to need a few more little patches. We're happy to help any way we can.'

Judith had a point. One that should keep a person awake at night. Today was my first day self-employed – no more working for someone else. And no more being paid for forty hours a week, sick pay, holiday allowance, or job security. At that moment, I had a total of one customer and ten hours' worth of work to get me started.

'I've designed some fliers,' I said quietly.

'Well, get them out there, lad! Me and Judith'll put the word around. Don't underestimate the value of good old word of mouth. Though, I can't guarantee you it will compare with your fancy-arsed banker wages.' He gave me a nudge and chuckled to himself as we stepped back out of the shed.

On that first afternoon at the Ruskin Park gardens, Ronnie had asked me,

'What do you do then? A well-spoken lad like yourself? Lawyer, banker, poncey beer maker?'

I didn't consider myself that well-spoken. Ellie and I had gone to a private school but it was down the road from our house in Wood Green and was more arty and weird than posh. But Ronnie did have one thing right.

'I used to work in banking. But quite a few years ago. I've been abroad the last few years.'

'Abroad? I've heard of that. 'Em foreigners come from there?'

'He's pulling your leg,' shouted a lady I would come to know as Judith. 'We're all very multicultural around here and very much proud of it. My parents were both Polish.'

Ronnie was practically bent double laughing as Judith shook her head and went back to her flowerbed.

'Whereabouts then?'

'The Middle East and Africa. Doing some... charity work.'

I hated the term 'charity work'. It sounded more selfless than it was. For the last four years, I worked in international development, doing project work for an organisation that technically was a charity. It was a job that got me out of London at a time I was struggling with a series of temptations.

'So where does a banker learn about hibiscuses? Your parents keen gardeners?'

'I helped run a farming project in Burundi. There's a lot of hills there. Surprisingly cold and wet at times. Like here. And before that, I would build little rooftop gardens and courtyards wherever I stayed in the Middle East. I did an online landscaping course to help pass the time.'

'So what brings you back here?'

We packed up at the allotment as the November sun began to set, the tools back in the shed, the large padlock on the door.

'So, is this you done with charity work?' Judith was fastening up her coat as we prepared to leave. 'You could always go back, I assume, if you get fed up doing other people's gardens.'

'I don't think so. It was surprisingly corporate, the charity sector over here. A lot of office politics. I don't think I really enjoyed one day of it.'

'And that girl?'

Six months ago, even alluding to Sarah would have been enough to send me into a spiral. Now, at last, a weight felt like it was slowly lifting.

'It was a relief,' I said. 'Knowing it was the last time I would see her.'

I thought briefly back to my last day, and Sarah doing the usual flick of her long brown hair and marching past me, determinedly ignoring me, as she crossed the office brightly telling someone how she was off to the south of France the next day.

'She didn't sound the right sort anyway,' Judith said diplomatically.

'It all works out for the best, lad. And take it from someone who knows, there's more to life than working in an office. People pay too much heed to computers and that these days. I don't know how you can stand being indoors all day everyday clicking and typing. It would do my head in!' Ronnie chuckled as the three of us walked up a path, away from the shed.

'In my day, work was about having a laugh with the lads. Out in the fresh air, the radio on and beers after. Didn't need a degree or memorising the works of Shakespeare. You just did what you enjoyed doing.'

And with that I thanked the Joneses, said goodbye – telling them I would keep them updated on progress – and set out back to my solitary flat and even more solitary life.

Researchers now say we should plan for up to five career changes over our lifetimes. I'm sure this would have shocked our grandparents' generation, who fastidiously stuck to one through wars, strikes, and recessions. I had turned thirty-five over the summer and, as of that day at the Joneses allotment, was already on to my third while everyone else I knew remained happy with their first.

I should explain how I arrived at my present situation. The first transition probably takes less of a leap – an investment banker who regularly partook in illicit substances giving it all up to do good causes, is perhaps a cliché these days. But then giving up charity work, both in the hills of Burundi and then at home, to become a one-allotment gardener in South London, perhaps takes some more clearing up. The crux of the matter began eleven months ago.

It was the run-up to Christmas and I was due to fly home. As I have said, for the previous four years, I had been doing various jobs around the Middle East and East Africa. Or to put it more honestly, I had not been living in London since I had woken up on the morning of my thirtieth birthday and decided to quit my stable, better-than-averagely paid job in the *City* to become a 'hippie do-gooder.' At least that was what my dad called it anyway. A sentiment shared by my sister though she preferred the term 'attention-seeking cock'. It was the first time in my life when I witnessed them actually agree on something. On the surface, everything in my life probably looked ideal, even aspiring. The thing about growing up playing strategy board games is, despite significantly diminishing the probably of losing your virginity before you are at least forty-one, it *does* make you better than average at *calculating* probability and the maths behind each roll of the dice. I, therefore, spent my twenties working for an investment bank, got paid enough to afford the mortgage on a nice flat in North London, and to most people – my dad (happily), my sister (begrudgingly), my friends from university and my friends from work – I must have seemed set to continue climbing the corporate ladder for the next twenty to thirty years.

My dad was in the same job his entire life. And he loved it. He was an academic and writer who wrote books on Ernest Hemingway and F. Scott Fitzgerald, lectured at a London university, and would occasionally be asked to appear on Radio 4 for some literature-themed documentary. 'How can you write *books* – i.e. plural – about Fitzgerald when he only wrote four, of which two were shit?' said Ellie one time, I think at a school parents' evening when her sixth-form English teacher had excitedly introduced himself to Dad. Anyway, Dad's field of study was early twentieth-century novelists ranging from E.M. Forster to Virginia Woolf to James Joyce, but it was *Hem* and *Scott* where he received most of his plaudits.

And Dad thought I loved my job too. I had always thought that neither Ellie nor I pursuing literature at a higher level would have disappointed him, but he seemed genuinely proud when I came home from university and told him I had been offered a job in a City bank. I guess it meant I would never be too far away, which I think he found comforting as I could tell that rattling along alone in the old house would bring him down at times. And when I would visit for Sunday lunch, always hungover, he would chuckle, 'Too much living the high life, eh?' He would then mix me up a Bloody Mary, grinning through his beard. 'Only one, mind you. Don't want you bankrupting them come Monday.' I still vividly remember those lunches. Three of us around the six-seater dining table, with Dad's sister, Auntie Pam, joining us, and both of them interrogating me on the ups and downs of the stock market.

So when I used Sunday lunch to tell Dad that I was becoming an aid worker and moving to Lebanon to work with an organization responding to the Syria crisis, he was understandably bemused. 'Since when were you interested in helping other people?' Ellie said indignantly, throwing down her napkin. Ellie and her husband Mike had joined us on that occasion driving up from Brighton 'just for something to do' as Ellie put it. I had naively seen their presence as an ideal opportunity to make my announcement with the whole family in one room. How was I supposed to know Ellie had her own announcement planned? That she was three months pregnant with Millie? In hindsight, Ellie saying no to wine, Mike not even allowing her to carry the weight of a plate by herself, and the fact that while Ellie's relationship with both Dad and me was vastly better than it had been in my teenage years, she had never previously made a spontaneous four-hour round trip visit for Sunday lunch *just for something to do*, all should have been somewhat of a clue.

Ellie walked out. Mike brought her back. Ellie begrudgingly told us she was pregnant. We were elated. I was also relieved at not having everyone staring at me like I was insane. And then gently after lunch, after Auntie Pam had gone home and Ellie and Mike had decided to stay the night rather than drive back to Brighton, we sat down in the living room and Dad and Ellie brought back up the subject of my new career.

I told them I wanted to travel. That apart from the occasional city break, I had never left London. I told them I wanted to do more with my life than enter numbers into a spreadsheet and read investor reports. I told them countless different reasons, all skirting around the real truth – that I was in therapy for drug and alcohol dependency and desperately needed a clean break from it all. And then I tried to appease Dad by saying it would only be for three months, I was only volunteering, I would be only on the border of Syria and in completely safe hands as, after all, who would let a maths geek from London anywhere near actual humanitarian aid? I would get the wanderlust out of my system and be back at a bank in no time. Three years later, I was making a Skype call to Dad, little Millie, and a heavily pregnant again Ellie from a town six miles from the Syrian front lines telling them 'Red Zone' status by the

Foreign and Commonwealth Office was a considerable exaggeration.

And then came that December day, eleven months ago. I was due to fly home for a family Christmas at Dad's. Millie would have just turned four, Ed was one year old. It would have been Dad, me, Ellie, Mike, the kids, and Auntie Pam all under one roof for a week, the house properly full for the first time since I was a child. Dad had even given me a call the week before, asking if I minded giving him a hand with the cooking. 'The Roberts men taking control of the kitchen,' he laughed, his voice sounding huskier as he got older. 'And *The Musician* has volunteered himself on procurement. He says farm shops in Sussex are saving the planet. Organic, and all that nonsense.' *The Musician.* That was Dad's name for Mike, an in-joke at having a professional rock musician in the family, which I thought perfectly summed up Dad's humour. It also, to my amusement, infuriated Ellie no end because *a*) she was also a musician herself – a classically trained pianist – and b) Dad was not scornful, sarcastic, or ironic. Ellie had been sure that bringing home a rock musician would have shocked and appalled our old-school academic of a father and further enhanced her 'wild-child' status. However, within the first hour of their meeting, Ellie took me into the kitchen to let Dad and Mike 'bond'. We were then suddenly greeted by a deafening wall of sound. Rushing back into the living room, we found Dad with a trumpet at his lips, and Mike with an acoustic guitar in hand, loudly accompanying a jazz recording that was turned up to full volume on the stereo. Ellie and I, Dad's children, who had lived in the same house as him on and off for almost three decades, had no idea he even owned a trumpet, let alone played jazz. I don't think I've seen Dad happier than that day. He was never one to be pigeon-holed, was Dad.

Even before making the trip, I had decided that I was ready to come home for good. I had spent each of the previous four years in a different country. Aged thirty, I was in a small set of apartments in Lebanon with its own little courtyard which I began beautifying with plants, shrubs and the help of an online landscaping course. Thirty-one, I shared a house in Jordan with an actual garden and learned what a kitchen garden was. Thirty-two, I was inside Syria, in a secure compound which we hardly left but had a rooftop which we gradually transformed into a mini oasis, again with the help from my part-time landscaping course. And then, aged thirty-three, I was offered the opportunity to leave the Middle East and project manage a very different project for one year. An agricultural farm in Burundi.

After the Burundi project was complete, I found myself in Nairobi, Kenya, with a plethora of other expats who had been given cushy office jobs in a tropical climate, put in charge of and doling out advice to vastly more experienced African colleagues, while they spent evenings and weekends at fancy bars or restaurants and exploring the African savanna. It had been a similar story in Lebanon and Jordan and was something I didn't really feel that comfortable with. Hence the amount of time spent gardening. I was ready to come home and make a life back in London.

Not that I had told anyone. That was going to be my surprise to Dad. Be back with all my luggage, and let him know he might have a houseguest for a month or so while I found my feet again. The day before I was due to catch my plane, I got another phone call. This time it was from Mike. There's no good, appropriate, or less horrific way to convey bad news but sometimes the act of telling becomes superfluous. 'Scott?... It's Mike...' was all he had to say. His pauses, his reluctant tone, the fact it was him calling me. In addition to being my brother-in-law, I do count Mike as one of my best friends but the only reason he would ever call me while I was away was if it was bad.

So I came home. To an empty house. Ellie and the kids stayed back in Brighton until Christmas Eve, the day of the funeral. Mike met me at the airport and briefed me that Ellie hadn't taken it well. He, strangely – or not strangely as grief affects all of us in different ways and all families are intensely complicated – acted as a go-between for Ellie and me. We didn't speak a word to each other until the funeral. I sat in Dad's – our – old Wood Green house with Auntie Pam making arrangements, and Mike would call asking what he could do. For some reason, it felt natural for this wall to develop between Ellie and me suddenly. Without Dad, what were we? After years of us gradually getting closer, it was no surprise that I had not heard from her. And neither did I want to. The longer her silence, the more justified mine, until the absolute horror show which was the day of the funeral.

CHAPTER 2

THIS ONE'S LIKE YOUR SISTER'S BEST FRIENDS

'Coffee?' Camille asked me as I put down my bag. She was at her desk facing the back of the room, moving stacks of papers around to create space for the cafetière and two mugs.

'Excuse the mess.' She said it in that comforting American twang with which I had become familiar. 'It's the once-a-decade day of admin where I shift through all my crap and finally give up on reading that paper I bookmarked back in '08.'

Camille's office was a small homely rectangular room with just about enough space for two armchairs and a desk behind them. Squeezed between my chair and the window was a compact side table with a carafe of water, two tumblers, and a box of tissues, which I very much hoped not to need. The walls were a happy cornfield yellow, and as I took my seat waiting for Camille, I glanced out of the third-floor window onto a tucked away old Victorian courtyard.

Camille's office was on the top floor of one of those grand London townhouses. Victorian, Georgian, Edwardian, I had no idea how one could tell, it just had a timelessness that reminded me of a period drama. Down below, a man wearing a crisp gun-metal suit and carrying an old-fashioned brown leather briefcase marched quickly into the building adjacent to us. He had no coat, hence the quickstep, I assumed. It had been below zero overnight and the frost left a shimmer on the cobbles.

'It's *bloody freezing* in here,' Camille said in an exaggerated British accent. She picked up the coffee pot and began pouring. I watched the steam flood out colonising the room's chilly air.

'Oh, the joys of working in a Siberian paradise. Why I gave up Monterey Bay for your eleven and a half months of winter, God knows.' Camille turned around, her shoulder-length blonde hair bobbing on what might have been a small animal cuddling her neck.

'Nice scarf,' I said, unable to suppress a smile. Camille was wearing a ridiculously thick cream woollen shawl the size of a poncho that had the home-made quality of a poorly designed child's safety blanket.

'My mother-in-law knitted it, douchebag.' She handed me a mug and looked down at the knitwear, lightly fingering it with her free hand. 'She's a lovely, lovely woman whom I adore more than anyone else in the world, but unfortunately, she has no concept of fashion whatsoever.' The scarf was an obvious juxtaposition to the rest of Camille's outfit – a smart navy blue dress with wide leather belt. She wore no tights despite criticising our English weather, instead opting for tall suede boots that reached the top of her shins.

In every way, Camille personified my mental image of the typical Californian. Tall, attractive, stylish, immaculate blonde hair, sun-kissed skin with perfectly toned limbs – probably from waking up each day to go surfing – and impossibly straight, white teeth.

'Oh, and if we are calling each other out on personal appearance, you may want to check the mirror. Jeez, Scott, what happened to your nose?'

Isn't there some kind of rule that says therapists are not permitted to call their clients *douchebag* or delve into open sarcasm as a treatment method? If so, it obviously did not apply to West Coast Americans. 'It's a Freudian term,' she smirked the first time she called me it. There was a spell at the start of our sessions when we were professional. I was polite and wanting to make a good impression as if it was a job interview. When Camille first stepped into the little waiting area and called my name, I have to admit, I was unnerved by how young and attractive she was. My previous therapist was a middle-aged man called Anthony. I had been seeing him for over six months, right up until the day I left for my new life as an aid worker.

'Anthony was my doctorial supervisor,' she had explained. 'We've known each other, God, nearly fourteen years. Five of which was working at the same practice right up until he moved back to Scotland.'

I am not saying an effective therapist cannot be young or attractive; however, Camille was a sharp contrast to Anthony's patient, coaxing approach. I also knew it would be strange talking to someone who was not Anthony about my thoughts, issues, the things I've done. So I was quiet, polite, determined to sit up straight and make a good impression. And if we continued that way, I very much doubt we would have made any progress.

'It's natural to want to be liked, to be polite, to be the version of ourselves we deem most appropriate in the specific situation,' Camille remarked probably after session two, 'but in the words of a great American poet, *'that ain't getting us nowhere'.*'

'Tennessee Williams?'

'Meatloaf.'

As Camille sat down opposite me, she reached over to the side table to pick up her notepad and pen.

'How did it go with Ellie?' she asked.

I groaned.

'It didn't.' I felt myself sink into the chair.

Camille reached over and poured me some water, a lock of blonde hair falling in front of her face as she did. I briefly retold the events of Exmouth Market.

'Have you tried calling her? Having the conversation over the phone?'

'Not really had the time,' I lied. 'With work, and that.'

Camille pulled a slight smirk as she made a note. Looking at her, I guessed Ellie and she would be around the same age. When I first met Camille, I felt strangely reminded of my sister's friends growing up. A three-year age difference was like dog years back then. They were the confident, worldly, mysterious girls who would hang out at our house, and the instant I hit puberty, I would place them on pedestals, afraid to make eye contact let alone be in the same room. I say *worldly* – more in the sense that they could come and go as they pleased and did not have to ask permission to go to Brent Cross shopping centre.

Camille then smiled at me, this calm, soothing therapist's smile of hers. If it is not something directly learned, it must be an art developed. How to reassure a patient without saying a word.

'Not to cast aspersions on someone else's workload, but do you think there might be another reason you've not called Ellie?'

I exhaled and automatically shrugged, shifting around in the soft chair. There were probably many reasons but even to me, saying, *because I don't want to,* did not seem the most constructive of answers.

'Shame? I still feel guilty, I guess. But I'm also seriously pissed off with her and don't see why it is always me who has to make the first move with us.'

Mature, I know.

'I'm pissed off at her and frustrated at myself – I know I didn't handle things well in the café. After six months of therapy I would have hoped I would have responded differently.' I sank further into the chair as if self-disappointment was like quicksand. 'I *could* have called her. Either when I got there to check she was coming or when she was ten minutes late. I didn't need to wait until she was *an hour* late to text her. And after, I should have done something other than run away.'

Camille smiled again.

'Scott, I tell a lot of my clients, therapy is not a vaccine. You don't take a six-week treatment and suddenly become immune. It's about working on something and allowing yourself more than a few stumbles along the way.'

I let out an ever-so-small snort.

'I had tried your idea of treating myself to a hot chocolate for each step of the way, you know, when doing things I would rather avoid. Like with the whole Sarah thing.'

'Hey, *sometimes* it does help.' Camille went a tad pink as she broke into a beaming smile. 'We all do need something just to get us through the prolonged bad times. Though I will take note of your critique of my therapy techniques.'

I laughed but also heard Ellie's shrill teenage voice in my head: *so this is all my fault?* She was yelling at Dad. She was standing, her arms by her side, her fists in balls, and positively livid. But the exact situation I could not recall. Memories all seemed blurred and hazy from back then.

I looked out of the window. In the courtyard below, a young woman was walking her bicycle across the cobbles. She was dressed in leggings and a fleece top and fiddling with the strap of her helmet. Suddenly I felt this pang of comfort or familiarity. I was recalling *Tender is the Night*. Dick Diver looking out the window of the bar watching riders of the *Tour* pass and dismount, resigned and determined not to pay attention to the scene unfolding in front of him: his wife and her lover telling him she was leaving him. I smiled, recalling just how good that novel was and how it alone would justify Dad's obsession with Fitzgerald, despite Ellie's taunts.

'I don't know if it's relevant,' I began, not sure if I was really addressing Camille or thinking out loud. 'Or why it's now suddenly on my mind, but recently I'm remembering this memory from years ago.'

Camille was still – patient. She stared calmly and gently with her brown eyes, and her blonde hair had fallen again past her cheek. She gave me the floor.

'As kids, Ellie was the talented one in the family. Like *really* talented – a musical prodigy. She was able to play Bach and Chopin at the age of seven. Her instrument was the piano and Dad and Mum ended up buying her a baby grand for the living room. It satisfied Ellie's tutor's conviction that she needed the best to practise if she would be the world-famous concert pianist she was destined to be, and Mum liked having something stylish on which to display family photographs. But the most remarkable thing about Ellie's talent was that it was a natural gift – she was one of those infuriating people who hardly needed to practise. Growing up, she would always have to be nagged to do her one hour of practice, though when she got into it, it was frightening how effortless she made everything.

'And then this particular summer – I think I was thirteen and she would have been sixteen – she wanted to practise all the time. But it wasn't effortless. It was loud and angry and constant, thumping the keys as hard as she could. One Sunday, I was studying for a test when she started up. I was getting more and more annoyed the longer she played hoping Dad would do something rather than just hibernate in his study as usual, or that the neighbours would complain. It felt like she was even louder, with all these crashing notes, and I just wanted her to give it a rest. So I went downstairs into the living room and tried to shout over the noise: "hey, Ell, can you quieten it down? I'm trying to do my home-work.' But either she couldn't hear me, or she ignored me as she kept playing with just as much intensity and ferocity. I shouted a couple more times, 'Ellie, *Ell*, can you give it a rest?' but if anything, she just got louder until I had enough and marched over and grabbed her wrist.

'The next thing I knew, there was this primal scream. I then had this sharp blinding pain above my right eye and was lying on my back unable to breathe – Ellie's knee was pressed into my chest, her fist wedged into my mouth, and her other hand repeatedly slamming my head into the wooden floor. 'Jesus Christ!' I then heard. Ellie was suddenly off me, and there was the sound of her screaming and shouting and furniture being kicked. My dad had finally entered the room and was dragging her away, but I couldn't see a thing. My eyes were closed and I was curled up in a ball. I just felt myself shaking, unable to move, and willing myself not to cry while the gooeyness of the blood started to spread.'

I gave Camille a matter-of-fact half-smile to signal the story was over. There was a small carriage clock also on the side table where we put our coffees. It let out a low chime for the half-hour. Camille was still staring at me with that gentle stare of hers. Her notebook sat closed on her lap. She then straightened up.

'Scott, where was your mom during all of this?' she asked in a more serious voice.

'Devon. It was September. Mum had left at the start of that summer.'

Camille leaned over and refilled my water glass from the carafe. My mouth was so dry I almost finished it in one gulp.

'What happened next, Scott?'

'Dad called Auntie Pam – his sister. She lived up near

Alexandra Park – she still does – and came round to stay with Ellie while Dad took me to the hospital. The sharp pain above my eye was from a metal photo frame. When I had grabbed Ellie's wrist, it must have been the first thing within reach. Luckily, Dad wasn't into claw-hammers...' I tried to smile but Camille was unmoved. She was looking at me, waiting for me to continue with her hand covering her mouth.

'Well, the doctor said I was lucky. I had stitches where the corner had embedded into my eyebrow, and they cleaned some fragments of glass that had shattered around my eye. I had another couple more stitches in the back of my head where it had hit our wooden floor and Ellie had hammered it back down repeatedly. Dad was worried my nose was broken due to the blood, but it was just a nosebleed from a glancing strike.'

I let out another snort of laughter describing the war wounds. I also reached for the tumbler and finished the solitary last sip before turning to the window. It was getting darker, and a storm looked to be setting in. Suddenly, as I got lost staring, the blackness seemed to flicker and transcend into a brilliant white. I closed my eyes, rubbed them, and then everything was back to normal. I suddenly had a craving for a cigarette.

I can't find a lighter anywhere. I'm going crazy. But I'm not crazy...

It took me a moment to notice Camille, her eyes also closed, her thumb and fingers rubbing her lids too.

'Sorry, Scott. I meant what happened between you and Ellie.' She gave another small encouraging smile.

'Nothing,' I said matter-of-factly again. 'Some lady did come to the house the next day and asked me what had happened. I didn't know why at the time, but I guess it was some kind of child-welfare thing. But it was nothing major, and after Dad took me down to the park for ice cream while the lady spoke to Ellie and Auntie Pam.

And then that night, Dad and I took a trip for a few days, a writers' conference – a trip he normally took a couple of times a year but usually we would have Mum there looking after us back home. I should have been at school, but they weren't as strict about that stuff in those days – it was actually the first time Dad and I had done a trip together, just the two of us.' I smiled – this time for real.

It became our thing, taking trips together. It started then, and it was just a few days in a nice hotel, but it transpired that when Dad was younger, he would do a lot of camping and orienteering – something else that did not fit his image as the bookish academic. You also wouldn't have got Mum anywhere near a tent, hence the lack of those activities until then. It also got me out of the house and away from my Games Workshop sets.

'I think I had already forgotten about the piano incident and wondered why Ellie had not come with us, or why she didn't kick up more of a fuss about having Auntie Pam stay with her and not being allowed to remain in the house by herself.

'And when we came home, everything was normal again – at least the *new normal* after Mum. The only thing slightly odd was that first afternoon back. When I got out of the car, I saw Ellie looking down at us from the upstairs window, but when I caught her eye, she disappeared – Ellie was never one to back down from a staring contest. Back then, she was – ' I looked around the room for the word. I was going to say *surly*, or *moody*, but no. 'She was a *bullying arsehole*. Anyway, that day she was quieter, no slamming of doors or sighs of exasperation or calling me stupid every time I said something. And at dinner, with the four of us, me, her, Dad, and Auntie Pam, around the table, she said nothing until after everyone had finished when she asked in this weird soft voice, 'please may I leave the table?' I can't recall her saying *please* until then.'

Camille had picked up her notebook and was writing. After,

she hooked the pen to its side and placed it out the way on the side table.

'Scott, I want you to do an exercise for me.' She sat forward, so my attention was only on her. 'Close your eyes.'

I did, letting her and the room slip from view. I also tucked my hands under my thighs as I became more acutely aware of the cold.

'Go right back to you and Ellie at the piano. Go back to that day and that specific moment.'

It was only on Camille's advice that I had even downloaded a meditation app. Visualisation exercises did not come naturally to me at first, especially if they placed me somewhere I did not want to be – in the same room as my older sister. If this was meant to be an exercise in how to get in touch with my resentment, it was working. I had thought Camille might pick up on the last bit I said about Ellie looking sheepish when Dad and I came back from our trip, and I could then point out that she never actually said sorry.

'Okay? Tell me exactly what is happening.'

'She's sitting at the piano, glaring at me as usual.'

'Okay. What happens next? What do you see?'

'Nothing. She sucker punches me and I'm on the floor.' The imagery slowly began to solidify. I could see our old living room. I could see Ellie kicking and screaming above me as Dad had his arms around her waist, restraining her as she tried to pounce. And then all I could see was the floor. I was huddled in a ball, cowering like a weakling.

'Scott, this is important,' I heard Camille's voice fluttering in as I nestled under the piano. 'What *exactly* are you feeling right *now*?'

'Nothing,' I heard myself say. I was looking down at the smooth, glossed wooden floorboard of my childhood home. I could feel the stickiness of the blood. A girl had just kicked the shit out of me and I had done nothing to defend myself.

'Ashamed.' My hands weren't as cold anymore, and instead of

clasping them under me, I let my finger press my eyelids down, keeping them closed, maintaining the image.

'Ashamed at letting her have that power over me. And betrayed for her doing it.'

I had not started seeing a therapist again to talk about Ellie, Dad, or well-buried childhood memories. I had begun therapy because of a girl called Sarah and how her ending our very brief relationship had sent me into an emotional tailspin. I could not sleep, I felt humiliated, I was hurt that someone I had grown close to could so easily cast me aside. I had felt ashamed with Sarah. I had felt betrayed. Suddenly I cringed at how Freudian the inter-connectedness began to feel.

'It should have brought us closer together. It wasn't my fault that Mum left, so why was she so determined to take it out on me? And now I'm on the floor, unable to fight back, overpowered, relying on my dad to stop her.'

I could feel the cold floorboards and the dull, heavy throbbing at the back of my head.

'Everything had to revolve around Ellie,' I heard myself whisper.

CHAPTER 3

IDEALISM, MARXISM, ROMANTIC FATALISM, AND SARAH

It *was* a breakdown. Part of me wants to say it wasn't, and that I was just down in the dumps like I usually get for one to two months every year. And part of me still feels ashamed for allowing it to happen. Ashamed and weak for not being normal and taking rejection on the chin.

But I did not *allow* it to happen. That was the whole point. The harder I fought, the longer I ignored it and I carried on, the stronger it became. It was like it fed off hubris, knowing I was too afraid, or too English, to admit there was a problem and do something about it.

Breakdowns are more complex than one single event, incident, or person. There has to be something else at work that makes you susceptible. They are like love in that respect. And a lot of the time the trigger for a breakdown is love, or what you had engineered to believe was love, because you were susceptible enough to fall.

Early into our sessions, Camille gave me a reading list, and on it was Alain de Botton's *Essays in Love*. I found myself lying in the bed of the Airbnb I had been staying at reading it from cover to cover. It was like all the mysteries of the universe suddenly revealed. It essentially listed the symptoms of infatuation and the three critical ingredients to believing you have fallen in love. And then points out how easy this is to do – but not so easy to undo.

Almost immediately after Dad's funeral Ellie and I received the news that everything was not straightforward with Dad's will. Again, this could have been us trying to pigeonhole Dad, but within days of arriving home with all my belongings and having planned to crash at Dad's for a few months while I got myself on my feet, we essentially found out the house was not wholly his. To cut a long story short, I was asked to move out while our family lawyer sorted through what was soon to become a messy situation.

I accepted the first job I was offered – working with a charity from its London office – so I wouldn't dip into the rather meagre savings I had set aside to afford the jaw-dropping London rents. The work was fine, the majority of the people were alright, but it was office work at the end of the day. I was sitting at a monitor for eight hours a day, just like I had done at the bank, and despite my being away for four years, nothing had really changed. And then came Sarah, to save me from it all.

Idealism: Something in mind, spirit or will is the ultimate foundation of reality. That our reality is actually what we make up in our own heads and a reflection of our own ideas. To badly paraphrase Kant, if we want to fall in love, reality be damned, we will make that someone worth falling in love with.

Not meaning to be unkind, but I would not describe Sarah as conventionally beautiful. Not in the Hollywood, immaculate features, turning-all-men's-heads-when-she-walks-in-the-room type of way. She had this slightly wonky face and this peculiar smile, of a girl not well rehearsed in the art of smiling. She would be dress pristinely around the office, with perfectly ironed blouses and pencil skirts always finishing an inch below the knee, and always look serious. She had an unsmiling focus, like she knew she was going places, and combined with her immaculate clothes, she was distinctly unattainable.

Marxism: Groucho rather than Karl. The anecdote goes that Groucho Marx had been furious at being refused entry to an elite club he desired to join but would, in turn, consider it an insult to belong to the club who would have someone like him as a member. Even if that club had originally been the one that refused him. Or to quote the old phrase, we want what we cannot have. Even in love.

Sarah had never worked abroad. In fact, I was one of only a few in my new office who had. I assumed that this was what first put me on her radar. So when I found myself sitting opposite that unattainable girl at work drinks and she first smiled at me, that strange, goofy smile, I was smitten. And soon began the secret meetings – the walks at lunch, the drinks after work – and then those countless text messages and phone calls. I became her confidant. The only person she said she could be herself around.

Romantic Fatalism: Or, put simply, the intervention of fate. After all, what else could kick-start love more than the firm belief that it was our destiny? For Sarah and me, that came one February evening as I walked through the snow to Dalston station. I had on my travelling backpack and was carrying a crate of all my worldly goods – a digital radio, Bluetooth speaker, a series of paperback novels, and a print of Van Gogh's '*Starry Night Over The Rhone*'. Admittedly, not a massive haul for what had been thirty-four years on the planet, but at the time, I was in between my third Airbnb so needed to travel light.

'Scott!' I heard a girl call. I looked up to see in the distance a girl beaming at me. Scott is not an uncommon name, and not immediately recognising the girl, I quickly glanced over my shoulder. I continued forward to avoid the embarrassment of misrecognition. 'Scott!' she called again, and this time stepped out in front of me. It was then I recognised her, but still only just. She was smiling this huge, beaming smile, like she was thrilled to see me. How strikingly different it made her look. Up until that point we had only spoken that once, at the work drinks, but there she suddenly was – the girl who I would glance at as she strode across the office – standing randomly in front of me at Dalston railway station, miles away from where we would normally see each other.

Sarah *said* she had met a friend who had just left to catch his train home. Later she told me she had been there to meet a guy from a dating app.

I told her about my living situation and she laughed. A whole-hearted giggle of a laugh, and looked incredibly pretty as she did so.

'Are you off home now?' I asked, finding myself hoping she would say no.

'I'm stranded!' she said, again beaming. 'I cycled here but just had two glasses of wine. They won't let me take my bike on the train for another hour!'

So I asked if she wanted to go for another drink. Purely to kill time. Sarah led me to the same pub she had just left, just around the corner from the station. I assumed we would have one drink, talk about work, and then we would leave, Sarah able to travel home with her bike. But it was past closing time when we both stumbled out of the pub.

. . .

My preconceived notion of Sarah was the ambitious, must-be-involved-in-everything young woman I saw at work. She was recently promoted, was about to manage someone for the first time, and seemed to be going places. But in the pub, with me, she was suddenly endearingly girlish and youthful.

We had taken two sofas in the corner of the pub and lounged about like it was our living room. She sat childlike, her legs crossed beneath her and feet on the sofa, laughing at everything I said and giving me a virtual tour of her life through the photos on her phones. In my day, it was considered a little bit rude to take your phone out while having a conversation but since returning to London this seemed now the norm, and her relaxedness in this brave new world added something to her charm. We were not hugely apart in age – six years – but she was very much the millennial and I was Generation X.

'I know I will never be a *pretty* girl,' she suddenly confided after telling me about her breakup with her ex-boyfriend. 'Not pretty like the other girls. But I would like the man I end up with to *find me* pretty. Just a little.' The other half of the Marxist (Groucho) view of love is, 'if that person wants me, there must be something wrong with them because no one beautiful or remarkable could ever love someone like me.' For me, this self-deprecating lack of awareness of how attractive I found her was like being struck by the proverbial thunderbolt. *Idealism. Marxism. Romantic Fatalism.*

CHAPTER 4

LOUGHBOROUGH ROAD

One thing Sarah said to me in the short window when we still spoke to each other was,

'I might go out with you if you still owned your flat.'

She meant it as a joke, but every little joke has that element of truth at its core, and that particular one seemed to epitomise the reason why I would never be good enough for her. I *had* owned a nice two-bedroom flat in Finsbury Park. Nothing fancy, but it was home, at least for a while. I had probably been happiest during my mid-twenties, just after my Exmouth Market years and when I was with Vicky. In the end, it just became a place where I woke up hungover and with feelings of paranoia and self-loathing from whatever I had done the night before.

I sold it when I decided to leave London, fancying a clean break and new start. I just about broke even after I repaid all the credit card debt I had accumulated from my banking lifestyle, and in my head I reasoned that when I did come home I would do things differently. How was I supposed to know that London property prices would skyrocket and four years later I would rent seven

Airbnbs in four months before gratefully accepting a room in a former squat?

After my session with Camille, I found myself again going against my ingrained instincts and taking the overground south of the river. I would leave a therapy session in one of two moods: a little calmer, more resolute, and slightly more confident of getting through the day; or completely drained and just needing to be by myself and process my thoughts. Alighting at Loughborough Junction, I made the short walk along the reassuringly quiet side streets back to Loughborough Road and the row of terraced houses I had most recently started to call home.

My plan was to sneak quietly up the stairs, throw some pasta into a pan, and then take a long hot shower to wash away everything on my mind. The only issue was avoiding my housemate, who had an annoying habit of leaving her bedroom door open – both an extension of halls at university, I assumed, and, also likely, a passive-aggressive gesture that this was more her flat than mine. Our usual protocol was to put on a fake smile and make twenty seconds of niceties before I disappeared. But lucky for me, my housemate was usually contented with a quick 'hey, how was your day?' using a big, polite smile to mask the fact that I was literally the last person with whom she had wanted to live. Fortunately for both of us, it was Thursday night, and she would usually be out with her posse of attractive, severe brunettes doing whatever it was that normal young people did with the weekend in sight.

Trying for a third time to unlock the front door, I finally felt the key connect with the ancient mechanism and engage. I rammed into the panel of red peeling paint with my shoulder, hoping not to take the whole thing off its hinges, and bundled myself inside. Our flat was the upper of essentially one house converted into two flats, and my room was right at the top, in what had been an attempt to convert the attic.

'Scott!' I heard my name called from above. Katie *was* in. I looked at my watch, and suddenly my heart sank. If Katie was still in then she had probably invited her entourage of female friends over, and as with so many evenings that summer, there would be a troop of three girls sitting drinking wine in Katie's room with her, preparing for a night out and, perhaps legitimately, staring daggers at me every time I passed that open door.

A pretty, petite brunette appeared at the top of the stairs. She was dressed in jeans and a large knitted sweater, not the type of outfit if she had been planning a night on the town – *night on the town?* When had I started talking like my dad?

'I thought you'd be home ages ago?' She had on a strange fixed wide smile.

'I had a doctor's appointment. Was I meant to put the bins out?'

'That doesn't matter!' she then yelled, strangely loud. 'It's just great to have you back!'

It was not like Katie and I did not get on as flatmates – we communicated well enough to make sure the bills got paid and did offer to make the other a cup of tea, though seldom drank it in the same room – but it had never been her habit to greet me at the door.

I carefully squeezed through our artificially narrowed hallway and onto the bare floorboards of the stairs. It would be no exaggeration to say that our flat had seen better days. The landlord had been quite happy to keep the same décor as during the Blitz, and the hallway was currently doubling as his private storage facility with boxes, books, kites, bicycles and even a 1970s storage unit that had been originally salvaged from a skip.

As I climbed the stairs, Katie remained at the top, her smile very unnerving and, upon getting closer, worryingly manic. 'We've got company!' she beamed, again theatrically brightly. As I reached her the smiled faded. 'Save me,' she mouthed and before turning back around and calling, 'Joan, Scott's here.'

Inside our kitchen, sitting at the end of the small dining table nonchalantly flicking through an old copy of *The Observer Magazine* was Joan, our landlord and currently by default, my best friend.

'Joan came by to check on the boiler,' said Katie, walking back into the kitchen, past the table, and then around the sofa, coffee table, and dilapidated armchair to the boiler cupboard in the far corner of the room. Here I should make known that when I say *kitchen* I mean the one room in our flat that served as kitchen, dining room, living room, and utility room in one. At the far wall were the kitchen cupboards, washing machine, small pantry, and stove. On the near side, immediately next to the door was the fridge, on top of which was a lava lamp and old hi-fi system. The sofa that Joan and his previous flatmate had rescued from the side of the road, a hand-me-down coffee table, and free eBay-acquired armchair, just about fitted in the remaining space. And last we had our large sash window, where Katie stood, which scarcely halted the flow of cold air over our barely functioning radiator.

'Prognosis?' I said, standing in the doorway, trying my best to raise a smile.

'Yeah, it's fucked,' he said, without looking up from the magazine.

Joan's real name was Jonathan, and I had known him since university. Since those days, very few things had changed about Joan. I was pretty sure the Beck t-shirt he was wearing over his skinny frame as he rocked back on his chair was the same he would wear to indie nights at the students' union. The only noticeable difference between Student-Joan and London-Joan was probably his hair. Now sporting long floppy brown hair, he had originally been given his nickname because of a short, pudding-bowl, *Joan of*

Arc haircut. A nickname he seemed not just to tolerate, but when he brought his parents along to one of our pub lunches during the Exmouth Market days, I was surprised to hear them refer to him as Joan too.

We weren't exactly close friends at university. We were more friends of friends. Also, I didn't really like him that much, to be honest. He always came across as aloof, would mumble rather than talk to you and had such a remorseless way of taking the piss out of people that it surprised me he had any friends at all. It was only when we graduated and lived on the same street with our other university friends at Exmouth Market that I actually got to know him. And it was only at a party when Aurora Vivic drunkenly burst into tears and threatened to cut his penis off with a kitchen knife that we first bonded. 'The room is gravitating to your arse,' Joan had whispered to Aurora as she was dancing. When the commotion had died down Joan looked genuinely confused. 'I thought it was a compliment,' he said.

'So any idea when you're going to have it fixed?' said Katie, now stretching up to the cupboards above the cooker and bringing down three wine glasses. *Oh fuck*, I thought. We were going to have to do *entertaining*.

'Meh,' he shrugged.

'Joan?' Katie was holding the glasses, her brow starting to furrow.

'I don't know, it's been like that for years. Leon never complained. Just deal with it.'

'I don't want to *just deal with it*. I want a landlord who actually bloody does things when you ask him and not just take my rent because he knew I was desperate.'

Katie's own relationship with Joan was slightly complicated by the fact that, in addition to being her landlord, he was also her older brother. She put the glasses down on the table. Eyes still on the magazine, Joan reached into a bag at his feet and brought out two bottles of cloudy white beer and slid one across the table to me. Katie looked unamused.

'Okay, well I won't then open the wine if it's going to be just me. I'll have gin instead or something.'

'You don't like beer anyway,' he said, lacking any real concern as Katie left the room.

I sat down opposite Joan, pushing off my coat onto the back of the chair.

'Did you really come round to look at the boiler?'

'Nah. Alison's got her book club round. I was bored so I thought I'd come round here. Katie's obsessed with this boiler thing.'

In a way, it was warming to have a friend who felt comfortable enough to pop round when he felt like it. So many of my friends had left London during my years abroad, and arranging to meet would take months of arduous planning. To give him credit, as a friend Joan was relatively low maintenance. At university, he was *cool* for not being *cool*. He did his own thing, went to obscure music nights, and when we all graduated and moved to London, it was he who knew the best clubs that were refreshingly not filled with other investment bankers but rather twentysomethings dressed in t-shirts and jeans, drinking lager out of plastic cups and jumping around a dancefloor. One of my original struggles with Joan lay with me, and that I have always been a people-pleaser. Any silence or lull in the conversation, I would deem a failing on my part. For Joan, these trivialities seemed to have no effect. Now, if he chose to put minimal effort into a conversation, it made him refreshing company, especially when you yourself were unable to be good company.

'Okay, I've got someone who can come by next week,' Katie said, returning with her phone against her ear. Both Joan and I looked at her blankly. As if to emphasise her point about the heating, she was now wearing a scarf. 'The engineer. He can look at the boiler next week.'

'It'll cost a fortune. Plus, you've got that.' Joan nodded down to the electric money-guzzling heater we had on.

'It's your responsibility! Scott and I are not putting up with this for the whole winter. I'll even contribute if it's excessive. I'll let them know next week is fine.' With that, she walked back out of the room.

It was not the most obvious pairing – Katie and me. It stemmed from us both being desperate for somewhere to live just when Joan chose to vacate his flat. Joan and his girlfriend Alison, another friend of ours from university, had been in a relationship for over a decade; however, it was only in the last few years that Ali had understandably owned up to the fact and then allowed him to move in with her.

All I really knew about Katie was that she was a graduate of Magdalen College, Oxford, she worked in a museum, and her long-term boyfriend was on a yearlong work placement at a Berlin law firm which meant she had also vacated their previous flat and took up her brother's generous offer of renting his. Though, like me, she was led to believe it was the whole flat she was renting.

I had no idea Joan even had a sister until we had known each other for about ten years. I knew he had a younger brother, Niles, who had visited him frequently when we lived on Exmouth Market, but Katie was an unknown. 'Well, she was a bit of a swot when we were kids,' Joan had said. 'Proper goodie-goodie teacher's pet and got sent to the posh girls' school. She was only twelve when I went to university, so we never really had that much in common.' And I felt that too summed up my relationship with Katie.

. . .

'You have to be fucking kidding me,' were Katie's first words to me as a flatmate. It was probably the only time I had heard her swear and was on a Saturday morning in late April. We had both arrived at Joan's flat with all our possessions and found out we were moving in together.

She came across as someone who did not swear a lot even then, as we stood on the street, Katie staring at me dumbstruck. We were outside on the pavement, glorious spring sunlight beating down on us like it should be a day for the beach rather than the strange stale-mate we were having at the old red door. Our respective entourages stood looking on, also wondering what was happening. On Katie's side was a large white van and three pretty girls, all staring daggers at me. On my side was Mike, Ellie's husband, who had rung up and offered me the use of him and the family car – an ol- school Volvo station wagon.

It had all started out friendly enough.

'Oh. Hello again,' Katie had cautiously said as we pulled up and were at the steps up to the house. 'Are you looking for Joan? You know he's living at Alison's now?'

'Yes, I know,' I said, about to have said the exact same thing. 'I'm actually moving in. Joan gave me the key yesterday...' I was taking the keys out of my pocket as proof, wondering why Joan's sister was then standing outside his old address.

'I think there's been some kind of miscommunication. No, you're not.'

She said it adamantly. Rather fiercely, in fact. I then told her of Joan's offer and the fact I had paid him the first month's rent, which seemed to trigger a slight explosion somewhere in her brain.

To be fair to Katie, I would not have been in the mood to have a calm discussion with me either. Considering the only time we had previously spoken, I had drunkenly put my tongue in her mouth.

Mike and I stood back as she paced the pavement on the phone to Joan. At one stage she seemed to be literally pulling her hair out, and as she did, one of her friends would give her a consoling rub on the back, hug or lay their head on her shoulder in support. Every now and then, a taller, skinny friend with sharp, attractive, but not the friendliest of features would make a point of looking directly over to me and glaring. Eventually, Katie put away her phone and announced to the tall, skinny girl and her other friends,

'My *brother* has properly screwed me. I can't afford the rent without *him,* and I really can't do another week sleeping on someone else's sofa. So this is it.' She then gave me a raised-eyebrows, it-is-what-it-is look, and proceeded to move in.

Mike and I decided it would be best to leave them to it and found a pub which did burgers and had a pool table. Katie told me that she and her friends were going out after they finished so we should 'have a chat on ground rules' the next day. While I stood outside waiting for Katie find an alternative to living with me, a thought began running through my head. If I didn't have Mike with me – joking around, telling me about an album he had recently watch mixed – it would have been humiliating. Six years ago I had done something stupid, and I felt awful and a complete idiot both at the time and after. Every time I would then see Katie, as she and her same friends attended more of Joan's birthdays, I felt rightly embarrassed and avoided even eye contact. But I was twenty-eight back then. Okay, that is the same age as Katie is now, perhaps twenty-nine, but I was a broken, immature twenty-eight. A drunken idiot. Not that I am now in any way wiser or sager. And not to entirely deflect the blame away from me, I am pretty sure she knew it was a misunderstanding and that I was set up by her twat of a brother.

I also quietly resented having to have a conversation on *ground rules* when I had no interest in Katie whatsoever. That might sound bitter, if not an exaggeration, but there were too many parallels with Sarah. They were both the same age and members of what I had deemed the superficial generation who lived their lives through their phones and social media – obviously, living my life sitting on park benches alone staring absently at communal gardens and spending my evening hiding in my room listening to vinyl, makes me the antithesis of shallow.

I just wanted somewhere to live, store my records, and spend my evenings alone brooding and playing acoustic guitar. So the reason why Katie and my relationship has not strayed any deeper than a polite *hello* was not solely because of her animosity to me or because of the *ground rules* we set out. But also because I didn't want to give her the satisfaction of wanting to live with her.

To make things worse, after the first awkward few weeks, Katie became quite friendly and polite. We weren't best friends, but she didn't have any reservations about leaving her door open, offering to make me a cup of tea, or waltzing into the kitchen while I was cooking and briefly tell me about her day. Whereas I would always gauge in the most cowardly way whether the coast was clear before even leaving my room.

Katie remained in her room, still on the phone trying to sort out more of the structural issues with our flat as I sat with Joan drinking the beer he had brought. To be fair, she had already transformed it from when Joan lived there. When he had first rented it the estate agent had called it 'a fixer-upper'. It was a one-bedroom that had been on the market some time due to the previous tenants being squatters. However, the agent hinted that it could be turned it into a two-bedroom flat by simply throwing all the living room furniture into the kitchen, so Joan and our other mate, Leon, took it, happy to overlook its defects in exchange for cheap rent. One day, a letter arrived informing them that their landlord had not been paying the mortgage, so Joan ended up buying the flat himself, probably at a knocked down price. However, homeownership was not a thing to suddenly make Joan house-proud. Everything else remained as it was – worn down, in disrepair, and with no surface looking like it had seen a cloth or vacuum cleaner.

In our first week, Katie had somehow managed to blitz the previous rustic and chaotic living room-cum-kitchen with cushions, place-mats, and artistically draped throws to give the flat an almost homely feel. She even brought with her enough rugs to hide away the exposed wood floorboards through which light from the down-stairs squat would shine through.

'Oh, Mum wants to know what you're doing for Christmas,' Joan called out.

Katie walked back into the room, gin and tonic in her hand, and put her phone into her jeans' back pocket.

'Now Ethan's... doing his own thing.' Joan stifled a laugh.

'What's that supposed to mean?'

'Well, Mum says she and Dad will be in France. But if you book your flight now, you could join them. Since you won't be spending it with Ethan's family anymore.'

'Ethan and I haven't discussed where we'll be spending Christmas yet.'

'Doesn't Tess Philips need to be involved in that discussion too?' Joan said quietly with a not too pleasant smirk as he sipped his beer and went back to *The Observer Magazine*.

There was obviously some private joke going on as Katie just stared at him, eyes slightly narrowed like she was sizing him up. She then rolled her eyes, muttered what might have been *'grow up'* and brushed past my chair, walking out.

'How's Alison?' I asked, breaking what was not an uncomfort-able silence.

'The same, I guess. She's got a lot on at work so I've been on dinner duties. How's whatshername?'

'No idea,' I said, and with it felt a small flicker of relief.

'Shame, I was enjoying the updates,' he said without any sincerity. 'By the way, *my* friends mean *everything* to me too?' And as if to prove it, he gave me a doe-eyed look and reached across the table to place his hand on mine, before doubling over laughing at his own joke.

I had forgotten I told him that. I think we had been in the pub at the time, and I was bitterly, drunkenly, having an embarrassingly indiscreet rant about Sarah to my *only* friend who would listen. Her overuse of platitudes had come top of my list. *Well, my friends are everything to me*, she had said, a little bit patronisingly, it felt. Her being young and arrogant, a close second as she described a weekend spent in the company of others at theatre matinees, ballet workshops, picnics, posh London bars, etcetera, and I remarked where did she find the time. What I wanted to say, as she flicked her hair to the side, and sipped her house white wine, was it didn't matter if they were everything to anyone. When kids came along, and the need for houses rather than flats, gardens rather than window boxes, those friends would disperse far and wide, no matter how important they were to her. But then, maybe she was right and it touched a nerve. My best friend was currently sitting opposite me, and I was counting down the minutes until he would fuck off.

Joan then smiled and took out his phone. He flicked through the screen and handed it to me. 'Here, I might have found the perfect girl for you.'

Guardian Soulmates was showing on his browser. 'Apparently the more pretentious girls who are sick of Tinder are on it.'

'Just back from living in Paris for four years and looking for someone to enjoy readjusting to London life with,' I read aloud and

scrolled up to a picture of a smiling girl in a floral dress standing in a park.

'See, practically made for you.' Joan then took back the phone and started scrolling again. I had to ask the obvious question.

'Joan, if you're happily living with Alison, why are you on a dating site?' Joan grinned – a grin that definitely did not look without ulterior motive. 'It's Niles' account. We found the link last weekend when we were back home for Dad's birthday,' he said, referring to his brother, and handed me back his phone.

'Okay, this one. Like I said, probably your ideal woman. Be a gentleman and make sure you read her biog first.'

He had scrolled so that I could see only a highlighted passage of text. I began reading aloud again.

'*I work in the museum sector which should tell you that I'm very clever and highly creative. I am very proud of what I have achieved so far in my professional life and also hold an MA from one of the more exclusive colleges in Oxford...*' I looked up at Joan. 'This girl does not really sound my...'

'Keep reading.'

'*My friends and family are everything to me...*' I raised my eyebrows, feeling more uncomfortable than amused. Reading someone's dating profile for sport actually seemed pretty low.

'Keep going. Just till the end of the next line.'

'*I've been described as an English rose and am a Home Counties girl growing up with two older brothers now living in the shabby-chic Bohemia that is Loughborough Junction...*' I immediately stopped reading and scrolled up but not quickly enough.

'What the hell are you doing?'

Katie was suddenly at my side staring down at me, livid. Her feet were apart and her hands balled into fists upon her hips. As I glanced back at the phone trying to see if I could quickly get rid of the evidence I saw Katie again, this time in the photo above the profile, standing in an identical pose but smiling and wearing a black bikini. Real-life Katie grabbed the phone from me.

'Where did you get this?' she demanded. I literally could see her nostrils flaring. When I gave no answer she turned to Joan, who had picked back up *The Observer Magazine* and was contentedly smiling, taking another sip of beer.

'Is this you?'

At getting no response from the smirking Joan she threw the phone at his chest.

'You are such an arsehole! How the hell did you... why are you even on a dating site? I'm seriously going to call Alison and tell her she's got a perverted creep as a boyfriend.'

'I'm not,' Joan smiled. 'Check the login.' Katie looked down at the phone. Her face suddenly went bright pink, as had probably mine.

'This is my account.' She stared at him open-mouthed. 'How...'

'Niles saw you checking it at Mum and Dad's last weekend. He said it wasn't difficult to figure out your password. Nice username, by the way.'

'You've hacked my account? My two older brothers have hacked my account and have been showing their pervy little friends my internet dating page?'

'To be fair, we hacked *Foxy Kitty's* dating page. And if you were so precious about being looked at, you probably shouldn't have put a half-naked picture of yourself online begging men to go out with you.'

Joan didn't seem to see the need to even fake remorse. He kept sipping his beer and went back to the magazine with a self-satisfied, highly amused grin.

'Were you part of this too?' She turned back to me, still glaring. 'I know he's a cretin but we're meant to be housemates...'

'Oh, give the self-righteousness a rest.' Joan let out an exasperated sigh. 'He thinks you're a bigger nightmare than I do.'

'What?'

All I had wanted at the start of that evening was to go home and lock myself in my room. Now I had somehow found myself in the middle of a brother-sister spat. Katie's voice was a lot louder and higher than I had heard it before. Her eyes were wide with pure indignation, and while I knew that she was entirely in the right, all I wanted was to retreat to my bedroom and fall asleep listening to *The National*.

Katie was still glaring at me, her face scrunched up. Before I could reply, Joan rolled his eyes and muttered,

'Oh, what's not to like? The bossiness, the sense of humour by-pass, and the *Douchebags of Eastwick* always in tow, you're the world's greatest housemate.'

Considering the circumstances, it was admirable how relatively calm Katie was. Well, compared to how I imagined that Ellie would react. She just stood there, like she was counting to ten. She then snatched the magazine out of Joan's hands.

'Right, I think this session of family bonding is well and truly over. Thanks for coming round, Joan, a pleasure as always.' Joan just rolled his eyes, picked up his beer, and took his phone back out.

'Alison's book club's still got an hour to go.'

Katie waited, hands still on hips, until it was apparent Joan was going nowhere. So she stormed out of the room. I saw her on the landing putting on her dark green coat, hat and gloves.

'We got it, Joan,' she said, standing in the doorway. 'It's your flat, you can come round whenever you want, stay as long as you desire and there's nothing I can do! So next time let me know, and I can make sure I'm somewhere else.'

She spun around and disappeared out of view. Before reappearing a second later.

'And, Scott,' she turned, looking at me far too passively not to be eerie. 'Terribly, *terribly* sorry for being such a complete bitch, I don't know how you put up with me.' Joan and I then heard the sound of her shoes thundering down the stairs and the door slamming shut behind her.

'What's her problem?' said Joan, sipping his beer.

Was it wrong that I found the whole brother-sister fallout both excruciatingly uncomfortable and yet entirely mesmerising? And was it wrong that while firmly believing Joan to be an arsehole, I was slightly envious of Katie for having an older sibling who cared enough to go to such extremes to make fun out of her?

Since we moved in together on that not exactly auspicious morning in early June, what I knew about Katie was the antithesis of what I knew about Joan. What I think sums Joan up is his inability not to laugh at anyone who takes themselves too seriously. At first, you find him a complete prick. But then, a bit like a deep therapy session, you gradually come away with something you did not know you were looking for – truth.

Joan's idea of a joke was cutting, but it was also honest. So honest, that the majority of us would virtually crumble at having our egos punctured. In the pub, we were all subjected to his casual smirks and one-liners. When Alison had experimented with an eighties hairstyle, it was Joan who pointed out she looked like a racoon. When Leon announced he was being promoted, Joan questioned if being asked to do more for the same money was just being told that everyone thinks you're lazy. And I won't even begin to relay what Joan has said about my love life over the years.

But when it came to the big things, he knew where to draw the line. When my dad died, he called and asked if I wanted to go for a drink. While I was in the Middle East, he posted so many genuinely supportive things about my work on his social media to his massive following – yes, Joan's ability to ridicule and take the piss had essentially made him an online influencer. That said, I would not have made such a generous character assessment of him six years earlier when we were out at a basement bar for a Northern Soul night on his twenty-ninth birthday.

That night, as was my tendency at the time, I had arrived much later than planned and everyone was already there sitting around a crowded table while the dancefloor was just about getting going. Nights like those would usually get busy after the nearby pubs had called last orders, so apart from our friends, the only people I did not recognise were a group of four girls who Joan was talking to at the bar. It was not entirely against the norm for Joan to hold court with good-looking girls – Alison being a prime example – but there were numerous juxtapositions about the scene that immediately caught my eye.

First, Joan seemed to be having a normal conversation with the girls just by himself. In as long as I had known him, I had never seen Joan ever make any effort with a women, let alone try to chat up a group of girls. He would usually hang back, laughing at people like me making nervous, awkward approaches in a club and then be in hysterics when it went sub-optimally. He would only engage when he could not resist making a comment that either cuttingly took the piss out of either one of us or the girls themselves. However, these girls seemed to genuinely not look that offended talking to him. And, if anything, he looked a bit bored talking to them.

The second juxtaposition was what the girls were wearing. These types of nights would normally attract those into vintage fashion with 1920s flapper dresses or waistcoats and flat caps. Or those who did not want to make too much of an effort but wanted people to know they were not making too much of an effort. So almost half the dancefloor, boy and girl alike, would be wearing chequered lumberjack shirts, or t-shirts with an ironic slogan. What those nights usually did not attract were four classically attractive brunettes in sleek black dresses who looked like they had mistakenly wandered into the indie scene.

Joan saw me and waved me over, and I suddenly felt the icy cold sensation of nerves as I joined the five of them. Anthony, my first therapist, had once told me that attraction was more about acceptance than beauty or sex. Unfortunately, I was not due to meet Anthony for another six months. Then, my life was a weekly collection of heavily drunken nights out in the hope of meeting someone who could replace the woman who a year earlier had agreed to marry me.

'This is Scott,' Joan said to the girls, over the music from a speaker just above us. 'He does banking stuff. He's single and loaded. Scott, this lot were just saying how they were looking for rich boyfriends.'

Two of the girls gave me an awkward smile and began fiddling with the straw in their drinks. Another tallish, skinny girl, probably the most attractive with sharp cheekbones and almond eyes, simply turned away to look across the bar.

'Don't listen to him. We weren't saying anything like that,' then said the fourth girl, giving me a warm, friendly smile.

'I'm Katie,' she said, offering me her hand. 'My brother thinks anyone whose wardrobe includes more than four t-shirts is a shallow egotist.'

As we shook hands I could not recall what surprised me most, that Joan had a sister or that he had a sister who was so ridiculously pretty. It might have been because I had not had a promising girl smile at me in what seemed an eternity, but I found myself smitten even before Katie had let go of my hand.

'I didn't know Joan had a sister.'

'We keep it well hidden. He thinks I'm a geeky swot, and I still hold a grudge against him for locking me in our downstairs bathroom when I was six years old.'

She was pretty, she was funny, she had referred to herself as a geek, and she was talking to me. She was perfect.

'Can I get you guys a drink?'

'We've just ordered actually. They don't do mojitos, unfortunately.' One of the other girls then said something into her ear and she nodded.

'We're going to dance. It was nice meeting you.'

As the girls left, Joan nudged me.

'I thought you'd get overly excited.' He nodded in the girls' direction. 'You do realise it's just a lot of hairspray and makeup? Most women also have legs and bums.'

'I wasn't looking – '

'Sure you weren't. They are also ridiculously dull. Katie's been inviting them to stay at my parents' every bloody summer since they all started at university together. Niles and I can't go to a single thing back home without one of them being in tow.'

'The tall one's alright,' I said, hoping to divert attention from who I was actually staring at on the dancefloor – she was smiling and trying to dance the best she could to *Joy Division*.

'I've got nothing against the Oxford lot, but with Katie it was like when the iPhone came out – you had to remind her that she just *goes* to Oxford, she didn't invent it.' He then tilted his head as he looked over again. 'The small, chunky one is pretty cute, I guess, if a little bit braindead. I'd go for her. The tall one's a complete up-herself bitch. What am I saying? That's exactly your type these days, isn't it?'

Joan had a point. After Vicky told me our engagement might have been a mistake, I began swapping indie nights for the clichéd nights out I had initially avoided while working at a bank. I would get invited out by brokers on expense accounts to the posh clubs of Soho and Kensington, ordering rounds of champagne to impress Sloaney girls and part-time models.

As I sat with my friends, my eyes would still flick back to the bar and the pretty brunette girl who was somehow related to my dickhead mate. It did feel a little bit disturbing knowing that this girl would probably share so many genes with Joan – up close would they have similar ears, the same nose, the same mannerisms around the dinner table? To be honest, I soon began to get quite drunk and forgot most of these reservations and just honed in on how much I had liked seeing her smile at me.

'Why don't you just go up and talk to her?' said a voice next to me. It was Alison. At that time she had bright pink hair, two lip rings, and a nose stud.

'Do you like Katie?' she said enthusiastically. 'She's super nice!' She grabbed Joan who had been having a separate conversation. 'Joan, Scott and Katie would make a cute couple, right?' Joan looked thoughtful for a moment and then laughed.

'Nah, I don't see it.' Alison slapped his arm. 'Well, she's high maintenance, and Scott's a bit little-boy-lost.' He motioned to turn away, but Alison caught him.

'By high maintenance, do you mean she washes up and hoovers more than once a century?' Joan simply snorted and smiled.

'Fair point. I don't think she's seeing anyone at the moment, and I suppose Scott actually talking to her would make a decent change than him just leering at her and her friends all night.'

Joan then turned me around to face the girls who were standing at the far end of the bar.

'Just offer to buy them drinks. They're technically still students so should be grateful.' I then felt an array of hands push me off towards them.

I stumbled forward, conscious that I was not entirely steady on my feet. I wished I was drunker to have more confidence, but also soberer so I could walk in a straight line. Four pairs of eyes were then on me as I interrupted them, taking Joan's advice, but shouting it at close range, 'CAN I GET YOU SOME SHOTS?'

'It's okay, thanks,' said Katie. She was sitting on a barstool, smiling serenely while her friends looked slightly alarmed at the random man shouting at them.

'We're good with these,' she smiled and raised the drink she was resting on her thigh.

'Don't worry, we're all doing them. It's Joan's birthday!' I felt my voice edge overly ebullient. Obviously, she knew it was her brother's birthday. I also noticed I was slurring a lot more than I could recall five minutes earlier.

'We don't want a crazy night,' she leant forward to shout over the music. I took Katie's response as an invitation to step through her friends and lean in closer to hear her.

'We've got to catch the nine o'clock coach back to Oxford tomorrow. It was the cheapest ticket.' She gave me a polite smile and tried to turn back to her friends. Two of the girls had backed away, laughing.

'Four vodka tonics and a round of tequilas.' The attractive tall, skinny one had pushed herself in between Katie and me and shoved her empty glass into my chest as she waved to the barman.

'You don't have to – ' Katie tried to say, but her friend kept blocking her and staring at me with a severe glare until the tequilas were poured. The tall girl and her two friends downed their shot while I did mine, and the shorter two ran off giggling to the dance-floor. Katie was about to get off her stool, tequila untouched, but the tall girl pushed her back down, mouthed *don't be rude*, and gave her a slightly villainous smile before leaving.

My banter did not improve. I asked any random question that came into my head as she politely answered, staring back at her friends, who were laughing as they danced. The music seemed to get louder and I could not hear her answers, so I had to lean in closer and occasionally shout, 'SORRY?' I knew it was not going well. I just needed a way to style out my exit, to seem like less of the creepy drunk guy who wanted to ply her and her friends with alcohol.

'How did it go?' said Alison excitedly as I rejoined her and Joan on the other side of the bar.

'Apparently the River Cam is in Cambridge. Not Oxford. Hence she does not go punting on it often.'

'Oh. But Leeds Castle isn't in Leeds, either,' Alison replied with an earnest smile. 'You were talking for ages, though. That's good. Surely?'

I ordered myself another drink and rejoined my circle of friends. However, I would still occasionally look over at the girls. I then saw Katie walk over and say something to Joan. They both then seemed to look directly at me.

'What did she say?' I asked Joan.

'She asked if you were going to ask her out or what,' he said, deadpan. 'And if her friends can go back with me if you and her go on somewhere else.'

I have to be honest. Only a complete idiot would have believed Joan. Even drunk to the point of teetering dangerously, I should have known better.

'That's great!' beamed Alison. 'I can help look after the girls and set them up in your front room.'

'I'm guessing that's your cue to join her, then.' And if I had been just one more drink sober, I would have noticed that not even that duplicitous arsehole was able to keep a straight face as he shoved me toward the dancefloor. All I remember was suddenly being on the dancefloor, standing in front of Katie, who was swaying to the music and looking away.

In the periphery of my vision I recall seeing Alison striking Joan on the arm repeatedly and angrily as he was positively wetting himself with laughter. I then looked down at Katie who had her eyes closed and head tilted to the side, still moving with the rhythm.

I was kissing her for about five seconds before I felt her pushing me away, and then I suddenly had three angry attractive girls all yelling at me and shoving me, hard, away from their friend and off the dancefloor.

At the *Jaqueline Celeste*, one of the nicer pubs in the flat's vicinity, Joan and I finally found Katie.

'Well, she's not going to be at the *Red Lion*, drinking cask ales,' Joan said as we spotted her through the window. 'She used to do this all the time as a kid. Go off in a strop and sit under a tree at the bottom of the garden.'

'Yeah, but she's not a kid. She's a grown woman, and you've been a prick.'

We watched her through the glass sitting at the bar nursing what looked like another gin and tonic. Joan pushed the door open as I grabbed his sleeve.

'Actually, maybe we should hold off.'

'Make up your mind!' Joan let go of the door, looking exasperated. 'You're the one who suggested this.'

'Because we *should* apologise. But now she looks quite...'

She looked sad. She was slouched, had an elbow on the bar, resting her chin on the palm of her hand, and was looking through her glass at thoughts unknown.

'She looks like she might want to be alone.'

Joan then also studied her.

'Nah, she's just a moody cow.'

The *Jaqueline Celeste* was a low-lit, upmarket bar, rather than one of the old-fashioned boozers or unrelenting craft beer pubs that were springing up. Candles lit the wooden tables, all of which were occupied, and the clientele looked too young and far too trendily dressed to be in jobs which paid enough to afford to drink there. In addition to a wine list upon a chalkboard behind the bar, was a craft beer menu complete with tasting notes, even stating which specific community in the British Isles the yeast came from.

'For fuck's sake, do you ever shut up about it?' Joan then said to me as we stood looking up at the board. *'Boohoo gentrification's a bad thing,* we get it. But seriously, how many working men's pubs do you think either of us would seamlessly blend in to?'

We were just far enough away to be out of earshot. Katie was still staring through her glass at some distant spot behind the bar.

'The sour is quite nice. They have that at Alison's local.' As Joan was about to order, I held him back once more. This time because the sad-looking girl sitting at the bar was now glaring at us open-mouthed, in total disbelief. She then turned away, shaking her head.

'Scott thought we should apologise,' Joan said, taking the stool next to her and also ordering two lagers.

'So it's Scott's fault you're *deliberately* a bastard?'

'As much as it's his fault you're *very clever* and *went to one of the more exclusive colleges in Oxford.'* There was a third stool next to Joan. I didn't take it. Instead, I opted to stand rereading the beer menu intently, pretending I was not listening to what I hoped would have been a more sincere heart-to-heart than Joan's opening gambit.

'Also, you know I'm a bastard. I've been taking the piss out of you your whole life, and the only time it's actually justified you throw a tantrum.' A blonde girl behind the bar put our pints in front of us as Joan pressed his phone onto the card reader.

'Justified?' she hissed sharply. 'How is it justified to show your friends private stuff about me?'

'First, I would describe him as more of an acquaintance than a friend.' I automatically felt my mouth open as I took my eyes off the board and stared at them.

'And because it's not private. That's the whole point of the internet, isn't it? And, because it's not even you. Either you've finally learnt what satire is, or you've totally got stuck up your own arse. Come on, even you have to see it's ridiculous?'

'I didn't even write it! Or sign up for it! If you must know it was Izzy, for me. To get me back out there.'

'Obviously. She even Photoshopped your head onto someone less flat-chested and boyish.' Katie made a grossed-out face and slapped Joan on the arm. Not affectionately. Hard.

'Listen, I'm not saying we weren't *not* being arseholes. And I guess I am sorry you got so pissed off. But you should either write something normal, yourself, or delete the thing. Otherwise, you will only get losers like Scott checking you out. Plus, the fact you haven't taken it down *and* were checking it at Mum and Dad's probably says something about you and Ethan too. Other than everything being fine.'

From looking like she was quietly listening to Joan's initial apology, Katie then rolled her eyes and looked away. I had finally decided to sit down though I still tried my best to look more interested in my pint and the bottles lining the bar than the scene next to me.

'How is it any of your business? What has our relationship got to do with anyone else?'

'I don't know. Because he turns up at family gatherings? Because you've hardly shut up about him for the last however many years? Because I keep getting asked about this fucking Christmas thing and the fact Mum's heard from Ethan's mum that *twatface* is probably working or some bullshit, so is not likely to spend Christmas with them after all. Hence Mum doesn't want you spending it alone.'

Joan let out a long sigh and took a large drink of beer. There was the jangle of a small bell as the bar's door opened and one of the young *hipster* couples left.

'So I said you could come with Alison and me to her parents if you didn't want the fuss about going with them to France.'

'You're asking me to spend Christmas with you and Alison?'

'It's more her asking. Plus, it would be the easiest thing all round.'

They didn't say anything for a minute or so. Katie just stirred her drink with a small black straw, and Joan then took out his phone and started scrolling. I glanced around the *Jaqueline Celeste* and its pleasant early twentieth-century soft furnishings, the well-polished wooden bar, and the other customers who all seemed more engaged with their conversation than we were with ours.

'You could just be supportive about the Ethan thing,' Katie then said quietly, still staring at her drink while she stirred it. 'You are meant to be my brother.'

'Why, though? Katie, you're the most mature person in our family, if at times predictably so with the whole five-year plans and overachieving. So what if one part of your life isn't working out like you expected it? Welcome to what it's like being one of the rest of us. Fuck, look at Scott.' Joan then leant back to let me into the picture. Hunching over the bar, playing with a beer mat, I looked up reluctantly, knowing it would be a tedious joke at my expense.

'When it comes to relationships, you're looking at someone who had one snog with a girl from work and as a result, spent six months having her wage a hate campaign against him. To the point that he's been unemployed a week digging holes in an allotment rather than see her again.'

For the first time one of us smiled. It was Joan, as he glanced my way. Katie furrowed her brow. 'You've told her about Sarah, right?' Katie looked puzzled and I shrugged.

'Scott gave up being a millionaire to save the world and now is digging up gardens for a living because he befriended some bunny-boiler who wanted him to come round and watch her getting railed by dicks she met on *Tinder*.'

'That's not remotely true, Joan.'

'It's all true! That's what makes it hilarious.' Joan then turned back to Katie.

'Scott dated this psycho who kept sending him risqué photos of herself mixed in with screenshots of guys from *Tinder* whom she was also seeing.'

I looked at him, unimpressed, but this time gave him the glare reserved for when he had gone too far.

'But you are still working, right?' asked Katie, this time looking at me puzzled. 'At a charity? That park garden thing is what you do in your spare time?'

'Do you two seriously never speak to each other?'

'No, I left the charity. I'm just doing some work with people from the community garden fixing up their allotment.'

Katie still had her brow furrowed. 'I thought you liked your job. You always seemed, I don't know, like you had a good day when I asked you about it.'

'No one likes their job, little sister. At least those of us not clever enough to work in the museum sector.'

Joan smirked again, but this time was standing up and pushing his pint away.

'Alison's done with book club, so I can go home. If I leave now, I can get in an episode of *Race Around the World* so tonight won't be a complete write-off.'

And with both Katie and me still sitting there with half-full drinks, he simply walked out.

Over the course of the night, we'd hardly had a two-way conversation. Joan had primarily been the focal point. In a way, that summed up our relationship to date. Now that it was just us, I had no idea what to say to her. I was about to ask her whether she wanted to leave the drinks and head back home, but she broke the silence first.

'It's not like he's autistic.' She picked up her glass and stared at me like she was intently trying to work something out.

'He's fully aware of what he's doing, and he does know when he's being a jerk. But I also genuinely believe he doesn't do it for pleasure or sadism. It's like he was born with the *arsehole gene*.' She sat up and swivelled on her stool, so she was fully face-on to me.

'I spoke to Alison about it drunk one night and ended up asking her what she sees in him. And she confided that she thinks they're still together because he pissed her off so much once that she punched him in the testicles. She said it was meant as a joke, but must have done it harder than she thought, and it ruptured something, so he had to go to the hospital. The worst part is when she told me we were both practically wetting ourselves laughing. I do love him – I must do, right? – but he doesn't make it easy. I think if he and Alison got married, I would cry all through the ceremony, not because it's what you do at weddings, but for Alison and how she's throwing her life away.'

For the first time since our initial meeting at that indie basement bar years earlier, Katie actually smiled at me. A real one, brightly and laughing, rather than out of politeness. She then half-frowned, a smaller, more apologetic smile.

'Do you really not like living with me?' she said.

'No! Not at all. It was just a bit of a weird start – I knew you thought you'd be living alone, so I thought I'd give you your own space. And I then had other stuff on my mind.'

'This Sarah girl?'

'To a less extent now. Now that I don't work with her. It's not a bit deal, I actually do enjoy garden stuff and have some savings to pay the rent still – '

'Scott, I'm not interrogating you! It's totally up to you what you want to share. But it would be nice if we could feel we could chat occasionally.'

We sipped our drinks again, a little bit more comfortable than when Joan had left us, as my lager and Katie's gin and tonic came close to their end.

Things with Sarah and me came to a head on Easter weekend. We were going to a gallery together on the Thursday. The trigger came a few weeks earlier after, having dated without openly acknowledging we were dating, she asked me, 'so what is this?' Perhaps I should have told her I thought us just friends, but considering I had taken her to a candlelit wine bar, I think we both knew there was something more going on. We started holding hands across the table and as we left the bar we stood under the streetlamps and had our first kiss.

But we work together,
What would people say if they found out?
I'm not sure how I'm feeling.
This is more than friendship but I don't know what this *is.*

It was not quite Romeo and Juliet, but rather two work colleagues both in a bit of a rut making much ado about nothing. Well, at least that is how I would describe our relationship in hindsight, without acknowledging what I was actually feeling at the time. I wanted her. Part of me craved the attention she gave me –

all the text messages, the secrecy, our self-importance. And then a week after the kiss, Sarah finally came to a decision.

I'm not sure it is just that we work together. I don't think that would stop me. I just don't think I have strong feelings for you.

At least it was a twist on the *it's not you, it's me* cliché.

What Joan had said about the photos of herself and the screen-shots from *Tinder* began happening soon after. We fell back into a situation where she wanted me to play the older brother role. At least the majority of the time. *This is more than friendship but I don't know what* this *is*, she repeated as she would still message me late at night, sending me pictures of herself; with friends earlier that night, and then of herself in her bedroom. Then, the next day I would receive screenshots from her Tinder account. *What about this one? What do you think?*

I tried to ignore her once when I realised it was not going anywhere. *Why are you ignoring me? This is not cool.* So we continued on, agreeing to remain as friends and even go to an exhi-bition together, one which she told me she went to every year but this would be her first time *with a boy*. Again, in hindsight, I don't know what is more embarrassing, the fact this whole melodrama caused me to spiral into depression, or the fact me and a grown woman were carrying on like we were in a poorly edited episode of *Dawson's Creek*.

I then made her cry. And I caused her to storm away from me down the length of London's Southbank. We had not yet reached the gallery, and she began telling me of a date she went on the previous night. I tried to act unaffected and asked how it went. She said promising. I stopped asking questions. We wandered further toward the gallery. 'Are you going to see him again?' 'Maybe tonight,' she said. 'He asked if I was free, so depending how long this goes on for.'

I can't remember how it started but she accused me of being

passive-aggressive. I think I said something about not fancying being a warm-up act. She said she had made it clear to me we were just friends. And I said she might want to read through her countless messages to me and look up the definition of friendship.

As I have said, this was after work on Easter Thursday. By the time Tuesday morning had come round I was sitting in the waiting room of a therapist's office about to meet Dr Camille Pendry.

'Do you know what the most annoying thing about tonight was?' Katie said as we walked back. 'I was really looking forward to opening that bottle of wine. I guess any incentive will do when having to sit through an evening with my brother, but I was genuinely quite excited when spending the extra money on it in the shop.' Under the dim streetlamps, I stared down at the uneven pavements trying to make sure we avoided the usual neighbourhood dog shit.

'I'm ashamed to say I chose it for the label,' she said, still talking about the wine as we stood on the landing, taking off our coats.

'I shouldn't admit it but that's how I choose. Despite being told countless times it's all just marketing and that I truly know nothing about wine.'

She quickly stepped into the kitchen and turned to face me with the bottle she now seemed obsessed with.

'Never judge a wine by its label. Never judge a book by its cover.'

She handed it to me and went to the kitchen cupboards.

'It's still relatively early, and I'm kind of feeling like I need to *de-Joan* myself – is it wrong to come back from a pub and *then* need a drink?'

She brought down two small tumblers. I might have been overly harsh about her obsession with the wine bottle. After all, she

was the one making an effort. If left to me, we would have walked
the whole way home in awkward silence. And it was a nice bottle.
There was something quite stylish about the symmetry and colours
– a light cream background with rows of embossed shiny circles,
five across and down, the colours changing gradually from red to
blue.

'What do you reckon? It is still quite early. One drink? Without
Joan. A very belated moving-in toast?'

Her relaxed smile faded as I groaned.

'I'm completely wiped out, to be honest. Another time?'

'Oh, yes, sure,' she said as I handed back the bottle. Early, to
Katie, I assumed meant any time before two in the morning, when
she would usually come home from nights out. For me these days, a
late night was what I had endured that evening – the clock just past
ten, and me not yet in bed listening to depressing indie music. I did
feel guilty, though, as despite smiling, she looked disappointed.

'Can I ask, who said that you weren't a good judge of wine?'

'I don't know,' she said absently, returning the glasses to the
cupboard. 'Probably Izzy. If there's an excuse to be snobbish, she'd
be first in line. Ethan too, come to think about it. But then his
parents do own a wine cellar, apparently enabling him to form a
critique of anything he desires. My taste in wine, my taste in music,
my overall qualities as a girlfriend apparently.'

She turned back from the cupboard and gave me a raised
eyebrows look.

'Do you want to talk about it?'

'About my bad taste in wine?' she said, tiptoeing to the top
shelf.

'About you and Ethan. I know Joan just stirs things up most of
the time, but if you did want to chat...'

'You don't have to. And besides, my brother has the *arsehole
gene*. We've established that.' She then bit her lip.

'Are you asking me because you already know? Joan's told you that Ethan's sleeping with someone else, hasn't he?'

The wine was pretty bad, it turned out. And it was ages before I got to go to bed. 'It's been going on for a month or so,' Katie said as I set back down my glass. 'Or at least that's the one I know about. Ethan had said that while he was away we should try to be non-exclusive. Still be together, but less intense. See other people while we were still young and before things became serious.'

'How long have you been together?'

'Long enough for me to assume things already were serious.' She finished her glass and slowly pushed the base back and forth. I picked up the bottle and topped each of us up. We both sipped and winced at the taste. Letting it breathe seemed to make it worse.

'So I said yes. But only because there wasn't much choice. That's really the conversation you want to have with your boyfriend who you have been with for over six years. Not, "let's talk about the future and the fact that we've been living together a year so maybe we should think about the M-word." No, instead, "I kind of want to get my end away but still have you as a backup".'

I was a little out of my comfort zone. When Sarah first told me about her breakup, I had held her hand. At the end of the night I hugged her and told her it would be okay. With Katie, we were strangers until an hour ago, and our only form of physical contact was when I had kissed her against her will.

'It'll be okay,' I said and found myself reaching out and patting her upper arm, a bit like I would have with my old friend Jeff Martin for a good presentation.

She had both elbows on the table, cupping her chin, looking thoroughly miserable.

'Thanks, but I'm in a relationship that I'm too embarrassed to get out of, and I spend my weekends clubbing and partying like I was a twenty-year-old trying to show the world I enjoy not being exclusive too. Things are not okay!'

She stared down at the table and put her face in her hands. Awkwardly again, I reached over, and this time tried a soft rub on her arm.

'It wouldn't be so bad if I didn't love him, but I do, and it's all so...'

I had honestly thought she was just having a rant and needed to blow off steam. But it was so sudden. Her voice cracked, I saw her lip briefly wobble, and the next thing I knew, she had burst into tears. It wasn't crazy crying. It was worse – the heartbreaking kind. Her face quickly went pink as the tears started to stream down her cheeks before she could catch them.

I got off my chair and moved next to her crouching down, this time my arm around her shoulders, still a little worried she would push me off.

'It's... shit. And he sounds... well, like a bit of a dick.' She started wiping her eyes. She just nodded and gave a half-smile acknowledging the attempt at reassurance. I tried to soothingly rub her back until I realised my fingers were rubbing the clasp on her bra strap, so I decided to stop.

'It was Joan who told me,' she said, pulling out a tissue from her pocket. 'In front of our parents. Mum had asked how Ethan was enjoying Germany. Joan just snorted and said she was better off asking Tess Philips.' She shook her head, tried to gently dab away a tear from her eye, which was futile – her running mascara made her look like a panda.

'He said after that he heard from... oh, you wouldn't know them. That's the thing when you grow up in a village. Everyone knows everyone. He now seems to take genuine amusement in making sure it is common knowledge that my boyfriend prefers regular sex in Berlin with someone who was two years below me at *my* school, rather than having a relationship with me.'

Katie finished drying her eyes. The crying was over, though I thought it best not to mention the huge mascara circles. I didn't think telling her *it would all be okay* really fitted the context. Again, I hardly knew her and had never even met Ethan. In hindsight, I perhaps should have seen it strange that he never visited, and she had only travelled to Berlin a handful of times since we began living together.

'I don't know him. Or Tess Philips. But I have got to know you a bit, and I think you're incredibly kind and friendly and warm-hearted. And pretty! Really, really pretty!'

This might have been too much. But complimenting her personality made her sound like the consolation prize. I was being weird, and Katie seemed to give me an odd sideways look to confirm this.

'What I'm trying to say is that he's making a huge mistake. And it's *because* you're kind, warm-hearted, and beautiful that he's doing this.'

She gave me another quizzical look.

'Once this beautiful girl agreed to go out with me and suddenly I was all *Mr Self-Confidence* and thought every woman on the planet must also adore me. I quickly forgot how much a chance that beautiful girl took, that it was her benevolence that plucked me from obscurity, and how lucky I was. Until I lost her, that is.'

We sat in silence for a bit until she smiled and said it probably was time for bed.

'Sorry to ruin your evening,' she said as she stood.

'Hey, it was not ruined.'

'Liar,' she smiled. As she left the room she turned. 'That girl. The beautiful one who took a chance on you. Is that the one from tonight? Sarah?' She smiled again, causing me to reciprocate.

'No,' I said. 'That was someone else.' For a split second, I saw Vicky sitting on a picnic blanket on a sunny afternoon at Regent's Park, smiling at me as if for the first time. 'She deserved better. And she found better.' Katie smiled sympathetically before saying goodnight and leaving.

CHAPTER 5

I'LL STILL DESTROY YOU

Is it possible to have a soundtrack to depression? The thing about depression is that once you're out of it, you're out of it. You're suddenly like everyone else again. It's very difficult to describe what it is like at its peak. When you start thinking rationally it is almost impossible to put into words the processes in your mind that make you feel worthless – that you would prefer not to live.

This might just be my experience, but I would not describe what I felt as sadness. It is not like the feeling you get when you listen to a *depressing* song. We all feel sad and melancholic at times but this was something more. It's like feeling so empty you can't bear one more day carrying around with you that expanse of nothingness.

The days before Easter weekend there was this intense paranoia and self-loathing. A voice shouting how worthless I am, how everything is my fault. It was like this switch flipped and I would hear it over and over. Flaws and failings. That's it. Numbness and supersensitivity because every little thing would be evidence of my worthlessness. *I might go out with you if you still had your flat. My friends are everything to me.* Throw away comments from Sarah, but I somehow saw them as evidence of my inadequacy and let them ruminate until something in me broke.

When I was transitioning through my teens, from the *Games Workshop*-obsessed board-gamer to what was effectively a wallflower at the *cool kids'* house parties, I traded up my little painted orcs and druids for music – rare albums on vinyl and an acoustic guitar – in an attempt to make myself *cool*. I had thought an obsessive knowledge of indie and rock music would be the key to getting girls to notice me. After all, did not all women secretly want to be the girlfriend of a budding rock star?

No, not *all* women apparently, and of those who did, the majority seemed to prefer global superstars to a seventeen-year-old whose greatest musical achievement was covering two Ocean Colour Scene songs.

My bedroom at Loughborough Road was the converted attic. With Katie finally gone to bed, I quietly passed her door and climbed our second staircase. I switched on only my small bedside lamp and put on my headphones. The album on my turntable was *Sleep Well Beast* by The National. Those not interested in indie music, *Pitchfork* or post-punk, would not have heard of them, and I have no desire in going all *High Fidelity*. Let's just call them an American rock band, now in their 40s, who sport suits and cardigans rather than tattoos or ripped jeans, and won a GRAMMY in the *Music for Solitary Men Approaching Middle Age Who Take Themselves Too Seriously* sub-genre.

This would be the way I would spend my evenings that summer and into autumn; lying on the bed, letting my stereo play, in my quaint little attic room, which I had converted into an emotional sanctuary. Before Sarah and I had so destructively parted on Easter Thursday, I had already planned to squat at Dad's house. Technically, the house was meant to stay vacant until probate had been decided – that was the agreement Ellie and I had made with the potential new owner. But at the time I was sub-renting at my fourth Airbnb in a five-person house share. The Sarah situation was already going south and I desperately needed time alone. After our argument, I felt alive with vindication, that she was the one in the wrong, she was the one who had led me on, she was the one with the pathological need to be adored. At least that was what my head was partially saying. Another voice was also telling me what had happened was all *my* fault. I was in my mid-thirties, homeless, with no prospects, in a job I had no passion for and with hardly any friends or family anymore either. Sarah did not want me because, put simply, I was not good enough for her.

This one's like your sister's best friends. In the bath. Calling you to join them.

The song played through my headphones as I looked up at the skylight above my head. It had its blackout blind drawn, but I occasionally saw it flicker as air would get through the seal. I should be too old for transcribing song lyrics and ascribing meaning to them, but please humour me.

We all need something at times. A quirk, a place to go or perhaps a hobby that completely and solely belongs to us, and no one has to understand or needs to know. 'Scott, I'd like you to make a list,' Camille said during our first session. 'Of all the little things that bring you joy. Be it a favourite meal, a place you like visiting, something you used to really enjoy doing. Then give yourself permission to go out and do them.' I think Camille had meant a walk around Highgate cemetery, or sitting in a Chinatown restaurant at lunch, or watching an old film just to feel something akin to myself again. All these were on my list. But so was this song.

This one's like your sister's best friends

Having a popular older sister with a set of pretty, well-developed friends, who would spend countless days sitting around the house, was a source of both fascination and self-conscious anxiety growing up. I'm sure they knew I would stare at them, especially which part of them my eyes would find themselves resting on. Rather than nurture my confidence with women, I became all too aware I was Ellie's geeky younger brother with thick glasses who built models of orcs and warriors in his bedroom. But it was a homely image. And like many a man growing up with an older sister, I very much related to that lyric. It reminded me of simpler times.

There were other lyrics like it. I have no idea where *The National* stand on copyright infringement but sometimes depressing songs can be just the antidote you need for battling depression. Each line transported me away from that friendless attic room and back to a part of my life I found altogether more reassuring.

This one's like your mother's arms...

When I began sorting through some of Dad's belongings I found the photographs of all our old holidays. We were at the seaside. Mum looked so young. She was ridiculously beautiful. She probably still is. I guess having one of your parents leave is not overly uncommon these days so that feeling of abandonment and longing can be considered pretty much universal. Perhaps too those feelings of regret and nostalgia when you look back to a simpler time when everything seemed so perfect, or at least compared to those weeks, months and years after when there was an unspoken hole in our lives.

It was only a song. I stared up at the sloping ceiling and the attic skylight. The never completely pitch black London sky kept creeping through the sides of the blind. There was one line though, which reminded me of Dad. I was back at our old house and inside our conservatory. It was a summer night and Dad was scoring into slices of orange peel and dropping them into glasses. 'It's the oils, you see,' he explained, adding a precisely measured amount of gin and topping it with tonic. He did make the best gin and tonics. When I was old enough to join him, we would sit there in these large wicker chairs with the conservatory doors open and look out on the garden as if the world and all its problems were a million miles away; *this one's like the wilderness. Without the world. I'm gonna miss the long nights, with windows open.*

I don't think depression is brought on by one single event like my argument with Sarah. As I would lie on my bed that spring and summer, most notably after my sessions with Camille, I thought back to those memories brought on by that song. What they all had in common was I was a little bit sad in each. The awkward teenager whose sister despised him and lacked friends of his own, let alone a girlfriend. The small boy whose mother was one moment loving and then absent the next. And the thirty-something whose best friend was a man in his mid-sixties who had left him too. It all felt a culmination. Like I said, it's not exactly rational. *The sky is getting white. I can't find a lighter anywhere, I'm going crazy. But I'm not crazy.* Perhaps that was the line in the song that made me love it. It was the only one who told me at the time that I was not crazy.

I was still fully dressed, but I closed my eyes, wrapped my duvet around me and switched off my lamp. I imagined depression as a young child standing with their heels against the wall having their height measured. I imagined it growing with me as I got older, a friend from childhood, in the room as I stood awkwardly staring at my sister's friends, watching over me in the days after Mum left, at the drinks cabinet as I stared at Dad's empty chair. Someone familiar, even nostalgic. Each time that little bit taller.

I then saw depression back in April hovering in the shadows at Dad's house as I took the first of the pills. A mythical Golem, lurking in the corner of every room, waiting, biding its time.

I woke up with a start as my phone buzzed loudly. Since Sarah and I had stopped speaking my phone was largely devoid of messages, especially late-night ones. Reaching over, I wondered if it was her, perhaps one last message, maybe she missed me now I was gone. I am not saying I would have welcomed a reunion with Sarah, but there are times when I did look back at those early days and did miss some form of human connection. Or perhaps it was my mobile network informing me I had run out of data again.

It was not Sarah. Or Vodafone. But a message from Mike, my brother-in-law.

You might want to go to the house tomorrow. Orletta's been in touch.

CHAPTER 6

OUR HOUSE

When I arrived back in the country for Dad's funeral, it was Mike who did all the driving back and forth between Brighton and London, helping with arrangements and carrying messages between Ellie and me. It was also Auntie Pam who did her usual stalwart job of seeing us through, getting us into line and somehow knowing the ins and outs of burying not just my father but her younger brother. That was something we took for granted over the years: Auntie Pam's steadfastness. She was the opposite of Mum in that respect. She had had a distinguished career as a senior anthropologist working all her life for the Royal Society. She was married once, had no children, but seemed far more content to dedicate her life to order and answering the big questions regarding the origins of man.

Growing up, we were the children who were permitted to run wild and free. However, a visit to Auntie Pam had us doing chores and eating pea soup for dinner – all chocolate was confiscated at the front door. 'I won't have them running around on sugar and e-numbers. You might as well be feeding them rat poison,' was one of her popular sayings. She was divorced and, as I said, had no children of her own. Only us, and we were not too thrilled at the time by the association. But what you dread when you were younger becomes a comfort as you grow older. Auntie Pam was always there for us and even more so when Ellie and I drastically let her down that Christmas Eve a year ago.

The service was at eleven o'clock – prayers at St Augustine's and then to the cemetery. Our family solicitor – Auntie Pam's first husband – told us Dad had left wishes for such a day, he was to be buried for eternity underneath the ground eight miles from our family home. That was its own relief as making decisions would have involved Ellie and me having to communicate, but, at the time, we seemed to both find comfort in each other's absence.

It had been six months since we last saw each other. I was in London for a couple of weeks at the start of the summer, and we had spent a weekend at Dad's taking the kids to parks and then sitting up drinking wine. When Mike had offered to pick me up from the airport, I had assumed Ellie and I would have some time to sit quietly and talk about Dad. Or if that was too touchy-feely just sit together in silence and try to acclimatise. But she had relayed to Mike that with having to get the kids ready it would be easier to all meet directly at the church. She, Mike and the kids would travel up on the day so I would not see Ellie until the funeral service itself.

In hindsight, it was not unreasonable of Ellie, and if I stepped into her shoes I would see the challenges of trying to balance childcare and grief. But at the time, I felt it gave me the moral high ground as it was her way of having yet another dig at Dad. I remembered those teenage years especially those days before she left for university. All she did was goad him and yell at him and do her very best to humiliate him before abandoning him. And he just allowed it to happen. However, I wasn't going to let it. Not that day. Not on his last day.

That day was never going to be all sunshine and rainbows, but for those attending, it would forever be remembered for one public spectacle. For me, yes, that moment would mark a low point in my quest for emotional maturity, however when breaking down the day's events, two other probably more significant developments also occurred. The first was seeing the girl I loved.

It's funny what we remember. And when. Those Proustian moments that arrive when you are doing nothing more than opening the garden gate to your once family home. I walked up the path looking up at the brickwork and the tall windows. I quietly opened the front door and felt a familiar air flow into my lungs. The hallway, always catching the light in the mornings; the staircase which we would come running down; the entrance to our long sitting room; Ellie's piano still in pride of place and, just beyond, our dining table, chairs tucked in and placemats still laid out. It was quiet, too quiet, no signs of life in those rooms and I didn't need to venture forwards to either the kitchen or Dad's study. Instead, I climbed the stairs and made my way across the landing to what I still referred to as Mum and Dad's room.

I saw her before entering. She was standing at the window looking out, the floor-length voile curtains blowing in the light wind making her look taller.

'She's taken the dresser,' Ellie said without turning around. 'And the ottoman. And the chest of drawers. But not any of the shit Dad got from Ikea, funnily enough. And she left the curtains. I guess whatever transport she had was already full from pillaging.' The room was indeed bare. Spacious and tranquil, and Ellie looked like a ghostly vision as the warm light filled the room, bouncing off the champagne walls. 'I thought you would be at work,' she said, again still absently staring out the window. I wondered how long she had been like that. There was no doubt she had seen me lingering in the street outside.

'I took the day off.' Not quite a lie.

'Lucky for some. What is it you do again? It's so difficult to keep track.' The first dig. It only took her three sentences. She was good – she knew just where to jab the knives.

'Ha. For a second you sounded just like Mum.'

We'd not even made eye contact and the passive-aggressive point scoring had begun. I looked around at what had been left behind: the bed and bedside tables, and the wardrobe. In the twenty years since Mum left, Dad had not changed the room one bit. And I never thought about questioning whether that was healthy until now.

'Fuck this,' said Ellie, spinning around and walking across the room, past me and out of it. 'I told Mike I would handle it.'

I followed her onto the landing and down the stairs as she went off on her low-level monologue. 'I didn't need him to postpone his session work. And that I didn't need my little brother tagging along while I sort this mess out.'

'But it's not really up to you to decide that is it, Ell?' Ellie ignored me, ducking her head into each room apparently looking for something. We made it to the kitchen and on the breakfast table was an official-looking letter. She picked it up and thrust it at me.

'*Mrs Orletta Imogen Roberts requests proceedings commence for the clearance of Number 1 Queen Mary Grove in advance of the sale of property,*' I read. '*All possessions deemed the property of Mrs Orletta Imogen Roberts will enter auction at Southgate Auction House on January 14th 2019. We ask you to hence remove all articles not deemed legal property of Mrs Orletta Imogen Roberts prior to the aforementioned date. All articles deemed property of Mrs Orletta Imogen Robert are listed as inventory on the enclosed annex and any such removal shall be deemed theft...*' I tailed off towards as Ellie stared at me.

'Did you know her middle name was Imogen?'

Ellie then grabbed a small collection of papers which had been under the letter and thrust them at me too. It was the *enclosed annex*. For someone who didn't want me tagging along she seemed pretty insistent I be kept up to date. There were a lot of pages.

'Hang on, when did she have this done?' Ellie shrugged. 'Like, someone's come in and looked at everything. This page has all of Dad's books – all of them. There's...' I did a rough count of the rows and columns '... nine hundred books. None of these are hers. Why does she...' I suddenly felt agitated seeing everything in the house listed in black and white. 'But this is *everything*. There's a watch I bought him for Christmas here.'

'Don't worry, Scott. There's some shit in the basement she doesn't want. We can sue each other over that if you like.'

Ellie walked around me and stood at the sink, her back turned again.

'But... we agreed to wait. That was the whole point of me moving out and mothballing the house. We'd see what probate comes up with and sort things out then.'

'Yes, Scott, you having to have moved out is the issue here. God forbid a thirty-five-year-old man should have to fend for himself and not still have to live at his parents'.'

Still surveying the list, I heard the tap running and glanced up to see Ellie at the sink pouring herself a glass of water.

'I called Maxwell. He's going to drop by and explain our options. But he said on the phone that if it's got to this stage then Mum's solicitors are pretty certain probate is now a formality.'

'Ell, Maxwell's not even our lawyer. He's more or less sided with Orletta this whole time.'

'You're right, Scott, why don't we just pool our fortunes and hire some fancy London barrister? Maxwell's our only bloody option.'

And so summed up the last year of our lives. The low level bickering, constant but consciously never enough to cause a proper scene. After the funeral we tried to get on. In fact the events at the cemetery seemed to bring us closer together. At least for the one hour before Maxwell sat us down in the study and told us about the will. Since then our only point of conversation had been the house and how to stop Orletta – our mother – getting her hands on it. Ellie then snatched the inventory from me. 'He'll be here in an hour. I'm going to Dad's study and see what's actually mine on this bullshit list. Oh, unless you want us to search for any more little notes you've left lying around? Perhaps something to Grandma confessing to war crimes?'

She did have timing, I had to give that to Ellie. Standing across the kitchen, she delivered sarcasm without a trace of the sardonic. But she had brought up the note and I was obliged not to ignore it.

'Ellie, we should talk about – '

'Save it, Scott. Like I said, I really, really don't care.'

The church was chaos. We had arrived with Dad before Ellie and Mike. After we had settled him inside, Auntie Pam had me standing outside with the Orders of Service. 'He never liked cere-mony,' said Auntie Pam at my shoulder as we waited, looking down the path where people would be coming from. 'He hated being late. Even as a boy he would want that time to himself – to survey the scene before all and sundry. He would be happy with today.'

I didn't know if Auntie Pam was emphasising that point because I had gone quiet. I was in my black suit greeting people who all seemed to know me and whom I vaguely recollected over the years. The majority of the time I was just staring out into the distance at the park over the road until I felt a body press into mine and a kiss on my cheek. And there she was, after seven years. Her yellow hair creeping out from under her hat, the black dress she was wearing making her look older but in such a good way. A beautiful way. This woman standing before me, an echo of the girl I once loved.

'Vicky?'

'I'm so sorry, Scott. My parents told me. I tried calling you but...'

'I don't have an English number anymore. I forgot to... I basically... How are you?'

'Tired,' she said with a careful smile. It was such a pleasure seeing her smile, even on that cold, damp Christmas Eve when everyone in that church should have been sitting at home with their loved ones feeling joyful and not huddled together waiting to say goodbye to someone they all cared about. She looked down at her stomach and the protruding bump.

'How many months...?'

'Five.'

'Is it your...?'

'Second. One girl so far. I think we're going to stop after this little one.'

'It's been...'

'Seven. Seven years. When I heard I felt I should come. I hope you don't mind?'

She looked great. She always used to wear her hair long, ever since school, but it looked like it was cut short under her hat. She looked exactly the same yet completely different. A stranger from a dream. Something about her face was suddenly complete, the cute-ness and that sweetness I adored as a boy converted into true beauty. We did not part on bad terms after the breakup. We broke up because she was brave enough to sit me down and tell me it wasn't working – something I already knew. We were never *high-school sweethearts*. At school she was the only girl to talk to me, largely because she was the only girl in Maths Club and she had asked me how to solve integrations.

We went to the same university but she slotted in perfectly with the boys and girls who ran societies, attended balls and hosted dinner parties, whereas I found my own niche with friends like Joan. We were still friends but lesser friends than school. And then came the return to London and the great leveller. London treated you as irrelevant irrespective of whether you had won re-election to the Student Union council three years in a row or if you had spent four years playing computer games.

We ended up at the same parties. I was always at my best at my drunkest, and I had a job that instantly meant I could afford a nice place to live and to go out without having to worry about savings or being able to afford rent. It was about then that I stopped deliberately looking for her.

In five years of London, post-university living, there was by no means a conveyor belt of young ladies at my door. But there were drunken fumbles, a few overnight guests, and a French quasi-girlfriend who liked staying at mine and was my first experience of weekly sex with the same person.

And then Vicky broke up with her boyfriend. She was alone at a dinner party, and I saw her in the corridor putting on her coat about to leave. I asked her to stay and for the first time in years we had a long chat. We arranged to meet for coffee the next day and catch up on our diverging lives. Coffee then became drinks the following week. Drinks became dinner. And a taxi back to hers became me believing my life was finally complete.

'How are you coping?' she asked. 'How's Ellie?'

'Are you coming to the...' I did not want to say the word. 'There will be something after, at Dad's. It will be nice to talk.' She squeezed my hand and walked into the church.

The service *was* lovely. I know everyone says that, but it was. It was astonishing all that Auntie Pam had accomplished without the help of Ellie or me. All I remember about the days before the funeral was sitting on the sofa in the living room, various different groups of people around me, and Auntie Pam talking, organising, while I stared petulantly into space quietly seething that Ellie had got away with not being there too. That probably says everything about me: my father had died and all I cared about was my sister having it better than me. And what did I actually do regarding the funeral arrangements? Nothing. There was so much I should have done but Auntie Pam had to step in at the last minute – telling the vicar about Dad so he could say some words about him at the start of the service; deciding on the readings and then contacting Dad's friends to ask if they would do the honours. Auntie Pam's first husband, Maxwell, did the eulogy, and it was perfect. He spoke of Dad's career, his friends, his interests, and how proud he was of both Ellie and me. Maxwell was an excellent speaker and he had people laughing through their tears, exactly what Dad deserved.

Then, to my right at the opposite end of the aisle was Ellie. All in black, and crying. I had only seen her cry probably twice before in my life. Even at the car, when she and Mike arrived, she was more tense than sad, preoccupied with getting the kids sorted, and we just shared a brief nod, 'alright' and just as we were heading in she said to me softly, 'surprised you could make it. Africa's loss is apparently our gain.'

And now she was bawling, after all she had done and all she

had said to him. All of us – Ellie, Dad, me – had somewhat patched things up in the last few years but there did seem to be a correlation between how broke she was and how often she would call or visit. At least that was what I was telling myself standing in the pew watching her as the church sang '*Amazing Grace*'.

By the grave side, she was the same. Unrelenting. We were throwing in a handful of dirt and she shook her head refusing, obviously wanting people to see how emotional she was. The kids didn't understand. Mike was holding Ed and, as the vicar said his final words, Millie ran off with Mike having to give chase. People started moving away. Auntie Pam was talking to the vicar and suddenly it was just Ellie and me, next to each other, looking down at Dad's coffin. She was still sobbing.

'You can tone it down now, Ell,' I heard myself say. 'Nobody's looking anymore.' She shot me a look. But I stared straight ahead, determined not to see her.

'You don't want to overdo it, after all,' I said again to my crying sister. In the corner of my eye, I saw her take a tissue to her eye. I then heard her say in a hoarse voice,

'Scott, why don't you do everyone a favour and go fuck yourself?' I turned around. Through our entire lives she would always have the last word. But that's the thing about grief and anger and trying desperately to hold back this intense rage that seemed to have come out of nowhere to run through my whole body: you say things you would normally keep well hidden.

'Anyone would think you actually gave a fuck about him.' I mumbled it and then walked away over the wet grass. The ground was soft and my shoes slid in the mud. I made to walk between the headstones to the cars where the rest had gathered. I then felt myself flying forward, my hands catching me as I hit the damp grass pressing into the mud. Flipping myself over I suddenly had Ellie on top of me.

'You self-righteous little...' she hissed. I'm not sure if she punched me. I don't think she did. I think with the wet grass and the anger it was a push with her whole weight – and grief – behind it causing both of us to tumble. But she definitely winded me as her knee landed into my stomach and I then felt her palm press on my mouth hard as she covered it.

'Shut up! You poisonous... waste of...' She looked livid. In hindsight, understandably so. I could feel the cold and wet of the grass soaking into my trousers and suit jacket. I also felt a déjà vu of helplessness lying on my back with my sister trying to suffocate me, but now had the indignity of being a six-foot-tall man who had just been flattened by a five-foot-seven, barely one hundred and thirty-pound mother of two. I felt my hand squidge on a patch of mud. I grabbed a handful. As Ellie pressed her fist into my mouth I smeared soft, runny mud across her face, into her hair, reapplying it to nose and cheeks as she pinned me down.

What happened next was even more embarrassing. If we were brother and brother, or sister and sister, it could have been a watchable punch up, but there was one of us pinning the other down and we both began grabbing handfuls of earth from the side of a grave and flinging it at each other. Ellie tried to push herself off me taking what mud was around her and practically creating a face mask for me. We tried to separate from each other but found our legs were entwined and slipping in mud. As she got up, I also tried to get to my feet, inadvertently pulling her back down as I had to cling to her, my shoes having no grip. I think it was then she did manage to get to her feet, having had to shove me off her in the process – which she did through one short, sharp punch to my eye. There we were, Ellie standing triumphantly over me, her high heels sunk into the mud, her black dress now a shade of mocha, and me flat on my back spreadeagled. She looked down at me panting, her teeth still gritted. I looked up, and rather than seeing Ellie above me I saw the

nine-year-old girl who was the sister I once hero-worshipped. I
suddenly found I was smiling. She glared at me, and just as
suddenly, she began laughing. Then there were people.

'What the devil?' Maxwell was first on the scene. Tall, grey-
haired and spritely of physique, he must have won the foot race.
Then came Mike.

'What the f...' He was carrying both Ed and Millie. Maxwell
reluctantly offered me a hand and helped me to my feet, keeping
my dishevelled body at arm's length.

'Mummy's all messy,' said Millie, grinning happily. Mike just
looked at us, dumbfounded. We were facing each other, still panting, smiling. 'It's nothing,' said Ellie. 'We just slipped.'

'Mud patch,' I confirmed, flicking my head and then suddenly
having to bend over to catch my breath. I stared up at Ellie. She was
covered in earth – face, hair, shins and knees. She looked bedrag-
gled and tired.

'Let's just go back to the car,' she said. As Mike and Maxwell
still stood looking like we were criminally insane, Ellie and I turned
away and began walking side by side. 'Sorry,' I whispered. 'Me too,'
she said. I felt our hands touch as we walked and, for the briefest
second, we held them. Ellie was talking to the kids: Millie walking
and Mike still carrying Ed. If you excused the fact our clothes were
ruined you would assume nothing out of the ordinary with the
scene. Then we saw Auntie Pam. She had not cried that day. She
had stayed strong. But I could see the tears in her eyes and in a
croaky voice she just said, 'the children can come with us,' before
she turned away and went to the car.

It was perhaps hypocritical of us chastising Orletta for taking an
inventory of Dad's possessions, as two weeks earlier, Ellie and I had

done the same. Since the funeral the house had been mothballed. The only person accessing it on a regular basis was Dad's friend Jane, a retired government spy from the Cold War era who, in what turned out to be Dad's last few years, helped him keep the house in order in return for intellectual company.

Ellie and I took great amusement in goading Dad over whether the relationship was *sexual* company – Jane had been a student of Dad's, taking up a doctorate in English literature as a pastime for her retirement. Dad would never rise to the provocation but watching his and Ellie's back and forth did amuse me. Ellie, for all her faults, knows how to master subtlety when it suits her.

'Dad, it must be a joy for Jane to have her literary professor in such close proximity. I'm sure a lot of girls would get starry-eyed at the prospect.' Dad, without looking up from his paper, would say, 'I wouldn't say that, dear. Having taken charge of our country's national security for over two decades, I very much doubt that now undertaking a PhD would turn Jane into a schoolgirl.' Ellie would not reply but take an interest in a book and lightly hum, '*Mrs Robinson*'.

Looking back, it was warming to know that Dad had someone in his life, even if it was just a friend. Auntie Pam was only a few miles away and available for Sunday lunch, but Auntie Pam was, well, Auntie Pam – a former anthropologist and antiquities expert who was not one to suffer fools gladly nor debate the merits of an egalitarian state over coffee. It was nice to know that Dad was not locked away alone in his study and had someone to share a gin and tonic with on summer nights in the conservatory. Dad's other friend of note was Auntie Pam's ex-husband, and our family solicitor, Maxwell. Maxwell and Auntie Pam had divorced when Ellie and I were barely old enough to really understand what divorce was. From what I remember, as a couple neither were that child friendly and I have only vague early memories of Maxwell being at Auntie Pam's when we would visit. I would more associate Maxwell with his visits to Dad and them sitting with a drink putting the world to rights. It was not that Maxwell was unfriendly, or strict like Auntie Pam, rather I don't think he understood children. When I was the age of eight or so he would be the only person to shake hands with me, followed by a pat on the head as he commenced a bright, enthusiastic conversation with Dad over the copyrighting of one of his books. It was both easy to see what drew him and Auntie Pam together and also why they were apart. Both held successful careers and came across as knowledgeable and worldly. One could imagine the allure of a similarly active mind just as one would see the frustrations and impatience at neither giving ground nor trying to understand the importance of the other's work.

As we waited for Maxwell, I swapped rooms with Ellie and went to Dad's study, a small room at the back of the house. Its walls were entirely lined with books, and Dad's desk sat at the back, still with his handwritten notes and stacks of papers piled up. For his sixty-fifth birthday, I had bought him a whisky decanter and glasses. These were placed next to Dad's record player on which we'd hear him play classical concertos, operas and, later in his life, jazz.

I sat in his leather chair. It was soft and comfortable as I rocked back. I then felt a jolt of dread. There in front of me was his letter writing pad, the last letter written, not by him, but by me. I could still see the indentions of his name and the first line, and found myself closing my eyes and rubbing my finger over the words to feel the letters I had jotted. Slowly I got up and moved to the door. The shelves next to it housed Dad's favourite books. Those weeks earlier, Ellie had been checking which were first and second editions and I was upstairs taking mental note of his things and what we should do with them.

It had been both Auntie Pam's and Jane's idea. 'It gives me something to do,' Jane had said to me when she offered to keep checking in on the house. 'I would hate to know that all of George's possessions were sitting dormant gathering dust. Houses are meant to be lived in after all.' Auntie Pam echoed that opinion in a pale blue air mail letter. I don't know if Ellie's or my behaviour was the trigger, but once the funeral was over she announced to us that she was stepping out of retirement to join some expeditions in Ethiopia and the Middle East. She might have realised that retiring to be close to her family was futile when the one she loved most was no longer there. I still remember smiling at seeing the *Par Avion* label on that very thin paper, which I did not think was still in circulation. *'It has become my concern that even considering the less than ideal circumstances regarding your father's probate, you both have left his home as a mausoleum and appear to be waiting on some other person to take charge and organise his effects'.*

At the shelves, I found both halves of a torn *Watership Down*. A novel out of place among the works of Aldous Huxley, George Orwell and Ernest Hemingway. I had put it back exactly where I had placed it that Easter weekend. Dad had read it to us when we were little, so I placed my note within its pages. To many it would make no sense, but even now, I feel it was the best way to reach him. I took the book out, the note now gone, and closed my eyes. The way I felt back then, I did not feel now, I told myself. Just sheepish at the state I had got myself into and then having my older sister find me passed out in my own vomit. In a way, part of me hoped we would lose the house. That it would mean Ellie and I could go our separate ways and would have no need to pretend to like each other which I am not sure we ever did. But then, if there was no house, what exactly did I have left? We all need an anchor, don't we? Mine had been Dad and this house. Now with Dad gone, I felt the wilderness fast approaching. Without Ellie, who else did I have? I then heard a tap at the front door heralding Maxwell's arrival.

When we arrived back from the funeral, Ellie ran straight up the stairs to wash the mud off and change clothes. 'My dress is ruined, by the way,' was the first thing she said to me as Mike drove us back from the cemetery. She then called me a dickhead under her breath and asked me, slightly disinterestedly but *asking* just the same, what my plans were now the funeral was over. As we got out of Mike's Volvo, and as Ellie took first dibs on the bathroom, I went to the kitchen, using the sink to clean myself up when Vicky came in with a tumbler of amber liquid in her hand.

'I thought you could use this,' she said, handing me the glass.

'Thanks. But I don't really drink the good stuff these days.'

'It's single malt,' she smiled. 'I could get you a gin and tonic if you prefer? I know tequila was more your drink but I wasn't sure of the etiquette.' She did have a great smile. I picked up a tea towel and wiped my face and wet hair.

'Thanks, that's kind of you. But I just poured myself something.' I saw her eyebrows rise in surprise as I nodded at my glass of water.

'Well there's plenty of wine.'

'Not today.' I tried to smile politely. 'I've been experimenting with sobriety the last few days. To be present for a change and not just let things drift.'

'My, things have changed.' She leaned against the kitchen counter as I rested a hand on the sink. 'Scott Roberts, the life of the party, turning down free alcohol.' She then smiled – tenderly like she had done when we would walk home from school. 'It's okay, you know. If you do want to drift off for a bit, today of all days. I don't think anyone is going to hold a glass of whisky against you.'

'I'd hold it against me,' I smiled.

'You should go back in. I'm sure a lot of your dad's friends would love to talk to you.'

'When Ellie comes down. In the car, we said we should show a united front and try to erase everyone's memory of the floorshow.'

'It was pretty memorable. Do you mind if I ask what it was about?'

'The usual. Who loved him more. Who, at heart, is a more screwed up human being.'

'Scott, I know it's not the best time but I am sorry about how things ended between us. You were one of my best friends...'

'Vicky, it's fine,' I said, cutting her off. I felt guilty enough at that moment without having to accept an apology I did not deserve. I could not bear to see her standing there, in her graceful black dress, with her bump, looking apologetic.

'You have nothing to apologise for. I was a waste of space back then. Like you said, life of the party, but not really that equipped for the day to day.' I smiled again and she looked up at me and ran her hand through my hair.

'You really need a shower.'

As we both laughed we were joined by Maxwell, carrying his own glass of red wine and looking uncharacteristically agitated. He was not the most patient, but he was always friendly and gave off the air of carefree confidence.

'Listen, old chap, we really must have a word,' he said, placing his wine on our kitchen table. He then noticed I was not alone. 'Victoria, isn't it? I do remember you.' He instantly beamed, appearing his jovial self again. 'Jolly decent of you to be here today. Scott, I've just asked young Mike to fetch your sister.' He then looked around the room. 'Perhaps we can take this to the study?'

Vicky squeezed my arm and excused herself. Maxwell and I walked through to the study.

'Apologies, old chap,' he then said, calmer. 'But it's best to do this now before you and your sister start partaking in any beverages. Ah, there she is.' Ellie, changed out of her dress into a black top and dark jeans, entered the room with Mike. Maxwell perched himself on Dad's desk as we gathered. 'Pamela allowed me a quick sift through your papa's paperwork. As expected, I found nothing.' We had no idea what he meant.

Maxwell's resting facial expression was that of an eerie grin.

'Old George and I go back a long way. I've represented him for, what, near forty years – not an easy feat when it comes to writers, publishers, agents and the like.' He gave a light chuckle, seemingly genuinely proud of himself. 'So in light of the unhappy event, I pulled out the files.' From his jacket pocket he took out a manila envelope and he handed it to Ellie.

'This is effectively George's will. There are instructions; of what to do in the event of a day like today; provisions for care when you were both children; bequests; it handled the day-to-day so to speak.' Maxwell waited for Ellie to look through the whole document.

'Okay,' she said, appearing to scan the pages like she wasn't sure what she was looking for. 'I guess these make sense.' She shrugged and handed me the pages, sitting down in Dad's chair while I perched myself on the windowsill.

'So, what's the big deal?'

'That's everything. Your father left those instructions, but he did not write an actual will.' Maxwell paused, poignantly looking at us both, as if to make sure we understood him.

'This, in itself, is not an uncommon event. Not many of us

believe the day of our passing is imminent, so we wait. Until we're on our death bed, and then we plan on calling fellows like myself and decreeing out our legacy. In fact, when there is an obvious next of kin there is simply no need, and even the most sensible of minds find putting it all in black and white rather morose. The simple fact is, we believe we have more time than we do.'

Looking over at Ellie, I saw she seemed as interested in Maxwell's conversation as she was in mine during our car ride. I couldn't blame her. Vicky was in the next room, apparently happily married and pregnant with another man's child, but all I wanted to do was talk to her, look at her, and find out everything that had happened in her life after she had walked away from me that day on Primrose Hill seven years ago.

'So you're basically saying that Dad didn't do his paperwork? So Scott and I now need to fight it out to decide who gets what?'

'Next of kin, my dear. *Not* his children.' Again, Maxwell paused, expecting us to be processing the significance of his remark.

'What's the difference?' As Ellie asked the question, I turned away and stared out of the study window, looking out at our back lawn.

'If you asked me a few days ago, say, purely concerning this case, I would tell you that there is no difference. I did advise your papa over the years on the merits of drawing up a will and naming beneficiaries, just as I did advise him on the drawbacks: changes in circumstances, grandchildren, a future partner, taxation. And through it all, *next of kin* would simply result in the house and any funds being left to you both. *Unless* your father had a legal spouse who would then usurp both of you as the sole recipient.'

I heard a snort of laughter from Ellie.

'Maxwell, is this your roundabout way of telling us that Dad and Jane eloped? That the two of them ran away together in the middle of the night?' Ellie clearly thought Maxwell was being ridiculous.

'No.'

'Or did he have another paramour we knew nothing about?'

'My girl, please.' Maxwell was beginning to sound annoyed. 'As your *family* solicitor, I do not act solely on behalf of your father, but have acted on behalf of your whole family. Your father, the two of you *and* your mother. When your parents separated, your father informed me that the two of them had agreed to handle the matter amicably. And privately'

Through the study window I could see that Auntie Pam had opened the conservatory and a gentleman in a pale blue suit was smoking a cigarette. *Gentleman* was such an appropriate word for him and a number of Dad's friends in the house; in their sixties and beyond, white hair, crisp suits, white shirts and traditional tie, and they held themselves in a way that seemed entirely proper. Our lawn and garden was very much winterfied with nothing in bloom and our trees lacking their leaves.

'Now, I do not know how much you would understand of the process, but there are steps required to legally end a marriage. With all your father's legal paperwork in front of me over the last few days I noticed something that came as quite the surprise.' As I continued looking out at the garden there was another pause. Maxwell took a breath.

'I found no evidence that your papa had formally finalised his divorce from your mother.'

Another pause. I stayed at the window, noticing some red berries on an elderberry bush.

'Maxwell, don't be ridiculous,' Ellie said, this time sounding fed up. 'Dad *was* divorced. Obviously. He's been divorced for almost twenty years.'

'No,' Maxwell said, again poignantly, but this time we could understand the significance. 'No, he was not.'

'Crikey, my dear, things are finally moving along, aren't they?' I heard Maxwell say jovially, like it was a good thing, as Ellie led him through the house. I left Dad's study and found them both in the kitchen, Maxwell in his typical grey suit grinning brightly as Ellie offered him a seat.

'My girl, it was likely to turn out like this. They were married and living in this house close to twenty years. The divorce papers were not signed.' Maxwell was sitting with his legs crossed at our small breakfast table, and Ellie was filling the kettle and bringing out two mugs from the cupboard.

'But they *were* divorced,' said Ellie. 'Or at least in common law, surely? She had left him for a longer period than they were married. You can't have someone appear out of nowhere and inherit everything belonging to a husband she left twenty years ago.'

'I am sympathetic, my dear. And it was worth a shot waiting for probate. But your papa was meticulously organised. If he had signed or processed the *decree absolute,* there would be filings, either in his records, or he would have sent them to me with his other legal affairs. Your only options are now to have a friendly chat with Orletta, or take the matter to court, which I would highly advise against.'

'Why?' I said. They both looked up at me as I lurked in the doorway. I picked up a mug by the sink and placed it next to the two that Ellie had laid out. The kettle had just finished boiling. 'Why can't we take her to court? Like Ellie said, it's common sense. Obviously, she had made some excuse not to sign her papers so Dad saw no point signing his. And, like you said about why he didn't have a will, he did not think he was going to pass away in his sixties so he never followed up on it.'

Maxwell just sighed and looked at me much as he would a tedious office junior.

'Firstly, my boy, there is no such legal term as a *common law divorce*. And secondly, this is not America. She is your mother and it is not the done thing. *Roberts and Roberts versus Roberts*? I think not.'

'Maxwell, she wants to sell Dad's house and use the proceeds to form a cult. Who gives a fuck about social niceties?'

I saw Maxwell wince at Ellie's use of a swear word. He then gave an apologetic shrug.

'My dear, we do not have the luxury of asking George what his intentions were. But your best option by far is to sit down with Orletta and thrash this out properly. She's a reasonable woman – '

Both Ellie and I scoffed.

'She is a reasonable woman,' repeated Maxwell. 'I'm sure you would be able to keep what is sentimental and who knows, between yourselves, you could negotiate a small sum which I am sure she would agree to if only to solve the matter amicably.'

'Maxwell, we don't want a small sum.'

Ellie looked like she was getting more and more wound up as she put down her tea and began to pace the kitchen.

'This is not some form of negotiation. This is *our* home. I want my children to have their Christmases in the house I had my Christmases. To play in the same garden that I played in. To have some form of family history and know something about their grandfather, and not walk past this house one day and see it converted to flats.'

'Listen, my girl. I can see you are bitterly disappointed, but your papa would not have wanted this. If there was ambiguity in the will then perhaps he wanted this feud patched up.'

'Well, that hasn't exactly gone swimmingly.'

It was clear to me why Maxwell was so successful as a solicitor. His calm manner and quick counterarguments seemed to have taken the wind out of Ellie. She sat down at the table and appeared to deflate, hunching over her tea, staring down irritably.

With Ellie looking worn down, I suddenly felt it was my duty to step in. Being the younger sibling, I would always tend to let others speak first, having ingrained in me a military-style hierarchy of not speaking out until my commanding officer finished.

'We've done what it says to do on all the various websites, but without a court or a judge, no one is going to understand that this is not normal. And isn't the whole legal system meant to be built on reasonableness, and interpretation and precedent?'

'My boy, the law does differ somewhat from what you may have glimpsed on television programmes –'

'But there's no other option.' I seemed to be finding a voice. I glanced guiltily at Ellie, who was still sitting slumped at the table. I then looked to Maxwell, who had begun staring at his watch. Our mum had left our father and us twenty years ago to become an established artist residing in an artists' colony in Devon. She became an important figure in twenty-first-century British art, and her rare visits would always be proceeded by a fanfare of pomp and ceremony as she would ask Dad to bring us to an exhibit of hers in London. We were never permitted to visit her. She didn't have time what with running that colony of hers and the European tours.

'This is *our* house. Ours, and Dad's house. How could he have wanted the woman who walked out so many years ago to come back into his life – after he's gone – and claim his home? None of this makes any sense, so how can we stand by and not do anything?'

'My boy,' Maxwell said wearily. 'If you want your day in court, then yes, you may have chance of contesting *Intestacy*. However, what all these legal programmes fail to mention is the cost of it all.

Going to court even when you have an open and shut case can be a bottomless pit.' He now sat upright, his hands forming a steeple. 'Cases like this can get stuck within the framework of our legal system for years, and even if you win, you would most likely have to sell the house anyway to pay the solicitor, the barrister, the juniors, and the court itself. If you are determined to learn more about the law I can suggest one work of fiction that gets the whole process spot on – familiarise yourself with *Bleak House*. There was only ever going to be one winner in the case of *Jandice and Jandice*.'

CHAPTER 7

AFTER THE FUNERAL...

I had not spoken to our mother in over four years at the time of the funeral. It had become five by the time we had received notice she intended to put all our father's possessions into auction. Ellie was three, then four years old. The final straw for Ellie was Orletta not showing up for Millie's christening.

What summed up the Roberts' family was that we rarely had fallings out. We simply stopped having conversations. We stopped calling our mother and our mother stopped calling us. No malice, just good old deep-seated resentment.

Our mother sent flowers on the day of the funeral. It was Maxwell who told her of Dad dying, asked to by Auntie Pam, together with numerous of Dad's friends who had spent their Christmas Eve at the church with us. Maxwell was not the type of man to let the breakup of his best friend's marriage stop him maintaining ties with one of Britain's most eminent artists, I sometimes say, rather scornfully, through this whole fiasco. But then, Maxwell was also not the type to let grudges and the taking of sides influence his relationships. How many of us can say that? After the funeral, he spent an hour with us breaking down exactly what Dad's will, or lack of will, meant for us. Neither Ellie nor I had spoken of it before that day. Nor thought about it. In my head I dissociated Dad with Orletta completely. 'Dad and Mum' were the parents I grew up with, and loved wholeheartedly. When Mum left, in a way, she never came back. The *artist, Orletta Roberts* was born. Mum always painted, and the same conservatory which had become where Dad would sip his gin and tonic was Mum's studio. Mum had always been exceptional and well regarded in her own circle. But then the Royal Society took notice, and she was off like a shot to somewhere in deepest Devon, to become the queen of some artists' colony whose benefactor, and her new partner, was a property tycoon named Conrad.

From my impression, and I don't think just because I was a kid I only saw what I wanted to see, my parents' split was not the conventional marriage breakup. There seemed to be no discussion of custody – we never spent a single night with Mum once she left. There were no teary goodbyes at the end of each visit. In fact, I had not seen her happier to be on her way and off to which social event had actually brought her to London. It was literally like she went away one weekend and forgot to come back.

The concept of Ellie and me inheriting Dad's house had blindsided me that day because, to me, it would always be Dad's. So to be told by Maxwell that in the eyes of the law it would now be seen as Mum's, was something I could not comprehend – there was no 'Mum', only *Orletta Roberts*. And Orletta Roberts had her own house and fortune down in Devon.

Not that it should have mattered. But losing Dad, and then losing Dad's house on a technicality felt akin to a betrayal. The only thing was, I was not sure who was betraying who – were we betraying Dad by letting his memory disintegrate into something to be lusted over on *Homes Under the Hammer*? Or was Dad betraying us by not shoring up his legacy? Either way, leaving it dormant for a year – doing nothing for a year – suited me fine. All I wanted was Dad's house to remain his. Not Ellie's, not mine, not Mum's. Just until I had gotten over my shit enough to realise that this house was an integral part of our family and Ellie and I had the right to call it our home. Unfortunately, Orletta Roberts was not of that same opinion.

Three days after the funeral, Ellie and I were both standing at the window watching our mother pull up. It was a sleek modern Jaguar with tinted windows, and though we could not see inside, it had to be her. We slowly made our way to the door, one last unifying nod and a deep breath setting us on our way to greet a parent who we had allowed to disappear from our lives. But it wasn't her.

'Apologies, Orletta is under the weather,' Conrad, our mother's partner, answered our puzzled looks as he gravely shook my hand and briefly embraced Ellie. He was very much the same as I had remembered him from my latter teenage years – the last time I had met him. Though with probably less of that snow-white hair decorating his crown, and, if anything, smaller than I recalled.

'You should have said, old chap. We would have gladly postponed.' Maxwell had entered the hallway, big beaming smile and towering over the rest of us.

Conrad removed his banker's coat, revealing a grey pinstripe suit as Ellie and I tried not to look bemused. He did still have that presence, stature, and chiselled face of a man not accustomed to explaining himself or suffering fools gladly.

'We thought it would be best if I make the journey. George's death has taken the wind out of Orletta and she very much wanted her respects paid.'

As we led Conrad to the sofa and armchairs of our living room,

Ellie screwed up her face to give me a what-on-earth? stare behind his back. I quickly shrugged an I-don't-know look.

'I understand this is a very difficult time for you both,' said Conrad, as we served tea. Ellie had got our old tea set out. It had been a wedding present to Dad and Orletta from Auntie Pam, and over the decades it had only seen the light of day in her presence.

'I won't keep you long. Orletta sends her love.' I shot Ellie another look. Neither of us had commented about our mother's absence and her sending a proxy.

'It was quite the shock for her, hearing the news. Even after the separation, she and your father were still very close.'

No they weren't, I expected Ellie to say. Or at least I hoped she would, as I did not have the courage to voice aloud what was bubbling beneath my silent, listening persona. Conrad then shifted forward, his hands making a triangle, cutting straight to the business end of the conversation.

'Maxwell has informed us of your father's will and your mother's position. As I said, these are difficult times, so I will make this brief, and we can start the ball rolling.' In my hands was my teacup. I had added three sugars, eradicating the taste of tea and creating a liquid that simply stung my teeth.

'Your mother acknowledges that she has no need for a house this size in London. We keep a flat more centrally when we do need to stay. She has also been keen to expand the artists' colony for some years now, so the proceeds can go some way to realising this. The only question is when. I am sure you both would want to free yourselves from all this as soon as possible and move on to mourn your father in your own way.'

'What do you mean by *proceeds*?' I asked, looking up from my teacup.

'The sale of the house. Your mother's and father's house. She has no need for the property as a primary address, and in this present climate it would release significant funds...'

'But, Scott's living here,' interrupted Ellie.

This time it was Conrad's turn to look bemused. 'Scott, I understood you were living abroad? The Lebanon, was it?'

'He came home at Christmas. And this is where he lives when he's in England.' It felt very strange hearing Ellie come to my defence, or what appeared to be my defence. Apart from me, everyone was now on the edge of their seat as Ellie moved onto the offensive. 'It's also got all Dad's things in it. And our things. You can't just sell it. It's not Mum's to sell! It's our home!'

Conrad looked unmoved as if it was a mere token argument from Ellie.

'Eleanor, I'm sad to say I'm at the age where I am getting increasingly more experienced with the affairs of close friends passing away. It is never an easy time, and financial circumstances always form a distraction to grief. As difficult as it is, decisions need to be made early and not drag on. Scott,' he then said as he looked at me. 'Be assured, we will not force you out of the house, but you will need to find alternative living arrangements as soon as is feasible for you. I am sure you would, yourself, want stability and your space after all your travels...'

As Conrad continued, I stared at Maxwell. It felt like there had been crossed wires somewhere.

'I don't think we have agreed on anything yet,' I said. 'I don't know if Maxwell's told you, but Ellie and I want to keep the house. As Ellie said, it's our home.'

I am not sure what I was expecting as a response. Perhaps an argument where we debated again the legal meaning of next of kin, and what rights our mother would have forgone when she left. But instead, Conrad gave a small, sympathetic smile.

'Ah,' he said. 'Of course.'

He then also looked at Maxwell. 'Max, I believe there is a conversation we then need to have. Perhaps some forewarning would have been appropriate.' For the first time, I then saw Maxwell look flustered as he stammered for an answer. Conrad cut him short.

'First, please accept my apologies,' Conrad said to Ellie and me.

'It seems both your mother and I were under the impression discussions were at a more advanced stage. I assume probate will now come into play?'

Conrad looked again at Maxwell, who again stumbled.

'In that case, I will leave you both and allow Maxwell to inform you more regarding the complete picture.' He reached down to pick up his car keys. Hesitantly, both Ellie and I rose with him, negotiations apparently at an end.

'Again, I am sorry for your loss. George was a very good man.'

I think only Conrad, with his old school demeanour and quiet authority, could have got away with such a line about the man whose wife he had coaxed away.

'I do have to say, Scott. I know it is a difficult time, but if we are going to continue discussions, it would be beneficial all round not having the prospect of a sitting tenant.'

I handed Conrad his coat as Ellie held open the door. It was all relatively cordial.

'It may seem rather heartless, but I have seen these situations escalate, as I am sure Maxwell can explain. It would be best if your stay in the house does not stretch too far beyond the New Year – at least until probate has come to a decision. Until then, I am sure your mother will be willing to accept the house as still your father's. Not hers. Not *yours*. Your father's.'

He gave me what I deemed a poignant stare, and then gave Ellie and me another sombre nod as he made his way back up the garden path to his Jaguar.

CHAPTER 8

THE DAY WE CAUGHT THE TRAIN

Once every month in the years before I left for university, Dad and I would do a trip. It had stemmed from the writers' conference I had joined him on the day after Ellie gave me stitches for my critique on her piano playing. We would throw tents in the car and head off to a campsite either on the coast or in the New Forest, just the two of us. It wasn't exactly stepping into the wild and battling the elements for survival, but it was hugely enjoyable and a diversion from our typical personas – Dad, university lecturer George Roberts, and his Games Workshop-obsessed son, now hiking, foraging and gathering firewood.

Over that same period, Ellie studied music at Bristol and completed her degree, and I hardly heard from her apart from the occasional call to check in with Dad. And over the phone all we would exchange was, 'is Dad there' and 'yeah, one sec'.

Ellie would spend the holidays with her new friends, even Christmas, either some trip abroad, a stay at someone else's home, or a series of festivals. Dad would visit her. I remember the first one barely lasting a few hours – he left mid-morning and was back in the early evening. He never brought me, but I was glad not to be forced to see her. I was resentful about how she had to have everything dictated on her terms. My *wild child* older sister had become dull and predictable in her determination to be unpredictable and untamed. Life was so much better without her around – no one-way shouting matches at Dad or slamming doors at all hours. No tension or snide comments regarding the 'bourgeoisie dictatorship' that was our home. I was glad not to see her for three years.

However, I wasn't. Not really.

As Ellie and I left Dad's house, I had hoped the alliance against both Maxwell and our mother had created some form of truce between us. But we remained in silence as we walked up the suburban roads to the main high street.

'Are you getting the train from Waterloo?' I asked as we entered Wood Green station.

'Yeah,' she muttered, taking out her bank card as we passed through the barriers and made our way to the platform.

'I was meant to meet Mike, but he has to work late. Every night this bloody week.'

We got on the Piccadilly line heading south. She yawned. Her eyes looked heavy.

'He's been in Hoxton at the recording studio. It's another generation of little bastards who can't play their instruments and are going to have one minute of fame before getting a one-way ticket to No-One-Gives-A Shit's-Ville.'

If I ignored the fact she appeared to be talking to the tube map rather than me, it was our first conversation in weeks.

'I know it's not his fault – I'm not *that* selfish.' She frowned, again looking away. 'He does fourteen hours' work for eight hours' pay, leaves at five a.m. and arrives home sometime after midnight.

Today was meant to have been just editing, but he's had to re-record nearly everything the untalented twats had laid down.'

She leaned on her forearm as she held the rail. I slumped against the tube door as we jolted along through the tunnel. 'And today I've got to be home to get everything done for...' She cut herself off and rubbed her eyes. 'Let's just say this wasn't great timing.'

'Is there anything I can do?'

'Yes, Scott, let's make this all about you for a change.' And with that, she turned away.

That was what it was like with Ellie and me since Dad died, even before the letter incident.

At Waterloo, Ellie marched into the main station and I tried to keep up with her.

'I don't need accompanying. I know where the trains are.'

'I thought we could talk. How long till your train?'

'For fuck's sake, which part of *I don't give a shit* don't you understand?'

She kept walking quickly. She had a stride that effortlessly took her the whole length of the concourse at pace, while I had to break into a jog to keep up.

'Let's just sort the house out. Can we agree on that? I need to make some arrangements for the piano. I don't care what she says, it's mine, and it's coming to Brighton even if we have to sell everything else in our shoebox to fit it in.'

'What about the letter, Ell?' I said, panting, as Ellie reached the ticket barriers and went through. 'My letter to Dad. I want to talk about it.'

Ellie came to a halt eight or so paces ahead. We were halfway down the platform. She turned around smiling – a calm, ironic smile that she saved especially for her enemies.

'There we are. Life has to be about Scott Roberts. Just like everything else. What shall I do, Scott, stay here with you, leave my kids to fend for themselves, make sure you're feeling better?' She walked closer, eyes narrowed, staring at me like she could not believe how stupid I could be.

'Scott, I'm going home. Back to my life. I suggest you go do the same.'

She shook her head, rolled her eyes, and walked away.

'Three years, Ell,' I heard myself call out. She turned around, giving me a what-the-hell-are-you-on-about look.

'I was fifteen and you left for three years. You didn't come back once.' Ellie looked back puzzled, with an undercurrent of surprise or anger.

'What has that got to do with anything?'

'We grew up together in the same house for fifteen years. And then one day you go and don't come back.'

'I was at university!' she hissed, cautiously glancing left and right – people had begun giving us a wide berth as they passed, walking down to the far end of the train.

'You were at university for like six months of the year! You never came back during the holidays, you never wrote, you never asked how I was, the only time we spoke was if I picked up the phone on the rare occasions you bothered to let Dad know you were still alive.'

I did not know where this had come from. I was suddenly so angry with her. She just stood there, perplexed, like I had lost my mind.

'Scott, I know you've got problems but get a fucking grip.' She grabbed my wrist hard and stared at me fiercely.

'I was a kid, Ell. You never said why, you never said sorry, and you just assumed we were okay.'

'Jesus Christ. Scott, that was a long, long time ago. I then spent the best part of my twenties looking out for you. Hanging out with you and your stupid friends. Where was all this fucking self-pity then?'

'I don't know, Ell, I think I was too busy developing a drug and alcohol problem in the hope it would impress my older sister.'

People were walking past quicker. It was the start of the Friday commute home and small suitcases were being wheeled along the platform by those in suits or smart winter coats.

'So this is my fault?' she said, not quite yelling, not quite not yelling. 'You're blaming me for how your life's turned out?'

'I just want to know why. What I did to make you hate me so much when we were growing up?'

In that moment I knew the answer. She gripped my wrist tighter. Her nostrils were flaring. I had seen her angry in the past, but this was nothing to the glare she was now giving me.

'It was your fault that Mum left,' she hissed. 'And it's your fault that Dad's...'

She didn't have to say the rest, and I'm not sure if she did. Through a red mist, I could vaguely see her turning around at the same time I did. I walked away, not turning back.

We were not always like that. And Ellie was right about my twenties. It was harsh to lay my problems with drinking and drugs at her door. We had become friends. Or at least drinking buddies. After university Ellie began her new, rather leftfield, career as a music journalist. Rather than composing or playing piano professionally like I thought she was destined to, she would go to gigs, interviewing the bands of our age, and tell Dad and me of life on the music scene when she would finally start dropping by. I was at university by then, but when I moved to London suddenly we found common ground.

'Fun area,' she said, sounding surprised when I told her I was living with friends on Exmouth Market. 'I have friends around there.'

She told me she might *drop by* and visit when she was next in the area. And to my surprise, she did. She would randomly turn up and drag my flatmates and me down to the Brazilian bar underneath our flat. She bought shots, she met my friends, she regaled us with tales of festivals, drinking with bands and endless travel, and everyone I knew loved her.

Al's Bar would usually be our final destination, drinking *Red Stripe* lager in plastic glasses on their basement dancefloor. Those were good years. I even associate getting together with Vicky as partially Ellie's influence as I was more confident and comfortable with people.

But over that period of belatedly getting to know each other, Ellie and I never *really* got to know each other. There were always other people around. At the end of a night she would crash on our sofa, and in the morning we would sit around drinking tea, hungover, watching one of the music video channels until she decided to catch the train or meet other friends for lunch. We never talked about the years before, we never reminisced on childhood memories, we hardly even mentioned Dad, and we never, ever, spoke of Mum. We never had an actual conversation, and I can only attribute that to fear – if we dredged up the past, it would break the present enchantment.

Ellie was also right with at least two of her other accusations – that I was self-pitying and that I was making everything all about me. It wasn't Ellie blaming me for Mum leaving or even Dad's heart attack that made me feel as shit as I did sitting on the top deck of the bus travelling back to Loughborough Road. It was the total embarrassment at goading her to explode at me. I wanted the argument. I wanted anger, resentment, self-righteousness, anything to end the nothingness and the impasse. I wanted to bring back the wild, militant, angry teenage Ellie who would scream at me and be the bad guy so I would feel something other than emptiness. Regarding those other accusations, I already blamed myself for Mum leaving – did not every child of divorce? (or *faux divorce*, if there was a term for it) – and for Dad's death. I never asked when his last doctor's visit was, and I took for granted that the age of sixty-five was the new forty-five, so I did not need Ellie stating the obvious on that occasion.

I had been lying on my bed at Loughborough Road for no idea how long when I heard the knock at my bedroom door. Miles Davis was playing on the record player as, reluctantly, I got up.

'Oh, sorry, were you asleep?' asked Katie.

'Asleep?' I ruffled my hair. I must have had bedhead. 'No, I've just been listening to music...' I stared curiously at Katie. She looked different – her eyelids were a shade of emerald green, and her lips a sparkly red. Even though I would see Katie and her friends getting ready for a Friday or Saturday night out every single week – it was impossible not to with her door constantly open – I would always make sure I was safely cocooned away back in my room by the time they eventually left so I never saw the final result. She had *a lot* of makeup on. And if I was being overly prudish, not much else.

'Are you on your way out?' I felt my brow furrowing as I tried not to look down at her outfit.

'Maybe. Eventually. Long story,' she sighed. She then held up a bottle and two glasses. 'I just opened a bottle of wine and wondering if you fancied a glass?'

'Err,' I said, probably unenthusiastically. Reluctantly looking at the bottle and glasses, I then saw her pleasant smile fade with uncertainty.

'Thanks, but I might not be great company.'

As Katie turned to go, looking somewhat embarrassed, I quickly realised how I was coming across. I was stalwartly guarding the entrance to my room, again turning down my flatmate on the rare occasion she offered to socialise with me. That was indeed the first time one of us had knocked on the other's door in six months. No wonder I only had one friend left.

'Actually, wait,' I said as she was about to retreat. 'I'm just being an idiot. A drink would be amazing.'

She smiled and handed me a glass. Either politely or cautiously, she stepped forward, looking about the room.

'Oh wow,' she then grinned and looked at me, surprised. 'I don't know what I was expecting, but I didn't see you as quite the collector. Are all of this yours?'

The shelves that lined the far wall housed a vinyl record collection that spanned twenty years – vinyl being my vice to replace my Games Workshop models. Wooden storage cubes from my old flat held the overspill and ran along the perimeter, with only my acoustic guitar and a mini sideboard breaking up the domino of records.

'I like the feminine touches too.' She nodded to the throws and cushions on my bed, also from my old flat, which now served to help me survive the winter in a poorly insulated attic room.

'Do you mind if I...?' Katie picked up the album sleeve that I had ceremonially placed on a 'now playing' stand next to the record player.

'The great Miles Davis.'

'You're a fan of jazz?'

I laughed a rather too forced laugh as she examined the record.

'I pretend to be. I think it makes me seem sophisticated, but most of what I listen to is indie-punk-rock.'

I was trying to act nonchalant like it was every day another human being, particularly a woman, took an interest in my record collection.

'So no dance or techno, then? And you play guitar!' She replaced Miles and stepped over to my acoustic, but this time her interest genuinely did surprise me.

'Yes, most days. Have you not heard me?'

'No. Unless, well, I do sleep with earplugs, and when I do hear music I assume it's the wannabe frat boys downstairs. Normally I just turn up my speaker to drown it out.'

I saw the corners of her mouth curl up into a grin.

'I'm kidding. I didn't realise it was you. If that's the case, I once actually turned down my music to listen to you. You were playing Damien Rice, right?'

I smiled vaguely, feeling a blush coming on. I then glanced down at her outfit, which I had been trying so hard not to stare at. She was wearing a small, low-cut white top with a printed red sparkly lipstick mark which matched her own lips. It didn't quite reach the top of her skirt, which tightly hugged her thighs and, in turn, did not remotely reach her knees.

'Oh, please don't. I know, I look ridiculous.'

'I didn't mean to stare. I've just never seen you dressed up before. Well, apart from...' I suddenly thought better than to go back to the time we met.

'You look great. Cool outfit.'

'I look like a prostitute,' she said, flicking her hair to the side and sipping her wine. 'This was Izzy's idea. We went shopping on Saturday and I got railroaded into trying something new. Per square inch of fabric it's by far the most expensive thing I've ever owned. We're meant to be going to a party and she convinced me to wear it.'

'Izzy's the tall one, right?'

'Not that tall. Her skinniness and short friends make her look taller.'

Katie then sat on the bed, placing her glass on my bedside table. She lay back, picking up one of my cushions and putting it over her face to stifle a mock scream. She smiled as she sat back up.

'Apparently, I look too much like a librarian when we're out. Or so Izzy has hypothesised. And despite telling her that I very much wanted a Friday night in watching crap TV and eating ice cream, she's got us both on the guest list of some club and has guilt-tripped me into going. Hence this.' She waved her hand down her clothes.

'Aren't Librarians meant to be sexy too?' I hovered, leaning against the wall with my wine. I did not have another chair in my room and was not sure about the etiquette of joining her on the bed.

'Now Izzy's messaged saying she's at work drinks. A client is there who she's trying to impress, i.e. sleep with. Some hedge fund type who she says does not know the first thing about the art but has decided he wants to start collecting. So I'm on call, in case Mr Hedge Fund doesn't work out. Arrgghh!'

Again she picked up the cushion to groan into. She then picked up one of my throws and placed it over her legs.

'So what happened today? What makes you bad company? Or worse than usual that is?' Again, another smile.

'Just family stuff. My sister and I haven't been getting on recently, that's all.'

'Is it because of your dad?'

Unconsciously I shot Katie a suspicious look.

'Scott, can I say something? I was speaking to Joan a few weeks ago and, I don't know how it came up, but I had no idea about your dad.'

She bit her lip and stared up at me so anxiously I suddenly felt on the back foot. I had deliberately never mentioned it and was glad Joan had said nothing as the flat was therefore sanctuary.

'I've literally felt terrible since, for not saying anything and being really insensitive when you first moved in.'

'It's okay.' I tried to smile. 'It's never been that straightforward with Ellie and me, especially when it comes to our parents.'

'Well, if you want a sounding board, I don't think Izzy's going to call any time soon.'

'Perhaps,' I smiled again. I shuffled my position against the wall and decided to instead perch on my bedside table.

'How is everything with you and Ethan?'

'Don't remind me,' she groaned. We'll talk properly soon, see what happens. Right now, I'm just done with the whole competition of it all – the nights out and *getting myself back out there* that Izzy and the girls have had me on. It's been super supportive of them, but I've spent a fortune on makeup and dresses over the last few months. Plus, my work has completely fallen off a cliff. I'm now slightly worried I might get fired.'

She flung herself back on the bed staring at the ceiling. Were we now friends? It felt like a trust was slowly forming – like she now saw me as one of the girls. Though, part of me still held a grudge about the whole moving-in weekend.

'I thought you loved life at the museum.'

Katie picked up the cushion again and cuddled it against her chest, still staring up at the roof beams and skylight.

'I had a run-in with my boss. It wasn't bad or anything. She just said she noticed I hadn't been quite myself – code for the fact I've been stumbling in late and sending things out unchecked.'

'It's fixable, though, surely?'

She sighed, slowly sat back up, and reached for her wine.

'At least I proved two things tonight,' she said, taking a sip. 'I neither have Izzy's confidence nor her impossibly small bum to pull off wearing something like this.'

'In light of past events, it's best if I don't comment.'

She picked up another cushion and lightly threw it against me, smiling. She then narrowed her eyes and bit her lip.

'I don't know if I should tell you this, but I don't think Izzy would mind you commenting.' She made a small snort and grinned.

'After all, she's checked out *your* bum enough times for it to start getting decidedly awkward.'

My wine went down the wrong way as I coughed and sputtered.

'The one we've just been talking about?' I frowned. 'Tall, skinny, and kind of rude all the time?' I tried to examine Katie's face for signs that she was winding me up. 'She glares at me whenever I'm in the same room as her! I've never even seen her smile!'

'She doesn't like smiling! She says it makes her look goofy.'

'That's just weird.' I could hardly hide my freaked-out smirk. It was both ludicrous and impossibly flattering.

'*Plus* she's *not that* tall! Or skinny – she plays tennis! Ultra-competitively and is ridiculously toned. In case you're interested.' It was now Katie's turn to smirk at me. Then the doorbell rang.

'Oh please don't let it be Izzy.'

Katie sat up, alert and listening.

'She does this. Changes plans and then turns up without warning. This is a huge favour, and I shouldn't ask, but could you tell her I'm asleep? Or ill? I really, really don't fancy being dragged out until four in the morning.'

I quickly descended both sets of stairs expecting to find an unsmiling, severe brunette with an impossibly small bum on our doorstep. Instead, as I opened our front door and looked out onto Loughborough Road, there was a tall, skinny musician with stylishly messy brown hair and the weary smile and dark eyes of someone who had hardly slept in days.

'Mike? What are you doing here?'

I looked over his shoulder to see if Ellie was somehow with him.

'Kidnapping you,' my brother-in-law replied and quickly squeezed past me and bounded up the stairs.

'Let's just say I'm making you an offer you can't refuse,' he said as I followed. 'You're spending the weekend at ours, and you and Ellie can sort this out for good. I'm not having another week with her wandering around like someone had put down her pet Labrador. Let's get you packed.' He then began bounding up the steps to my room.

'Hold on, Mike – '

'I take it *The Duchess of Bath and Wells* is out? What is it tonight? Shooting weekend at Hugo Sloane's...?'

Mike stopped dead at the doorway. Katie was standing up, glass in hand, and throw set aside back on the bed, about to leave. If possible her skirt looked an inch shorter as she stared at our unexpected guest.

Mike looked from me to Katie, confused. 'Oh. Sorry. Didn't mean to interrupt... anything...'

'You're not!' Katie said, somewhat defensively. She then screwed up her face. 'I, umm, do live here.'

'We were just talking.'

'Obviously!' Katie glared at me, not appreciating my explanation.

'Well, I guess that living room of yours is a tad on the cramped side to have a proper chat,' Mike smirked.

'Oh, grow up, both of you,' she said, pushing her skirt back down and squeezing past us both before then stopping in front of me.

'*Duchess*? Seriously?' She rolled her eyes and set off back down the stairs.

. . .

For Easter that year, I had suggested to Ellie that we spend it together at Dad's. She declined for what were good reasons at the time. 'Easter? We never do anything for Easter, and I'm not driving three hours each way just for a glorified Sunday lunch.' I suggested we could all stay the weekend. 'That's a bit morose, isn't it? And we agreed to leave the house alone, at least until this bullshit probate is done.' But I did so anyway, against her wishes.

On Easter Monday, livid at knowing I had been staying there, she drove into London to check I hadn't trashed the place. She found me passed out on the floor of the upstairs bathroom apparently having gone on a bender and having thrown up in both the toilet and the sink.

'Selfish', 'irresponsible', 'useless', and 'wanker', were just some of her words as she got me to my feet and bundled me fully clothed into the shower. From then on, she wasn't that keen on my ideas, thoughts or offers to visit or meet up, apparently not wanting her waster piss-head brother around her children. I thought it was imprudent to say I only had three cans of lager.

'I thought you didn't get on?'

'We probably don't now.'

'I'm just saying, if Ellie came home and found a girl dressed like that in our bedroom, divorce proceedings would be underway. That's if I hadn't fallen to my death from our bedroom window.'

'You're only on the first floor. There's very little chance the fall would kill you.'

We were on the A3, the lights of the motorway leading us to the coast. I had thrown a bag of clothes in the back of Mike's Volvo – not the most rock and roll car for a musician, but he said it more than reaped dividends when it came to transporting guitar amps and drum kits to recording studios and gig venues. He also said it came in handy when ferrying around two young children and their plethora of accessories.

'Millie and Ed are having a sleepover at Mrs Rawlins. We're having Millie's birthday party tomorrow so Ellie and I were going to use the child-free time to wrap presents and bake sugar-filled crap to dose up a dozen or so screaming five-year-olds. Rock and roll, man.'

'Ellie never said she was having a party.' I had the present I was going to post to Millie in my bag though I felt put out that Ellie had banished me from my niece's birthday party.

'You know, your sister's not the battle-axe she makes out she is. Sure, she's got her issues with sarcasm obviously, but at heart, she's a lot more fragile than she lets on.'

A drizzle began to fall as Mike flicked on the wipers and indicated to take the A27.

I knew Mike's plan was terrible. He had spent all week in a recording studio laying down riffs and guitar solos for a new teenage punk band so the last thing he probably would have wanted was to seek out his waste-of-space brother-in-law. As we wound our way through the traffic-free night roads, he described the band as 'still a bit raw'. That was Mike's way of describing them as musically incoherent. As Ellie would say, he was a die-hard member of the *Musicians' Union* and would never utter a bad word regarding another musician's abilities. People liked working with him, so as the music industry declined he was still in demand, though he still had to contend with irregular hours and the long commute.

As headlights and brake lights shone ahead of us, I asked Mike if he had thought about a comeback with his old band.

'It's a hobby, now. We never really stopped playing together, we just had our day and I think more bands need to realise that or else madness lies in wait.'

Dual carriageways became a single lane. 'There are still eight or so folks who remember us,' he grinned. 'And that gives us around two gigs a year where we can play what we want. The rest of the time we have weeks like these, and we *are* lucky. Between this and Ellie's teaching, we just about keep the wolves at bay.'

'You must miss it, though?'

We turned off onto a dark side road.

'We were all pretty done with it ten years ago – the record companies, the touring, having to release utter crap you've written in a day without your heart in it. Like I said, man, the band's a hobby now. And pretty much the best hobby in the world. Now just give me a cold lager, an evening in, and some time with Ell and the kids. That's the new dream. Rock and roll for the old and knackered.'

And when he should have been at home with his wife and kids, Mike was now having to chauffeur his douchebag brother-in-law around with him, at the risk of triggering his wife's wrath, because he believed it the right thing to do.

Mike once told me about the time he first met Ellie. We were on his stag do at the time, a weekend on the Cornish coast with ten or so of his other mates, surfing during the day and at night monopolising the bar in a remote country pub. Interestingly, the tale was a completely different story to the one that Ellie told Dad and me. She had said that they had met when she reviewed one of his band's shows – she had seen him at the bar after and asked for some backstory for the piece. But according to Mike, as he and I sat hunched on bar stools drinking another of the infinite ales the pub had on draft, they did not meet at that gig. Ellie was only at the concert because Mike had invited her the afternoon before.

'She was auditioning at London Guildhall,' Mike said while the others were either at the pub's dartboard or resting their limbs in the big armchairs by the fire. 'She was in the main auditorium. Just her sitting at the grand piano and a panel of three administrators in the front row. And one shaggy-headed stoner with a guitar case over his shoulder skulking in the shadows right at the back, just out of a meeting with an old tutor. She was sensational. She played something so melancholic, but with these notes of hope, I knew right then I needed to speak to this girl.'

Mike then leaned on the bar looking strangely starry-eyed, as if he was fully picturing the moment or about to doze off after a long day's surfing and drinking.

'After she finished, I followed her out and caught up with her by the noticeboards. It had been years since I'd been that nervous. I don't know what I said, I think I mumbled something about hearing her play and told her how moving I thought it was. She looked amused, probably startled that this random grungy guy had been hiding in the dark spying on her. But I could also see her turning this cute shade of pink so I took that as a good thing.'

I followed Mike into their house. I could see Ellie moving between their little dining area and the kitchen. I don't think she saw me. She was setting the table and I was standing out of the way, by their sofa and fireplace, with toys and games piled up alongside it. There was also an electric keyboard that had been Ellie's piano for the last decade or so, crammed into the corner of the cosy room.

'Jesus, Mike, you said you'd be back two hours ago!' said Ellie, busying herself with the cutlery. 'You're not going to see the kids now. Mrs Rawlins would have put them to bed hours ago. You better not have eaten, I've...' She then saw me.

'I called Mrs Rawlins on the way. I said I'll drop round now and look in on the kids. She's offered sherry and leftovers so....' He trailed into silence as Ellie just glared. I thought I should say some-thing to take the heat off Mike.

'I asked Mike if I could tag along. I've got something for Millie. I thought I might be able to give you a hand setting up.' Ellie remained glaring at Mike, who then went over and whispered something in her ear. As he did, I pretended to busy myself looking down at the books laid out on their small coffee table. One of the books was *An Introduction to Financial Accounting*, which seemed a strange choice for two musicians. My phone buzzed with a message. Looking up to see Mike and Ellie still whispering, I took it out and saw a message from Katie:

Hope all is going okay? K x.

I felt the hint of a smile. I thought the *Duchess* comment would have irradiated any goodwill we might have built up. We didn't normally text each other pleasantries – our previous exchanges glancing back up the message history were all regarding the boiler. Ellie then marched out of sight into the kitchen, coming back with a bottle of wine and one glass, which she banged down on the table and poured. Mike then kissed her forehead as he turned to leave.

'It could be worse,' Mike whispered to me on his way out.

I heard the door of Mike's Volvo shut and the engine restart. Ellie then started laying the table.

'Scott, sit down, make yourself at home. Glass of wine?' She marched back into the kitchen. Approaching the table I could see black smoke coming out of the oven.

'Actually, is that wise?' she said, returning with a steaming, charcoal coloured dish with a substance bubbling out of the sides. 'I hate to think I'm fuelling your drug and alcohol problem again.'

This *was* going to be a nightmare.

'Ellie, any chance we could just fast forward to me apologising?' Through the journey, I had been getting more and more anxious. We did not do confrontation. That was how our family worked.

Ever since Ellie came back into the fold after those oh so joyful teenage years, our relationships were based on a fragile unspoken truce. We'd ride things out, keep the alcohol flowing, until one of us – usually Ellie – forgot why they were pissed off.

'I shouldn't have said what I said at Waterloo. It was stupid. Really stupid.'

We were standing at opposite sides of the table. I was leaning against a dining chair and Ellie was holding her wine glass at her mouth, masking her expression.

'I guess the reason it's been on my mind is because everything seems to stem from back then. We were close when we were kids. I miss that. I feel sad that we lost it.'

I felt my voice go quieter. She seemed to gulp down her wine and then walked away, but this time came back with a serving spoon and another wine glass. She set it down in front of me and returned to her seat.

'I'm sorry for what I said about Dad,' she said, also quietly, not looking up.

She then took the spoon and cut into the dish.

'You're going to want to pour yourself some wine,' she said. 'This looks truly dreadful.'

CHAPTER 9

THIS ONE'S LIKE YOUR MOTHER'S ARMS

When I was ten, Ellie was my hero. She was the world's greatest older sister, a fact which was emblazoned on a mug I had bought for her from the Muswell Hill card shop. She was bossy and forthright, declared and dictated, but with kindness always being her underlying motive. 'Tomorrow we'll go walking in the hills and for dinner tonight we'll have pizza because that's Scott's favourite as last night we had Chinese which is Dad's and mine.' That was my overriding memory from our family holiday to Exeter and the coast. Be it on the beach, the moors, or in town, Ellie would march ahead like a general leading her army with me beaming and rushing to keep up, and Mum and Dad laughing.

When we were very small, she would build us a den in the living room out of blankets and sheets. She would make up stories and give recitals on my Fisher-Price Xylophone. She would hug me when I was tired, upset, or scared and tell me she would keep all the monsters away. At that age, she seemed to love having a little brother just as much as I loved having a big sister and protector.

Mum had this tendency of being there but not being there. Even on those family holidays, she would leave us lagging behind with Dad, and head off somewhere saying she just needed some alone time. But she did it in such a way that she'd smile this radiant smile of hers watching Dad pick up Ellie and me, both of us giggling hysterically, and calmly say, 'Now, George, I'm going to get one of my heads again.' She'd wag her finger jokingly causing Ellie and me to giggle more, and Dad would give this soft nod and watch her walk away, probably knowing what we didn't – that it was only a matter of time.

Mum, or Orletta, as I now call her, was beautiful. When they would have dinner parties, Ellie and I would sit on her and Dad's bed watching Mum at her dressing table delicately applying her makeup smiling at us like Audrey Hepburn, iconic into the camera. 'Up?' she would ask, coiling her blonde hair into the shape of a tulip and raising it above her head. 'Or shall we let it drape and flow?' She would give a mock quizzical expression as if it was the most serious of dilemmas for us, her stylists, to deliberate, which inevitably caused her small children to start rolling on the bed giggling, so proud to have her as our mother.

During the dinner parties, Ellie and I would sneak downstairs past our bedtime to watch and listen. Mum would sit at the head of the table and have this expression, hanging on every word of another guest. She would then spot us and give us a wide-eyed look of shock, before beaming and then returning to her guests. When Mum spoke it was then our guest's turn to hang upon every word of hers. Everything she said rang to an easy rhythm. Her passion was art. Her studio was our conservatory where she would paint and sculpt and then at those parties relay her inspirations and aspirations, all those around the table entirely captivated – Orletta, the beautiful artist, George, her intellectual academic husband, and Ellie and me, the doting adorable children completing the perfect family.

And then came the summer I turned thirteen. I walked downstairs and found suitcases by the door. It was still another two weeks before our usual holiday, so I had not anticipated us going away anywhere that day. I then heard Ellie coming out of her room. She was approaching sixteen years old and had transformed from the sweet, bossy, caring older sister to the stereotypical monster, stroppy teenager. 'For Christ sake, Scott, can you stop leaving your Games Workshop shit everywhere, I almost impaled my...' Ellie stopped at the top of the stairs, her eyes fixed on the suitcases. She didn't move, just stayed frozen to the spot and silent. I was simply happy that her rant was cut off and wandered off into the kitchen. That's when I really knew something was wrong. In our conservatory I could see three large wooden crates. All of Mum's paints, materials, and canvases were nowhere to be seen.

Ellie was sitting at the bottom of the stairs when I came back, and before I could ask her what was wrong, I heard Mum call, 'Eleanor, Scotty. Please come upstairs.' Ellie stared at me, wide-eyed. I had never seen her look scared before. I was the soft one – the mummy's boy – not her. In their bedroom, Mum was packing a holdall at the edge of the bed, and Dad was standing at the window gazing out. Dad half looked around when we entered and then returned to the window. They had long, draping voile curtains, so it was a little strange that Dad was staring into them rather than pushing them aside to look at the road or whatever he was staring at. Mum looked up from her holdall and beamed at us as if we were wonderfully unexpected guests.

'Please sit, dears.' She smiled her dinner party smile and gestured to the bed. I pretty much jumped on, eager to know what the surprise was, whereas Ellie, again, approached it reluctantly. For the last year or so, Ellie had been obsessed with being 'cool'. Everything we did was boring, and she was not afraid to make it clear to us that she would rather be anywhere else than hanging out with her family when we were all together. But at that moment, she genuinely did look like she would rather be dangling from the edge of a cliff than climbing onto the bed to hear what Mum had to say.

'Sometimes it is very difficult for a person to spend their whole life only ever being one thing,' began Mum, sitting herself down on the edge of the bed, smiling calmly at us. I had no idea what she meant, but her tone was soothing and reassuring, natural and effortless. Mum then told us how wild and wonderful the world was, that there were so many incredible people out there we were yet to meet, and that there were adventures we were yet to have.

'I would never want either of you to feel you have to stay in one small place or that our lovely, lovely home is all there is for you to see.' She kept smiling, and I became mesmerised. She was just as captivating as I had seen her at her dinner parties.

'I love you both so truly, so madly, so completely, you will always be the most special people in my life. And I loved your father for years and years and wonderful years...' Dad still had his back to us, facing the window but not looking out. He seemed to be staring downward, trying to be both present and absent while his wife told his children she was leaving them. As Mum continued to speak I looked to Ellie who seemed to have stopped listening to Mum and was also staring at Dad.

'As we get older our dreams diverge. What made us happy once can no longer make us happy anymore, and that is absolutely nobody's fault. The person who was your world can, in turn, become a wonderful friend whom you will always love, but in a different way, and treasure the memories forever.'

I looked over to Ellie again, and she was still staring at Dad, but this time her eyes were narrow and fierce. Mum told us she wanted us to be happy and do what we loved. She smiled contentedly as she described how she was going to become a full-time artist. She was joining an artists' colony somewhere on the south coast. 'You can come to visit any time you like,' she added, beaming. It was run by someone called Conrad – a friend of hers – and they would spend half the year there and then travel all over Europe seeking inspiration. She made it sound like the most wonderful of adventures.

And then that was it. The fifteen-year-old Ellie sitting next to me could not hold it in any longer. She erupted in tears. Streaming down her face, she flung herself into Mum's arms. 'Darling!' exclaimed Mum as if this reaction from her only daughter had come out of the blue. The moody teenager Ellie evaporated in our mother's arms, her face nestled into Mum's blouse crying her heart out. Perhaps it was because Ellie was fifteen, whereas I was twelve, that she had seen the warning signs in the months leading up to that day. Maybe she was old enough to see through Mum's tales of happiness and *wonderful* adventures. She wailed so uncontrollably that Mum looked visibly shocked. She tried to muffle Ellie, holding her close, rubbing her back, and making soothing shooshing sounds. She shot a look at Dad as if imploring him to intervene. Dad had remained with his back turned. As Ellie's wails began to calm, he finally turned away from the window eventually. 'Excuse me,' he said quietly and softly walked out of the room.

Over dinner, Ellie and I talked mainly about Millie and Ed. To be fair to Ellie, dinner would have probably been dreadful even if it wasn't burnt. I think it was meant to have been a pasta bake, but I kept finding stray chunks of raw cauliflower and carrots and solid slabs of tuna that had welded themselves to the bottom of the dish.

'Do you want some more?' she asked, picking up the spoon.

'Yes. Thanks,' I said, hoping she would not notice the reluctance. 'How do you make it so... creamy?'

When we eventually finished, Ellie got up from the table, pulling a crushed packet from her jeans pocket.

'I didn't know you still smoked.'

'I don't. Have you tried *telling* people you're bored and want ten minutes peace and quiet outside? It spares everyone's feelings.' She pulled out one of the Marlboros and a lighter. 'Come on,' she then said to me.

We stepped out onto the patio. Ellie and Mike had a small garden with a little area of grass occupied by the kids' Wendy House. Ellie offered me the packet, but I declined. She then lit up, looking at the half-moon, clear from clouds or whatever it was that caused it to shine a little less bright in London. She took another step forward, away from me.

'You would spend hours in your room playing with those stupid, model soldiers,' she said, holding the cigarette away from her.

'You would make these idiotic sound effects and commentate to an empty room totally in your own world.'

'Well I was a kid – '

'It meant you missed things.' Ellie took a drag of the cigarette and flicked away the ash.

'Mum would have these phone calls. I'm not talking about secret liaisons, even though she most likely had those too, but phone calls to friends and she would always sound so radiant and at times so self-deprecating it was charming. So I would hide behind the door listening.'

Ellie paused. She brought the cigarette back to her mouth but instead of inhaling she just dropped it to the ground and stubbed it out. The next voice she spoke was not hers, but our mother's.

"Oh, Claudia, she should wait until she has two! *Two* is when it all starts to unravel."

Ellie took another step forward, her arms now crossed. Her voice had the overly posh intonation of our mother's. '*Two*, she would say. 'The second one takes up everything and more. It is all roses until you have two.'"

She then turned around. 'That was all complete bollocks, Scott. I know it, you know it, but what the fuck did I know back then? *Two* was difficult, and then she left. So I went back to one.'

We both started looking up at the moon. It was a beautiful night and warmer than it had been in weeks. I thought quickly of Katie and that our boiler problems would not be an issue tonight. I then walked up to my sister so we were side by side.

'Scott, I know you were a kid. I know you were only thirteen, I was there, I'm not delusional, you do not need to remind me. But I wasn't a kid. I was meant to have been a woman. I was meant to have grown up and become not a dependant anymore but instead Mum's equal, her friend, a mould she could now form something out of and teach me how to be like her. We worshipped her. You know we did. And then I had finally reached the age when I could be taught how to put on makeup, get my ears pierced, try on her jewellery and perfume and even wear one of her dresses outside the house. Instead, all of those things got packed in a crate and sent away.'

I started picturing Ellie again as that girl at the piano. Her hair was straighter back then. Shinier too, like brand new hair. I looked at the Ellie standing there now – the mother of two, dressed in a baggy knitted sweater and comfortable jeans. I then thought back to post-university Ellie – a punk-girl with spiky hair and a nose stud who knocked on the door when I was seventeen and reintroduced herself as my sister.

We were not those kids anymore. All those physical characteristics were long gone, and with them, the people we once were. Perhaps for the better.

We weren't huggers. The only time we did was in front of other people, such as Mike's family, to appear normal. But I wanted to hug her. Or her to hug me. Like when we were kids. So I stood there, next to her, and gently let my arm press against hers. Hopefully, she saw it as a symbol of solidarity, not her brother being weird. But we stayed like that, in silence, both just watching the moon, until she said,

'I'll let Mike know it's safe to come back.'

CHAPTER 10

AUGUST AND EVERYTHING AFTER

Being a summer baby made me one of the youngest in my year. While this meant I was the last one to get legally served in a pub, by the time I turned eighteen, my A-levels were done, and I had a lazy summer in store of computer games, camping trips, and doing what at the time was my dream job – working as a steward at Barnet Football Club. And on such a lazy summer day, while Dad was at work, I answered the door to a stranger. A young woman, a bit older than me, with short spikey hair and a nose stud. And she stared back at me, her cautious smile turning into a frown.

'Scott?'

'Ellie?'

I let her in, and she wandered first into the hallway and then the living room very much like a stranger would – slowly, and glancing around her, at the walls, the framed pictures, the ornaments and clutter, taking everything in just for a second, appraising and acclimatising to her surroundings. I followed and then waited at the doorway, giving her the room. There was so much that I could have said or asked but because I could not decide on my first question – *'what are you doing here?'* seemed a little hostile, *'how are you? How's university?'* too trivial – the accumulated silence made it more difficult to say anything at all to the sister I had not seen in three years.

Ellie then reached her piano. The baby grand. The focal point of the long room. As it had been when she used to practise, the top was covered in photo frames, but with some additions since she had last sat there. She picked up one of me and Dad at the football – me in my Barnet top and him wearing their orange and black scarf – both of us beaming. She kept looking at it, examining it as if there was some hidden meaning in something that was essentially a selfie in a silver frame, and then placed it back down.

'Still not lost your virginity?' she called over her shoulder.

When I retold this story to Vicky while we were dating, she was borderline horrified. She sat up and accused my sister of being typically deliberate, cruel and emotionally bullying, looking to cull my self-esteem as soon as she had walked in the door. But the reason I told Vicky the story was not to chastise Ellie or for her to pity me, but to explain to her why Ellie was none of those things. Ellie had *remembered*. It was no coincidence that her first words to me echoed her last words before she left. Standing in the doorway, I watched her gradually turn around. She looked at me without any of the fierceness or the dismissiveness of the seventeen-year-old Ellie. I walked over to her, and for the first time in probably a decade, I hugged my sister.

Millie ran to hug me and asked me to throw her up in the air. It was easier to do when she was smaller, but I very much tried to oblige. It still overwhelmed me how much Ed *had* grown since I saw him. But no sooner had Mike brought them home, than the house began to fill with fellow parents and five-year-olds darting everywhere at once.

Ellie was in the garden with the other mums watching the kids. The sun was bright and warm. Even though it was the first day of December, winter had seemed to be put on hold for Millie's party. I caught Ellie's eye and smiled. That morning, by the time it took me to put away my sleeping bag and have a shower, Ellie and Mike had transformed the whole house with decorations, present wrapping, and baking. Ellie then excused herself and walked over to me.

'You're missing out,' she said, a paper cup of what looked like juice in her hand. 'Angela's just been enlightening me on the firmness of her nipples since she stopped breastfeeding.'

I sipped my beer, looking at the group of women standing cradling wine glasses on the patio as their small children chased each other around Ellie and Mike's garden.

'Is that normal? Do all women say such things to each other? Am I now meant to share details of my body parts with these strangers that I am now bonded to until Millie turns eighteen?'

'Don't forget about Ed. You're probably plugged into the matrix until he's finished college.'

'Thanks,' she said as we stood back watching the other mums. I felt bad for deserting Mike in the kitchen with the other dads. They were interrogating him about being a rock star in the *noughties* and Mike was trying his best to understate the fact, while looking slightly cornered.

'Jeez, how is it possible to have two children and still have a body like that?' Ellie nodded to a brown-haired woman bending over, pulling exaggerated faces and nodding overly enthusiastically at two toddlers. To be honest, I had already noticed her. She was wearing tight-fitting jeans and a loose top, which emphasised both the slimness of her waist and the fullness of her chest.

'Yoga?' I smiled as Ellie raised her eyebrows.

'Rumour is she and her money-bags husband have an arrangement. I should probably introduce you. Maybe she can be the one to finally pop that cherry of yours.'

I couldn't help laughing. After all, it was as heart-warming a moment as it gets for us. The sun was shining, I was wearing a t-shirt in December, and for the first time in recent years, my sister was taking the piss out of me in a non-emotionally hostile way.

'They're all going to fuck off home in about an hour. I'll get Mike to do the clearing up, and we can go for a drive. Talk about that letter.'

We parked up along the coast. The sun was setting over the sea as we climbed down from the road to the pebble beach. We were one of what looked like a dozen small groups enjoying the unseasonable warmth. People had come with picnic blankets and were staring out at green waves under a sky that was orange and red. Ellie sat down, and I settled myself into the smooth round pebbles next to her, my knees against my chest. We both looked out at the sea and the apocalyptic horizon.

Neither of us said anything at first. We just sat there as the tide rolled in, gulls screeching above our heads and other people around us doing all what normal, happy people do.

'I don't know what I'm meant to say,' she then said, massaging her eyelids. 'I'm not even sure I remember what you wrote in that stupid little note. All I know is my carefree, feckless younger brother was telling our dead father that he couldn't handle life anymore, so was throwing it in like he's done everything else.'

Her tone was less harsh than her words. She sounded more matter-of-fact and weary than typically sarcastic.

'Don't hold back then,' I tried to laugh it off. But rather than looking at me, Ellie was still staring into the distance, looking bored and irritated

'You've got no big commitments. You don't have kids. You're able to travel all over the world. Life for you is idyllic. It always has been.'

'Yeah the Middle East was a real cakewalk at times. Seventy-hour weeks, active gunfire, not being able to leave the compound without an armed guard, people who have lost everything resenting you being there – '

Ellie then started slow-clapping me.

'There's Golden Boy selflessly saving the world. Desperate to be everyone's favourite.' She mock-saluted the sea and put on a sardonic voice. 'Scott! The steady one who did what he was told. Got his degree, settled down into a job, and his one act of rebellion was to announce he was off to save humanity, but you weren't, were you? Turns out you were just a fucking hypocrite.'

With that, she turned and stared at me. A couple passed by in front of us. They were holding hands, both in shorts and sandals.

'Secret alcoholic and drug user,' she said with apparent delight. *'"Dad, I've done a lot of things I'm not proud of".'* She deepened her voice, which I assumed was to mimic me though she sounded like a cartoon bear.

'"The only relationships I've had since Vicky have been with dancers and girls I've bought drugs for." By *dancer* I take it we're talking ballet? Experimental modern? And using drugs to pay for sex!' She gave a triumphant *ha!*. 'Good loophole. Classy. Our father would be proud.'

I cringed, having had the latter years of my twenties replayed in front of me. Ellie leaned back, casually satisfied. Down the beach, some small kids, wrapped up still in winter coats, were playing chicken with the shoreline running back to their parents, laughing loudly as the tide rushed back at them.

'Have you paid for sex?'

'No.'

'Oh, so just bribed girls for it?'

I wearily rubbed my head. 'I don't know,' I mumbled. It might sound as if I was clutching at straws to make myself less pathetic than I was.

'I was the type of guy who hoped spending a lot of money on drugs, and doing them with girls would make them like me. Would make someone like me.'

Like Vicky once liked me, I wanted to say. Ellie was right however – I was meant to have been the nice one. That was what Vicky had said she liked about me. And then I became the man who spent his evenings in dodgy strip clubs. Among my broker colleagues at the time, it was called *Pretty Woman* syndrome – falling in love with the girl who danced for you, believing in their eyes you were special and that you were the one to rescue them and ride away into the sunset. The same happened in the fancy, high-end clubs. My broker friends would take the VIP tables and groups of women who would join us, champagne flowing on expense accounts. I would fall under a spell with any girl who would speak to me.

'I had a therapist back then. His name was Anthony, and we spent all our time talking about all this. I got into this cycle where I needed all the nights out and drugs because I didn't know what else there was. I didn't like spending time alone, and I wasn't very good at talking to people – girls. Christ, Ell, there were so many times I would leave my real mates and go on to a club to get high because I didn't want to go home. I *did* loathe myself. For both not having the willpower to stop, and not being like the other guys who had girlfriends or were genuinely popular without the need for drugs.'

Ellie was staring at the sea. A large wave was coming in and splashed the small children. They all burst out laughing as one of their parents ran out to bring them back up the shore. There was a group of twentysomethings just down the beach. They had just let out a cheer, and I could hear them clinking bottles as I looked across to see them celebrating something – their joyous voices full of possibilities.

'Ell, the whole reason I wrote that letter was that I am ashamed. You were right. Everything was a lie. I tried to go away and redeem myself, but everything I did was to make myself feel better. And when I was finally ready to come home, it was too late. Dad was gone and I didn't seem to have anything left that was worth anything.'

Ellie still looked bored, staring into space.

'How much did you spend? In total.'

I shrugged. 'Enough not to have a flat anymore.'

'And now the money's gone, that's you fixed, is it?'

'Being popular with women doesn't seem important anymore,' I half-snorted. A revelation that took me far longer to realise than it should have. 'Ironically, I just miss everything I used to have. My old friends. Sunday lunches at Dad's. I took for granted all those nights and deemed them not enough – you have no idea what I would now do for an evening in a warm pub playing a board game.'

With the sun dropping, the warmth of the day was starting to fade too. Ellie must have wanted to get back to Millie and Ed – I recalled just how happy Millie had been with her party. Ellie and I even seemed not to mind each other then. She had now said what she needed to say, and with it, could walk away knowing she was right about me all along.

'When Mum left you got it easy,' she suddenly said. I looked back at her, surprised. She was still simply staring out at the water.

'You didn't feel it as hard.' Her voice was quieter. 'Mum leaving brought you and Dad closer together. I, on the other hand, gambled on the wrong parent.'

She rubbed her eyes and rested her chin on her knees.

'What you said to me at the funeral, *you* were right. I spent years blaming him for Mum going and treating him like shit – '

'Elle, I lost the plot that day. I didn't mean anything – '

'And it doesn't stop there. You *did* make him proud. All the fucking time. All my life I used to look at you and I was so fucking jealous. You were the *Golden Child* and I was the screw-up – '

'Ellie, you're a trained concert pianist, for fuck's sake. I think you won regarding who was the more talented one.'

'Scott, I've not played in public for a decade. I've become a middle school piano teacher. This is what I've achieved in life. The musical equivalent of fuck all.'

Another family, this time the one nearest to us, began to pack up their belongings. Ellie folded her arms over her knees and hugged them.

'I used to want to compose, to write film scores, concertos, to one day write a symphony. When I was seventeen, I had interviews at music colleges where I would get to play on a Steinway. A *Steinway*, Scott. Now I play on that electronic piece of shit at home. At seventeen I was asked to join some really good schools, probably the best schools, but I moved to Bristol to be closer to Mum, to be able to visit on weekends or stay during the holidays. And I did. At first. And it was great.'

'You stayed at Mum's?'

This, I did not know. Orletta would come to London, and we would meet her at a gallery. When it came to visits to her new house and life down in Devon they always got postponed. I felt my brow furrow.

'She was in her element – queen of artists! Teacher, patron, the one everyone looked to for inspiration. And then she was either abroad all the time or having some exhibit dedicated to her, and we could never cross paths, which,' Ellie gave one of her ironic snorts, 'never seemed to be that great a hardship to her. I even suggested she come and visit me, but she never found the time.'

'You and Mum?' I frowned. 'In Devon? Without me?'

I felt a sharp pang. After being on the defensive so long, I was suddenly taken aback.

'Like you and Dad spent all that time without me.'

'Ellie, that is not the same,' I said, surprisingly steadily. 'You see that, right? You chose not to come back and spend time with us. I begged Mum to let me visit her...'

I suddenly felt cold. Like someone proverbially walking over my grave.

'I never told anyone this, but during my first week in Bristol, I was standing outside the practice rooms and heard Beethoven's *Piano Sonata* 32. It was Son Jii, a Korean student from my group. *Sonata* 32 is next level. It requires composure, patience, this clock in your head for the quiet parts and then impossible hands to keep up with it as it explodes. And Son Jii crushed it. It was so beautiful I wanted to cry. We had had this lecture the day before when a pompous stiff had put a slide up with the amount of hours practice done by amateurs, professionals, and those who won awards. My hours were below that of an amateur. Three to five hours was the standard, which I scoffed at as a typical university scare tactic. When Son Jii came out, I asked him how many hours a day he did. He said eight. I just looked at my hands and knew I would never be able to compete. While I was out at the bar with my housemates, Son Jii and the others would be in those practice rooms, doing more hours a day than I did in a week. Scott, I took up journalism because I wasn't a good enough pianist. I was not even a *could-have-been*. I was an anonymous *never-could-be*.'

Ellie closed her eyes, and as the sea breeze picked up, wound herself tighter into a ball.

'I guess what I'm trying to say is that none of us are that happy.'

She screwed up her face and then threw a hand out, gesturing to the sea. 'We all screw up and have regret after fucking regret. And no matter how much we would like to blame others for screwing us up, a lot of the time, it's because we chose the easy way out.'

Ellie then pushed her knees down and shook her head, sitting cross-legged.

'And when I feel like that, the next thing I feel is this massive sense of guilt because I'm one of the lucky ones. I'm so lucky for what I do have with Mike and Millie and Ed, and I am ashamed of how resentful I am for wanting these other things. And I am so resentful at you, my brother, who got the career, got to travel, and lived the life so many people could only dream of, and then suddenly decided to end it.'

'Ell, it was just a letter – '

'Scott, I was there! You put a date on it! *Easter Sunday*. The day before I found you passed out on the floor, sick everywhere, and two empty bottles of pills in the bin. You *did* try to kill yourself. You tried to leave.'

I couldn't respond. She was staring at me so intently I felt both flushed and suddenly cold and sick. It was not that she knew my secret. It was that she knew something I had erased from my mind. I closed my eyes and tried to remember, but I ended up just shrugging even as I imagined the family bathroom.

'I don't know, Ell,' was all I could say. 'It may sound a cop-out, but I don't. I wanted to feel numb and I took them to see if I could. But I just thought taking a load of pills would make things go away. Just for a bit.'

'Jesus, Scott...'

Neither of us said anything more. We just sat watching the sea and listening to the waves until Ellie raised her eyebrows and pushed herself up and off the pebbles. We walked silently back to the car, leaving the twentysomethings to the beach.

'We all have our shit, Scott,' Ellie said. 'We all fail. That's what life is. How do you know it's not going to happen again?'

I shrugged.

We remained there, Ellie not yet starting the engine.

'I'm seeing a therapist again. This one's Californian, a bit New Age, makes me talk about stuff. How I feel. Why I feel the way I do. Where it all stems from. I know that no one is perfect and that no one has that perfect relationship or career or life, but it's difficult to remember that. When things were really bad she made me write this list of ten things I like doing. Just really little things, like going for a walk in Hampstead, playing a record on my turntable, having a really good Chinese in Chinatown. I don't know, it just helped.'

The waves looked bigger from the car park. I felt my own one wash over me.

'It might sound stupid, but I forgot how nice all those things were. That I could just close my eyes on Primrose Hill and feel what warm sunlight felt like. Or how uplifting the taste of really good Chinese food is.'

After another moment of silence, Ellie finally turned the ignition. She reversed out of the parking space and then put the brakes back on. She turned to look at me.

'Scott, just because I think you're a dickhead doesn't mean I don't give a shit.'

CHAPTER 11

FRIENDSHIP

'Scott, what do you think should be the role of a therapist in the client-therapist relationship?'

Camille had asked me that question early into just our third session. It was early May with English springtime well in bloom, so it was only appropriate that through the window, I would see low black skies looming over the courtyard below and hear the low rumble of thunder in the distance.

'To talk things over?'

'That's what we use bartenders for,' she smiled, looking down, making a note. 'At least we do back in the States. Why have you come to see a *therapist*? It's not the cheapest way *to have a chat* after all.'

It was also the first time I heard Camille's terrible British accent. It was so terrible that I let out an involuntary laugh. *Because I'm going crazy and I'm scared this might be permanent*, I wanted to say.

She then closed her notebook and placed it on the side table.

'Freud's legacy when it comes to psychoanalysis is that we as therapists play a similar role to archaeologists, excavating the cata-

combs of the mind and the subconscious. What lies behind awareness and what is the root cause of our drives, desires, and ambitions.
Our job is to be neutral – some would say withdrawn – to offer no
judgement and provide an uncensored sounding board.'

Camille shuffled slightly in her seat before casually crossing her
legs and leaning back.

'But, one of the first things we also learn at therapist school is
that Freud is not one hundred percent applicable to all cases, and
there is no one size fits all manual for the human mind. Let's do a
quick exercise.'

Camille sat back up straight and reached again for her
notebook

'Word association. No time to think, first word that comes into
your head: Time.'

'Management.'

'Scar.'

'Face?'

'Therapy.'

'Wellbeing.'

'Love.' The others had been quick-fire but I hesitated.

'Loss.'

'Trust,' Camille carried on.

'Friendship.'

'Thanks, Scott. Exercise over. We've got pretty much half the
session left. How about we put on hold trying to make that all
important psychological breakthrough?'

She got out of her chair and walked over to her desk at the back
of the room.

'Are you a fan of good old *Java Joe,* or should I be making you
an *Earl Grey*?' She came back with two mugs of coffee.

'Trust and friendship,' she smiled, sitting back down. 'Not very
Freud, but then if you lined up every client who made an appoint-

ment with me, and asked me what proportion came back for a second session, I would have to say...' She blew out her cheeks and did an elaborate shrug. '...twenty percent. Perhaps twenty-five if I'm feeling self-generous. And then there are those that go beyond the magic third session. We're down to single digits then.' Camille picked back up her mug, smiling.

'So, Freud may have given us the keys to the kingdom, but what use is it if nine out of ten clients turn back around and walk out the door because they have no interest in baring their soul to a non-emotive sounding board?'

It's probably not important, but I did get a half-price discount for that session.

It was weird at first, but we drank our coffee and had that *chat*. Camille asked about which part of London I was from, and when I said Wood Green she told me that her husband grew up in Barnet. I asked if he happened to follow, as I called them, the *Great Barnet* Football Club.

'Oh my God! So you're the other one!' Camille beamed, quite uncharacteristically for the calm, professional therapist I had known up until that point.

'I constantly goad him about his relentless devotion to a sport that won't let you drink a beer at the ground and to a team followed by only one other *bloke* and his dog. And, here we are! The other *bloke*! Please tell me you have a dog, Scott.'

It was unconventional and would definitely have had Freud turning in his grave, but I did come back the next week.

'Scott, I'm going to pick you up on two points,' Camille said as I tried to convince her of the merits of my adolescent passion. 'First, the game is called *soccer*. Football is a sport where the participant does not fall over crying when someone taps them on the shoulder.' She then leaned forward, shaking her head.

'Second, is that this is not Monterey Bay! Where I grew up, my whole school would rock up to the kick-off carnival with a cup of *SoCo and Lime* in eighty-degree warmth. You guys stand outside for two hours in this!' She gestured to the window where outside it was now pouring with rain. 'Watching a game that, from what Paul tells me, usually finishes one-to-nothing to the other team.'

Camille handed me the usual mug of warm coffee as we both settled into our usual seats. Since that glorious weekend of sunshine and warm weather at Millie's party, the temperature had plummeted, making a Thursday morning in December more of an ordeal.

'We're spending Christmas together,' I told her, feeling something unburden as I said it. Camille was still wearing her giant knitted cream scarf, this time being juxtaposed over a light pink blazer. I was suddenly conscious that I was wearing the same jeans I had been wearing to dig the Joneses' allotment and could not guarantee the mud stains would not be rubbing off onto the armchair.

I told Camille how when Ellie and I returned from the beach, rather than collecting my things and going to the railway station, she said I could stay another night. The kids had fallen asleep on the sofa, and once they were carried to bed, Ellie ordered a take-away. A Chinese.

'It *is* good, isn't it?' she said as we sat around the table.

'You're probably right about the house,' Ellie then said, sounding annoyed as she served Singapore noodles. 'We do need to get a solicitor. This whole thing is ebbing away from us.'

We spent much of that meal with chopsticks in one hand and our phones in the other Googling probate law.

'We can contest probate, even before it's granted,' I said, finding one link that delved deeper into inheritance law. 'It puts a caveat on

Dad's estate, which means nothing can be sold or got rid of for at least six months, with an option to extend for another six.'

Mike leaned over, examining the website with Ellie, holding his bowl and chopsticks out of the way.

'This is what I hate about the bloody law,' sighed Ellie, scrolling through the information. 'There's no common sense involved. You can't just get on with it – tell someone what the problem is and have them just sort it out. Instead, you have to pay a solicitor to dig through archaic books, and whoever has more money to spend usually wins. How is that *fair*?'

'Christmas?' smiled Camille, trying to bring me back to the point.

'Realistically, from all we read that night, we could end up having to sell the house even if we do win,' I said, trying to keep my hands warm as icy cold air radiated from the windows. 'Just to cover the legal fees. So Ellie suggested we spend Christmas Day at Dad's. As one last hurrah.'

It might have been the wine. There was a lot left from the party, and we had been refilling our glasses throughout dinner and the researching of solicitors.

'We should do something,' said Ellie, getting more animated. 'It's *our* house. If she's allowed to have valuers trample around, I'm allowed to have a last family bloody Christmas. The one that Dad tried to give us last year.'

'So, yes,' I smiled back at Camille. 'It looks like we're having a family Christmas.'

Camille sipped her coffee, still smiling. 'Congratulations,' she said, crossing her legs and flattening down her skinny black trousers. 'Those types of discussions are a lot easier to avoid than face head-on. I know it is early days, but you are allowed to pat yourself on the back.'

I wanted to say I was still feeling cautious rather than exuberant. After all, I had proved to Ellie that I was the feckless hypocrite of a brother portrayed in the letter.

Camille put down her coffee and flipped open her notebook, pen in hand.

'Scott, when was the last time you spoke to your mother?'

I puffed out my cheeks.

'Five years ago.'

'That's a while. And there's been no contact since your father passed away?'

'No. No, we've not.'

'Relax, I'm not criticising. I know it's sometimes best to allow time to run its course before picking up the phone. But a lot of our issues do stem from our younger selves. And, again, not to get too Freudian on you,' she gave her characteristic smirk whenever she mentioned Freud, 'the events of our childhood and the actions of our parents do shape us as an adult.' Camille then picked up the carafe of water and refilled both our glasses.

'Scott, in those initial months after your parents split up, what was your relationship like with your mother?'

Again, I puffed out my cheeks, trying to shift my train of thought from Brighton and Ellie to something that happened twenty years ago.

'Those visits to London would always coincide with a gallery exhibition featuring her. We had to get dressed up and when we arrived she ran up and greeted us like we were royalty, everyone in the room looking at us. We were then paraded around and had these well-dressed people telling us how proud we must be of our mother. Ellie and I would be the only children, and everyone else would surround Orletta hanging on her every word. Even Ellie, who worshipped her, looked bored, and no one would notice if we wandered away and waited outside.'

I shuffled about in my seat and picked up my glass of water.

'It was not like we weren't proud of her. We always loved our mum, but that woman at the gallery was not our mum. It was the *artist* Orletta Roberts.'

'Did you ever talk to your mum about these experiences? Did your sister?'

I thought back to the last visit of that era, and gave a small snort. I was sitting in the atrium of the National Gallery by myself, and Ellie had gone off to smoke outside. It must have been an hour until Dad arrived and collected us. He took us back into the exhibit to say goodbye and we both reluctantly accompanied him. When Mum saw us she beamed like she always did, like we were the most important people in the world and came over and hugged us both saying how lovely it was seeing us and she could not wait until the next time. Neither Ellie nor I replied, and Orletta Roberts, *the artist*, continued beaming and returned to the people in suits and fancy dresses who were surrounding us. In what had been a two-hour visit, those had been her only words to us.

'It's just a small gig,' Mike had said when he dropped me at the railway station, the day after Millie's party.

'It's flattering, but the promoter does need to have his head examined. The only crowd we can muster these days are fellow staring-down-the-barrel-of-fortysomethings, who can get a babysitter and want to spend a Saturday night pretending we're still in our twenties.'

His band had been invited to headline at the Blues Café in Brixton. Typically Mike played it down and I assumed that was partly because in their heyday they were regulars at the Hammersmith Apollo and Shepherd's Bush Empire. Still, for a band that Mike said only played for friends and family, this was one of

London's popular new music venues, and a quick look on its website showed Mike and company prominently.

'This Saturday?'

'Yep, why? Expecting another nocturnal visit from young women in short dresses?'

No, I wasn't. But I did find that I was not *dreading* returning to Loughborough Road. It was usually only for a moment, but I would approach the house and instantly feel a sinking in my stomach if I saw Katie's bedroom light on. It was the politeness that got to me over those months. The scripted niceties underpinning small talk as I would have to pass her open door. I did know this was largely in my head and some form of transference for what had happened with Sarah, but for the first time I actually looked forward to going home and having someone to talk to.

'She's not that young,' I said, trying to divert attention away from my newfound cheeriness.

'Yeah, perhaps not lead with that when you walk in the door.'

However, I did not have much chance to tell Katie of my weekend. *Really want to catch up,* she was kind enough to message when I had not seen her for a couple of days. *We've got a thing at work this week so I'm trying to redeem myself by staying late. Are you around Thursday?*

I too had been up to my neck in my own work – literally – as I shovelled trenchfuls of mud all week in the allotment. 'Hmmm, so you're going to do patch by patch?' said Ronny Jones when he stopped by at the start of the week to have a cup of tea and check on progress. He was looking at the plot pencilled in for turnips which I had rotated and replanted. 'It looks very nice, lad. But you do realise one at a time means you'll be having to dig up the latter beds in January? If I was you I'd make the most of the wet weather and dig up as much of this place as you can before a frost sets in.'

I had been up each day before sunrise and struggled to stay awake long enough to hear Katie return from work. All for what I calculated to be around half that of minimum wage due to the fact my gardening business still only had one client – not many potential customers were thinking about their gardens while it was cold, wet, and dark the majority of the day. So, on Thursday, as I returned from my session with Camille, I bought a bottle of wine from the Loughborough Junction off-licence, hoping to have that long-awaited catch-up with my housemate.

However, it was not Katie with whom I had that first conversation. When I arrived upstairs, I saw the bathroom door closed and heard the shower running. As I put the kettle on I heard the door of the fridge open behind me.

A woman, Katie's age but taller, skinnier, and with black hair as opposed to Katie's dark brown, was bending over rummaging around the bottom shelf. She was wearing what looked like a tennis skirt, had slim tanned legs and a now noticeably small bum – a fact that made me swiftly turn back around and stare resolutely at the kettle. Without a word, Katie's friend Izzy then brushed past me with a small bottle in her hand, opening the kitchen cabinets.

'Anything I can help with?' I asked.

'No.'

She didn't elaborate or look at me. She just stood on tiptoes and sifted through our glasses until she brought down two small tumblers. Over the six months I had lived with Katie, I had met or been in close proximity of Izzy probably a hundred times. And that was the first word she had ever spoken to me.

'Have you and Katie had a game?'

'Game of what?' She opened the bottle and poured a thick lemony liquid into the glasses. 'Tennis. I assumed from the outfit.'

'I play. Katie doesn't.'

She quickly shut the cabinets, picked up her glasses, and marched out of the room, not once even looking in my direction. If that was the behaviour of someone who Katie thought fancied me, then I would hate to see what she thought *despise* and *loathe* looked like.

'Hey!' then came a friendlier voice. In her dressing gown and towel wrapped around her hair, Katie put her head around the door.

'Don't go anywhere! I'll just put some clothes on.'

As I heard the bathroom door close and the shower run again, a fully dressed Katie joined me in the kitchen. She was wearing a blue dress with tights and a thick black belt. She had a towel in her hand and was applying it to the tips of her hair.

'It's an annoying work thing,' she said, throwing herself down onto the sofa. 'A private exhibit for one of the high-end donors, so we're all dressing up and losing our Thursday night to pretentious chatter about three-thousand-year-old antiquities.'

'And Izzy's your plus one?'

'Of course, she would have killed me had I not invited her. If there's an excuse to dress up and be pretentious, she's first in line.' She gave a mock eye roll and smiled.

'So, are things okay with you and Ellie?'

I tried to give a light-hearted smile.

'I think we've still got issues to work through. We're not the best at communicating.'

'Scott, you? Uncommunicative? Surely not.' Katie laughed, finishing flattening out the kinks in her hair. The room suddenly seemed a lot brighter with her in her blue dress, and I was about to ask her if she fancied a quick glass of wine when we were interrupted by the sound of heels on our wooden floorboards.

In front of us stood the embodiment of an Egyptian princess. A white sleeveless dress, bronzed tanned skin, gold necklace, and painted green eyes made her the second coming of Elizabeth Taylor's *Cleopatra*.

'I've ordered an Uber,' she said to Katie.

'Oh. I'm not quite ready. We've still got a bit of time. Perhaps we could have a drink with Scott?'

'No,' Izzy said impatiently. 'I do actually want to see this exhibition. I'm not the one who works there and can view it any time she wants.'

Katie unsurprisingly looked a little perplexed by the sudden outburst.

'Okay... I didn't know you were that keen. I'll just find a pair of shoes and get my coat.' Rather than saying thank you, Izzy rolled her eyes and stomped back out of the room.

'She doesn't want to see the exhibit,' Katie then smiled and whispered as we heard the same heels walk downstairs. 'She just wants to make sure she's there on time to be seen by any eligible men. Rain check on that drink?'

'Unless you want to ditch your friend and just hang out here?' It was rhetorical, but I was half hoping she might say yes.

'Don't tempt me,' she said, slowly rising from the sofa. 'Seriously, she's been ratty all afternoon. I really do not have high hopes for tonight.'

CHAPTER 12

BOILER

The thing about therapy is, at times, not only does it have to get worse before it gets better, but it also unravels the stitching above forgotten scars. It was five, maybe even six years, since I had a conversation with my mother. The last time we spoke had been over the phone. Though I say she had been absent pretty much since she left that day twenty years ago, there would be an occasional glimpse of the woman who we loved more than anything.

I last saw her when I was twenty-nine – it was my birthday – and it was lovely. It was at another art gallery, another of her fleeting visits to London, but it was different from when I was a kid. She was not exhibiting but had come to give a fellow artist moral support, and for the first time it felt like it was just us. I was typically hungover, unshaven and unkempt, but it was perhaps the residual alcohol in my system that made me less guarded, awkward, or resentful than I normally was when I saw her. And when I saw her waiting for me, beaming at me at the gallery entrance, I could not have been happier.

We went to the gallery's little café, and she asked me my news, and we sat for over an hour just chatting. She bought me a slice of cake, calling it birthday cake, and I saw her again: Orletta Roberts, *the mother*. Again, it might have been the hangover, or it might have been me having my own life, but it felt a new start. There was something less of a whirlwind about her. She was content just to sit and hear about my job and my friends, like we were something like equals. For the first time since I was a child, it felt like I had my mum back. Even if it was just for a fraction of one day.

I stirred and woke to the sound of clicking and light metallic banging. I then shivered. It was freezing in the room. My nose and cheeks were icy cold and I wrapped my duvet and throw tighter around me. I looked to my skylight and there was no trace of daylight, only the familiar orange of the streetlights coming through the blind. However, there was something different. A supernatural glow seemed to be emanating from the glass, and I sat up on the bed and pulled up the blind. It was snowing. Flakes were slowly coming down and had already settled around the perimeter of the skylight's frame. Then I heard the banging again and, putting on a jumper, went downstairs to investigate.

The kitchen light was on and I heard what sounded like whispering.

'Oh, why now, you stupid thing?' Cautiously, I looked around the door. 'Oh come on!'

Katie was standing across the room next to our sash window wrapped in an enormous brown dressing gown. The boiler cupboard was open, and she was agitatedly and repeatedly pressing knobs and buttons. She then spun around.

'Please don't tell me I woke you?' She didn't look as bright as she normally did. Her shoulders were slumped and she spoke more as a sigh than a question.

'A little bit, yes,' I grinned. 'But the cold would have killed me in my sleep otherwise, so I should be thanking you. What's going on?'

'Don't get me started.'

She turned, and we both looked outside the window where the snow was tumbling down. Standing together, we watched it settling over our downstairs neighbour's garden.

'It is pretty,' I said.

'Not when you've got a one-to-one with your boss first thing in the morning, and you've not had a wink of sleep because the bloody boiler your arsehole brother was meant to fix has decided to pack it in!' Katie then thrust her hand through a circular hole and the clicking noise started up again.

'He said this was meant to restart the pilot light.' She looked either in deep concentration or extreme pain as her hand disappeared. 'What kind of sadistic engineering requires you to do this?'

She removed her hand, grimacing, massaging her wrist.

'Stupid, useless thing!'

'Do you want me to try?'

I did not know what I was hoping to accomplish. Joan had shown me too how the boiler was meant to work, and Katie had pretty much done everything. So it was more for moral support that I stepped in front of her and examined what lay inside the ancient device.

'I'm sorry,' she said in a calmer but slightly croaky voice. 'For all I know I'm getting fired in the morning, and I don't really fancy it happening on zero hours' sleep.'

'Fired? What?' My hand was now also inside the boiler, pressing whatever it was that made the clicking noise. Katie ruffled her hair.

'I don't know. That might be an exaggeration, but you know how I said that I've been a bit lax at work? I've been trying to catch up, but my manager's still asked to see me tomorrow and won't say what it's about.'

'Oh,' I said. 'Well, that doesn't necessarily mean trouble?'

'It's annoying. If I had got my act together two weeks earlier, this chat may not be happening.'

She pressed herself next to me, trying to peer past my wrist through the hole. 'The light's not coming on. This is useless. Let's give up.'

We both stepped away and stared defeated at the cold, lifeless machine.

'Do you have an electric heater?'

She shook her head. 'Energy sapping.'

'Why don't you just take that?'

We had a heater in the kitchen. It was an enormous old thing, definitely pre-1980s, which Joan had inherited from one of his and Katie's great-aunts. It had a dial at the side which worked like an egg timer causing its mesh front grille to glow bright red with raw heat. Standing too close for even a few seconds would lead to burnt calves and ankles.

'Bertha?' That's what we called it. 'You're kidding. I'll be afraid she'd ignite my room while I was sleeping!'

Katie bent down to switch it on and we stared at its unpredictable red glow.

'Also remember Joan's wired that himself. I'm not touching the plug.'

'I've got an old sleeping bag I've been using as an extra duvet. You can have that?'

'Thanks. But what will you use?'

'I don't know. I might just stay up down here. Sit in front of Bertha and read while watching the snow. If you ignored the inconvenience, it is quite mesmerising.'

We turned back to the window. It was a proper snow globe out there coming down in droves. I then felt the soft fluffiness of a dressing gown against my arm as Katie stood close watching too.

'I've got an idea,' she said and left the room. She returned a moment with her duvet.

'This is totally girly, but let's just camp out here for a bit. It'll be just like being back at uni. Izzy, Sophie, Tara, and I used to do this all the time. I can make us hot cocoa, and we'll at least be warm.'

She had this bizarre eager smile. I couldn't help but look at her like she had lost her mind. 'Oh, come on! This is the first time all day I've not been a sad-sack about this bloody meeting. We'll stay awake, we'll both be warm, and neither of us will die in a house fire.'

We sat at opposite ends of the sofa. I had my legs stretched on the coffee table and Katie sat cross-legged turned towards me.

'Do you *really* think you'll be in trouble tomorrow?'

'Honestly? Probably not. But I feel I should be. I'm just so, so pissed off at myself at the moment. I love my job! I've loved going to museums since we all went on a family trip to London. I must have only been six or seven, but for a country girl, I was absolutely awestruck. And I still have that feeling now. I just haven't been showing it.'

'You *have* had other things on your mind.'

'Ethan?' she smiled. 'You can say it. I'm not going to burst into tears again. Oh God, we spoke last night, and he actually brought up kids.'

She rolled her eyes. Her understated reaction somewhat annoyed me.

He sounds like such a complete dick, I wanted to say. Ethan came across as the stereotypical arrogant, had-it-easy posh boy who thought he was God's gift to women. To be honest, not much more than a week ago, I would have said they were relatively well suited as Katie was the typical shallow, overachiever whose life went according to a set plan. But I did not know her then.

'What do you see in him?' I found myself saying.

'Scott!' She stopped smiling and stared.

'I didn't mean it like that,' I tried to brush it off quickly. 'You're kind. And understanding. Fun and independent...' I was trying to be nonchalant, staring out in the direction of the dangerously glowing red heater. 'Like you've said, you've got a career of your own you want to focus on. I don't think he's that supportive, that's all.'

I glanced over at Katie. She still looked pissed off as she sipped her cocoa.

'Easier said than done, Scott. I do love him after all.' She looked away from me, into the red glow.

We sat in silence as the heater made a faint buzz. I looked at the window, at the snow.

While still staring at the window, I felt Katie move. I expected to feel the duvet dragged off me and see her walk back to her bedroom. Instead, I felt a soft mesh of hair on my shoulder.

'Sorry,' she said. She had put down her cocoa, and stretched her legs onto the coffee table. 'You have just told me I'm going out with a useless twat, which effectively makes me a useless twat. But, it was sweet of you.' Katie then raised her head from my shoulder and I felt her wriggle back onto her side of the sofa.

'Oh my God.' She wriggled. 'Sorry, I'm taking up all the space with my oversized bum. You wouldn't have this problem if it was Izzy here rather than me.'

'I think you might have a warped opinion of what constitutes *oversized*,' I grinned, noticing her light brown locks fall in front of her hazel eyes. 'And I hardly think that Izzy and me ever sharing sofa space is likely.'

Katie picked her cocoa up and looked at me.

'You know, you and Izzy have more in common than you realise.' It was now Katie's turn to grin as I saw her try to mask a smirk while sipping her hot cocoa. 'Your physiques, for one. You and your constant gardening and, hmmm, how you seem to choose when my friends are round to come back all sweaty and manly, muscles bulging...'

'I do not!' I almost spat out my cocoa, unsure whether to look horrified or burst out laughing.

'At least Izzy doesn't deny she goes to the gym every single day. Plus she plays tennis twice a week. And she doesn't even like tennis! She only plays because she enjoys thrashing people and because she can legitimately wear short, tight skirts that show off her amazing legs and bum. Oh! Sorry! You're still adamant you've never noticed them.'

Katie smiled and rolled her eyes. The frostiness in the air was starting to thaw due to the heater. In fact, I cautiously checked how close Katie's duvet had got to its grille as my toes were beginning to cook even if my heels were still blocks of ice.

'Oh come on, you and Izzy are two sides of the same coin. You both outwardly dress like you don't give a shit – you with your I'm-Definitely-Not-A-Hipster indie-kid clothes and her with her deliberately provocative skirts. Because you both want to be seen as different.'

'I guess you've seen right through me,' I smiled. Katie just sighed.

'I'm just saying that Izzy isn't the shallow mean-girl people make her out to be – she's got a First from Oxford despite not having the easiest time of it.' Katie frowned and turned on the sofa. 'Her parents split up just as we got to university. She puts on this cold, frosty exterior, but there have been times where she's not been able to stop crying. When it comes to guys, her type seems to be *pathological arseholes*. Either the member of the college rowing team voted most likely to become a sex pest, or someone heavily into drugs and who sees nothing wrong with screaming abuse directly into her face at parties or physically putting her hands on her. She's been out with some real winners.'

I sat up further to be closer to Katie's eye line.

'I just thought, *he's* not as bad as we first thought.' She gave a childish grin. 'And *she's*... well, at times she's a total pain in the arse, but actually one of the kindest, most loyal, most fun best friends I could ever have.'

Katie's grin had turned into a warm smile. She sipped her cocoa, the steam rising over her nose and eyelashes.

'Thanks for saying I'm not as bad as you first thought. That's probably the nicest thing a woman has ever said to me.' We both smiled. 'And I'm sorry your friend has had a hard time. They really do not sound nice guys.'

We listened to the faint hum of the heater. The flat still had an icy chill, but it was a lot warmer than when we were standing by the boiler.

'Scott?' Katie said, in a tired sounding voice. I suddenly realised how heavy my eyes had got. 'Thanks for this. I was freaking out.' She paused to yawn. 'But now... I'm...' I looked over to see that, instead of finishing her sentence, she had her eyes closed and was breathing deeply, fast asleep.

I stirred just before her. I felt her warm face on my shoulder, and her smooth hair had crept against my mouth. Our feet seemed to have entwined in our sleep as had our arms – I was hugging her arm as in the night she must have rolled over and laid an arm across me. The problem was where her hand had ended up and what she was cupping.

I lightly picked up Katie's wrist and placed it on her own leg.

'Urrrrrgghhmm,' she groaned. I felt her face turn and press into my upper shoulder. Her hand then shot to her mouth. She jumped up.

'Oh my God, how long have I been asleep?' She stared around the room and looked to the window, squinting as if trying to get her bearings.

'Oh. I am so, so sorry.' She stared down, horrified, at my shoulder. Across my upper arm was a large wet patch.

'I can't believe I did that. I've *drooled* all over you. Scott, I honestly do not know what to say.'

Looking further at the patch, she had gone to town. In places her saliva had sunk through my top. I couldn't help but laugh.

'Why didn't you wake me?' she then said, sounding irritated.

'I was asleep! I had no idea you were even here, apart from this weird dream I had that I was drowning at sea.' As I grinned, she shoved my arm. She then jumped up and turned around, her dressing gown flicking the side of my face. She reached up to our stereo on top of the fridge, which had a clock on it. She sighed.

'Half six,' she said and sat back down. 'I'm not late. We've been asleep for almost five hours. So much for staying up and making sure neither of us died in a fire.'

We both sat up and looked down at Bertha, who was still glowing raw red. Katie seemed to cautiously push the duvet off her as she shuffled away from me. The belt of her dressing gown had come undone sometime in the night and, noticing, she began tying what looked like a double knot. I felt it best to leave the sofa.

'How about a cup of tea?' I said, crossing the room to the kettle.

'Thank you,' she said as I returned, handing her one of the freshly made teas. I looked out of the window. The neighbourhood gardens were a sea of white. I sat down in our dilapidated armchair as Katie remained sitting upright in the corner of the sofa.

'Sorry for being grumpy,' she said, taking a sip. 'A bit disorientated.' She gave a small smile, glancing at me briefly before returning to her tea. 'It's been a while since I've woken up next to a strange man.'

'I wouldn't worry about it. At least we both survived the night.'

'No thanks to my dickhead brother.'

'I'll call him today and tell him we're going to get someone in.'

'No, I'll call him. I could do with shouting at him,' she smiled, looking a bit brighter. 'I should be getting dressed. Get today's meeting over and done with. Urrrrgh,' came another groan, but she broke into a smile.

'Thanks for keeping me company. I was a complete pain. Again. Hey, what are you doing tonight? I can make you dinner as a thank you – I do a mean bolognese.'

'I'm actually going over to our old house tonight. There a few things of my dad's I said I'd look for and sort out.'

'Oh. Okay. I don't think I've been stood up for an empty house before. I guess it will be a whole a lot warmer than here anyway.'

The steam from our tea formed spirals through the atmosphere right up to the ceiling. I felt a pang of gnawing guilt.

'I'm going to see my brother-in-law's band tomorrow. Why don't you join us – Joan and Alison will be there too!' I found myself hastily adding the last bit.

'I told Izzy I'd spend Saturday with her – I've been putting her off all this week. Maybe I can bring her? I promise it won't be a setup.'

We both smiled. I felt this weird shyness just like when I was sixteen and first asked Vicky to the cinema.

'I better get dressed. I could do with getting in early and mentally preparing. Thank you again for last night. I probably would have spent it wide awake both freezing and freaking out in my room.'

As Katie left, I couldn't help feeling something familiar. Her large dressing gown reminded me of an old unfashionable raincoat Vicky used to wear. Vicky said she knew it was hideous, but it was almost essential over the British winter and served as a comfort blanket. To me, it made Vicky look beautiful, especially as she assumed she looked the opposite. She would have forgotten that I had fallen in love with her back when she was the maths geek sixteen-year-old without makeup on, her shiny yellow hair bundled back, and her face screwed up in concentration as we tried to solve refraction problems. As Katie and her enormous dressing gown left the room, I couldn't help thinking of Vicky and that day she and that raincoat left my life for good.

CHAPTER 13

BRUCE

When Vicky and I broke up what now seems so many years ago, it was not a case of no guilty parties. While Vicky was the one who eventually pulled the trigger, I would be first to admit that I had not given her much of an incentive to stay. Part of me still thinks that our relationship might have solely served as the wake-up she needed. She had swapped charismatic but controlling douchebags for what she thought was safe and stable. However, neither proved themselves emotionally capable of making her happy.

I should have been Vicky's knight in shining armour. But, by the end of our relationship, I had become both too insecure to feel comfortable in an adult relationship, and too drunk on the success of having one girl like me that I forgot how lucky I was to have Vicky in my life. What I did was not a question of fidelity, but something more pathetic. I had begun to question whether *she* was good enough for *me*.

When Vicky and I first started dating, I was the competition winner who could not believe his luck. When I was away from her, I would feel this sense of foreboding that she would come to her senses at any moment. I would dread those birthday parties with her friends – the glamorous, well-spoken, self-confident set that I had attended university with who seemed so much more mature and sophisticated than me. They would surely see what a charlatan I was. But then, away from this crowd, with my own friends and workmates, my ego got the better of me.

I started having these thoughts, about which I am frankly aghast when looking back now. They would be when the lights were out and Vicky and I were being intimate. I would be stroking her face and find myself suddenly thinking about the blonde girl working on reception at my bank. This girl had finally remembered my name after years of working there, and I would suddenly look at Vicky and feel I was settling for second place. That, in that bedroom twilight, Vicky was rather plain.

Or it would be a small redhead who I started talking to while out at work drinks. Until Vicky, I rarely had the confidence to approach women at bars. Suddenly I was all smiles.

Nothing happened between me and any of these women. But looking back at my twenty-seven-year-old self, that does not excuse any of it or make it any less of a fortunate escape for Vicky. I stopped appreciating her. I had made the cardinal mistake of believing that just because one girl was foolish enough to believe in me, I must be irresistible.

Broker drinks, networking drinks, team building drinks, I would be out up to three nights a week, and on the occasions that she joined us, I could tell Vicky would rather have been anywhere else than having my drunken banking friends repeatedly offer her Jäger-bombs and tequila slammers. I lost sight of the qualities Vicky prob-ably saw in me in the first place. She had liked the wallflower in me, the fact that I was not full of myself like her other boyfriends, the fact that I listened to her, that I was her friend. And eventually, she realised she had no desire to continue dating someone still going through an extended adolescence.

. . .

I had lied about having to go to Dad's house. When Katie offered to make me dinner, I instinctively hit the panic button. I had spent the first part of the year as a shoulder to cry on for Sarah, so I did not fancy repeating the experience. But sitting on our sofa, drinking cocoa together, was an image I could not get out of my head while I stood at the allotment trying unsuccessfully to dig frozen ground. I kept thinking back to the feeling of her head on my shoulder.

But as I returned to Dad's and descended into our dark, dusty basement, torch in hand, to bring old boxes out of storage, my phone buzzed. It was a message from Katie:

OMG – I've been offered a promotion! My boss is taking a sabbatical and she asked if I would like to fill in. Temporarily, obviously. But it means I'm not getting fired!!! xx

Obviously she was not going to get fired. From what I had started to learn about Katie, her definition of slacking off was doing the standard forty-hour week instead of her usual sixty. Putting the storage boxes on the dining table, I felt this sense of guilt and missing out. Dinner could have been celebratory. I pictured Katie's beaming smile sitting opposite me, holding a glass of wine. I wondered if she had already told Ethan. I hoped she hadn't. I found myself hoping I was one of the first people she told. I found myself suddenly hoping for a lot of things.

'Hey!' Katie beamed a huge, surprised smile. She was coming out of her bedroom as I reached the top of the stairs. She was wearing a baggy sweatshirt and what looked like pyjama bottoms. I smiled back at her, taking off my gloves and then my coat, catching my breath and letting my face regain feeling from the icy conditions outside.

'I thought you were staying somewhere snug and warm?'

'That wouldn't make me much of a team player.' I smiled a bit of a nervous smile. 'Abandoning you in a time of crisis. Is it me, or is it warm in here?'

'Oh, yes, Joan came round. There's a trick with the pilot light. *Another* stupid trick! I swear, he's deliberately done things to this house to make it impossible for normal human beings to inhabit. But seriously, why didn't you tell me you were coming home? I would have made dinner!'

'Well, it's late. I thought you'd either be asleep or out celebrating.' I smiled again.

'No, not out. Trying to be good and limit nights out to once a week.' She had on an intoxicating grin. I didn't need to ask about the promotion for how ebullient she looked. 'And as for being asleep...' She raised her eyebrows. 'Scott, it's nine o'clock on a Friday night. I think we can both stretch to staying awake until at least eleven.'

I was about awkwardly ask if she fancied opening a bottle of wine when Katie stepped forward and then put her arms around me.

'Oh, thanks for coming home,' she said, mid hug – a prolonged hug where I felt the warmth of her body pressed against me and her arms on my back.

'I have to admit, it was starting to feel an anti-climax hanging out here by my lonesome. Come on.' She then released me and led the way into the kitchen.

I watched her and waited behind for just a moment. Nothing was going to happen, I told myself. Ever. She was my friend and purely just my friend. But after what had felt an entire year under a cloud, I had a sense of awakening. Like I could breathe again. For the first time in I did not know how long, I had looked forward to coming home. As Katie tiptoed up to collect two wine glasses from our kitchen cupboard, I wanted to bottle up that moment. The next time those dark clouds descended, I needed to remember that feeling of warmth, contentment and belonging of simply drinking wine *with a woman I can call my friend,* to quote the other great American poet, Mr Bruce Springsteen.

CHAPTER 14

WILL YOU STILL LOVE ME TOMORROW?

The first time I met Mike, Ellie had uncharacteristically omitted to say what he did for a living. It was toward the end of my Exmouth Market years when she had been working in music journalism, and we would end up having a night out together almost twice a month. My sister was usually never shy about name-dropping. Or at having my awestruck friends hanging on her every word as she regaled stories of partying with the indie and rock bands they were obsessed with. She was also the master of throwing choice titbits that would have us all look at each other, sufficiently wowed, and say, '*you* know James Hetfield? From Metallica?'

Some of it was embellishment, some of it bullshit. Obviously, James Hetfield from Metallica did not have my sister's name in his iPhone contacts list. Rather, she had been in the same room as the band at a press event and had the moxie to approach him and have a three minute conversation – an achievement in itself considering I would have been star-struck to the point of paralysis. But at that stage in our lives, Ellie was the cool one, always going places and meeting iconic people. And she knew full well her stories would make her the centre of attention and a superstar by association.

Therefore, dating the lead singer and guitarist in a pretty decent and well-respected band surely should have made her unbearable, right? But when she brought him down to the Exmouth Arms, and we sat around our usual table drinking pints with my flatmates, she just gave a spiel about having met at a gig and that Mike just worked on the music circuit rather than, according to articles in *Melody Maker*, that he was the frontman of *'Britain's answer to the Black Keys'*. It was only when I was travelling through Oxford Circus tube station and I saw him staring back at me on a poster advertising their new album, that I had an inkling who Mike was and how well respected he was as a musician – four stars, *Q* and *NME* had rated it.

In that respect, it was not a surprise that when I arrived early to see his band step out of their hiatus, the Blues Café was completely full with barely even any standing room left for the sea of people who Mike was certain did not know who his band was anymore. It had the vibe of a mini arena with tables piled up at the side, making room for the crowd in front of a stage. From a far corner of the room I saw two arms wave to me, one eager like it had not seen me in years, the other – Joan's – disengaged performing a public service.

'Hey, stranger,' said Alison. They were on stools at one of the few remaining small, tall tables against the far wall. 'We thought we'd get here early and find somewhere to sit. Is it getting old that the thought of standing for a whole gig sends you into a cold sweat?' As a couple, Alison's natural enthusiasm gelled well with Joan's genuine disinterest. Her petite bubbliness, and free spirit with multi-coloured hairstyles, paired well with his tall, skinny lethargy of succeeding through minimizing efforts.

'How's you?' asked Alison. 'How's the house of horrors? Sorry I haven't been round to visit. That place still gives me PTSD from when Joan and what other life forms were living there.'

'You'd be pleasantly surprised,' I smiled. 'Katie's transformed it.

There was a spell when you could smell nothing but disinfectant, but it is quite cosy now.'

'How is Katie?' she smiled. 'How are you both getting along?'

'I think that's Alison's way of asking if you've tried to get into her knickers yet.'

Joan briefly smirked but then went back to staring at his phone.

'That's your sister!' Alison stared up at him, looking truly appalled. Joan shrugged.

'Well, you're the one so interested in how they're both getting on.'

'She's fine,' I interrupted. 'Actually, she's had some good news at work. And things between her and Ethan seem on the mend...'

I tried relay the last piece of news without visibly sneering. Waking up that morning, I could hear Katie downstairs rummaging around in the kitchen and talking to someone. It was not an unpleasant sensation, being woken up by a very cheerful tone and a lot of enthusiastic laughter. When I ventured down to the kitchen, she had made breakfast, spooning poached eggs onto a plate, with a huge smile on her face as she pressed her phone to her ear.

'It will also be more money, which always comes in handy,' she grinned.

I walked past her to put on the kettle as she gave me a quick smile and mouthed good morning before laughing again into the phone.

'Thanks!' she beamed, sounding mock-sarcastic but happy. 'I'll try to remember you think your girlfriend is basically a ninny.' She grinned again, this time her cheeks going pink as I pretended not to be glancing at her and busied myself making tea.

'I better go. I'm starving. Plus, I need to speak to Scott about this music thing with my brother. I'll call you back in an hour or so. Love you. Hey! Sorry about that – Ethan called. Wanted to hear about the new job.'

'Ah, okay. Things sound better?'

Her eyes rolled up to look at the ceiling thoughtfully before she answered.

'Yes. He's being quite considerate at the moment.' She then sighed, shook her head, and ran her hands through her hair, scrunching it up, but all the while smiling what looked like a very relieved smile.

'It is still early days, but he's been a bit more attentive this week. It's...' I saw the pink glow return to her cheeks. 'It's encouraging, anyway. So tonight,' she then said, picking up her plate of eggs and the mug that was next to it. 'I'm meeting Izzy for drinks first, so we might have to meet you guys there. What time is Mike on?'

Katie said she would try to get to the venue as close to nine o'clock as possible with the caveat of *Izzy being Izzy, so who knew what would happen.* In turn, I spent the day glumly moving between record shops and cafés half-heartedly trying to expand my 1960s Motown collection while scribbling some basic equations of how many new clients my fledgling gardening business would need before I went bankrupt. My conclusion being a lot more than the one client that I currently had.

It should not have been so disappointing to overhear Katie's joy when speaking with Ethan. Nothing had changed in the status quo – she had a boyfriend whom she loved. But I did find myself walking from Loughborough Road to the Blue Cafés with less of a jauntiness than I had the night before.

'It's great you're getting on,' said Alison. 'Katie really is lovely, which is surprising considering who she's related to.' Alison nodded to Joan, who had stopped listening and was looking out to the stage. He then raised his hand to get someone's attention. Through the mingling crowd, Mike was coming towards us, and just behind him a woman who looked identical to my sister.

'I didn't know you were coming,' I said to Ellie as we hesitated, then hugged awkwardly as everyone else was hugging.

'Mrs Rawlins said she didn't mind having the kids. Apparently, they are little angels for her...' She frowned as Mike smirked. 'Plus, I deserve the occasional night out, and why not treat myself to an evening chain drinking flat lager and ruining my new boots on a sticky floor.'

'She's been looking forward to it, really,' smiled Mike. 'I better go back to the band. We're meant to be on in five. See you all after?' We said yes, and Mike went back to the stage. Joan then offered to buy a round and took Alison with him to the bar.

'It's like old times,' Ellie said. 'Basement bars, bad lager, sweaty people jumping up and down. To think this was how I made a living, writing up gigs of bands who thought signing their first record deal would make them the next Stones. I really *don't* miss this.'

We stood watching the activity of music technicians moving leads around and fiddling with equipment.

'What about playing? Have you thought about composing again?' Ellie just snorted.

'I think that ship has sailed. Plus, when am I going to get a chance? I seem to spend most of my life either teaching scales or running around after Ed and Millie.'

At that moment, I felt my phone buzz. Assuming it was Katie, which it was, I quickly read the message as Ellie looked on at the stage. *So so sorry. It doesn't look like we'll make it. Izzy is being a nightmare! Will tell all tomorrow. Have a great night!*

Putting my phone away, I felt relief cancel out some of the disappointment. Her conversation with Ethan was still in my head. It was going to be strange especially in this awkward 'group hang' setting I had engineered that would have included the eclectic mix of her brother, her best friend, my sister, my brother-in-law, and

Alison. But I found myself lost in my own world, staring down at the soon-to-be sticky floor as the packed crowd got even more packed.

I then realised where I was. I was on a night out with two of my best friends and my sister, watching my brother-in-law's band play to a full house. I had not had a night like this in years. I listened to the noise, the eager conversations around me, the sound system in the background, and felt the brushes of people coming through with drinks, jostling for space. I turned around to see Joan and Alison being served drinks at the bar and then looked at my sister next to me, dressed up for what she said was her first night out in months. I then closed my eyes and let myself appreciate that moment.

'The piano at Dad's is just there not being used,' I said to Ellie. 'If we're going to be spending Christmas there, you might get a chance to... I don't know, pick up where you left off.'

Before she had a chance to answer, the lights dimmed and I felt a plastic pint glass of lager being thrust into my hand by Joan. There was a roar as my brother-in-law and his band stepped out onto the stage.

What I have come to find incredibly unhelpful in my relatively short life is how people with drinking and drug problems are portrayed by films and media. On the screen, people struggling with the lure of all-night benders only kick the habit after attending a weekly meeting in a church and confiding to a group of strangers that they are an alcoholic and stating how many days or months they have been sober.

In fact, during my late twenties, the one thing that drove me further into the arms of drugs and alcohol was trying to give them up completely. I could go through the day without the need for a drink. I could go three weeks without a drink. But if I saw my friends, I would run out of things to say while sober and feel an outsider, unable to join in the merriment. And then all it would take was one beer to have me craving more and leading me to order cocaine and making my way to the nearest strip club.

It was Alison who recommended therapy to me. I was a tired, sad kind of drunk, and we had found ourselves sitting on a booth in a quiet corner of an indie club while our other friends were on the dancefloor. It had been my third night drinking in a row, and the previous two had involved a lot of white powder, meaning when it came to seeing my actual friends, I was typically hungover and jaded. 'How are things?' I asked her. 'Pretty shit, to be honest,' was her reply, but with her characteristic warm smile. 'I've been feeling a bit lost recently. Work, life, men. It's been a bit shit for a while now – probably why everyone thinks I'm such a head case.' I turned to her and noticed there wasn't the same zany spark. Instead, she sat back subdued, sipping what looked like water from a plastic glass. 'It's okay, you don't have to be kind,' she said after I tried to reassure her that we all thought she was wonderful. 'I drink way too much on nights like these. I wake up hating myself as I usually finish the night having a stand-up row with someone off my face, or bursting into tears for no reason at a random bus stop.' She gave a little shrug as *'Parklife'* by Blur kicked off a mini-riot on the dance-floor. 'I'm seeing someone now. No, not another man,' she smiled. 'A therapist. Someone to talk things over and help me realise what this all means.'

Two months later, I had my first session with Anthony, a middle-aged Scottish man with a soft, patient voice. I wanted to blame my drinking on my split with Vicky. I wanted to blame going to strip clubs and doing cocaine on my drinking – as if it was the beers and beers alone that made me some kind of fiend. But the first thing Anthony pointed out was everything usually ran a little bit deeper.

Anthony and I spent six months talking through my recriminations and relapses to why I wanted to do cocaine or go to strip clubs. The hardest thing to admit were the words 'because I was lonely.' I also stayed out in part because I did not want to go home. I had no hobbies, I had no purpose. Somewhere along the line, I had started believing that I needed to drink to speak to other people – to have confidence, for people to find me interesting, and to meet someone new. Anthony and I then gave it a new word. Rather than *addiction,* we used *dependency.*

It probably sounds like an excuse, and maybe with hindsight it is, and the truth was that it was easier to pay for stimulated confidence and for women to talk to me.

'What do you like about drinking?' Anthony then asked me, but not in a sneering, what-on-earth-do-you-see-in-it type of way. 'Socialising is a big part of our lives. Think back to when you enjoyed a drink for what it was, and you did not have those recriminations the next day.'

I recalled those nights at indie clubs and dancing until the early hours of the morning. I remembered the taste of a cold beer after a long day and also standing in a warm pub on a cold night with my friends, just enjoying being there.

'It's not simply a case of stopping drinking and then life becoming better. You also need to find what you're passionate about, slowly filling your life with other things and experiences.' Anthony then let out a small laugh. 'Then, you will find yourself both enjoying those beers with your friends and wanting to return home to, who knows, bake banana bread in the morning.'

. . .

Rather than baking banana bread, I found myself spending more time in Dad's garden. It began one Sunday when I arrived for lunch and saw him sweating, trying to unearth what looked like the whole front flowerbeds, and as Anthony described, I found myself gradually coming home earlier so I could spend the next day learning to plant things I had no idea the name of yet.

And returning to Loughborough Road after the Blues Café, I had that similar sensation. Instead of wallowing about Katie, I spent the evening surrounded by people I truly loved. It had been completely euphoric. Mike's band had the venue erupting, and the crowd were whooping and jumping like they would have done a decade earlier. There were times on stage you could see Mike lost for words as his vocals were drowned out by a thousand voices singing over him. After the set, Ellie embraced Mike, and neither looked like they were ever going to let the other go, and we all stood around basking in the glow as random people would come up to the band asking if they could take a selfie with them.

As we all hugged outside and said goodbye, I was reminded of the heyday when we would go indie clubbing and, at the end of the night, stand on the pavement about to go home, just waiting that little bit longer so we could keep absorbing that natural high. I hugged Joan, Alison, Mike, and even my sister, with a giant bear hug – Ellie did groan but squeezed me back just as hard. And then I let the buzz carry me home, back to Loughborough Road.

As I climbed the stairs up to the landing, I hoped that Katie might be back from her night out so I could share with her how euphoric the night had been. There was a soft light coming from the kitchen, but otherwise, the house was still and quiet and I could see Katie's door was shut. It looked like one of us had left a lamp on. As I entered the kitchen and went to switch it off, I was startled.

'Yes?' said a voice from the sofa. Lying across it was a girl in a short black skirt and small white top staring at me through shiny fresh makeup – Izzy. Her legs were nonchalantly stretched out, her shoes off, and her head was resting on a pile of cushions sitting up just enough to sip from a small glass tumbler.

'Can I help you?' she then said, not overly politely considering who lived there and who did not. She raised her eyebrows and gave me a *'well? I'm waiting'* stare.

'Is Katie here?'

'In bed,' she said, rolling her eyes and looking away. She raised her tumbler to her lips and let it touch the bottom one. 'She said the gin was yours.' She tilted her head to a bottle on the coffee table. It was about half empty, which was not the case the last and only time I had poured myself a glass.

'You're both back early,' I said, walking to the sink to pour myself a glass of water.

'Well, Spoiler didn't fancy the club.' I assumed that from the look on my face Izzy saw that I didn't understand her reference.

'It's what we used to call her at Oxford,' she said lazily, stretching out one of her legs fully so her bare foot dangled off the end of the sofa. She started making circles with the tip of her toe, staring absently as she did.

"Spoiler of all things fun'. The sensible one who said no to anything remotely interesting. Weed, pills, house parties at random men's houses at four o'clock in the morning. Threesomes.'

With the last one, Izzy glanced over with a hint of what might have been a smile – the first time I had seen her do so. 'Probably for the best. At least it meant she was there to hold back one's hair when one was throwing up stoned. Or hold one's hand when freaking out on acid. Shame about the threesome, though.' Again, another glance and smile as her eyes kissed mine.

I tried to smile politely, not quite sure of the etiquette for a random girl drinking alone in my living room. She was still absently making circles with her toe as I tried not to glance at her long legs.

Izzy was attractive, very few could argue the contrary, but there was something off.

'You *can* join me. I don't bite. It is your gin after all.' Again with minimal effort, she waved a hand to the bottle.

'I was going to bed,' I said, picking up my water. Izzy then let out a sigh and impatiently flicked her hair to the side. 'At midnight? On a Saturday?'

I knew I shouldn't be so easily goaded. I also had a feeling that having a drink with Izzy was not the thing to do, and the safe play would have been to smile politely and go upstairs to my duvet. After all, it was not the friendliest invitation, and sitting at an arm's length drinking with a girl who seemed in a strange mood was unlikely to be a jovial experience. But I didn't go upstairs.

'Have you got any tonic?'

'It's your house,' she shrugged.

I turned around one of our dining chairs and sat opposite Izzy. She was staring at her toes, indifferent to me taking her up on her offer.

'Spoiler's having a sulk. In case you're wondering why I'm here by my lonesome.' She sipped her glass of neat gin.

'We had a tiff. Her fault, but Little Miss Morality decided she would still offer me the benevolence of her room as a place to crash. I'd rather enjoy the remainder of the evening out here.'

The tonic we had in the fridge was flat and had a bitter after-taste, but I sipped it anyway as I looked at the strange girl with nice legs.

'We're meant to be at a party. Friends of mine from work, but Spoiler is apparently above all that now.' Izzy then did look at me. A non-friendly accusing stare. 'You know about Ethan, I take it? Of course you do. You both are so chummy now.'

'Is that what your *tiff* was about?' I made the mistake of smiling. After all, it did sound a little trivial. But Izzy then smiled too – the first full, irrefutable one I had seen from her. However, it was not a kind smile.

'No, Scott. It was because Spoiler doesn't want mean old man-eating Izzy to *fuck* her sweet, sensitive housemate.'

She made a sarcastic pout, holding eye contact. Through its modern overuse, rarely does the word *fuck* tend to shock. But put so deliberately, in her public school accent, it hung in the air.

'Don't look so worried.' She then rolled her eyes and lay back again, sipping her gin. 'I don't fancy you, if that's what you've been led to believe.' She narrowed her eyes, staring at me uncomfortably closely. Things had started to feel weird – or at least weirder than they already were. I gulped down more of my gin and tonic so I could politely leave.

'Katie hasn't led me to believe anything. She might have been overzealous on the matchmaking front but that's just because – '

'Spoiler's got a big mouth,' she continued, cutting me off. 'Big, and unfortunately disappointing, I'm reliably told. In case you were wondering. What with all your late-night chats and that.' She finally broke her stare and looked away, now irritated. She suddenly looked a lot younger, like a teenager having a bout of petulance. A lot less sexy. She reached over for the gin to top up her glass.

'Do you think you may have had enough?'

'I have a certain type, Scott, you see,' she said, ignoring me. 'And sadly, you don't fit the bill.' She seemed genuinely happy relaying the news. 'You see, all this,' she waved her hand around in a circle, 'the *shabby chic* lifestyle is not my thing. Just thought you should know.'

I could only smirk and let her go on.

'I'm not one of the Katies of this world who finds charm in a man-of-the-people or someone who goes to festivals or watches *has-been* bands. And let's face it, spending an afternoon record shopping – Scott, I hate to be the one to tell you, re-enacting the past is hardly sexy.'

She wasn't exactly offending me – I don't like the word, but there was something about her being too much of a bitch to be a bitch. Rather, it was weird how she seemed to know so much about me. Weird and irritating.

'You see,' she said, sitting up. 'I like men who don't act like boys. Who achieve, take what they want, and have something to show for it. If that makes me shallow...' She simply shrugged to end the sentence. I had come to the end of my gin and tonic. Placing the glass down on the coffee table, I stood up to leave her.

'Thanks very much for the heads up, Izzy. I'll make sure I cross your name off my list of potential girlfriends.'

I felt a cushion bounce off my face as I was about to walk out the door.

'Oh, grow up,' she said with a snort of laughter. She reached over and picked up my empty glass and the gin bottle. She poured another and then offered it to me.

'You *are* quite the sensitive soul.' She made the pouting face again. Did she think her childish, demeaning gestures were sexy? Obviously, they were. I tried to at least scowl as I took the glass.

'And you're a little bit hostile.'

'Oh, really?' She smiled, this time without an undertone. 'Well, then. Here's to neither of us wanting to fuck each other.'

Even before I could decide if I wanted another drink, let alone sit down, Izzy flung herself to her feet and said,

'Come on. I want to show you something.' She stepped past me and surprisingly took my hand. She led me into the hallway and to Katie's door.

'Oh, what do you think?'

There were a pair of shiny black high heels on the floor, and she put her toe into one. 'I just got them. The effect is greater when on.'

Still holding my hand, but this time for balance, she bent down to do up the straps.

'Well?' she said.

'Yes, great,' I said, unsure why my opinion on a pair of shoes was needed.

'Cost a fortune.' She spun around, apparently enamoured with her new purchase, looking down at them at all angles. Then, she opened Katie's door and wandered in.

'It's fine. She's asleep. Come on,' she smiled, pulling me by the hand. This time it was a different smile – conspiring and happy. I took one step forward, Izzy's fingers soft and delicate in my grip. I stopped just on the threshold.

'I'll wait here,' I whispered

Izzy shot me a look – a huge smile – and then playfully tugged me forward.

'Look.' She then said softly and pointed at the bed. There was Katie, unsurprisingly sleeping. What was surprising was despite the cold, she had her duvet kicked off and was lying on her side in her pyjamas, deep silent breaths coming from her. I quickly turned away and made to leave but felt Izzy's hand grip mine more forcibly, and her arm yank mine hard like it was a child's game.

'Don't worry,' Izzy smiled again. 'She's dead to the world when she's asleep. We used to have a lot of fun with that at university.' I felt Izzy's breath on my ear. Her heels made her taller so her lips were at my earlobe. She then turned back to Katie and stepped towards the bed, kneeling in front of her.

'Look at Little Miss Maturity. Thirty years old and still wearing rabbit pyjamas.' The streetlight was illuminating Katie, casting a glow through her curtains. They were full-length pyjamas and had some pattern on the front. She also had on thick socks, so I could not see any skin at all, which I tried to tell myself made this situation less *pervy.*

'I'm going to go,' I said, releasing myself from Izzy's grip.

'Ooooh, look at her white knight!' Izzy beamed up at me, again looking manically happy.

'She won't even stir. Oh bless! Such an untroubled mind.' Izzy's hand lightly stroked Katie's face.

I felt I now needed to stay and get Izzy out of the room, making sure she didn't do anything like draw on Katie's face with mascara pens or put her hand in a bucket of water. Or worse. I had a vision of an unhinged Izzy pinching Katie's nose to impede her breathing and Katie waking up gasping for air. But Izzy then got up, walked past me and around the bed as I partly stood frozen, her accomplice, but still noticing the pendulum swing of her hips.

'Matching slippers!' She reached down and turned around with what appeared two large balls of fur. 'So Little Miss *Wascally Wabbit* can be a bunny. Not quite what Ethan imagined when he suggested cosplay, I'm sure.'

At that moment, I was not sure who I despised more. Izzy, who seemed to enjoy the cruelty she was inflicting on her best friend, or me for being complicit. I glared at Izzy, who was still beaming, and then put her hands together and made a scurrying pawing motion with the slippers. I stepped over and took the slippers off her. She gave me a pouting face and dramatically fluttered her eyelashes.

'You *are* her white knight,' she whispered and stepped very close.

She raised her arms and put them around my neck. She smiled once more as she leaned her head to the side, and I felt her mouth on mine. Her teeth pressed my jaw open. Her tongue playfully brushed mine, and I felt it push against the inside of my cheek.

I had let go of the slippers and had my hands on her waist. I felt her take one and move it behind her onto what Katie termed her *impossibly small bum.*

'The zip's at the back,' she whispered, biting my neck. Her

hand had rolled down my chest and was at the top of my jeans. My eyes then glanced to the sleeping Katie, and I quickly let go of Izzy.

'We shouldn't,' I whispered. 'Not here.'

'Oh, stop talking,' she said. She angled her head again to kiss me, but when I didn't return the gesture she dramatically dropped her arms. 'Seriously?' She put her hands on her hips and stared at me. She was actually looking angry.

'Fine,' she said. Both her hands pushed into my chest as she shoved past me and marched out of the room. I was alone with the sleeping Katie – somewhere I definitely should not have been, so I turned around and followed Izzy out. I had expected Izzy to return to the sofa, and I would awkwardly say goodnight – most likely get ignored – and go to bed. But instead, I found Izzy waiting five stairs above me, on her way up to my room.

'Coming?' she scowled.

'Oh my God,' she said, in exasperation rather than pleasure. 'Oh, it *is* like making love to a virgin.'

I was on top of Izzy. I was naked, and her skirt and underwear were somewhere on the floor. What goes on behind closed doors I would, under normal circumstances, say should remain behind closed doors, but unfortunately, what happened afterward would make little sense without knowing what took place in that room. Plus, it hardly constitutes being crass or boastful if I am effectively externalising the single most humiliating sexual experience of my life.

'Oh. My. God. Am I supposed to undress both of us?' Izzy had said after having, I had thought seductively, lifted my t-shirt over my head. We did kiss, but there was no beaming smile as there had been in Katie's room. Instead, she kept on the same scowl from the stairs.

I then mistakenly thought it would be erotic to start by kissing the inside of her thigh. As I did, she grabbed a fistful of my hair and pulled my head up. 'Scott, can we please up the pace? It would be nice for something to happen sometime tonight.'

As I moved up her body, slightly reluctant to obey, we then kissed, and all felt forgiven. As she delicately and rhythmically put her mouth to mine, I tried to lift the white top she was still wearing. She snatched my hand away and pulled her top back down.

'Oh my God, *I'm* lying underneath you. *You're* lying on top of me. I've already removed my own underwear, and now you want to play with my breasts, like a fifteen-year-old! I'm seriously five seconds away from calling this off and getting the deed done by myself.'

Those romantic imageries of lovers gazing longingly into each other's eyes came to mind as Izzy and I glared at each other. We had reached a level of intimacy unprecedented for two people who hardly knew each other: that of mutual loathing and disdain. My arms were outstretched on either side of the mesh of her long black hair spread across the pillow. As I reluctantly obeyed and moved my hips closer to hers, I muttered:

'Well, I'm not sure how disappointed I would be if you did.'

'Oh *honey*, I kind of already am!' she said patronisingly.

'Now, I'm not sure if you have ever done this before, but that teeny little part of you probably should not be rubbing against my leg. That's call *not* having sex, Scott.' She put her hand to my face and her fingers squeezed my bottom lip nodding it up and down. With her other hand, she then reached for my wrist.

'Why don't you take this hand and help move your little friend somewhere he might be a bit more useful?'

'You know you could be a bit nicer.'

'I'm starting to get bored now, Scott.'

So I did what she asked. Without saying another word we

began a staring contest of who could glare at each other longest as our hips moved together.

'Are you doing this deliberately? Making the experience as dull as possible?'

'You're not exactly breathing like someone bored.' As we were doing *the deed* I could hear her breaths through the glare, usually a sign that at least something is happening. Even as I said my retort I could tell that I was not breathing normally either.

'Is this your first time?' she said, in a slight whimper, now biting her lip. 'Should I be making allowances?'

'You're not exactly doing a great deal yourself to enhance the experience,' I breathed, adjusting my arms to hold myself higher, conscious of my technique.

'Oh really?' she announced slightly louder, with a little more venom in her glare. I then felt one of her legs wrap around my waist. Then the other. The improvement was immediate as even staring down at Izzy's surly face, I felt us starting to move together more intently. Then she kicked me. Hard.

'Arrrggh! For fuck's sake, Izzy!' I keeled over. 'WHAT THE HELL!' Blinding pain was in my side. Izzy had just kicked me with the sharp three-inch point of her shiny black heel, which I had forgotten she was still wearing. She had managed to stab me straight in the fleshy part just below my rib cage – an area I'm pretty sure contains my kidneys. The pain was excruciating.

'Oh, I am sorry,' she said, smiling, sounding delighted. 'I thought you could do with encouragement. *Giddy up!* and all that.' She was on the verge of giggles, so not to give her the satisfaction, I closed my eyes to block out the pain and tried to carry on with what I was doing.

'Could you breathe a little less loud?' she said. I knew I was wheezing. I don't know where she had kicked me but I was starting to feel sick and dizzy. She had already implied I was a wimp. I just wanted to get it over and done with. The good news was that, despite the sarcasm, she was beginning to sound out of breath too.

'Oh my God,' she said again, but this time more of a heavy whisper. Her nails dug into my arms. 'Anyone would think you'd never done it before. That I'm taking your virginity. I'm not taking your virginity, am I, Scott?' And there it was, the final piece to the evening's festivities. Izzy bringing my sister into the proceedings by echoing the exact same taunt. Did I have to track down Greta Morgan and ask her to tell all my doubters that I lost my virginity to her during our last year of university?

'Your rhythm is appalling.' She then let out a moan, probably involuntarily. She closed her eyes and arched her head back. I felt her legs wrap around my waist again.

'Oh my God, you really are a shit lay – I've honestly never had sex *this* bad. Ha! Congratulations, you are officially the worst sex I've... ever... had...'

'Well... I'm sure half the male population of Oxford would be relieved to hear that.'

In light of the exchange, I had expected another insult hurled back. Instead, she slapped me. Hard. I looked down, and she was not just glaring up at me, but her teeth were gritted and her face slightly more pink versus her usual cold white.

'Fuck you,' she whispered, and then covered my face with her hand. I could just make out that her eyes were closed and her face scrunched up as she grabbed me and rose up.

'Uhh!' she squealed. And then again. Her arms were around my neck and her face was to the side of mine as she shuddered.

'For Christ's sake, slowly now, you idiot,' she whispered. She lay back down and began to squirm. 'Oh, my God. Oh, it *is* like making love to a virgin.'

I know I should not have been surprised, but with all the glares and insults, it was difficult to remember the purpose of what we were doing.

'I told you not to stop!' she yelled, arching her neck again and flinging her head back. I then felt another kick to my hip. Still hard, but this time more irritating rather than painful.

'My God, have you still not finished?' she then said.

I hadn't. But I had had enough. I stopped what I was doing. 'To be honest, if you're done, I think I'm going to call it a night.' Tired and deflated, I rolled off her.

'Ahem! If *I'm* done? Well, thank you for your benevolence.'

I got out of bed and put on my jeans, clutching my side.

'Where the hell are you going?'

'To the bathroom, Izzy,' I answered, slow and tired, my hand where her heel had landed.

'Did I *actually* hurt you?' she asked, not sounding concerned but surprised that I was being openly a baby about the incident.

'No.'

'Excuse me? Are you not at least going to offer me a t-shirt or something to change into? Or do you expect me to spend the night in my clothes?'

'You want to sleep here?' I assumed she was joking.

'Oh, just pass me a t-shirt and go.'

By the morning I had a bruise that was pretty much covering my side, as I examined myself in the bathroom mirror. It had a solid dark centre and reassuringly looked quite the war wound. I don't care how tough a man or woman thinks they are – try not being felled when a high heel is jabbed into your side. If Izzy had chosen a pointier pair, the mood would have been further spoilt by both of us having to sleep in blood-stained sheets. As it was, I was currently hiding in the bathroom with my surprise guest still asleep upstairs.

In my perhaps limited experience, the first time spending the night with someone could quite aptly play out to the soundtrack, 'Will you still love me tomorrow?' by The Shirelles. Obviously, with Izzy, it would be more a case of, *would you still despise me tomorrow*. Still, while I stood in front of the bathroom mirror, I could not help drifting back to my first night with Vicky. I had been awake for hours already, this ball of euphoria turning to nervousness and uncertainty, as I waited for her to wake. As I seem to enjoy pointing out, this was not my first night with a woman – Greta Morgan, please get in touch – however it was the first time I had been truly and overwhelmingly in love with the person lying next to me. Vicky stirred and gave me a sleepy quarter-smile. My mind raced, desperately trying to avoid an awkward silence. Did she have regrets? Was her quietness simply her knowing she had made a mistake and wondering how not to hurt my feelings?

I anxiously glanced at Vicky as she stared up at the ceiling. 'I have so much to do today,' she sighed. 'I really should go to Jemma's. I promised I'd carry some boxes to Tony's.' I did not know who Jemma and Tony were, but in that moment I assumed they were just characters in the brush-off. As we lay again in silence, she then surprised me by rolling over and laying her head on my chest. 'Why is it so early?' She yawned again, but then I saw her smile – a full, relaxed smile. She looked up at me and then placed a kiss on my mouth. It was just one kiss, but I felt the biggest weight lift from my shoulders.

There were going to be no such tender moments with Izzy. During the night, we unsurprisingly did not bask in the afterglow of our first time together. The only words we exchanged were, 'move over!' (Izzy), 'stopped hogging the duvet' (Izzy), 'stop kicking me!' (me), 'stop being pathetic then' (Izzy), and 'seriously, perhaps you should call an Uber and go home?' (me).

I put my t-shirt back on. What made the situation worse was

when I had got out of bed, I saw her lying asleep in a blue t-shirt I had given her. In the night she had thrown the duvet off her, mumbling she was too hot. She looked peaceful, sweet, and unnervingly sexy, and despite all my protests, I was still a little awestruck about how beautiful she was.

I was still drying my hair as I left the bathroom, about to make myself a cup of tea, when I was greeted with a friendlier voice.

'Hey, you're awake,' said Katie, in her dressing gown, clearing the coffee table and still looking half asleep.

'I could say the same about you.'

'Didn't sleep that well. Had a nightmare evening with Izzy. I thought I would clear up the collateral damage before you woke up.' She held up the two glasses and the bottle of gin. I suddenly felt a flash of guilt. 'This is yours, isn't it? I'm really sorry, I told her not to, and I will definitely replace it – God, yesterday was awful. And I'm so sorry for missing the gig!'

I was hovering at the door, not allowing myself to go in until I had unburdened my conscience, but Katie looked so worn out and preoccupied I just waited.

'It's fine. It was a great evening. Are you okay?'

'Kind of.' She placed the glasses by the sink and put the bottle of gin back in the cupboard.

'I'm just reaching my limit with Izzy at the moment – to be fair, we usually have this once a year where we get a little bit tired of each other. Either I'm suddenly too boring for her, or I get to the point where I just don't want to hear another mean-girl comment come out of her mouth.'

As I hesitated and failed to interrupt her, Katie picked up a cloth and began wiping down our small dining table.

'It started with me mentioning the gig, and we had a brief falling out about her not dressing up to go hang around at, I quote, some dive with grungy middle-aged men – I'm so sorry. I then said I didn't fancy going clubbing again, especially if she was just going to ditch me and hook up with some guy, which is usually true but *was* a low blow on my part. That pretty much unleashed the beast. She immediately brought up Ethan and said how if I didn't want all men I'm with to go looking elsewhere, I should stop being such a prude and follow her lead.'

She finished with the table and placed the cloth back by the sink.

'And perhaps she has a point.' She sighed and leaned against the counter. 'But then I think I'm quite happy *not* having the nurse at the local STD clinic know me by my first name and ask if I want the *Izzy special* every time I walk in. And she wants to have a go at me about life choices! You have no idea how relieved I was to wake up and find she'd not stayed the night. It'll blow over, but literally, last night was so close to being the last straw.'

I eventually did enter the room. To belatedly face the music.

'Actually, she did stay the night.'

She looked up at me, puzzled.

'In here? Did you see her then? Before she left?'

'She hasn't quite left yet. She's still asleep. Upstairs.'

It took Katie a few moments to compute what I was saying. It didn't help that I was acting like a schoolboy, being as indirect as possible – after all, Izzy and I were both single. She then screwed up her face.

'As in, *in your room* upstairs? In your bed? Seriously?' She just stared at me, like she could not believe what she was hearing.

'Well, you both don't waste much time. And here was I quite enamoured by that spiel you gave about having nothing in common.'

She turned her back on me, pouring the kettle.

'Well, I hope you had a nice time.'

'Are you pissed off?' I asked. She turned around, looking like she was weighing up the question.

'No, not pissed off. You both are free to do whatever you want, but I am a little annoyed at the timing and the hypocrisy. If you like her, say that you like her, don't just lie to me and pretend to be above it all. Or if you choose to go to bed with someone, perhaps not choose the one girl who was...' Katie puffed out her cheeks and stretched her arms out. 'Who was adamant about self-destructing and thought she had a personal vendetta against me.'

Katie then shook her head and brushed past me to the fridge.

'As I said, it's none of my business. But it is a coincidence that Izzy and I get into a fight and the next moment she jumps into bed with you. I'm not pissed off with you, Scott. I'm just pissed off at how typical this is.'

'Care to elaborate on that, *Spoiler*?'

Wearing just the blue t-shirt I had lent her, Izzy stood in the doorway. Looking at neither one of us, she confidently marched past Katie to bring down a mug from the kitchen cupboards.

'Oh, and Scott, in case you didn't know, that door of yours is not exactly soundproof. There's nothing quite like waking up to the World According to Spoiler. Quite the hour of morality.'

Katie's look of exasperation turned to one of wide-eyed alertness as she then glared at me – a *why didn't you warn me* look.

'Izzy, I don't know what you heard, but I was just a bit annoyed – '

'No time to chat, dear. What with the number of men I've apparently been shagging, the clinic has the full spectrum of testing in store for me today.'

'I didn't mean – ' Katie put her hands to her eyes, looking like it was far too early to be having this three-person conversation. Izzy then turned around with her mug at her lips, the blue t-shirt barely hanging halfway down her thighs.

'What I will say, though, is Scott's version of last night did omit some crucial details. For one, as much as I would like to consider myself the seductress, it wasn't *me* who got him all hot and bothered and ready to burst. More like those sexy *wittle miss wabbit* pyjamas of yours.'

Izzy looked over at me, smirking. Katie also turned to look at me.

'It had all started so, so innocently. You were dead to the world, and I invited Scott in to see what normally goes on in these slumber parties of ours. Then we're having quite the make-out session at the end of your bed. I don't know if I should mention what we did with those fluffy slippers. Perhaps that's one thing to leave to the imagination.'

Katie folded her arms and glared at me.

'Is any of this true?'

'Oh, don't be angry at Scott, honey. Take it as a compliment. At least some guys find what you've got on offer worth the punt. I hear Tess Philips is more a French maid's outfit type of girl – a bit obvious, but it must be comforting to finally know what makes Ethan happy.'

With that, Katie finally had had enough.

'Seriously, you can both do what you want.' Shaking her head, she brushed past me. Her bedroom door then slammed as Izzy just stared at me and winked.

CHAPTER 15

IN THE AEROPLANE OVER THE SEA

'We're not speaking,' I told Camille. We were sitting in our usual chairs, and from the office window, it was like morning had bypassed the courtyard and thick dark clouds masked the winter sun.

'It's not like we're avoiding each other,' I tried to explain. 'It's like it was a month ago apart from we skip the polite inquiry into each other's day – her door is more often closed than open now.'

'Have you tried talking to her about it?'

'No real opportunity. Our paths haven't crossed in the last two weeks.'

'No, Scott, have you tried *talking*? Knocking on her door, saying you are making a cup of tea and asking if she wants one? Small gestures. To test the water.'

'I'm not sure I'd like the answer I'd get,' I smiled. 'Also, I'm not sure how much I want to apologise.'

I frowned and crossed my legs, squidging myself more into a ball as Camille sat patiently, her pen in one hand and her trusty notebook on her knee.

'I want us to be friends, but two weeks of the silent treatment feels an overreaction. It's like when I was trying to be just friends with Sarah – shouldn't friendship *not* be this fragile?'

Camille smiled and flicked back her dark gold hair, a trait I noticed about her when transitioning from listening mode to analysis.

'You and Izzy are both single adults and, hey, it is good that you're noticing parallels with Sarah – shows you're getting your money's worth from our sessions. But remember, not every situation is like-for-like.'

She put her pen to her lip and chewed the end for a brief moment. I stared down at the carpet while she did.

'The great thing about us human beings is that we are full of contradictions. We acknowledge that our lives are constantly evolving and changing. That we meet new people and seek out new experiences, all the while failing to recognise that we also live our lives through a series of parallels. That, emotionally speaking, we take these unique moments and respond to them pretty much in that like-for-like way you've just described.'

Camille flattened down her dress and leaned forward, her pen held out like a wand to emphasise her point. 'What I mean, Scott, is too often all of us revert to repetitive modes of behaviour, and this can stem from a long way back.

'If you were consistently screamed at as a child by your parents, you may develop a chip on your shoulder and revert to a highly defensive manner whenever any form of confrontation arises. This will then become your default mode in any relationship throughout your adult life. That's just an example, but noticing when we've felt something before is key to understanding our triggers. I'm not saying there's anything wrong with what you're doing but does this two-week period of not talking feel familiar? With Sarah? With

Ellie? And if this is solely a case of Katie overreacting then why are you here?'

Things did not exactly improve after Katie had walked out on Izzy and me. As if nothing had happened, Izzy brought down the cafetière from the cupboard, tiptoeing as she did, her legs exposed beneath my t-shirt.

'Don't look so worried,' she said casually. 'If you're wondering what nasty things you could have caught from man-hungry Izzy. Or exactly how many men have accessed that apparently revolving door down there.'

She opened a small pack of dark roast I vaguely remembered Katie was saving for a special occasion.

'But then Spoiler's definition of *a lot*, or sex for that matter, may have even my local vicar classified as promiscuous. Bit of a lay-back-and-think-of-England girl, truth be told.'

She took down another cup as the kettle finished boiling. 'I suppose it's just us for coffee now Spoiler's gone off in a sulk. She does that. In her head she believes she's taking the moral high ground, but a sulk is a sulk.'

'That was quite heated.'

'Oh, the white knight again! But whose aid is he coming to? His sanctimonious landlady or his *slutty* conquest?' She plunged down the cafetière.

'It was just the heat of the moment. She didn't mean any of it.'

'Oh, she did.' Her smile faded, and she looked away.

I remembered my *half the men in Oxford* comment and felt a hard pang of guilt. As by way of an apology, I reached for her hand. She made a small, ironic snort and raised her eyebrows as she looked down at it. I was going to remove it, but she then held my fingers and smiled. She turned to face me.

'I have mine black,' she then said, turning back to the cafetière, pouring the coffee. 'I'll leave yours to you regards milk and whatnot.'

She picked up her mug and walked over to our sofa. From the side, she retrieved a small purse.

'I'm going to get dressed. Oh, even though I was not under the impression references were required, you are only the second man I have slept with in the last nine months. It was...' She lightly shrugged, her coffee in one hand and purse in the other, and left the room.

A few moments later, I heard the sound of heels running down the stairs and the door slam. I arrived downstairs to see Izzy getting into a car – I assumed Uber – ignoring me as I called her name, which then disappeared around the corner. I then felt that same pang of guilt burst forth again. For making Izzy feel like she needed to sprint out of the flat without a goodbye, and for the aftermath that it left.

One thing I left out when I relayed the story to Camille, was that I did knock on Katie's door. Or at least I was centimetres away from doing so.

The last years of my life, working abroad, had brought many new people into my life and a wide, if sometimes rotating, network of friends. But there was also plenty of time to feel lonely. Over the last few weeks, I seemed to forget about this loneliness. Rather than wanting to hide away in my room, I had found a friend with whom I could talk.

Standing outside her room, I was about to knock when I heard her. It was not loud, so I understood what Izzy meant about our flat's lack of soundproofing. It was the sound of sobs, travelling through the cheap wood. There were no wails, just the unmistakable sound of someone crying as if we were in the same room. Lowering my hand, it felt like one breach of privacy too many.

What I had done that morning – not telling Katie that Izzy was still in the flat while she was having her rant, standing by and letting Izzy say what she said about Ethan, holding Izzy's hand after – was not the behaviour of a friend. Two weeks of the silent treatment was the least I deserved.

As Camille alluded to, confrontation has never been something at which I've excelled. I've probably had only two arguments with girls in my dating life, and neither were with Vicky even when she ended our short-lived engagement.

I knew she was unhappy. I saw the warning signs, but I ignored them and continued as I was, hoping I was reading too much into her silences and occasional distance. I could have confronted her about whether she did want to get married, but perhaps I should have confronted myself regarding whether I needed to do some growing up first. I asked her to marry me one sunny day at the top of Parliament Hill, and she said yes, probably because she cared too much for me to humiliate me in front of those glancing eyes when I popped the question.

We never spoke about the future. I just thought saying the words would lead to us living happily ever after. Unlike Vicky, I had not considered what it really meant: living together, having conversations about who would do the laundry or if we should take turns making dinner, or even whose flat we would move into. Instead, I took her *yes* as an affirmation that I had finally achieved something in life and carried on, blissfully ignorant that Vicky had greater self-esteem than ever to be someone's achievement.

As a kid, it was Ellie who was the confrontational one. I don't think I even had an argument with Dad, or Mum, for that matter. When she was shouting down the house, I was determined to be nothing like her. I would be the good one. And because she was so determined to make Dad's life a misery after Mum had left, I was determined to be easier. I stuck with my Games Workshop, Barnet Football Club, and a bit of sport on the weekends – that was my bubble. As children, Ellie and I would have arguments like all brothers and sisters, but after the incident at the piano we stopped fighting. Bar the occasional insult, we basically ignored each other for the next two years.

So that became how I dealt with confrontation – to stay silent and watch my relationships either wither or implode. And two weeks of not speaking to Katie, I felt I was repeating this pattern. So for once in my life, I had to do something.

It was only a few days before Christmas, and Katie and I seemed to have developed an unspoken time-share agreement on the flat. I would come home to find evidence of her having spent the day working on the kitchen table with her notes, museum layouts, and printouts strewn about. But the closest we got to interacting was when I heard the careful opening of the front door long after I had gone to bed. In the morning, the house would be in silence, not even the sound of her radio alarm, as she seemed to be waking up later, and I would leave for the allotment before she had stepped out of her room.

I hoped it was her new promotion causing her irregular hours, not that she was so keenly determined to avoid me. The kitchen table always seemed to have multiple copies of leaflets advertising a *Christmas Extravaganza* at her museum. Exhibitions *across the ages* and *late openings* with champagne receptions in the run-up to Christmas were emblazoned. Katie had scrawled repeated notes and circled various events and rooms. So at the start of Christmas week, I bought a ticket to said *Extravaganza* and made my way to

Bloomsbury – London's museum district – just so I could ask my flatmate if she would be my friend again.

I didn't approach her at first. I stood outside the room where I had finally found her. She was in the northeast wing in a collection she had circled as *Flight – From Wings to War Planes*. It was one of the paid exhibitions and guarded by two friendly-looking young people, probably students, checking tickets and directing people to a table immediately through the door where another young man was serving champagne.

I had not been to a museum in years. I had always found the high ceilings and white walls far more soothing and alluring than what was usually on display – pots, bronzes, and glittery rocks from what I remembered when dragged around them as a kid. But Katie's was nothing like I had remembered. For one, people were drinking. Even before the table of champagne, there was a bar at the entrance. This then led into what looked and sounded like a dancefloor – it was actually a reinstallation of a 1970s fashion exhibition that had taken place earlier in the year. All over the museum, people were talking and laughing and paying no lip service to whispering. And in the room where I had found Katie, a crowd surrounded a middle-aged lady who smiled and joked, giving what appeared to be a talk regarding a series of model aircraft.

Katie stood back smiling, listening to the talk. She was holding a glass of champagne to her chest and looked serene – happy and amused. I noticed she had dressed up for the occasion. Her lips were redder, her cheeks a more subtle pink, and her eyes slightly darker along the contours. Her brown hair fell sleekly onto a very pretty dark green dress, very apt for the Christmas theme. The dress ended at her thighs – not too short, but eye-catching – and she was wearing black tights. She looked stunning. She reminded me of the girl I had met at Joan's birthday all those years ago.

Standing next to her was a girl with strawberry blonde hair wearing a similar dress, but in black. They would whisper something to each other during the talk and smile delightedly. Suddenly the room, including Katie and her friend, began applauding. I jolted out of my trance and realised what a bad idea this had been. Looking down, I was the most underdressed person in the building in my jeans, old trainers, and, dangling at my side, was a plastic shopping bag I had brought with me.

And then something started to wash over me. A sinking feeling. Of dread and that I didn't belong. Katie looked stunning. I, on the other hand, looked like I could barely dress myself. And was I not trying to repeat exactly what I had done with Sarah by saying I wanted to be friends with a girl who, at heart, I liked more than that? The only difference was that, in that moment, I could clearly see how large an idiot I was making of myself.

I have said it before, it is almost impossible to describe depression unless you're in it. In that moment I felt this familiar spiralling sensation that glued my feet to the floor. I was not good enough for Vicky, I was not good enough for Sarah, I was not good enough for Izzy and I would never be good enough for Katie, this voice started telling me as I needed to breathe heavier. I could feel my face burning like it was about to crack and split, and could feel the air in my lungs chill and then stifle. And suddenly all I wanted to do was disappear, to not exist, to not feel.

To apologise for invading her privacy, I was intruding once more, interrupting Katie at work when she was meant to be focused and where she seemed to be happy. I needed to leave, to disappear, but when I looked up, she was staring at me.

The stare turned into a glare. Katie said something to her friend as I showed my ticket to a smiling girl at the entrance.

'What are you doing here?' she hissed, trying to keep her voice low and letting her eyes flick self-consciously around her.

'I came to see the exhibition,' I said, a tad defensively. I had rehearsed what I had wanted to say but had lost all train of thought. Katie scrunched up her face and looked at me like I was mad, or worse: like I was going to do something mad.

'I was talking to Joan yesterday,' I tried to explain. 'He said you were off to Wiltshire. That you were spending Christmas with Ethan's family, after all.'

'Yes,' she said sternly, not seeing the relevance.

'And we've not seen each other around the house in a while – '

'Scott, I'm meant to be working.'

'Yes! Sorry!' I put on a beaming smile hoping a burst of positivity would thrust me out of the awkwardness. 'And that's what I wanted to say. That I'm sorry.'

Katie was still staring at me impatiently.

'I don't have any excuses. In fact, I don't have much more to say. I shouldn't have been in your room with Izzy and should have acted a lot more mature both then and in the morning. I just didn't want you to go without clearing the air. And giving you this.'

Even more awkwardly, I gave her the plastic bag. She gave me another confused glare and reluctantly took it.

'Oh,' she then said, softer, looking inside.

'It's a bit childish, but it's one of those adopt-an-animal schemes, so they've sent you a certificate and a book telling you about a panda somewhere in China who you are now helping look after.' As I spoke, Katie retrieved from the bag a small cuddly toy.

'Like I said, it's childish. I thought you might like the eco-wildlife idea...'

'No, it's sweet,' she said, less impatiently. 'Really sweet.'

'There's also chocolates as I wasn't sure you'd like it.'

She then brought out a box from the bottom of the bag, but this time frowned.

'Hang on, Scott. These are really expensive.'

I had gone to Bond Street to try to find something more grown-up than a cuddly toy, and panic-bought the chocolates from an actual chocolatier. She was right about them being expensive. I had not looked at the price before the shop assistant rang it up on the till.

'It's a lovely thought, but I can't accept them. You're meant to be broke...'

She winced, as we had now moved on to a different form of awkwardness – my financial situation.

'It's okay. I've got some new work. Part of the reason I've been making all the early starts recently. Plus, I really did want to leave things between us on a better note and say that I've enjoyed living with you.'

'Listen, Scott.' She raised her fingers to her face, pinching the bridge of her nose. 'I may have overreacted. There are things about Izzy and me – we're friends, best friends – but we're not that similar and sometimes wind each other up. Deliberately, it feels like with her, and we definitely know where to land the punches. The night before, your name may have come up while we were having drinks, and it seemed to trigger a row that had been bubbling for some time. That I was somehow implying she'd been acting *trampy* with all the *city boys* she'd been seeing, and she didn't need dating advice for me because my love life wasn't exactly a shining light. It just blew up. And then I find out that she's had a one-night stand with you, just to show me she could if she wanted to. No offence.'

It was a little bit offensive, but not surprising.

'I kind of thought she was. Have you heard from her?'

She shook her head.

'I *am* sorry for what I said about her, and I should apologise, but

I'm sick of all the snide comments about my appearance, and my boyfriend, every time she's feeling a little insecure, which has recently been all the time. Frankly, I'm enjoying a break from the drama where I can focus on nights like this.'

And she had a point. Around us, people were sipping champagne merrily discussing the models, maps and photographs precisely arranged to give the room a busy, excitable feel. If it had not been the need to have this heart-to-heart with Katie, I would have liked to explore the exhibition myself, such an impressive job having been done.

'What about the drama with Ethan? Is that all sorted?'

I tried to ask the question casually, continuing to look about the room, hoping it would not come across as a taunt.

'It's okay, let's just say that.' She seemed to give me a relieved smile as she followed my eyes to the scaled-model buildings at floor level, which looked like something from LEGOLAND.

'That's JFK Airport. A bit geeky, but we had it especially made. And regarding Ethan, there's no one else on the scene anymore. He says he's been swamped with work and... well... I didn't ask the question directly, but we agreed not to lie to each other, so I should take him at his word.'

'Are you okay, though?' I didn't want to pry too much further. If I were Katie, I would not have appreciated the constant dissecting of her relationship.

'Yes. Yes, I am. We'll be at his parents' from the 23rd. Me, Ethan, his family, and definitely no one else. Listen, I know my boyfriend's been an arsehole, and I know what I've told you about him does not paint an awe-inspiring picture, but I love him. I believe he loves me, and I can't constantly question his fidelity as that just makes the whole situation rather pointless.'

She drained the last mouthful of champagne in her glass and then looked back at me.

'But thank you for listening. And putting up with me. It does mean a lot.' She placed her hand on my arm and gave me a small smile, a much kinder smile than I had expected to receive when I was nervously floating on the edges of the room. 'Now, you do realise there's free champagne? How about I get us a glass, and you tell me if a night with Izzy was worth all this drama?'

CHAPTER 16

LAST CHRISTMAS

Mike and I collected the tree on the morning of Christmas Eve. I had stayed at the house the previous night to rummage around for our old decorations and to do some light shopping for anything Mike could not get from the farm shop. I also wanted to be there when the four of them arrived and witness the moment of pre-Christmas excitement when the kids burst through the door. Millie ran in circles around the living room while Ed tried to waddle after her, and their combined exuberance managed to turn an otherwise cold grey December day into officially the season of goodwill and festivities.

Our Christmas tree was a specific tradition dating back to my earliest memory. Nowadays, it would have been far easier for the tree to have been delivered, but Dad always bought his from a small farm just outside the M25 where he would spend at least an hour chatting to the old guy who owned it about the state of the economy and how things were better in the days before big corporations ran everything. So Mike and I were morally obliged to empty the station wagon and spend an hour and a half in traffic and then trying to force a Norwegian spruce into the car.

'Your dad not with you this year?' said the farm owner as we eventually tied closed the boot with rope, allowing part of the tree to stick out. 'Putting his feet up while you youngsters do the heavy lifting?'

It was a shock suddenly hearing someone ask about Dad. For a moment, distracted by the tree, I forgot he wasn't there at the farm with us. The realisation, and then having to tell this man who we saw once a year what had happened, sent an icy feeling down my spine and seemed to take the wind out of him.

'He was younger than me,' he said, having to sit down on a stool. 'You wouldn't believe it. You wouldn't believe it,' he kept saying, shaking his head, and to be honest, I was not sure I really believed it either.

Back at the house, as we forced the tree through the door, we were welcomed by the sound of squealing and screaming.

'Seriously? Did you both have to cut down the thing your-selves? You've been bloody hours!' Ellie was carrying a very pink-faced and agitated Ed and thrust him into Mike's arms.

'What happened?' said Mike, concerned.

'Nothing happened. Obviously. He took her toy. She started crying. She snatched it back, and everyone's been screaming their lungs out for the last hour. We call it *Thursday*.' Ellie then changed her voice as she started stroking Ed's hair as he remained silently sobbing in a bewildered-looking Mike's arms. 'It's alright now. Because Daddy's going to look after you while Mummy and Uncle Scott go and make sure dinner tomorrow is not only organic sprouts and nut loaf.'

She took the car keys from Mike and kissed both him and Ed.

'Come on. The butcher's closes at three.'

'Don't look at me like that,' she said as we got into the car. 'He knows I'm teasing, plus if I had another minute of pre-Christmas histrionics, I would lose my mind.'

Ellie put the Volvo into gear, and we set out on our road trip.

'Were we like that?' asked Ellie, indicating onto the high street. 'Do you remember all the bloody fuss you caused accusing me of locking you in the downstairs loo?'

'You *did* lock me in the toilet.'

'I held the door shut for about ten seconds, as a joke. You're the one who then got hysterical and broke the lock so you couldn't get out.' Ellie had a rare serene smile as we drove south down Green Lanes.

'You also turned the light off.'

'I asked if you were okay! And it was for two minutes, max! And I did run to get Mum, who just turned the lock from the outside with her nail. You came out, tears pouring, and said I had locked you in there for half the morning!'

'I was six.'

'And such a little backstabber even back then.' She again grinned, reminiscently.

We were passing Newington Green. The traffic was light heading towards London and we were approaching Islington and another Roberts family tradition. Farrell's was on the same road as Sadler's Wells theatre. It was where Mum had bought any meat if we were having a special occasion, and Dad would do the same even after she left.

'Seven,' I then sighed, gazing out of the window. 'Seven what?' she asked, parking the car.

'It would have then been seven more Christmases before she left. She seemed so happy at Christmas. We all were. Or maybe I'm imagining it. Were we happy, back then?'

'For fuck's sake, Scott.' Ellie put the handbrake on and unfastened her seatbelt. 'Oh, why not properly put us in the Christmas spirit by dredging up our parents' breakup.'

'I keep thinking about those days. More and more recently. It just seems more relevant all of a sudden.' I was thinking about what Camille said about the events of our childhood influencing the adults we become. 'Was she that unhappy?'

'Tell you what, when we get back, I'll let you tell Millie and Ed the story about Auntie Pam's divorce. Let's share these glad tidings all around.'

'They're just up here,' I said as Ellie followed me up the stairs at Loughborough Road.

'Scott, I didn't exactly expect you to live in a palace, but this place is pretty grim.' I turned around, and she was staring down, pressing her foot experimentally on the creaking floorboard as if it might give way beneath her. She reached out about to hold the handrail and then thought twice, wincing and then looking around at the faded wallpaper.

'It's just a bit... rustic. You should have seen it while Joan was living here. *That* was grim. Since Katie moved in, it's really quite cosy.'

It was an unplanned visit, but coming out of the butcher's, I had realised I had forgotten the games and the crackers for Christmas Day. 'Are they that important?' said Ellie. 'The game's half of Millie's present. It's meant to be a really good family one.' I had assumed Ellie would say I could not be trusted to do a single thing and tell me to go find something from the Wood Green Sainsbury's. Instead, 'How far away do you live?' she said looking at her watch.

As we reached the landing, Ellie still did not look impressed. 'Seriously, Scott, I've seen squats nicer than this. Mike's gigged with heroin addicts who live less out of squalor.'

'Ellie, I get it, you're not a fan.' I turned my back on her, surpris-

ingly more annoyed with her than I expected. After all, this was
Ellie. I should be used to her shooting her mouth off.

'I'm not being a bitch. I'm just a bit... taken aback. Your last flat
was so... well, I've got gay friends who would have killed to have
your skill at soft-furnishing.'

'Do you want to see where I live, or do you just want to linger
in the hallway?'

I walked into the kitchen preparing for more comments on the
décor. I knew I wasn't exactly living the life of a man my age, and
that if I kept hold of my old flat I would be in better shape financially. But Loughborough Road seemed to fit who I was. Dishevelled
on the surface and a mismatch of chaos and warmth. The place had
begun to feel more of a home than when I had my own flat.

'I was reading through the instructions on the sofa, so the game
is just in here – '

The first thing I noticed was a large canvas bag on the dining
table. Then the sink full of dirty plates, pans, and mugs. *Seriously, it
does look like we live in a squat*, I thought. I then realised I was the
last one in the flat the previous day, and Katie had said she was
going directly to Ethan's parents from work. So who the hell was in
our flat?

A laptop was open on the coffee table, a mug of what looked
like tea next to it, and then beyond it, on our sofa, was a gigantic
duvet covering so fully what was underneath I could only see
tangles of long brown hair coming out the top. The duvet stirred.

'Hey,' said Katie, sleepily, emerging from under the covers.

'Oh. Sorry, did I wake you?'

'No!' She crawled up into a sitting position. 'I was just
watching some rubbish.' She had been curled up, head on a pillow,
and as she rose, I could tell she was still wearing her pyjamas – at
three o'clock in the afternoon.

'I thought you were away,' she said, still sounding slightly groggy and a little hoarse.

'Just came back to collect a couple of things.' I was conscious that I was still staring at her like I had found some weird homemade science experiment incubating in our living area.

'Aren't you meant to be in Wiltshire?'

Before she could answer, I saw Ellie enter the room and her eyes also landed on the sink full of dirty dishes.

'This is my sister. Ellie. I was showing her the flat...' From comments made by other guests, I was well aware that our flat was hardly soundproof. I assumed Katie to have heard Ellie's words and expected a similar reaction to when Mike had referred to her as *The Duchess*. Instead, she smiled politely and stood up briefly to shake Ellie's hand, saying it was nice to meet her.

'You've got a nice place here. Very... cosy.' I would have at least hoped Ellie would try to sound sincere when offering up a half-hearted compliment, but thankfully Katie still seemed too sleepy to notice. Or to see that Ellie was staring at her pink rabbit pyjamas, part quizzically, part concerned.

'We didn't mean to disturb you...'

Katie still had the duvet wrapped around her lower half and held it in place as she closed her laptop.

'Scott, where's your bathroom?'

I directed Ellie, and she left me and Katie, who now seemed to be anxiously glancing between the sink and the duvet wrapped around her legs.

'Are you off to Wiltshire tonight, then?'

'Change of plans. Ethan's apparently working on a deal that needs to close by the end of the year. So he's still in Berlin. There wasn't much point going down to his parents by myself.' She spotted something on the other side of the sofa; her dressing gown submerged under the duvet. 'He said he would crash

Christmas at a friend's or at colleagues'. I can't really remember the details.'

With her dressing gown now on, she moved to the sink and began running the tap.

'What about you?' I asked.

'I might take Joan up on his offer to join him and Alison and Ali's parents, though it is a bit of a pain what with the trains. Plus it's been quite liberating to have a pyjama day and watch trash telly after a long week. What? Hey!'

She spun around, frowning. I had let out an involuntary snort and was holding a Marks & Spencer turkey meal for one I had pulled out of the bag on the dining table.

'I think duvet days are what Boxing Day is for. Or New Year's Day. Or any day in between. Not Christmas Day and definitely not with a ready meal for dinner.'

'Scott, it's Joan. And someone else's family. Would you want to sit around a table with him and wait until he decides he's bored enough to start telling complete strangers the details of your private life?'

'Well, why not join us?'

'Ha! Thanks!' she laughed. 'I appreciate the offer, but I am okay here by myself. Plus the last thing you guys want is a moody stray crashing your family event.'

'Of course we would,' said Ellie coming back into the room as if she had been part of the conversation the whole time. 'We're more than used to coping with one moody sad-sack so another just stops him bringing the rest of us down. Plus the more of us we are, the less time I need to spend with *my* dickhead of a brother. So you're doing me a favour.'

Ellie absently wandered the room, still sizing up my living conditions and perhaps checking for damp and mould.

'Seriously, it's a kind offer, but I'm quite looking forward to some me-time. Work has been crazy recently, so this is a chance to unwind, read a novel, or watch some trashy films.'

As Katie began washing the dishes, Ellie moved over to her, leaning casually against the counter.

'I know we've just met, but you don't seem the stay alone and brood type, and believe me, I've had the misfortune of being related to one my entire life. We all get into ruts and think Christmas on my own would be amazing but take it from someone who knows, it gets pretty shit pretty quickly. It's annoying and irritating, but it's the one day a year you realise that you don't want to be alone.'

Katie put down the pan she was washing and stared at the sink.

'Plus, and I have to say I really like what you've done with the place – all the homely touches are lovely and that – but you can't spend Christmas in a shithole like this. That's just masochistic.'

It was an unlikely car journey back to North London; two parts of my life that I did not foresee intersecting, navigating through the traffic in the low afternoon sun. In the last of the fading winter sunlight, as the streetlights switched themselves on, we arrived back in Wood Green. The temperature seemed to have plummeted since we left South London, and I particularly felt an icy shiver trying to carry into the house the games, crackers and meat I had piled up in my arms to avoid a second trip to the car. Ellie led the way with keys, and as we reached the gate, I could see our Christmas wreath was now on the door, and soft light was coming from the living room window.

'You have got to be bloody kidding me,' Ellie exclaimed, peering through and then shoving the key into the lock.

'You put up the tree?' She stood in the doorway of the living room, staring at Mike. 'And these two are sitting doing a jigsaw puzzle, like bloody angels? Are you deliberately taking the piss?'

As I joined Ellie we were then confronted with delighted screeches of 'Mummy!' as she picked up Ed, and Millie battering rammed herself into Ellie's hip, hugging her like she had been gone a month.

'Jesus, Mike, we were meant to do the tree together. You could have put your back out, and we'd all have ended up spending Christmas Eve in A&E.'

'I bowed to peer pressure,' he smiled, nodding at the kids. 'It was the only way to stop World War Three, and the tree's only half done, isn't it, Millie?'

'We left gaps for you and Uncle Scott, Mummy!' Millie was beaming up at both of us. 'And Daddy said we could do the angel when you were back.'

Mike's grin got broader and then peered quizzically over my shoulder into the hallway.

'I'm sure there were just two of you when you left.'

Ellie shuffled the kids forward to let Katie through who, understandably, looked somewhat hesitant at entering the surprise Christmas scene.

'A Christmas stowaway,' she said with an embarrassed looking smile, still clutching her overnight bag. She then gave a bigger smile and wave to Millie who had suddenly gone shy and was half-hiding herself behind Ellie's legs staring wondrously at our new arrival. 'My own plans went a tad wayward.'

'The more, the merrier,' grinned Mike and took the boxes from me.

'Katie, you'll be in Scott's room. We'll have Millie in my old room, Ed will come in with us, and Scott will be in the study on the camp bed.'

'Oh no, I'll take the camp bed.'

'It's fine, he's used to it. Every time anyone would stay over, he would take that bed – he's the outdoorsy one, so better him than us. Scott, why don't you settle Katie in?'

Not being in possession of the meats, games or crackers anymore, I took Katie's bag and led her upstairs. Or more accurately, I thought it would be chivalrous to let Katie go first, requiring her to awkwardly keep flicking looks back at me to ask in which direction she should head.

'It's to the left,' I said as she giggled at my attempts to direct her, looking about the landing and stopping outside each room in case it was mine.

'This one?' she smiled and cautiously peered inside. As she was about to walk in, I hesitated and wanted to reach out and stop her, saying she should take the camp bed after all.

'Oh wow, nice colours.' At this point I should mention something about my room; the wall opposite the end of my bed was painted bright yellow, the two adjacent, sky blue; and the wall behind my headboard was black with brilliant white dots.

Katie stood, turning in a circle, mesmerised. I hung back at the door, one hand masking my face, hardly able to watch for what next she would notice. Obviously, when I left that morning, I would have had no idea anyone else would explore that room.

'Oh my, these are all very cute.' It was impossible for her not to see them. Nearly every wall had some form of shelving unit, either tall book shelves or low frontless cabinets, and along every stretch of wood lying arranged in meticulous order was my collection of Games Workshop models. Towards the end of my teens – yes, the *end* of my teens – I had got up to roughly 1,342 models. I would have dreaded to know what Katie was thinking as she realised where she was spending the night.

'Oh wow, do you mind if I have a look?' Her politeness was unnerving. We both just needed to acknowledge this was the room of a complete freak and take her back down to the car so I could drive her back to Loughborough Road where I'm sure she was wishing she never left.

She picked up one of the more grand pieces; a three-inch model of Orc Commander, Tiberius Olff, with his bloodthirsty eyes, emerald-green skin, sabre sword, and battle shield. He was at the head of his Orc battalion. Next to the orcs were Galactus Maximus III, the space travelling Roman general, and his legion of inter-galactic soldiers. To be fair to Katie, she was being very kind, examining each piece like it was from one of her exhibits, rather than what a teenage boy did during his spare time for six years.

'You've got quite the collection.'

'I like to keep it as a shrine to my virginity.'

'And did you paint all of these?'

'Me. Dad. Mum. Even Ellie did one on a day we weren't being hostile to one another...'

'Oh my! Who are these *babes*, Scott?'

Katie's face lit up as she discovered and picked up Estella, the Warrior Queen. Obviously, in any form of marketing aimed at teenage boys and young men who prefer to stay indoors playing games, there is going to be at least one set of female warriors who have significantly larger than average breasts and do not believe in the virtues of clothes when entering battle.

'My, she must struggle to find a cup-size to hold those in place.' Katie was unashamedly smirking. 'God, I would kill to have legs like that. Good taste, Scott. And I see she has friends.'

'I know, it's a little sad...'

'No! I'm only teasing! They are wonderful. Each is so intricate. They must have taken you hours...' She grinned again, putting back Estella and turning around her kinswomen, who had apparently chosen to wage war in a silver bra and matching pants. 'And must have helped get you through those long winter nights... Oh! Wow!'

Her tone suddenly changed as she reached beyond Estella and

the Coven of Magda. She brought out a large fragment of rock with a snail-like spiral embedded in it.

'You collect fossils?'

'I used to. It was something my dad and I did. We used to go camping out by the coast near spots where you could do fossil hunting – only small ones, mind. That one we bought in a fossil shop.'

I had hidden the fossils at the back of my shelves but, recalling the memory of Dad and me on the beach as the waves crashed around us, I remembered just how happy I had been and how much fun it was. I bent down and picked up some of the others we had found.

'This was from the summer after GCSEs. Other kids at school were heading off on their first clubbing holiday to some Greek island, and I was somewhere on the foggy Kent coastline in a tent. Like I said, it's a bit sad.'

'There's nothing sad about that at all! You're talking to a girl who all she wanted to do when she grew up was work in a museum. Examining these is how I chose to spend the last ten years of my life. Plus, it must have been nice to spend time with your dad. I have two brothers for competition, and don't get me wrong, I love my dad to bits, but he does switch off when I start talking about exhibits or anything feminine. Our way of bonding is when he insists on picking me up from the local village if I meet an old school friend for a drink whenever I'm home. It's only a twenty-minute walk, but it's the only time it's just us, and then we take a detour and buy a burger.'

Again she smiled this wide, happy smile. Still holding on to my fossil, she went over to the bed and sat next to her bag.

'So,' she grinned, a similar grin to the Estella and *Coven of Magda* grin. 'Does this mattress have a tale or two to tell? Any young ladies get their world rocked within these four walls?'

She stretched out her leg and leaned back, sexily. Provocatively.

'Oh now I know you're taking the piss. I think we both know the exact number.' I smiled, rolled my eyes, giving her a mock glare.

'I'm serious! You'd think listening to your self-deprecating nonsense that anyone who built models, liked fossils, or played role-playing games was doomed to be alone forever! For your information, a lot of the boys in my college at uni were into these wizard card games and Dungeons and Dragons, and I know *a lot* of girls who had sex with them. Present company included.'

She went slightly pink as her smile went very childlike.

'Yes, I won't divulge the details, but let's just say in my first year, way before Ethan and me, and not exactly only once.'

She proceeded to get more scarlet as I leaned back against my shelves, wondering what *not exactly only once* meant.

'Wood Green isn't quite Oxford. We may have still been too middle-class to get mugged for our lunch money, but I cannot recall one girl who said two words to a member of the GWWA. Apart from maybe, *piss off.*'

'GWWA?'

'Games Workshop and Warlocks Association.'

Katie almost somersaulted as she threw herself backward laughing. She had to wipe a tear away from her eye as she sat back up.

'So, never? Not even post-school? It is a double.'

'It's a double because I was too tall for a single, even at thirteen. And post-school, well, Vicky did stay over a couple of times when we visited Dad, but I think the thousands of tiny eyes put her off, so we just slept. Besides, I did live elsewhere in London, so it's not as abstaining as it sounds.'

'Okay, point taken,' she smiled and held her hands up. 'I just saw it is a rite of passage, having your first illicit encounter under your parents' roof. Mine was a boy called Toby Ludgate from the boys' school sixth form.'

Still smiling, she had a faraway look that I was not sure was purely to give the story some extra colour.

'It was...' She put her hands to her face. 'It was both disastrous and a relief. We didn't really talk about it – I kind of assumed he'd done it before – but as we started undressing, he looked as terrified as I did, and I've never seen someone concentrate so much while we were in mid-act. Oh God, I can't believe I've just told you that! I've not even been drinking!'

'Well, it is five o'clock on Christmas Eve. I think we're all allowed to start drinking,' I said from the shelves. Her cheeks were rosy and she looked like she needed a minute to regain her composure. 'You're looking a bit brighter than you were an hour ago.'

'I feel brighter. We should probably go back downstairs before they start wondering what's happened to us.'

Mike and Ellie had started on the wine, and we found them with Millie and Ed on the living room floor in the midst of a game of Hungry Hippos.

'Uncle Scott's back! Uncle Scott's back!' cried Millie, almost sending Ellie's wine flying as she leapt up.

'Don't let it go to your head,' said Ellie. 'We told her we had to wait for you to finish the tree.'

Millie ran up to us, holding out a bauble in each hand.

'You're pretty,' she said to Katie shyly, grinning, looking up at the newcomer with awe.

'That's very kind of you,' Katie said, squatting down, so she was at eye-level with Millie. 'Would you like to help me put this on the tree? Where do you think it should go?' Millie nodded and grabbed Katie's hand, taking her to the tree.

Mike and I stood at the dining room table, pouring additional glasses and watching Millie and Katie, and Ellie and Ed, making the tree sparklier by the second.

'I hope she knows what she's getting into,' Mike said, nodding at Katie. 'I can't imagine Millie giving her new best friend a moment's peace.'

'True,' I smirked. 'We should probably just leave them to it and go down the pub?'

'What do you mean *we*? You're on Ed duties, mate. Ellie and I are going to get shitfaced.'

Resisting the call of the pub, we spent the evening sitting around the tree. Christmas songs playing on the hi-fi and glasses being refilled, Mike was right about Millie not giving Katie a moment's peace. But it was sweet to watch. Katie would have a wide grin or look playfully astonished when Millie would excitedly tell her one of a thousand different things. I then saw Millie hand Katie something and whisper conspiratorially in her ear. Katie whispered back and got up, walking over to me.

'I need your height.'

She showed me a piece of mistletoe, and Millie began pointing eagerly at the door frame.

'Put it there so Daddy can kiss Mummy, please!'

'Why can't Mummy kiss Daddy?' called out Ellie from the sofa. She and Mike both slowly got to their feet and made a show of dragging their tired bodies to the mistletoe. They then kissed to the cheers of the kids and Katie, and laughter from me.

'Now Katie has to kiss Uncle Scott!' shouted Millie. I spurted out my wine.

'I don't think it works like that, Millie,' I said.

'Yes it does! You were standing underneath it and she was next to you. Katie has to kiss you!'

'Yes, Scott. Please don't defy such a well-explained Christmas tradition,' Ellie beamed, not at all trying to hide her amusement.

'Katie's our guest, Millie, and we don't ask guests to go around kissing people.'

'But it's not fair, Uncle Scott!'

'Oh, come on, *Uncle Scott*,' said Katie, holding my hand and then dragging me back to the mistletoe. 'Don't be such a Grinch.'

As I reluctantly stood under the doorframe, a clap began from our onlookers. I knew I had gone the colour of Ribena and I saw that now she was in front of me, Katie was going slightly pink too.

'You don't have to...'

'I'm game if you are,' she said and then jumped up and planted a one-second kiss on my mouth.

Millie was jumping with glee, as was Ed, though I was not convinced he fully understood what was going on. Katie then turned to Millie, scrunched up her face and stuck out her tongue.

'Yuck! Boys are horrible!' She beamed at her little companion and took her hand. 'I'm never kissing another as long as I live.'

I realise now how lucky I was growing up. Christmas was always the best day of the year by far. Church, carols, even little parties, we spent the day together and it felt magical. As kids, Ellie and I would race downstairs to see if Father Christmas had been. The night before, our tradition was to hang large embroidered stockings above the fireplace, which did happen to be electric but did not diminish any of the joy or wonder we felt. Each stocking had our name on it, and when we both reached the bottom of the stairs we could already see they were overflowing with bulky shiny presents. Under the tree were more wrapped boxes, and we would suddenly see Dad and Mum emerge from the kitchen wrapped in dressing gowns, cups of coffee in hand, smiling at our delight. Very clichéd, very stereotypical, and very much taken for granted.

But that Christmas morning, I woke up arid-mouthed, blurry-eyed and feeling like someone had been at my temple with a hand-drill. Wine, gin, apple schnapps, Baileys – it was quite clear that Dad and Mum had achieved their sunny disposition on Christmas morning by not getting shitfaced on Christmas Eve.

I wasn't the only one. I stumbled off the camp bed and balanced myself in the narrow path of remaining floor space in Dad's study. Downstairs was still quiet as I made my way to the upstairs bathroom so I could have a more comprehensive wash and get rid of the smell and taste of stale alcohol that seemed to have marinated my face and gums. On the landing, I heard the sound of the taps running, and after a second, the latch clicked and my sister emerged from the bathroom looking very much like I felt.

'Merry Christmas,' I said, in a gravelly voice, a more tokenistic gesture as I was unable even to force my face to smile.

'Fuck off, dickhead,' she muttered and shielded her eyes from the light, returning to their bedroom.

When we were kids, early morning present opening was followed by church. We weren't exactly a religious family, but our school was tied to St Martin's, and the parent-teacher association organised a Nativity play during the morning service. Mum practically ran the PTA so we were forced to get excruciatingly dolled up in our best and most unrecognisable clothes. One year, I almost cried at having to wear a red bowtie, and Ellie would not stop shoe-gazing from the embarrassment of having to wear a green velvet dress. At ten o'clock we would then line-up outside the church entrance and sing 'Away in a Manger' with half a dozen or so fellow classmates, hoping not a word got back to anyone at school.

At ten o'clock that morning the living room was covered in wrapping paper, and four adults were slumped in armchairs and across the sofa watching two small children run around the room with their new toys seeing who could scream the loudest. Earlier that morning, Mike bribed Millie and Ed to go back to bed by letting them open one present and offering them a selection box of chocolates for breakfast. A short-term fix – Ellie usually being ruthless regarding their intake of sugar, which bought us enough time to shower and feel human enough to sit upright in a chair.

'Whose idea was it to open the drinks cabinet?' groaned Ellie, huddled on the sofa nursing her coffee and letting the steam waft up into her ashen cheeks and pink nose. 'Scott, want to take any responsibility?'

I was huddled in an armchair with a hot drink. Katie, by far the brightest looking of the four of us, was beaming away at Millie and Ed from our other armchair next to me. When the kids had been put to bed, we had gathered around the dining table to do the present wrapping. Believing we should save the remaining bottles of wine for Christmas Day, I suggested gin and tonics, which then turned into us sampling every other spirit and liquors that Dad had accumulated over the years.

Millie and Ed began chasing each other with flashing mini light-sabres.

'You'll be fine. I'll go put the bacon on.' Mike made to get up, but Katie bounced up before him.

'I can do that,' she said in a far perkier voice. Katie had stuck to wine the previous night while we wrapped presents and peeled potatoes and sprouts, hence how much fresher she looked in her sparkly grey and silver sweater.

'Rub your youth and alcohol tolerance in our face, why don't you,' was Ellie's groaning response.

. . .

Despite the hangover, it was enjoyable to drink with my sister again. No part of me wanted to go back to the days when one beer would have me going from bar to bar to club to who knows where in the search for deeper intoxication, but it did feel empowering to now have these one-offs and not feel a yearning for more. It was also lovely to sit around a table with my sister and my friends, not wanting to be anywhere else, and stop because it was past midnight and I was tired rather than because we had run out of alcohol.

And soon, the hangover faded. Largely due to the heat from the kitchen as I was placed in charge of cooking duties. However, it was not exactly the short straw considering the others had two hyperactive children to round up and pacify. From the living room came the sound of Louis Armstrong, put on by Mike to generate a calming atmosphere. A commendable idea in theory, however that soothing raspy voice was soon drowned out by two other high-pitched ones screaming in stereo.

'Can I give you a hand?' Katie had come in as I washed a lettuce in the sink. Millie's voice was still screeching above Louis' from the next room.

'Is it finally getting too much in there?'

'No! Well, maybe a little, but they're only excited, and now they're hitting the overtired phase. Ellie's putting them down for a nap.'

'I bet Millie's thrilled about that.'

'Oh, bless! She started crying! I don't know how Ellie does it. I wanted to start blubbing just watching her, hence offering you my assistance. Where shall I start?'

I smiled as she stood soldier-like in front of me, awaiting orders.

'Well, the beef's just about ready to go in the oven – I don't know if I said but that's our traditional Christmas dinner as none of us like turkey that much. Kind of a more ornate version of Sunday lunch. Is that okay with you?'

'Sure. Apart from, you know that I'm a vegetarian, right?'

'Oh.'

'Just kidding. I make a mean Bolognese, remember?'

From the clutter upon our breakfast table I picked up my to-do list and read out what had been done and what still needed doing.

'Oh my God, how organised are you!'

'You sound surprised.' Katie took the list from me and ran her finger down the tasks.

'Obviously! You've listed the timings to military precision; carrots go on at *seven* minutes past one? This from the man who has so far spent the winter wearing the same jumper.'

Playfully, she poked said jumper and me in the chest. Then, surprisingly she let her fingers linger, lightly stroking the cotton, letting out a small, faraway laugh.

'Have you heard from Ethan?' I asked, taking back the list. Katie seemed to snap out of her trance. Her smile fading as she sighed.

'I've been ignoring his messages. Before you arrived yesterday, we'd been speaking on the phone and I ended up hanging up on him. When he had told me he had cancelled his flight, I thought that meant he had to work today. So when he said he was spending the day with friends, I accused him of deliberately messing me about, that he could have come back if he wanted and that there was one particular friend he wanted to spend time with. He accused me of being melodramatic, paranoid and unreasonable, so I politely told him to go fuck himself and hung up. Mature of me, right?'

'I wouldn't say *immature*, though. You are entitled to ask questions.'

'Perhaps. But let's not talk about it now? It's Christmas, and not the day to pour your heart out over a boy – to kind of paraphrase your sister. Hence ignoring him.' She smiled and took the lettuce from me.

'What about you, then? If we are discussing each other's love life. Have you heard from Izzy since your night of passion?'

Katie began chopping the lettuce. Considering it was the reason that we had stopped speaking for over two weeks, I wasn't overly enthusiastic about divulging details.

'No. She was out the door as soon as she could. Didn't stop to swap numbers.'

I went back to the to-do list, picking up another chopping board.

'I never said you two shouldn't date. It was her motives for that specific night I questioned. You're nice. She's sociopathic at times but somewhere under all that ego is a really kind heart. If you guys were to pair up, you wouldn't need to worry about me throwing a fit or anything. That's all I'm saying.'

'Well, I don't think there's any danger of that being an issue.'

'If she was up for it, would you?' I could see a vague hint of a smile as I began peeling the little shallots I had set out.

'Actually, no need to answer that. I think we both know the *real* answer.' She grinned and flicked a piece of lettuce at me.

Still getting the vegetables ready, we heard the doorbell.

'Auntie Pam's early,' I said, leaving Katie in the kitchen and meeting Ellie in the hall as the welcoming committee.

'Seriously, we said two o'clock. Which means at least half two when you've got two small children to get dressed and get changed yourself.'

But it wasn't Auntie Pam. On our doorstep in his usual dapper suit, tie and unflappable grin was Maxwell.

'Merry Christmas,' he beamed. 'I was in the area and thought I would drop by seeing that you were both in residence.'

We retreated into Dad's study. Fortunately, my camp bed was

folded away, and I had been able to air out the room, so it was less pungent than it had been six hours earlier. Maxwell said yes to the formalities of coffee and mince pies, which had Ellie none too subtly staring at her watch.

'You've engaged a good one, you'd be pleased to know.' We both stared at Maxwell blankly. 'Your solicitor. The new generation always seems to have a get-up-and-go to them that I do have to admit shakes things up.'

As he had done when conveying to us Dad's will, Maxwell perched himself on Dad's desk, this time cradling his cup of coffee.

'I have to say, still, it was not the method I would have advocated for, and it could have backfired quite substantially. But it has certainly shuffled things forward. Orletta would like to meet.'

Neither Ellie nor I said anything. I sat myself on the windowsill sipping my coffee, and Ellie sat unmoved in Dad's desk chair. It was like a stalled negotiation, and Maxwell's brow soon furrowed, probably expecting more excitement than we offered.

'When?' I asked.

'Whenever,' he shrugged. 'Conrad called me yesterday to suggest you both go down for a visit and spend a few days with your ma in the fresh air. He told me that they were putting on a small show at that retreat of theirs, and that would be an ideal opportunity. I do have to say, you could both look more cheerful. Your bluff paid off. You've won!'

'How is this winning, Maxwell?' Ellie said calmly. 'How is a mother who hasn't spoken to her children in years, asking her partner to put thirty minutes in her diary a win for anyone?'

'I have to say, my dear, it does work both ways. You could have made that phone call yourself and not resorted to legal proceedings.'

'Scott, are you going to say anything or are you going to sit in your corner and leave everything to me?'

Despite my not appreciating her rounding on me, as if knowing Maxwell would bat her accusations away all day, Ellie did have a point. I had stopped looking at them and turned away, gazing out of the window. Outside, two young children – probably five and eight – were running happily while their mother, in her 80s summer dress, delightedly chased after them in what would have been the August sun. Everyone was laughing and the mother caught up with the boy picking him up, telling him he was too big to be carried and asking him never to grow any older. *This one's like your mother's arms...* Where were those happy people now?

'Scott! For pfff's sake – '

'Yeah. Okay. We all know we're going to do it, so we might as well just say yes and get on with it.'

I was still watching my 80s mother so I had no idea if Ellie was rolling her eyes, shaking her head, or giving me the V-sign – she preferred the V-sign to the finger. Ellie took after Mum, inheriting her blonde hair and smile, though with Ellie you would not know it. I took after Dad, being told that I had his jaw and nose. I had inherited my dark, black hair – the witchcraft gene, Ellie had called it – from our next visitor, who rang the bell, curtailing our conversation.

'Great,' mumbled Ellie as we both left Maxwell. 'It's now two o'clock, and I'm still wearing a coffee and baby puke stained t-shirt. Auntie Pam's really going to think we've got this day under control.'

As we entered the hallway Ellie paused, took a deep breath, and put on a big forced smile, before opening the door to our aunt.

'Apologies, dears, I know two o'clock means three o'clock and all that,' she said, coming through the door and kissing us on the cheek. 'But I didn't want to faff about wasting Ahmed's time as well as my own. Lovely boy, I use him every time I have to fork out for a journey, but he does assume every person north of sixty has some form of dementia. I reply, 'better old than zombified by one of those mobile phone thingies.' Look, you're not even dressed.'

Ellie and I had not even had a chance to say Merry Christmas as Auntie Pam handed me her coat and Ellie her canvas rucksack, which she carried with her instead of a handbag. She then left us in the hallway and proceeded into the living room, continuing with her story.

'Persian. Family is from a town outside Tehran. Left just after the revolution, around the time I was over the border doing my first dig in Iraq. Excellent driver. Punctual. He'll pick me up too. Right then. Mill-Mill. Edward Woodward.'

She clapped her hands, and we caught up with Auntie Pam as she stood above an understandably daunted Millie and Ed. 'Eleanor, bag please.'

From the rucksack she brought out a selection box of mini chocolate bars and a large tin of sweets.

'Auntie Pam, you never gave us chocolates when we were kids. You said they were bad for us.'

'You turned out alright, didn't you? Oh, do stop whining, Eleanor, it's unbecoming.'

As Auntie Pam crouched down to open the box, and coo over her grandniece and grandnephew, I smirked at Ellie. Her face had literally gone red with indignation.

'Back then, you were both constantly stuffing your faces with E-numbers and commercialised rubbish. It's a wonder you're both not obese. These days it's the nanny state and careerist bureaucrats telling you how to raise your children and how everything is bad for you. Oh, have another, dear, oh you are growing into quite the little lady.'

'None of that remotely makes sense,' Ellie said to me, as Auntie Pam was still talking to Millie and Ed. Mike, a lot more sincerely than his wife, got up and greeted Auntie Pam, offering her his chair. Ellie then glared at me, as if to have someone to glare at, or because it was too obvious I enjoyed the effect Auntie Pam had on her. She then took another couple of deep breaths.

'Auntie Pam, would you like a drink? Mike was about to pour some *bubbles*.' Ellie's use of the word *bubbles* was also comic. Her voice had suddenly gone posh, as if she had recently graduated from finishing school.

'Oh, don't be such a suck-up, dear.' Auntie Pam was smiling and grinning, focussing more on the children than the adults around her. 'Of course I would like a drink. I didn't spend fifteen pounds on a taxi to sit teetotal twiddling my thumbs.'

During that chaos, I had almost forgotten that Katie was still in the kitchen, let alone that we had Auntie Pam's ex-husband squirrelled away in Dad's study. Bringing in Katie to introduce her to Auntie Pam, I went back for Maxwell, but he was not where we had left him. Instead, I found him in the conservatory, standing there staring into space.

'Maxwell?'

'You never appreciate it, my boy.' His voice was strange. The assertive cheeriness absent.

'And you never know when it's going to disappear like a puff of smoke.' He nodded over to the large wicker chair, which used to be Dad's. 'Many an evening your papa and I would sit here, a glass in hand, putting the world to rights. Bloody awful year, this has been, I don't mind telling you. Bloody, bloody awful year.'

I had never seen Maxwell that agitated before. Uncertainty had replaced his usual composure and he looked pained and angry staring at the chair and the drinks cabinet where Dad would make his signature gin and tonics.

'There's not many of us now, Scott. The male divorcees club. At a certain age you come to enjoy life on your own. The gentle solitude after a long day. But you do not realised until very much late in the day that it was never true solitude. True solitude is being in the car and thinking to yourself, 'I'll just pop in on old George,' and then turning the car around because you realise he's not with us anymore. Your friend has gone. That is true solitude.'

We remained as we were. I could hear murmurs from the living room – no shouting or screaming fortunately, so Ellie and Auntie Pam must have been kept at bay. Through the conservatory glass it was a lovely December day with bright sunlight shimmering off the lawn. Maxwell then abruptly seemed to snap out of his gloom.

'Right, dear boy, I've taken up enough of your time. I better be off. Promised to drop in on a couple of colleagues and share a glass or two.'

'Or you could share a glass with us?' I found myself offering. 'Auntie Pam's just arrived and we've opened up some cava. Why not stay for lunch? There's plenty.'

I had planned on dining in the jumper I had been wearing that day, and for the whole of winter according to Katie. But everyone else had gone upstairs to change, so I belatedly realised that dinner would have a formal vibe. I even had Katie anxiously take me to the side and whisper, 'I was a bit thrown yesterday, so just packed the first dress I found. It might be a bit informal – like, a night-out dress rather than dinner with family.' She flicked her head over to my aunt, who had a knack of putting the women around her on edge.

In the end, Ellie invited a relieved Katie to do hair and makeup with her. This did effectively throw all my Christmas dinner timings out of the window, but it gave Mike and me a chance to move Auntie Pam and Maxwell into the conservatory and have a pre-dinner gin and tonic just as we would have done if Dad was with us.

'Friends and colleagues, Pamela. I really did promise to do the rounds.'

'I'm sure you have, Max. Or, for once, you could refrain from being the life of a dozen different parties and stay where you are. He was like this when we were married, you know.' Auntie Pam sat with her tumbler and turned conspiratorially to Mike and me. 'Infuriating. Never one to settle. I'm sure there are at least two manila folders sitting on his passenger seat with documents awaiting signatures you were planning to get this afternoon.'

Maxwell rested his chin on the palm of his hand and smiled. He certainly looked more at ease than when we stood in that room moments earlier.

'Pamela, age has certainly not blunted you.'

I can't precisely remember Auntie Pam and Maxwell divorcing. Back then it seemed a case that one day he lived with her and then he didn't. I assumed all was amicable as Maxwell did remain one of Dad's best friends, and I did recall them both turning up to dinner parties Mum and Dad would host. As they began talking about Christmases and friends gone by, Mike and I decided to leave them to it and stepped outside for some brief fresh air.

'The Duchess is taking her time. Maybe preparing for another mistletoe moment?'

'We're just friends,' I said, ignoring his grin. 'She's got a boyfriend, and it was your wife who invited her.'

'Yeah, spending Christmas with some random bloke's family, completely platonic.'

We could hear Auntie Pam berating Maxwell about some trip he once joined her on and Maxwell cackling at the anecdote.

'They get on well, don't they? Considering they're divorced.'

'Probably better than when they were married. I guess it just didn't work out. From what I remember at the time – or from what we overheard from Mum or Dad – Auntie Pam was constantly abroad with work and Maxwell was always at the office so they never saw each other.'

'Tell me about it.'

Mike gently shook and swirled the ice in his glass, looking like he was trying to dislodge the orange peel I had been heavy-handed with.

'Ell said you were having to rack up the hours lately.'

'That's the thing with the music industry now, you accept the work while it's there and put up with the hours that come with it.'

Mike shrugged, rather more pessimistically than I could recall seeing him. It felt a bit invasive watching him, so I looked out onto our lawn, which I needed to cut at some point; everything looked wintery, slightly overgrown, and unloved.

'But it comes to a point when you have to ask yourself if it's worth it, or if it's something you can see yourself doing for the next twenty years. And recently, I don't think it is.'

He shrugged again, and I remembered my conversation with Ellie on the tube.

'Either I'm in the studio all hours with session work, or if I get asked to play gigs, I'm on the road for a week solid playing riffs in a dark corner of the stage trying my best to look inconspicuous so the audience doesn't question why their three-piece indie-rock band has a fourth member twice their age. It's not exactly living the dream anymore.' He gave a small laugh and sipped his drink again.

'Ellie's pissed that she's the one who ends up doing the lion's share with the kids, and I seriously miss the little menaces. I'm tired of all the bedtimes missed and having to say goodnight over the phone. So I've been taking this accountancy course and been looking around for full-time jobs back in Brighton. Something nine to five. Like a proper adult.'

He did smirk at the end. A light smile that was perhaps there to combat the fact that I must have looked completely crestfallen.

'Fuck.'

'Joining the real world, man. Time to grow up.'

'Fuck.'

I honestly don't know if I would have felt more shocked or devastated if instead, Mike had told me he was seriously ill. I just stood there, staring at the grass in disbelief. Mike was the Musician. He lived the dream for all of us. Accountancy was for people who never had any dreams – people like me! Those who left university and went straight into a bank because they did not know what else to do with their life and never bothered to think about it. We couldn't lose Mike to that world. Not Mike. Not the Musician.

'Jeez, dude!' he laughed and put his arm around my shoulders. 'It will be alright. We'll still be friends, I'll still write, I'll still call.' He then began cackling with laugher as he put me in a light head-lock and rubbed his knuckles into my scalp.

'It will all be okay. Plus they can't be all bad, right? The dreaded accountants?'

It felt like Mike was literally and proverbially breaking up the band. If the Musician had to grow up and get a real job, what hope was there for the rest of us? At the end of the day, did we all have to wind up coming back to something that made us miserable? Would I myself soon be admitting defeat and hanging up my gardening gloves, crawling on my knees back to some faceless bureaucracy to spend my life filling in spreadsheets and writing the same report each month that no one would read? As Mike at least seemed in better spirits, still laughing at my despondency, we walked back inside and then, suddenly, I completely forgot why I had been so melancholic.

Black dress, deep red lips, and immaculate flowing hair, I would have been curious to see what Katie's idea of formal was if that was informal. I kept saying Katie and I were just friends, so I really should stop staring at her the way I was; that star-crossed look of awe as she stood in the conservatory doorway, my eyes going from her mouth to her figure and then quickly back to her eyes, like she was my date to the end-of-year ball. Katie then smiled at me and mouthed, 'do I look okay?', and I tried to nod understatedly. From behind her then came Ellie with Millie and Ed, all of whom looked equally dressed up and made me feel that my effort of putting on a shirt might have been a bare minimum. Millie quickly grabbed Katie's arm, dragging her away, and Ellie caught sight of Mike and me, rolling her eyes.

'Jeans? Seriously? We spend an hour with curling tongs and hairdryers going full pelt, and all you both do is button-up a shirt. So much for gender equality.' Mike and I both grinned but there was something about Ellie I had not seen before. She was standing wearing a long green and gold dress, elegant enough to outdo Auntie Pam, her hair flowing and the gold shimmering in the sunlight. I felt this bizarre sensation of pride. This was my sister, all grown up. I remembered what she had said about Mum leaving. It had not mattered in the end. She had done it all herself. I could not stop thinking how proud Dad would have been.

The table was laid, playing on the stereo was an ancient version of *Now That's What I Call Christmas*, and assembled were the build-your-own crackers we had rescued from Loughborough Road. Unfortunately, I had put them together while I was more than a little squiffy the previous night, and I could not remember which one was booby-trapped, containing at least six times the amount of snappers as recommended.

I sat Maxwell and Auntie Pam at the heads of the table – I was never sure if that was the correct term as surely being the head, or the foot, was subjective. It felt right that Maxwell sat in the place Dad would have had, considering he was one of his oldest friends, and also considering none of the rest of us felt ready to take on the role. On the other sides of the table sat girls and boys respectively, with Millie wedged between Ellie and Katie, and Mike and me flanking Ed. And all could not have gone better. Well, apart from the inevitable blip.

Halfway through lunch Auntie Pam asked me if I wanted to finish the slice of beef on her plate.

'It was far too large a portion. That would have fed us for a week in Ethiopia, as you can now testify too, young man.'

'I was only there ten days.'

'Scott tells me you've just come back from Oman, Mrs...' Katie helped Millie with a mini puzzle from her cracker as she tried to address my aunt.

'*Dr* Lloyd-Roberts, my dear, if you were writing me a letter but I told you, please call me Pam.'

I saw Ellie turn her head away from Auntie Pam and roll her eyes at me.

'Not that I like using my prefix. Doctorate in Anthropology and Archaeology, you see. I had been with the Royal Society since probably when Edward Heath was Prime Minister, being sent to God knows where however many times a year – Max will vouch for that. I retired five years ago and am now seeing the world on my own terms. Oman, Ethiopia, Egypt, with former colleagues the last year, lending a hand wherever I can at some dig or the other. Amman and Jordan in January, so no rest for the wicked.'

'Yes, Katie, Auntie Pam is really just like one of us at heart. Woman of the people.'

I'm sure I was not the only one who could feel the twinge of tension at that moment. With anyone else Ellie's sarcasm would at least be subtle, but with Auntie Pam she seemed to take every innocuous comment as a personal dig. It might have been because Ellie had lived a lot of her life as a free spirit – her mother's daughter, a musician following a path in the arts – and Auntie Pam for all her travels and worldliness was definitely not. She had always known what she wanted to do and pursued her career in one organisation with unwavering dedication. It might have also been that Auntie Pam was never one to mince her words, especially after Mum left, and especially about Mum.

'Academia is not for all of us, I do know that, Eleanor, but this young woman seems to have a steady head on her shoulders.' Auntie Pam then turned directly to Katie. 'I have nothing but the greatest respect for curators, if not for you the wonders I unearth would never see the light of day.'

'Auntie Pam, if I knew you were still keen to unearth wonders I would have asked you to help Scott and me sort through all the junk in the basement.'

Auntie Pam calmly let her face go deadpan. Like I said, usually Ellie's jibes would be subtle and cutting. Here even Mike, who was trying to spoon feed Ed some carrot, was giving her an anxious stare as she was beginning to sound like a bit of a dick. Millie, obviously oblivious to the conversation, was trying to regain Katie's attention by showing her the necklace she had on.

'Maxwell tells me your mother wants to come to an arrangement with you for the house? That must come as some relief to you both.'

'Not exactly a relief, considering she has no claim to anything of Dad's other than trying to exploit a technicality.'

Ellie's voice was slightly louder than normal, and there was a forcefulness about how she helped herself to another serving of Brussel sprouts. It was Katie's turn now to give me an anxious stare.

'That technicality being that this is now her house in the eyes of the law. My dear, I would have been as indignant as you, but you've had a year now. Perhaps you now need to think about what you would want to walk away with and finally put this to bed.'

Again, Auntie Pam looked undeterred by Ellie as she picked up the wine bottle and offered me a top-up.

'Walk away? This is our house.'

Ellie dropped the serving spoons back into the ceramic dish with a heavy clutter.

'Whose side are you on, Auntie Pam? Is it him whispering defeatist nonsense in your ear?' Ellie threw an arm out at Maxwell, who up until that point had been trying to have a quiet side conversation with Mike and Katie, perhaps to distract his half of the table from the scene beginning to unfold.

'Do not point like that, my dear, it is incredibly rude!'

I was transported back in time to when we were children and Auntie Pam had last used her stern voice on us. It seemed to attract Millie's attention, who stared open-mouthed.

'Now, I have never claimed to see eye to eye with your mother, but as your father told me more than once, I did not have to – that was his job. And until you can better understand his motives – it does pain me very much to say this – who are we to dictate who rightly gets what? It's not like George was prone to bouts of carelessness at the end of the day.'

'Well, it's not like we can go and ask him, is it?'

I really wished Ellie had not said that. It was my turn to clutter my cutlery loudly onto my plate. I stared forcibly at Ellie, glaring at her so I at least caught her eye. No one said anything apart from Millie, who was still telling Katie about the charms on her necklace.

'I mean, it's been a year.' Ellie's voice was quieter, her more usual sulkier one. 'If we knew why he hadn't signed his divorce papers, or why he hadn't drawn up a bloody will, well someone should have said. Unless you do know, Auntie Pam, and didn't think it was worth mentioning?'

Ellie began stabbing a roast potato with her fork and didn't notice what I did; Auntie Pam frowning and fidgeting in her seat.

'Nobody benefits from wild speculation, girl. I'd only say George always had a reason, was a rational man, and definitely not a bloody fool. If he wanted you to be calling solicitors and dragging your own mother to court, well, that's a side to him I'd not seen in my sixty-seven years, I can tell you that.' She stared down at her plate.

'I had naively hoped you would sort things out between your-selves, but instead we're sat here dredging up the past no matter the consequences...'

'Dredging up the past?'

Ellie's voice tailed off as Auntie Pam threw down her napkin. She began squeezing the bridge of her nose. Ellie and I stared at each other wide-eyed, giving each other the look of *we've broken Auntie Pam*. We'd seen Auntie Pam annoyed over the years – to be fair, that was her norm – but we'd never seen her flustered. Or as tired as she suddenly seemed. I leaned over to her.

'Auntie Pam, can I get you a glass of water – '

'And by Jove, that's exactly why we're here today,' Maxwell cut over me. 'To not dredge up the past but to raise a glass.'

He gently pushed back his chair and rose to his feet, picking up his glass of red wine.

'I could not have been more fortunate to have had a friend like your papa, and we have all felt his absence acutely in our own way this last year. But he would not have been prouder to see his chil-dren, grandchildren, friends and family – all who love him and all who miss him – here today.' He made the strategic pause of someone highly accustomed to making speeches, which allowed the rest of us to raise our glasses and look at each other – embarrassed in most cases. I half-smiled at Ellie, who returned it and looked over to Auntie Pam with a far kinder smile. Auntie Pam nodded, a far more peaceable, accepting nod. I then glanced over to Katie. I'm told the ancient Greeks had numerous words for the different types of love there are, so I find it strange that nowadays we seem to have so few. And for looks. And for smiles. Katie caught my eye and smiled this big reassuring smile, and in one moment, I suddenly felt that everything was going to be okay.

'So here's to all of you. And here's to George.'

I have to say, I was delighted that after lunch we ended up playing the board game I had got for Millie and Ed, and they seemed to enjoy it thoroughly. I felt it slightly made up for my status of absentee uncle for so much of their life. I also had to thank Joan of all people who had recommended the game – board games were one of his niche passions and he subscribed to some newsletter saying which new ones had won awards. In the one we played, each piece was meant to be a camel that could connect to another person's, forming a double-sized camel as you went around the board trying to unearth hidden treasure. I wasn't sure Ed would be old enough to understand, but Millie's expressions and leaps in the air every time she found treasure were enough to keep him constantly giggling too.

After, the adults played another game I had bought; this one very much charades-based and had us up on our feet, miming books and films in front of the Christmas tree.

Auntie Pam told Maxwell to collect his car in the morning and that Ahmed would drop him off on route. She told us she would keep in touch while she was in Jordan, and if we needed her, all we had to do was call her old office landline, and one of her old team would provide us with the number of whichever hotel she was staying, at which point I had to squeeze Ellie's wrist to stop an argument regarding the merits of modern technology.

The excitement had all got too much for Millie and Ed, who fell fast asleep in adorable bundles on the sofa. Ellie and Mike picked them up and put them to bed before briefly coming back downstairs, looking exhausted on the sofa and eventually submitting to tiredness themselves, saying goodnight with some large yawns.

It was just Katie and me, each of us occupying one of the living room armchairs sipping our glasses of wine, just the Christmas tree lights on as the house seemed to slowly settle and the echoes of an epic Christmas day gently faded away.

'Thank you,' she said, curled up in her chair, looking over to me. 'This has been a wonderful day. Truly wonderful.'

'Thank you for joining us – seriously – you've been run ragged by children for two days straight, and I think you have captured someone's heart forever.'

'I have no idea who you mean,' she laughed, and for a nervous moment I thought she might have realised I did not mean Millie.

'She is so adorable. I wish I could keep her.'

'Don't let Ellie hear you say that. She'd have her bags packed and sent your way every school holidays.'

'Well, I will then try to be the coolest aunt possible.'

As she giggled, my phone buzzed. Not wanting to interrupt the conversation, I just allowed my eyes to glance over it.

'What is it?'

I must have outwardly looked puzzled. As the screen lit up, I quickly saw a message from an unknown number saying, *So aren't you even going to wish me a merry Christmas?*

'Anyone special?' asked Katie.

'I have no idea. Probably a wrong number.'

'I may be able to help you.' Katie uncurled herself and rose from the chair. She had her phone with her as she came over to me. 'A Christmas present of sorts.'

On the screen was a conversation between her and Izzy that day. The messages were mostly from Izzy; *I expected you to apologise by now*; *God you are a tedious prick*; *Can you send me Scott's number? I should apologise to him too*; *Please*; *Merry Christmas btw. You know full well I miss you so stop ignoring me xxx*. Then a reply from Katie with my number, and then five minutes later two small x's, and a reply from Izzy with a smiley face.

'You'd better reply. It would literally make her implode. She doesn't normally ask for a guy's number. You're quite honoured.'

'I thought you were pissed off about her and me?'

'It's Christmas. Not really the day to hold a grudge. Plus, if she does actually like you...'

'If she *actually* likes me!' I laughed, almost spilling my wine.

'I didn't mean it like that! I'm the one who tried to set you both up, remember?'

She was giving me a comically stern glare as I continued to beam back at her.

'She *is* a lot nicer than she comes across. And you're...' She seemed to be taking longer than was complimentary to find a compliment. 'Lovely. Really, very lovely.'

Katie began clearing away the remnant glasses and small plates of snacks dotted across the room.

'It's okay, I can do that.'

When she got to the kitchen sink, I gently tugged her arm to pull her away.

'All that can wait until tomorrow.'

We went back into the living room and stood observing the evidence of all that had taken place that day; the toys and games neatly piled in the corner, the board game back in its box and placed under the tree. Katie yawned, a big yawn with her whole hand trying to cover her mouth.

'I guess it's time for bed.'

Katie nodded, suddenly looking dead on her feet, her hand still covering her mouth as if anticipating a second yawn. I watched her from the doorway as I flicked off all the light switches.

'Thank you,' she said again, stopping in the doorway and then reaching up to hug me. As I placed my hands on her back, she held me for longer than I expected.

As she finally let go, she then looked above my head and smiled.

'Uh oh. Looks like someone's found themselves under the mistletoe again.'

'Well, at least Millie isn't here to see it. We can probably get away with just the hug.' I felt myself slightly blushing as I looked back at her beaming face.

'No chance! Do you honestly expect me to betray my new best friend already?'

She smiled again, but this time it was different. It was less jokey, and soon it faded. She kept looking at me. I expected her to jump up and quickly peck me like she did the day before but she didn't. She tiptoed up, and I leaned down. The next thing I knew, I had my eyes closed, and her lip was between mine as she tilted her head and let her mouth open.

CHAPTER 17

CRUSH

The thing about having a crush on someone is that we do not expect it to be reciprocal. We fantasise about that moment when the other person says it had been you all along, and you walk off into the sunset together. But at heart, we know that is all it is: a fantasy. After all, if we were so confident that something would happen, it probably would have already happened.

With Sarah, and one of the triggers to that whole Easter weekend saga, I did not think anything would happen. Sarah was pretty, athletic, trendy, and her previous boyfriends were one step below professional athletes. She told me that she had put her last boyfriend on a pedestal as he was a triathlete who had once cycled from London to Sydney. With Sarah and me, it was me who put her on that pedestal. It might have been my tales of life abroad that put me on her radar, but when we kissed – when she knew for certain I wanted her – her interest in me seemed to dissolve instantly. I'm not saying I know what lay behind her motivations, but for someone used to putting others on pedestals it must have removed the mystique and created that Groucho Marxist dilemma; if this club wants me as a member, could I not do better?

A lesson I learned from Sarah was that the most destructive attractions are not those that allow us to kiss our crush at once, as we soon take them for granted. Or those who we do not kiss at all – we inevitably forget the infatuation as soon as our love is gone from view. But instead, those somewhere in the middle. Those we kiss just the once and find ourselves perpetually lost in *what could have been.*

Katie was already awake, dressed, and curled up in an armchair writing in what looked like a journal as I emerged from the study.

'Morning,' she said, a little too awake considering that I was still bleary-eyed and my back felt like it had recently come out of spasm after another night on the camp bed.

'Ellie and Millie are already up. I heard the distinctive sound of little feet scurrying between rooms being chased by bigger feet just before I came down. How did you sleep?'

'Fine,' I lied. 'It's very cosy in there. You?'

'Yes, okay thanks. To be honest my head was spinning a bit as I got into bed. I definitely had more to drink than I thought.'

She went back to her journal, and I was left standing there – most likely in need of a shower, knowing my hair was probably a wild mess – feeling awkward. Just for a change.

When I had gone to bed the previous night, all I could do was replay that kiss over and over, not wanting to fall asleep in case the memory would diminish. I had thought she would relinquish as soon as our lips had touched. But instead of jumping down and grinning like she did the night before, she remained as she was. It was like a bolt of adrenalin as she then gently pressed her mouth against mine. She leaned back against the doorway taking me with her. I felt her hands rest themselves on my stomach as we stopped kissing briefly to look at each other.

Neither of us smiling or giggling. And then we began to kiss again, this time my hands holding her hips and hers finding their way underneath my shirt.

'It's late,' she whispered, bringing the kiss to an end. She gave me this sad-looking smile. 'I really should go to bed. To sleep.' She removed her hand from under my shirt, and I took my cue to let go of her hips. 'I really did have a great day.' And then, as if like contemplating an experiment, she furrowed her brow and placed another kiss on my mouth, watching me curiously as she did, before saying goodnight.

After brushing my teeth, tidying myself up, and then making coffee, I returned to the living room where Katie still had her nose in her journal.

'Anything interesting?'

'Just some ideas for work. I woke up with them forming in my head, so I wanted to get them down on paper. There's a couple of work trips in January – Florence and Copenhagen. My boss would have gone, but as she's on sabbatical, there's an outside chance I might get the gig.'

'Excellent news,' I said, noticing that it came out rather down-beat. I was taking my place on the sofa opposite, coffee in my hand. I wondered how long she was going to be away as January was only a few days away.

'Fingers crossed. I might even be able to pop over to Berlin and visit my long-lost boyfriend. Remind him I exist.'

She wasn't looking at me but still gazing into her journal. I tried to disguise an involuntary sigh. I did not know if she thought she was being subtle.

'You've heard from him?'

She nodded.

'He kept bombarding me with messages as I was getting into bed. Nothing bad. Actually they were quite funny, quite self-deprecating. And then he called.' Hesitantly, she closed her journal, put it to the side and picked up the coffee I had brought her.

'Apparently he had spent the whole day at his boss's house. They had a quick Christmas meal with his family and then spent most of the afternoon and evening trying to put the whole thing to bed so his boss could go skiing with his children.'

She pulled an it-is-what-it-is face, with a shrug.

'So it was legitimate then?'

'Apparently so.'

With that, she raised her eyebrows, looked down, and got on with her writing. I sipped my coffee, our conversation now over. From the subtext, I knew Katie did not want to talk about the kiss. The fact that the first thing she brought up was her boyfriend's lack of infidelity probably said enough. So I probably shouldn't have then been such a dick about it.

'I probably should get going relatively soon. It's been a fun few days, but I better get myself back into work mode.'

'True. That way we can avoid talking about last night. Or how you seemed to have reconciled with Ethan minutes after.'

She didn't say anything. At least not with her mouth. She finally looked me in the eyes with an incredulous stare, which simply said: *fuck off you prick*. And she held that glare as we heard adult footsteps slowly come down the stairs before Ellie entered the room, looking like she would have preferred to still be asleep in bed.

'Katie, someone is asking if you would like to play dolls with her in her room. You'd be forgiven for not and hiding out down here.'

'Of course, I'd love to.' Her voice jumped into cheerful mode as she smiled and sprang off her seat. As a hardly appreciative Ellie gave a tired nod and went towards the kitchen, Katie made to leave the room and I opened my mouth to apologise. However, as I did she glared at me, shook her head and mouthed something; either *get lost* or *fuck off*, I couldn't tell which.

. . .

'We'll pay you fifty quid,' whispered Mike over the screaming. We were gathered in the hallway to see Katie off. She was standing at the door with her coat on and her bag at her feet looking entirely overwhelmed. Between us was the small figure of Millie, her eyes and face bright pink as tears streamed down her cheeks, staring down her mother, believing her the wicked witch of the situation.

'I don't want her to go!' She stomped her little feet as hard as she could into our carpeted floor. Ellie raised her eyebrows as if saying, this is what it's normally like. She then quickly stepped past the wailing Millie to hug Katie goodbye.

'Don't look so alarmed. This is a compliment. She hardly ever throws a tantrum when I leave the house, do you, Mill-Mills?' There was more stomping until Ellie tenderly kneeled down to put her arms around her daughter, letting her wail into them.

'Quick, run while you can,' she whispered.

Closing the door behind us sealed a vacuum on the crying. I followed Katie down the path to the gate in silence, not trusting myself not to repeat something stupid. As we reached the gate, we both turned to each other, took a large breath, and simultaneously exhaled *sorry*.

'Earlier was stupid,' she said with an awkward quarter-smile. She puffed out her cheeks and looked around like she was searching the quiet suburban street for what she wanted to say.

'The thing is, it's been a while since my last drunken snog – not saying that's all it was!' She seemed to go pinker. 'But I think the last time I've had a snog outside a long-term relationship was when some wasted guy accosted me at my brother's birthday.' She let a small grin slip across her face and seemed to them nervously look at me to see if I would reciprocate.

'It was nice. The *snog*. And it was a really, really nice day with your family. I just...'

'Feel guilty about Ethan?'

'Yes. But not just that.' She again puffed out her cheeks and frowned, staring at our low garden wall for inspiration.

'It was a bit of a classless move on my part, using you to cheer me up and then hoping to brush it under the carpet – '

'You've got nothing to apologise for. It was Christmas, there was mistletoe, and I think we've both had such a time of it recently when a snog was a super-nice way to end the day.'

Snog? Super-nice? I don't know why these words had re-entered my vocabulary for the first time since I was a teenager. Perhaps it was because I wanted to put both of us out of our misery as soon as possible with one push of casual positivity.

'I'm sorry for this morning. I got caught in this moment of – do we talk about this, do we not talk about this, and just freaked out. I'm really no good at this.'

'I don't think anybody is.'

'I mean the whole concept of *polyamory*. It's just not possible to do what you want and not hurt other people.'

'We may be going too deep.' I tried to smile, and even though she was now smiling too I still wanted to pull away from the conversation and have her just leave.

'Friends? Still?'

'Yes,' I smiled. 'Still friends.'

We hugged – a friends hug – and she stepped out of the gate. She asked if I would be back later, but I told her that Ellie and I had some plans, and I would be home the day after.

Mike took the kids to the cinema by himself in the afternoon, allowing Ellie and me to drive to Enfield cemetery. The last time we had set foot there we were caked in mud, wrestling like adolescents. I felt an enormous pang of guilt as we reached Dad's grave – I had not been to see him in over a year.

I would have thought all those years of enforced Anglicanism would have shored up my belief in the afterlife, but somehow Dad's departure felt all the more final. Plus, how could I bear to visit him when I had let him down so badly? The funeral, Sarah, Easter weekend, *Watership Down*, letting my life slip away and erasing anything he could have otherwise been proud of me for. It was now a year later, and I was looking down at his headstone, wondering if he was there in the ether surrounding us, feeling we had abandoned him.

'Scott? Are you alright?'

Had I not known my sister, I would have mistaken this for concern.

'Just a bit weird being here again.'

In the blur of memories, I do not think I properly looked at the stone or what we had chosen to put. 'George Geoffrey Robert, Beloved Father, Brother and Friend.' There was so much about him we could have also said. Such as all he achieved: all those many books and accredited papers; even the Radio 4 culture documentaries would instantly fill me with this surge of surprise and pride when I would hear his voice; the fact he did his best to make a shy, nervous, nerdy teenager come out of his shell without ever making him feel there was something wrong with him.

'You've gone pale,' said Ellie.

'Probably still hungover. We didn't pick a bad spot, did we? Look's beautiful, even in winter.'

Even with the trees bare and the grass damp, it was spacious and peaceful. I could imagine that in the summer it would be green and full of light.

'Are we really going to do this thing with Mum?'

'I thought I was the flaky one?'

'Well sorry for not being sociopathic but I'm not exactly looking forward to seeing my only surviving parent just after I've sent her a letter announcing my intent to sue her.'

Despite the clear sky overhead, it was bitterly cold out there by the grave. Ellie had her parka wrapped tightly around her and her thick gloves on. I buried my hands deep into my jeans pockets for warmth.

'We can't avoid it forever,' I said, knowing it would annoy Ellie hearing me lecture her on avoidance. 'Why keep putting ourselves through the crap of second-guessing her motives? Plus, I'd like to ask her why she's doing all this. The house is *our* home, not hers.'

We stood quietly, staring at the memorial, and the wind began to pick up.

'Mike says he's giving up the session work.'

'It's something we're discussing. Nothing's final.'

'Have you thought any more about starting composing again?'

Here I assumed I would receive the traditional snort of sarcasm with Ellie responding along the lines of, 'oh yeah, like I get so much time at the moment with two kids under six years old.' But instead, she sighed.

'Thought about it. Thinking about it. It's not like you can just rock up at the Albert Hall and throw down, though, is it?'

She shivered and wriggled her legs, for warmth I guessed.

'But I don't want Millie and Ed to grow up and one day hear how both their parents were once good at something that was rare to be that good at, and then both gave it up to become like everyone else. Even thinking about Mum, oh God, I despise her at times, but she went for it. She put her art first, above everything else. Above everyone else. I'm not saying I want to be like her, but I do want to show her it is possible to follow your dream and not abandon your children to do it.'

I suddenly felt a few droplets of rain. The clear skies overhead were not as clear anymore. Ellie looked like she was freezing. I could hardly feel my hands. I was going to suggest we go back to the car and perhaps get a hot chocolate from town – what we called Wood Green high street – while we waited for the kids' film to finish, but just as I made to move away, Ellie called me back.

'Scott, this thing with Katie... Be careful.' I had expected her to goad me, as Mike had done. But instead, she looked genuinely concerned.

'No one's that perfect. Or has their life that together. I'd watch yourself with that one.'

It was a strange rhetorical warning and probably the first time Ellie had ever talked to me about a girl that didn't merely imply I was and would forever remain a virgin. She also gave me this weird stare like she was making sure I understood before she too turned towards the car park.

The rest of our Boxing Day was pleasantly subdued as Christmas seemed finally to take it out of Millie and Ed. They spent the evening curled up on the sofa as we stuck on some old records and sat in the warm glow of the tree. Ellie was standing at the piano looking at the old picture frames. I was about to get up and put on another as Mike had both children lying on him, but instead, Ellie sat down on her old piano stool. Without a word she gently tapped the keys, like testing it still worked.

And then, it was like an incredible wave of soothing notes. She didn't take a second to warm up or get her bearings. The silence was filled with this delicate movement that evoked this memory of staring out at the rain on a gloomy day. It both had a pitter-patter rhythm and something else going on, building, ascending. She claimed she never practised and not to have the technical ability of others, but she was a phenomenon. I could have been at the Albert Hall, or sitting in the cinema being moved by the soundtrack to a film. She was faultless.

The music stayed with me long after we all said goodnight. I went to bed ready to sleep for a week with the notes and tones gently swimming around my head. I closed my eyes and drifted off, gently and peacefully. Then, a message on my phone woke me. Despite what I had said that morning, my heart jumped hoping it was Katie.

So you're not going to wish me a merry Christmas? It was the same number that Katie told me belonged to Izzy.

With the mistletoe and the kiss, I had entirely forgotten about her message. Obviously after what had happened the previous night it would have been a little bit insensitive to have kissed someone I claim to like and then start a text message conversation with her best friend. I then received another message. Well, more accurately, a series of punctuation marks.

???!

I remembered what Katie said about Izzy not liking being ignored. I also remembered what Katie said she had done right after she kissed me and how she didn't allow her phone to go unanswered.

Sorry. It's been an epic couple of days. Merry Christmas. I knew it sounded dismissive but that was partly the intention. I wasn't really sure what her motives were, but from our night together and the morning after, I was pretty certain it wasn't going to be a straightforward, *let's be friends.*

Haha obviously! Oh what a jet setting lifestyle I'm sure you lead. I should be honoured to have received a response at all.

The soothed state in which I had gone to bed was beginning to diminish. I put the phone down and closed my eyes. But my phone kept buzzing.

Are you pissed off with me? God you are a sensitive soul aren't you?

No, it's just strange to hear from you. You didn't seem overly keen to keep in touch.

Who said anything about keeping in touch? I'm just bored. I thought you could entertain me. Or the other way around x

I assume for those born into what is termed Generation Z, the smartphone is more or less a necessity when it comes to seduction. When I was in my twenties, we would go to clubs hoping to swap numbers with a girl, text her a few days later and arrange a date. Now that all seems superfluous as countless apps exist to cut out having to walk up to another human being and make those introductions. Obviously, we did have photo messages, and friends of friends particularly in my banking days would pass on stories of *sexting*, but I never belonged to a crowd where late-night *entertaining* was anything but folklore.

When I was with Vicky our late night behind-closed-doors message exchanges would be of the intensely cringe-worthy nature – I would tell her how beautiful she was and how I missed her when she was not around. With Sarah, there were *so many* messages but they were all from the script of an incredibly clichéd Romeo and Juliet adaptation, telling each other how we mustn't, that what we had was more than friendship, blah blah.

Am I not your type? Do I need to put on some bunny pyjamas and go to sleep cuddling my fluffy slippers? And there it was. As I held my phone in the darkness of my room, I would admit, I did want something to happen but not if she was going to do the whole Katie thing again. At least, that was what I tried to tell myself. I did, for once, want to create the pretence of not rolling over and doing what I believed the other person wanted.

No, it's just a bit weird you bringing someone else into this.

Get over yourself. You know you are really starting to bore me now.

I responded that she was the one who initiated the conversation, determined to stay strong and have her at least say one nice thing to me before I inevitably succumbed.

You're a really shit lay, you know that right? Like you are genuinely quite bad in bed.

Thanks for the feedback.

That's okay, I'm sure you hear it all the time.

The irony was that it was a little entertaining. Izzy's ruthlessness was both intensely annoying and actually quite witty. We seemed to find some form of mutual pleasure in winding the other up. Realising I was probably getting off too much from not being nice to her I put my phone down. There was not being a walkover, and there was being a dick. I was starting to become the latter.

I did come though. In case you were interested.

Suddenly I was interested. All my moral objections evaporated.

So it can't have been that bad then.

Oh it was. I just like letting it happen. Sometimes it's easier.

So that's why you asked for my number?

This time there was a pause before her response.

On second thoughts, it turns out you are pretty much an arsehole. Go fuck yourself.

PARENTHESIS
VICKY

This might sound slightly stereotypical, but having grown up in a house with two women, I have been exposed to my fair share of romantic comedies and period dramas. Before Mum left, Friday evenings would be movie night, and during the summer, we would host the Roberts Film Festival, which was a tradition started by Ellie, and had all of us gathered around the television to watch a film of each of our choosing over a week. Even though I did inflict such classics as *Space Balls* and *Bill and Ted's Bogus Journey* on my family, romcoms won out three to one – Dad's favourite films included *Nabokov on Tolstoy*, an old black and white interview with the *Lolita* author sharing his thoughts on Russian literature, so his choice was vetoed and taken by Ellie. Therefore we had to watch something that had her and Mum in tears and Dad snoring heavily in his armchair.

But having sat through Hollywood-esque love stories such as *The Notebook, Four Weddings and a Funeral, Brief Encounter* and some of *The English Patient* (I fell asleep through that one) it had become clear to me that the key to true happiness was not wealth (*The Thomas Crown Affair*), status (*Overboard*) or a high-achieving career (*How To Lose A Guy In Ten Days...*) but rather through finding true, all-encompassing love.

So then, by that logic, the reverse must be true: that if you are not lucky enough to find someone to love and who loves you back, you will never be happy. Therefore, my quietness as a teenager would have been nothing to do with my parents splitting up or my sister occasionally using me as an emotional punching bag, but was purely because I had not yet met the girl of my dreams. And then, at age sixteen, as in those Hollywood films, she suddenly walked into my life.

Vicky joined our school midway through the first term of sixth form. Our school was not exactly typical compared to others. Amberton Grove was a fee-paying independent school, but where to many this would conjure up images of blazers and collared rugby shirts, Amberton was founded in the late 1970s, part-funded by the Arts Council, shunned uniforms, and was determined to be so nonconformist it probably became the same as everywhere else.

It began life as a small arts school. If your child was gifted at drawing or music, or wanted to dedicate more lesson time to sculpture rather than maths or science, Amberton was the place to send them. It was founded, and then governed, by a Parent Teacher Association which comprised of London and Home Counties artists, actors, classical musicians and patrons who wanted the school to become a haven for nurturing talent at a young age. An arts college, but from the age of five. Away from those who would burst the creative bubble. Some of my friends ask what my creative gift was that needed nurturing. That was easy: a sister who was a musical prodigy and a mother whose name even back then carried some weight in the arts community.

However, by the time the 90s came around, having a private school developing Britain's next generation of Turners and T.S. Elliots had become a pipedream. I suppose this was because there were already numerous academies in Central London dedicated to either music or drama, so sending a child all the way to Wood Green when they were barely three foot tall might have been considered excessive. When I joined Amberton, I was not the only student who lacked in musical or artistic accomplishment. The PTA had to balance out wanting to attract the crème de la crème of the next generation's artists with being able to stay in business, so it became a relatively cheap posh school who would just about take anyone.

We did have to keep up the pretence, though. Amberton paid far more attention to the humanities, art, and drama than STEM subjects, with exhibitions and readings held in greater esteem than, say, afterschool sports clubs. Our school play was the social event of the year, with parents even attending in black-tie, as they would to the opening of a West End show, which coincidently shared a similar budget. To give it its due, it was impressive with its post-modern set designs and a symphony standard orchestra. And by necessity rather than design, each three-hour epic performance had a reverse-Elizabethan quality, with the majority of male parts being played by girls due to a lack of talented boys. We did have Christoph Koller and Owami Tskinae, who between them were Amberton's equivalent of Affleck and Damon, and were able to stage-snog – and real snog – probably every girl doing drama, hence ninety percent of girls at our school. However, even they were upstaged by Julia Hudson and Amelia Montrose from the year above, who in their performance of *Les Liaisons Dangereuses,* pushed boundaries with a very heated and tender love scene in the middle of the stage. It lasted in excess of five minutes and brought both a standing ovation from the PTA, thrilled that Amberton would be seen as ground-breaking, and a jaw-dropping silence from an audience of teenage boys who unsubtly then spent the rest of the play queuing for the toilet cubicles.

When I chose my A-levels, the published class list told me I would academically come into contact with just four girls, all of whom were in my economics class. However, Christoph and Owami were also in the same set and, in a school where somehow the drama kids had become the American high-school equivalent of jocks and cheerleaders, it was needless to say that the GWWA was pretty much the bottom rung on the social ladder.

Then one day, as my all-male maths class climbed the stairs to Room 4.B at the top of our Modern Languages and Sciences block, we all had to do a double-take as in that usually sterile classroom was the unthinkable: a girl. She was sitting at the front of the class, her exercise book and pens already out, working away as we lingered outside. Unsure what to do, whispers went back and forth, as none of us had seen her before. We silently looked among ourselves to gauge who dared to tell the pretty girl with shiny blonde hair and who seemed to be wearing another school's uniform she was in the wrong place. Instead, we just bundled our way in, everyone navigating to their own desks talking louder and with deeper voices than normal, ignoring the new girl. All apart from me. She was in my seat.

'Sorry, do you usually sit here?' she said, looking up at me as I nervously hovered.

'Oh, here, please.' She pushed her books and stationery a few inches to her left and squeezed her legs together, tightly wrapped in a grey pencil skirt, slipping her bum off her current chair and onto the next one, offering me the seat next to her. I have to say, I watched this movement very much as closely as my classmates had watched Julia Hudson and Amelia Montrose.

'Mr Trioski just put me here. He said most of the desks were free. I guess it's bad luck I took yours.' She smiled this glowing, perfect smile as I forced myself to stop looking at her pencil skirt.

'Are you... new?'

'Yes!' Growing up with a sister should have made me far less awkward around girls than I was. But, as Ellie had both devoted herself to being an uber-bitch since I hit puberty and left for university the previous year, my exposure to girls had eroded completely. I felt this strange lift as she answered my question so enthusiastically. 'First day! First class! In fact, this is my first week back in England and living in Wood Green.'

The girl told me her mother was a diplomat in the Foreign Office, based at the British Embassy in Cape Town for the previous two years, and before that their family had spent time in Malawi, Thailand and Mexico.

'I actually grew up in Hertfordshire, at least until I was eight. It's been fun but I'm a bit nervous about being back – I've been at international schools and there are so many of us with nomadic parents, this definitely now feels like I'm the odd one out. I'm really far behind. I have no idea how I'm going to catch up.'

And so began our friendship. She didn't need me tutoring her. Vicky had already covered most of what we had done at her previous school. But she didn't seem to mind having me as a study buddy, and her work ethic was such that we spent every single lunch break together in the library with our maths books out. And as in most love stories, I fell more and more in love with Vicky with each second we spent together, and I resolved that one day I would win her heart and marry her. And I came so close.

Then, one evening after school, I thought that day had come.

'I can't make lunch break today, I'm afraid. But how about this evening? I have netball, so if you don't mind waiting around, maybe we could go for dinner or something?'

As I have already said, my position in Amberton's social pecking order was pretty much firmly at the bottom. The actors and drama kids ruled the roost and us Games Workshop junkies were pretty much shunned. But unlike my GWWA counterparts, model building was not my only hobby. From age fourteen, I was a regular starter in our school football team. Not just for my age group, but for the ENTIRE SCHOOL. But being the best foot-baller at a school like Amberton was like being the best golfer on the moon.

I was the best because Amberton did not play football. Or any sports. On Wednesday afternoons, priority was given to art and drama and those not gifted, like me, were lambs to the slaughter. As a box-ticking exercise, we had to have one school sports team and hence our oddball XI were pitted against eighteen-year-olds who were at a county standard. Our best result was an 8-3 mauling by Muswell Hill. I won't describe our worst result.

So when Vicky told me that she played netball, I thought this again was fate bringing us together. We together would be the sports geeks. I had never been more nervous and excited as I arrived at the local leisure centre to watch Vicky's match, already mentally preparing all the superlatives I would tell her about her perfor-mance. I sat in the front benches brimming with pride, seeing my beautiful, almost-girlfriend sprint from one side of the hall to the other. That sense of euphoria then melted away as Christoph Koller suddenly appeared. 'Hey,' he grinned, that confident grin of his, and took the seat next to me. He then nodded over to the girl on the court who I thought was the best-kept secret at Amberton. She beamed up and waved enthusiastically back at him. As it turned out, Vicky and Christoph were the best-kept secret, and that night was their first official date as a couple. And what better way to make it official than to invite another couple. So I did end up going on my first ever date that evening. But not with Vicky. Rather as part of a double date, and with a short, redheaded girl from Vicky's netball team called Tiffany Matthews who went to Wood Green High and I had only just met.

Considering the events of later, I should be a lot more

respectful when I think back about Tiffany. After all, she seemed just as enthralled to find out I would be joining her and Vicky at the American-style diner Christoph had suggested we go to. It ended up being four of us in this red leather booth, Vicky and Chris on one side, his arm around her and his jacket covering her shoulders. Christoph would make Vicky giggle, and she didn't mind how he would monopolise her attention, turning her around so she would only face him. On the other side, Tiffany was slumped with her elbow on the table, looking thoroughly bored as I entertained her with philosophical banter such as, 'Have you been playing netball for long?' 'Yes.' 'What's Wood Green High like?' 'Like any school, I guess.'

We left the diner with Vicky and Christoph holding hands, and then Vicky made it clear to us why she had chosen netball over drama by doing an elaborate fake yawn and saying how tired she was and that we should call it a night. Christoph, most gentlemanly, offered to walk her home and the two then left, leaving Tiffany and me alone outside the diner with the neon signage making up for the lack of stars in the night sky. Or at least I thought we were alone. It turned out *I* was alone. While I was debating whether I should ask to walk Tiffany home, she had already departed and was a hundred yards down the road walking quickly by the time I realised she was gone.

With such an inauspicious of evenings, it might be hard to believe that in addition to being my first date, Tiffany Matthews also ended up being my first kiss. This was also largely set up by Vicky, and at a house party just before the start of final exams. Over the two years of sixth form my relationship with Vicky became very much owner and pet. The geeky new girl was soon one of the most popular in the school, but she still kept her study sessions with me and did her best to integrate her weird, loner friend into her new scene of cool arts kids and drama stars. She invited me to parties with her and Christoph, at the majority of which I would drink juice and stand in a quiet spot putting on this big fake smile whenever Vicky found me and asked if I was having a nice time. I have to say, in hindsight, this was incredibly sweet of Vicky, and though at the time I quietly resented having to hang out with people I hardly knew, I see now it would have been easier for her just to ditch the awkward hanger-on.

But one night I was not the only wallflower at the party. Vicky had invited Tiffany, and perhaps acknowledging that having two socially awkward friends at the same party was a challenge even for her optimistic nature, she reintroduced us and then quickly disappeared off with Chris. In all honesty, our second meeting probably went just as well as our first.

'Any idea where Vicky's gone?' I tried to shout over the shit music.

She just turned to me, nodded at the stairs and made a circle out of her finger and thumb on one hand, and then made the motion of inserting two fingers into it with the other. After what felt like an hour of silence sipping some terrible wine from plastic cups, Tiffany then turned to me, scowled and unexpectedly pressed her tongue into my mouth. We continued to do that for pretty much the rest of the party rather than bore each other talking.

I never saw Tiffany Matthews again after that evening. Or at least *that* Tiffany Matthews. When I asked for her phone number, she just scowled again and left the party. Soon we were all leaving for university and I was to say goodbye to Vicky and the Amberton crowd forever. Or so I thought. Christoph and all her other friends at Amberton were going to drama and arts colleges. I expected Vicky to join a fancy London university, somewhere near Goldsmiths to be near Christoph. However, when I shyly showed her my admissions letter to a far less fashionable institution she seemed strangely interested.

A few weeks later, she came into school and excitedly told me we would be 'university buddies'. As she jumped to hug me in the common room I remember feeling intensely flattered and thinking that fate might have another twist in store for us. Sadly, what I also remember about that day was that it was the first time that Vicky had hugged me in such an enthusiastic way and I could feel her bra and breasts press into my chest. She squeezed me tight, euphorically continuing our conversation as I had my hands on her sides, up until the point at which she stopped talking, slowly let go, and gave me an embarrassed smile. She said she should get to class, leaving me to, as subtly and quickly as I could, rush to the toilet cubicles to do something about what Vicky had unmistakably felt pressing into her.

Sadly for me, university caused Vicky and me to drift further apart rather than bringing us together. We ended up in entirely different scenes as her worldliness had her thriving among all the societies and social events. Christoph was long gone, but there were others, and soon she and Paul Gross, the student union president, became the glamour couple. She still made an effort with our friendship, and bizarrely we did share some friends in common – Joan, strangely being her friend first – but my infatuation with her fortunately diminished.

And then came the years after university and the night I met Tiffany again at a London party. We would have been graduated four years by then, and Vicky and I had finally drifted apart, only seeing each other every few months at parties hosted by our university friends. Vicky was still with Paul and it very much looked like they were set for a life of success, marriage, and then beautiful successful children. I had found a bit of a niche of my own too at the bank, enjoying earning money and a widening circle of friends due to the fact that I enjoyed drinking, nights out, and staying up late, talking nonsense with anyone who would listen. For me, post-university was the one big party that university should have been, and suddenly I did not feel as insecure around those who had run societies or student unions. In fact, after a couple of drinks, I did not feel insecure around anyone.

At that particular party, a group of friends and I had barged in late and declared the party had officially started, passing around bottles of gin and vodka and then taking over our host's sound system.

'What you playing?' smiled a girl as I was on the decks. I think it was because she was smiling I had not recognised her. She then laughed.

"I know! It's been years!'

Tiffany Matthews was now a woman, and what's more, a rather charming woman and definitely not the girl I had kissed what would have been a whole decade earlier. We were not moody, melancholy teenagers anymore at a teenage party. I asked what she had been doing the last ten years – university in Scotland, moved to London only recently – what she was doing now – she was copy-editor for a magazine – and what she wanted to drink.

'I was about to go. Vicky and Paul are having one of their deep philosophical conversations in the kitchen and I don't really know anyone.'

'You know me!' I was smiling so hard I hoped it was infectious and I took her glass from her and made her an excessively strong gin cocktail.

The South London flat we were in got more and more crowded as we moved away from the decks to find a quiet corner to talk. She returned from the bathroom and said that it looked like Vicky and Paul had left and perhaps she should too. Again I tried to convince her to stay, but instead, she suggested it would be easier to talk back at her flat. So we did. And so we became the unlikely couple.

What came next is uncomfortable for me to admit. I've always tried to portray myself as the nice guy with geeky tendencies, however what I did to Tiffany really wasn't that nice. We had been invited to a dinner party. Tiff and I had been dating a couple of months and were at the stage where she had asked me to go visit her parents with her in Norfolk. The dinner party itself was hosted by a close friend of Vicky's whom I also knew from our incestuous post-university scene.

On that particular night Tiff had a deadline and didn't manage to leave her office before midnight. Under more normal circumstances, being the only single surrounded by couples would have unnerved me. However, I was not the only single. Vicky was there too. Without Paul. We were hence sat together and what I immediately noticed was how quiet she was. Vicky and I were still friends, but we had long since stopped meeting at lunchtime to do our maths homework together. But that night, I managed to stop her in the hallway before she was about to sneak out the door. She told me about Paul and their breakup. We had our first *real* conversation in years.

'How long has it been going on?' Tiffany screamed at me when we returned to her flat after another dinner party weeks later. This time both of us had been in attendance as well as the newly single Vicky.

'Do you think I'm an idiot?' She had found out about coffee meetings and a dinner between Vicky and me, which I had neglected to tell her. I tried to shrug it off, saying we'd been friends for ten years and it was pretty normal for us to meet for coffee. I had never seen Tiff angry before. Her face literally went as red as her hair.

I was adamant I had done nothing wrong. Even at that dinner, all I had done was sit next to Vicky and make her laugh a couple of times. At one point, she did put her hand on mine while she laughed and then hastily removed it, looking over at Tiffany, who was staring daggers at us.

'Everyone knows! You've made me look a fucking idiot!' At this point she was shouting so hard her voice broke. I tried to maintain this look of astonishment like what she was saying had come completely out of the blue. I was not cheating on Tiffany with Vicky, I was adamant about that. Nothing had happened with Vicky while I was seeing Tiffany. Apart from the secret meetings. And that I held her hand as we drank wine, and she told me about Paul's repeated attempts to diminish her confidence. And that we had a rather prolonged hug after getting a bit drunk and emotional together. And that I had gone to Tiff's straight after, told her I had been at work drinks and had sex with her thinking entirely of Vicky.

'Seriously, Tiff, nothing's going on. Vicky would never look twice at me.'

I don't think the absolute stupidity or hurtfulness of that remark really dawned on me until years later, which said a lot about me at the time. She looked at me in disbelief. Her anger then seemed to crack and she burst into tears. Tiffany and I had been together for nearly three months and in that time, had never argued or really faced any set of trying circumstances. We got on, she seemed accepting of my company, seemed to like having sex with me, and altered my social calendar to do more grown-up things like brunches and dinner parties rather than just hanging out with my flatmates and going to bars. And then, my last memory of her was this sobbing young woman, covering her face and screaming at me to get out. As I said, it was not until years later when I truly appreciated what an arsehole I was, or the irony of then having my heart broken by Vicky.

Vicky had told me that while at university, Paul was passionate, articulate and always determined to get things done, but when they moved to London, she began to see another side of him. One that left her dreading to be alone with him. Behind closed doors, his smooth and suave exterior turned into a moodiness every time he could not get his own way. At university, he was top dog. And suddenly, he wasn't anymore. He had to start again in London like everyone else, but this time all the stars were not revolving around him. Vicky said he hated her work friends and, though always charming at first, if the conversation moved into work-related topics, he would roll his eyes looking bored, keep telling her they should leave, and the minute they were out of the door, go off on a rant about every one of them. Then came the tirades in public.

The night I had held her hand and she had given me that prolonged hug was when she had confided in me that he had started acting aggressive toward her, especially in the bedroom. He began mentioning her previous boyfriends and once, in the middle of the pub, joked with their friends that her popularity at Amberton was because she had given oral sex to the whole drama department.

I knew I was falling back in love with Vicky the evening she had told me she had broken up with Paul. After Tiffany and I had broken up, Vicky and I waited a few weeks before meeting at a restaurant. *Sorry about Tiffany. She told me it didn't work out.* Either Tiffany felt too humiliated to tell her best friend her boyfriend was obsessed with her, or Vicky and I were each as delusional as the other. I wore my best shirt and shoes, and she wore full makeup and a heart-stopping red dress with a low neckline. Rather than hugging, as we had always done when we saw each other, she kissed me on the cheek, like a woman would a man.

We reintroduced each other to our parents. Her dad seemed to look bemused when I turned up, wondering why Vicky's hanger-on, Scott Roberts, had suddenly turned up at his house after all those years. I didn't mind this, though. It was Vicky's mum who perversely made me feel awkward. She was friendly, polite, complimentary, and offered me seconds of apple crumble, all with this knowing, contented smile. Like she knew she would be repeating this exact dinner in a few months with Vicky's real boyfriend and that I was just the warmup act.

But Vicky and I were very much still together those months later. Just long enough for me to take what we had for granted and, in Vicky's eyes, become just another version of Paul. Whereas Paul had ridiculed Vicky in front of his colleagues, I treated her like she was my star prize. When she would see her friends, I would have nights that finished at three o'clock in the morning – my reward for making a success out of my life. And after nine months of not seeing the warning signs, believing I was God's gift to women, of fantasising about other women while sleeping with Vicky much as I had fantasised about Vicky with Tiffany, I asked Vicky to marry me.

I chose to do it at the top of Parliament Hill. Vicky was surprised, to say the least. Everyone around us saw what was happening and with all eyes on her, she said yes when in fact, that was the evening she knew she had to break up with me.

The strangest thing about our 'engagement', to be frank, was the amount of sex Vicky and I started having. Instead of talking or making wedding plans she'd just quietly lead me to bed. At the time, I didn't pay much attention to the fact that she would not kiss me. Just lightly on the lips to start and then kind of getting on with it as she gave me the same somewhat embarrassed smile she had done when we were teenagers and had felt my erection stab her in the thigh. It was like as long as we were having sex, everything was fine. Talking and planning could wait, as could telling other people that we were engaged. But when I suggested we throw an engagement party, she went quiet. I told her I had already told my dad, and for the first and only time, she got angry with me. She said I hadn't consulted her, and my dad would tell her parents, and then she told me that I had ambushed her at Parliament Hill and she needed time to think.

'It's not you, it's me,' she said in the kindest cliché possible as we sat on a park bench. Even a prick like me knew it was coming. We were on Primrose Hill on a cold overcast day, so there were not many other people around. I remember that she was not wearing any makeup and looked sombre in an old boyish jacket and plain turtleneck. We both knew it was a lie and it *was* me. I tried to negotiate saying we should just have a break and catch up in a couple of weeks. She said she loved me very much but as her best friend and she was being unfair to me. And then she left me alone on the bench where I probably stayed for the next three hours. And even though I knew it was coming, I could still feel the bottom fall out of my entire world.

My only consolation was that I deserved it. For how I treated Tiffany, and for treating Vicky like she was a prize rather than a human being with her own dreams and aspirations, which I never bothered even thinking about. And in a way, the whole experience taught me a valuable lesson that would stay with me for the rest of my life. That I deserved to be alone. I complained so long about girls not noticing me and implying they were too shallow to see beyond my geekiness. And when two incredible women finally did, it turned out there wasn't that much worth seeing. I hence deserved to fall in love with someone like Katie and have her not like me back, and I deserved to desire Izzy and have her point out how wanting I was to my face. I want to think there is a *happy ever after* out there for each of us. But not for a prick like me.

CHAPTER 18

HELLO ETHAN

I had regressed to the twelve-year-old who thinks it okay to be mean to girls he actually fancies. And I resented the fact that it was Izzy who was contacting me, not the girl who over the last few days had genuinely made me feel something other than alone and the geek who collects fossils and model orcs. But either way, why would Katie trade in Ethan for someone in their mid-thirties who had had only one proper relationship in their adult life? And why would a girl as attractive and materially centred as Izzy be interested in a recluse who spent his days caked in mud digging allotments?

We all bundled out of the house at midday the day after Boxing Day. Ellie and I broke the habit of a lifetime and voluntarily hugged as we said goodbye at the car.

'I'll call you about Mum.' Millie and Ed were fastened into their car seats and placated by games as I waved the four of them off. Mike had offered me a lift, but I told him they could get stuck in traffic for hours getting through South London. We both also glanced into the back where Millie and Ed were having a contest of who could shout loudest to get Ellie's attention, and Mike gave me a look that he might have preferred to join me on public transport.

On my way back to Loughborough Road, I felt both apprehensive and, if I'm completely honest, a little crushed. Soon that kiss between Katie and me would be forgotten, and we would go back to being as we were. It would be a little awkward at first, but I would eventually return to being Katie's weird flatmate who was too busy running a failing business and playing average guitar to fancy her.

But when I arrived home, the first thing I heard was voices – plural – coming from the kitchen. I had assumed Joan was still at Alison's parents' as there was definitely another man in the house. On the landing, I saw a suitcase outside Katie's room.

'Hello?'

'Hey!' said Katie, staring up at me, a bit startled, across from me at the head of our small dining table. 'I didn't hear you come in.' She had a mug in her hands and some papers in front of her. A boy, probably her age, was sitting next to her. Katie hastily got up.

'Scott, this is Ethan. You've met before, right?'

I shook my head. Ethan, slim, good-looking in a boyband kind of way with well-styled hair, had his phone in front of his face and did not immediately look up at me.

'Hey.' He swapped his phone to his left hand and leaned over to shake mine.

'I told you, babe, we were at Fish's and Bel's last time I came back and Dan and Dani's before that.' He then put his phone down and looked at me with this all-too-comfortable grin. 'Hope this one's not been too much of a pain in the arse.'

'Ethan!'

'Well, you are.' He smirked to himself and then went back to his phone. I said it was really good to meet him, but I'm not sure if the prick noticed from his phone-based reaction.

When I was sixteen, my dad tried with minimal success to tutor me in English literature, perhaps hoping if I understood more about what went into writing a novel, I would appreciate them enough to at least take English for A-level. Most of it went over my head, apart from the term *unreliable narrator*. I liked it because it sounded perverse for an author to tell a story from the point of view of someone untrustworthy. 'It's because we all see things from the way we want to see them. Not necessarily the way they actually are,' Dad had tried to explain. I mention that because when meeting someone for a maximum of thirty seconds, referring to them as a prick probably says more about you than it does about them.

'Scott, Ethan's visiting for a few days. He finished the deal he was doing at work, so he thought he'd surprise me – '

'Here, that's the train we need, not the one you were saying.'

The prick flipped his phone around and held it in front of Katie's face as she gave one or both of us an uneasy smile, her eyes darting between the two of us. Taking that as agreement, he then crossed his legs and rocked back on his chair, his eyes back on his phone.

'We're probably going to be travelling around the next week or so, so we won't be in your hair, hopefully.'

'Yeah, I'm not sure this place could handle a third person. Your brother's really screwed you over.' Again, Ethan smirked and chuckled to himself.

I felt my eyes narrow. Okay, the flat was a shithole, but it was mine and Katie's shithole. I realised it was weird me loitering in the doorway. The original plan was just to say hello, act positive and normal, excuse myself, and go to my room, all of which I could still do. I looked at Katie. She was giving me the sympathetic smile I felt I had seen so often.

'Okay, maybe I'll see you tomorrow morning. I'm a bit shattered from today, so...' It all came out monosyllabic, and I stopped because no one was listening to me. Ethan showed Katie something else on his phone that held her attention, so I left them to it.

. . .

So that was Ethan. The strange thing was I think I would have liked him if I met him three months earlier, before Katie and I had become friends. He seemed to have a high opinion of himself and probably grew up too entitled to understand the concept of manners. A perfect match for the up-herself *Duchess* I tried so hard to avoid. But as for the woman who I had recently come to know, I felt a little bit disappointed in her. Ethan was good-looking, confident and, from both meeting him and hearing Katie talk about him, a bit of an arsehole. What did that say about her?

I knew it was probably envy turning me sour. I was the one determined to be the arsehole, so I thought it best all round to stay in my room. Having spent three nights sleeping on that old, uncomfortable camp bed, I closed my eyes and let fatigue take over, falling asleep fully clothed.

I awoke to hear the house in silence and find a substantial patch of drool on my pillow. Desperately needing a wee, I groggily stumbled to my feet and cautiously opened my bedroom door. Downstairs, all the lights were off, with only a glow coming from beneath Katie's door. I quickly used the bathroom and was just about to go back upstairs when I heard it. It was a yelp of pain. I stopped where I was – between the bathroom door and Katie's. I heard it again. It wasn't loud, but it was undoubtedly a high-pitched yelp, followed by another, and another. Was Katie alright? I instantly thought, looking at her door. *Is that bastard hurting her?* I can only blame the cocktail of sleeplessness and grogginess for taking even longer than a split second to guess what the sounds obviously were. Perhaps part of me did not want to put the sounds I was hearing into context. So I stayed rooted to the spot, suddenly thinking back to Izzy's assessment of our flat's soundproofing.

'Fuck, babe, I've missed this. You're so fucking doing it...'

I raised my foot quickly to get away from Katie's door. As I did, an ear-splitting creak sounded from our ancient floorboard. I pushed my foot immediately back down, looking horrified at the door, paranoid they had heard me. Fully aware now how even the lightest muttering of noise could travel between rooms, I stood frozen, trying not to make another sound. There was silence. Oh fuck, they *had* heard me. I felt a coldness shooting through me as I tried to lift my foot again gently. This time the creak was slower and more pronounced. I squeezed my eyes closed, anticipating Katie's door being thrust open and Katie glaring at the creepy pervert listening outside. Instead, I then heard more yelps. And then a little more commentary.

'Yeah, babe, just do that. I'm so fucking close.'

I had to go. I seriously had to not be there. I slid my foot back quickly, unable to avoid another creak, but thrust myself onto the next floorboard. I then did a weird dance taking enormous, wide strides on tiptoes to the stairs, hoping the boards' edges would creak less than the middle. I got back to my room, closed the door, and stood with my back against it, horror-struck at what I had ear-witnessed.

CHAPTER 19

BARNET FOOTBALL CLUB

Barnet. The Up n' Under. Football at its most pure. The art of bypassing flair and skill and instead hoofing the ball from midway inside your own half into the opponents' penalty area every single time one of your players wins possession. There was something to admire in our commitment to it. Even when we had one of the most skilful players in the world – admittedly aging – Dutch master Edgar Davids, we would throw bodies forward, aim to jump higher with more gusto, and bundle the ball into the goal. But even for Barnet Football Club, as I stood at the North Stand with my orange scarf around my shoulders close enough to the action to audibly hear our centre-half say, 'piss off, you wanker' to their forward, this was football at its most dire.

It was a freezing cold December afternoon, and we had just had forty-five minutes with no reason to shout, cheer, jump, or remove our hands from our pockets. Those around me were moving towards the exits for a half-time pie or warm drink. We were two-nil down to... to be honest, I had not even heard of the other team – we had been relegated the previous season all the way out of the football league and were playing against teams I was pretty sure were still of an amateur status. And to make things more humiliating, it was their fans who were singing at us, *who are ya? who are ya?*

Something I'm pretty sure most football fans are aware of is that usually when your life is shit, your team typically chooses that moment to pile the misery on, and that day was no exception. I was well aware that Katie and Ethan were both consenting adults, and they had not seen each other for months, hence the only surprise should have been that they were still fully clothed at the dining table.

At that exact moment, Katie would be on the train to Ethan's parents, huddled in his arms, thoughts of me highly unlikely to flitter across her mind. Apart from maybe how much she hated me and how seethingly angry she still was. In my defence, I didn't exactly walk into the kitchen and tell her that I had spent part of my evening listening to her having sex with her boyfriend. It just kind of came out.

'I'm so sorry,' she said, looking up from a rucksack on the dining table as I entered the kitchen that morning. For the briefest of moments, I thought she was apologising for me having heard her lovemaking. I had not got a wink of sleep. I had stayed awake the night watching my watch move closer to dawn, feeling more and more tired yet unable to close my eyes without seeing them both doing what they were doing.

'Ethan takes super long showers. I meant to remind him that he's sharing the bathroom.'

'Oh. No problem,' I mumbled a little groggily as I moved to the kettle, trying my best not to look at her. 'I guess he probably needs it.' I caught a quizzical expression on her face, but she returned to her rucksack.

'We're catching the eleven-thirty train. With all the changes we need to make, it will probably take us most of the day. And I think we're coming back the week after New Year as some uni friends are doing a barge trip. I had time off booked anyway, so we might as well do something fun. Do I have everything?'

She stood up staring at the bag, frowning and then rubbing her head.

'While he's in the shower,' she said, lowering her voice. 'I wanted to say, I hope this isn't weird, Ethan staying over? Because of Christmas. We've become such good friends recently, and I didn't want there to be any awkwardness?'

'Don't worry about it.' I turned my back, pouring the kettle. 'Can you pass me the milk?' I don't think she expected such a matter-of-fact reaction. She went back to her rucksack, hunching over to stare into it. She then stood back up, covering her mouth with her hand while she stifled a big yawn.

'I don't know what's wrong with me today. I'm so tired I can't think straight.'

'I bet you are,' I said, kind of under my breath but audible enough to hear.

'Scott, is there something you want to say?' She turned toward me as I put the kettle down. Her hands were on her hips, very similar to the stance she gave Joan and me for another invasion of her privacy. For some reason, I thought honesty was the best policy.

'No. It's just the flat's not soundproof, remember.' I gave a raise of my eyebrows, which I think might have been to indicate that I was trying to be subtle. Perhaps I thought she would laugh about it and then say something like, *I'm so sorry! I didn't realise.* Even if I had had just two hours of sleep I think I would have known that that was not going to happen. Instead, she pretty much let me have it.

'Excuse me. If you have something to say, please come out and say it and not make a series of innuendos that I am somehow meant to understand.'

'Well, I think you might already know what I'm talking about, so there's not much point in me saying it.'

It was a cartoonesque moment where her jaw actually did drop.

'Were you... listening? To me and Ethan... Urrggh! You creep!'

'I didn't have much choice. Like Izzy said, sound travels.'

'No it bloody doesn't. Not if you don't want it to and not all the way upstairs. What were you doing, getting your little thrills while you snooped on us?'

'It wasn't like that.'

It was all a déjà vu of the whole dating profile fiasco. She was both livid and hissing things at me, probably keeping her voice low so the conversation didn't reach Ethan in our non-soundproofed bathroom.

'Oh this is low even for you.'

'What's that supposed to bloody mean?'

For some reason, that really touched a nerve. It was like the last couple of months had not happened, and I was still the flatmate who had once snogged her against her will. I tried to screw up my face to look both hurt and annoyed. We then locked eyes and stood silent, each of us glaring at the other

'I'm not doing this. You're not worth it. We can discuss this when I get back.' She started thrusting a series of items from on the table into her bag, including our dishcloth and my vitamin supplements. 'We can also discuss which of us is moving out because I really can't stand the sight of you right now.'

They deserve each other, I petulantly thought, slumped on the terrace as Barnet's subdued North Stand got emptier. If she still thought I was the creep she had met six years ago, then I was determined to see her as the shallow snobby-nosed little girl whose life revolved around nights out and an arrogant pretty-boy boyfriend. But I didn't think that of her. I was actually thinking about how I could apologise again. For two relatively mild-mannered people, this was our third fight. I only had two ever with women prior to moving in with Katie, and in both I mainly stood back, made one dumb comment, and watched while the other person got upset.

It began to feel even colder without as many people around me. I looked out at the pitch and saw a couple of our subs doing line drills, perhaps going to come on at halftime. Usually, the banter around me would be boisterous, but our team's lacklustre effort seemed to be infectious. I knew I should get a tea to warm me up, but the queues would have been ridiculous, so I stayed slumped on the terrace railing, wallowing in regret, hoping it was an empty threat her saying one of us should move out. I knew I should leave it a day or two to let her cool down, but I got my phone out anyway.

Listen, I got up in the night to use the bathroom. I was disorientated and heard weird noises as it's usually dead silent. That's all. When I realised I went straight upstairs and put my headphones on.

I wasn't going to apologise. She was at least half to blame for the argument. And I was not going to be called a pervert. In hindsight, the headphones bit was a bit much.

I then slumped further, feeling as empty as the stand I was standing in.

'Howdy, stranger,' came a familiar and yet completely surprising voice. Standing behind me with an uncharacteristic orange and black Barnet scarf wrapped around her, and linking arms with a smiling man in thin silver-framed glasses and a smart black coat, who I vaguely recognised, was Camille, my therapist. I did a double-take. I had never seen her outside her therapist's office before, let alone at the last place I would imagine her – a Barnet football game.

'I told Jim we might bump into you. After all, how many of you guys could there be?'

'Excuse Cammy's sarcasm,' smiled the man, offering me his

hand. He then gave me this look of faint recognition. 'You drink at the Dog and Duck, don't you? Post-match?'

'Yes!' I said, suddenly cheering up at being recognised by a fellow Bee. It was surreal seeing Camille in a non-workplace setting. Like two different worlds colliding.

'This is my Christmas present to Jim. Buying the tickets and sharing the experience. I have no idea why I did not do this earlier. Just think of all those cafés, museums, and galleries I've been wasting my time at.'

'I've been trying to tell her it isn't always this bad. The midfield's been non-existent, and Underwood's had an absolute shocker even for him.'

I instantly liked Jim. He was very much the gentleman football fan and would look more suited to a corporate box at Twickenham than alongside the rest of us rabble.

'Right. Coffee?' He pointed at me. 'I told Cammy the steak and kidney pie would make all this worth the ordeal. One for yourself, too?'

'No don't worry, it's – '

'Yes he will. If I'm getting food poisoning, I'm taking both of you down with me.'

Leaving us, Jim joined the queue for the exit and Camille joined me at the terrace rail.

'So here's a first. The therapist stalking her client. This could be that screenplay I always said I'll write.'

She had on her usual beaming smile and was bobbing on the spot. Her hands were deep in her pockets as she stood.

'I thought you were ardently against coming to a game?' I smiled.

'Sometimes you have to spice it up. Step outside the comfort zone. Plus, dinner will be his treat, and I fancy something very stereotypically American that would have Jim cringing at the cheesiness.'

Around us, a couple of fans were coming back to the terraces with drinks and pies.

'So, I feel I'm going to end up donning my therapist's hat, or we're just going to stand here awkwardly while you pretend to be all cheerful. So let's cut to the chase?'

She was still smiling while I stared back blankly.

'I saw you a while back. I have to say, Scott, even considering what we were watching, you looked pretty miserable.'

'I didn't realise.'

'And why should you? It's not every day you have a health professional spying on you. You're entitled to look and be miserable. It's healthy. In a way.'

I gave a small laugh and then leaned with my hip on the railing.

'Housemate issues.'

'What, again?' she said kindly, a touch jokingly which made me feel a little more at ease. 'New issues or still related to you and your night of passion with her foxy best friend?'

'We kissed.'

'Shocker!' beamed Camille.

'I'm sorry, Scott, I'm not the kind of therapist who can shift back and forth into my highly professional manner at the drop of a hat. You may have to deal with a hybrid of Camille, the obnoxious Yank. But that's generally a good thing, isn't it? To kiss a girl who you like a little more than just as a roommate.'

'Not when her boyfriend then comes over for a conjugal visit.'

I briefly relayed details of Christmas and the events after. Camille listened patiently with a slightly off-putting amused smile.

'I'm sorry, I am sympathetic, but this is progress. You're getting back out there. You've made it clear to someone you care about what your feelings are. That's brave. And if it is any consolation, we don't normally have these arguments or fights with people we're indifferent to. I guess the next step of the journey is dealing with it when our bravery hasn't quite paid off. Letting it hurt for a while. But knowing it will end. And that with each one we get a bit closer to finding the person of our dreams just as long as we don't give up. But, yeah, it takes a lot of work, so I'm booking you in for another six months of sessions at least.'

Camille grinned at me and then looked over my shoulder, waving to who I assume was the returning Jim. She then, surprisingly, punched me on the arm. 'But for now, cheer up! You got to first base with a hot chick. Worry about the rest tomorrow.'

I tried my best to let Camille's advice resonate. The problem was, and I have found this before with therapy, that while you can have these Eureka moments of emotional understanding, rogue feelings and unhelpful monologues do not come with an off-switch. Just the thought of going back to Loughborough Road reminded me of the idiot I was, so I made my way back to Wood Green and revisited another area of my life that was slowly going downhill.

'Margery would be very pleased to see this,' Jane said, handing me a cup of tea as I removed the weeds from her front lawn. 'She will be back from France next week and asked me to tell you that you can start work on Tuesday.' Bringing with me from South London a hoe and set of medium-sized trowels and forks which I knew Dad did not have in his shed, I spent the first afternoon down the road from the old house, in the garden belonging to Dad's best friend.

Jane was in her mid to late sixties, I think, retired and had probably been our family's one point of continuity over the previous year. She had a large house with a spacious suburban garden just a few streets away. However, she would still be the one to attend

Dad's house on almost a weekly basis and make sure the junk mail had not built up, the dust had not accumulated, or burglars had not ransacked the place. All in exchange for access to Dad's study and library of books.

Jane had also become my agent regarding my gardening business. My door-to-door leafleting campaign was not having the response I had hoped – or having any response at all – so Jane had spread word amongst her friends, which had resulted in two phone calls, and I was set to start work on one the following week. In return, I offered to de-weed and restore her flowerbeds, partly as a thank you, and partly as a distraction.

Sorry for being an arsehole, read the apology I finally sent Katie – I received no response from my blunt explanation message. I had sent it while the Piccadilly line was still overground as I completed my three-day North London hiatus and returned south to spend New Year's Eve crop planting on the allotment.

That day I spent eight hours trying to make up for my time in North London, busying myself physically so I would stop checking my phone to see if Katie had replied. I also wondered if I should just call her, remembering the days before mobile phones when you had to dial someone's number and wait in anticipation to speak to somebody. I could still call her – I'm pretty sure phones did still have that function – but it would tell her it was me calling, and if she didn't answer my message, why would she pick up my call? So, standing over a trench I had just dug, and my foot on my garden fork, I dialled her number.

It took only two rings before my call was diverted to Katie's answerphone message. I had my answer. The light had faded entirely by the time I decided enough was enough in the allotment, but not before stabbing myself in the foot with the fork, tearing my trainer up in the darkness.

I tried to console myself with the thought that Katie was on a barge with friends and, in such close proximity, taking such a phone call would have been somewhat uncomfortable. So, limping back to Loughborough Road, I tried to push away all unhelpful, disheartening thoughts.

Our flat had been in darkness for almost four days when I unlocked the door and climbed the stairs. There had been a light rainstorm in the afternoon, and my now bloodstained trainers were caked in mud. My forehead and hair were in a similar state from when I kept trying to wipe the steady mist out of my face. There was also something of the wet dog odour to me as I immediately went to the bathroom for a much needed hot shower.

'Nothing's happening, mate, it's just clicking away,' I then had to say to Joan, phone pressed between my shoulder and ear, my clothes back on and my hand inserted into our boiler.

'Hold it down for three seconds. Let go. Wait. Do it again. Wait, and then press and let go. I've already told Katie twice. It's not difficult.'

'How did you even come up with this? It's not the most logical thing especially if you're bloody freezing and can't feel your hands.'

'Don't be such a baby. And it's fucking obvious. Same principle to starting a car. If you flood the engine nothing's gonna happen.'

'Jesus!' I suddenly heard a mini combustion and felt an intense heat on the back of my fingers as I tried to get my hand out of the boiler as quickly as possible.

'Oh yeah, you might want to watch out. Too much gas and you've got a fireball.'

I looked into the boiler and saw a blue flame. Though it would be at least an hour until I had hot water or a warm flat.

'How are you guys spending tonight?' I asked Joan, a little more grateful as if not for him, I'd be washing in a bucket of water and then spending New Year's Eve trying not to freeze to death.

'Some lame party. Alison and I are still at my mum and dad's.

We thought it would be cheap, plus Ali now knows a couple of Katie's old school friends who will be there, so she's happy.'

I couldn't help thinking that this was as selfless as it could get for Joan.

'At least Katie's out of the house now. She came down yesterday with twat-face – I forgot what an annoying suck-up she can be.'

I half-smiled.

'He's not grown on you?'

'Nah, but who gives a fuck. I'm not the one doing him.'

I stopped smiling. I could hear some background noise on Joan's end as I perched on our windowsill, not wanting to get mud on any of the chairs. A hairdryer was going and someone seemed to be calling out to Joan as he replied muffling the phone.

'And she's back to thinking you're a total nob-end again, so well done on that front.' I could picture the smirk on his face as he chuckled. I asked him what she had said.

'Nothing, just did the typical Katie thing and rolled her eyes, shaking her head like it was too beneath her to discuss, like she does with Niles and me. So I assumed you've not been using coasters for your tea or something equally barbaric.'

It probably says something about me when a conversation with Joan cheers me up. I had confirmation that Katie was openly pissed off with me – enough to tell other people. But I at least had someone on my side – because he was a complete prick too. She and Ethan would be on the barge getting ready for what, truth be told, sounded quite a romantic New Year's.

I paced the flat, tapping radiators waiting for the water system to warm up. I could hear music coming from somewhere down Loughborough Road. Someone was probably having a party. However, I had my night planned: shower, then reread *Essays in Love*, hoping a bit of modern philosophy would help plug that hole I was beginning to feel somewhere within my chest. But before that, I picked up my phone again, went to my unanswered messages to Katie, and wrote one more.

Sorry for how we left things. I really didn't mean to act the way I did. Hope you and Ethan are having a good break and hope you have an enjoyable New Year's.

I then dropped my phone on the sofa cushions and let it disappear from view.

I had just taken off my mud-stained jumper, relieved at the sight of warm steam coming from the shower, when the doorbell rang. I thought it was just belated Christmas carollers or someone with the wrong address for a house party, so I ignored it. Whoever it was then rang again. And again. And again.

Irritated at my long-awaited shower being postponed, I ran down the stairs gritting my teeth and telling myself not to tell whoever it was to fuck off.

'Oh. You *are* home.' Izzy was standing on my doorstep arms folded, staring at me, looking annoyed.

'Thanks for picking up your phone.' She gave me a surly look and then turned around and waved to someone. I saw a car flash its lights and pull away.

'Katie wasn't sure if you'd be in but I was in a cab anyway. I need one of my dresses back. Ahem, can you let me in?'

It wasn't a request. She stepped close and glared at me for being in her way. As I eventually moved, I noticed she wasn't exactly dressed for standing outside on a cold night. From what I could see, she was only wearing a black skirt – no tights – and whatever was underneath a thin-looking green leather jacket.

'I wasn't sure if you'd be out doing whatever it is you do,' she said, climbing the stairs. 'I would have given you more warning but I didn't fancy wading through another gulf of sarcasm.'

She twirled around to look at me as she reached the top.

'Drunken error over Christmas, by the way. Katie implied I may have hurt your feelings, so my present to her was to say sorry to her *wittle fwiend*. Very much not happening again.'

She made her way into the kitchen and unzipped her jacket, throwing it onto the sofa. She stood in the middle of the room, looking around with a sneer, like she didn't know what she would catch if she were to touch anything. She then stared at me, really scrunching up her face as she examined mine.

'Is that mud?' It came out like this was the first time she had ever come across it. Which would not have surprised me. 'It's on your neck. And in your hair!' She stepped forward looking borderline horrified, and really began peering at my mesh of dark locks. With the heels she was wearing, we were at eye level.

'Oh my God, and you smell. You actually smell.' She stepped backwards making, to me, a rather tedious show of recoiling.

'Thanks.'

'Like a hockey field, or a friend's mangy wolfhound. You realise that, don't you? You're covered in dirt and smell like a dog?'

I stood as I was, close to the door. Cold, muddy and hungry, I regarded having a surprise visit from Izzy as one of the last experiences I was looking to have that evening. It was also rich that she accused *me* of being sarcastic. I tried my best to maintain eye contact and look as passive as possible. Eliciting no response, she rolled her eyes and walked to the window, glancing out. Seeing that she was only supposed to be picking up a dress, I wondered how long we were going to have this stand-off.

'You know, I was spending Christmas at my father's when I messaged you. Well, his place in Chamonix. Me, his girlfriend, a couple of cousins. Standard Christmas – drinking wine, remaining on best behaviour, getting a bit bored late into the evening so I thought I might have a bit of fun with you. Be a bit of a prick-tease. Turns out I wasn't the only one.'

She spun back around, arms folded and grinning – a wide, slightly psychotic smile rather like The Joker in *Batman*. She then marched up to me and shoved her phone in my face.

'*Will Scott be in Katikins?*' she read, seeming to have memorised a WhatsApp exchange she was showing me. 'That's my pet name for her. Well, one of them. *Sorry I don't know.*' She put on a girly voice to mimic Katie. *I thought you were BFFs*, was Izzy's response. *Just ask him if I can collect my dress, or better still tell him which one it is and have him leave it in a Selfridges bag on your doorstep so I don't have speak to the cretin.*

'*Things are a bit complicated between us right now. We're not exactly speaking.*' Izzy had taken back the phone and was narrating, beaming away, apparently wholeheartedly entertained. She placed her hand on her wide open mouth to emphasise the drama.

'Here, read the rest yourself.'

Self-satisfied, she thrust the phone into my hand.

OMG! You slept with him! You total slut and hypocrite!! – there was then a series of smiley and winking faces.

No! Nothing like that. We just had a moment.

Shame. We could have compared notes. He was pretty dreadful to be fair though. I couldn't help scowling but also needed to read on.

We kissed. While Ethan and I were having a fight. And now it is super weird. I don't know why I'm telling you this. Please don't call him or go over.

There were more messages but I held the phone out for a delighted Izzy to collect.

'You seem really pleased at yourself for someone who has just found out her best friend is feeling like shit.'

'It's called vindication. This is the same best friend who called me a slut for doing exactly what she's almost done but was too lame to go the whole hog.'

'I thought you had both made up?'

Izzy's smile diminished slightly. Instead she folded her arms and then, still standing, crossed one leg over the other like a ballet dancer.

'Perhaps I was a little bit hasty. After all, what's worse, occasionally doing something sketchy and apologising for it after. Or making someone feel like shit for a month and then doing exactly the same thing? Like, which is worse, Scott? To be the slut, or the prick-tease?'

The smile had now fully disappeared.

'You know she's boning his brains out?'

It was a sudden shift. No belittling sarcastic reply, as per last time. Straight on the offensive.

'They're with the old Oxford set. Apparently it's been quite the giggling point. You see the walls on a barge aren't overly thick apparently and the happy couple have been at it like rabbits morning, noon and night. Wouldn't have taken Spoiler for a *nooner*. I assumed it was birthdays and Christmas only.'

'I think you've made your point.'

'Oh, touched a nerve, have I?' The big, wide grin returned. And for the first time, I think I surprised her by doing the last thing she might have expected. I smiled back. Not a huge, I'm-having-a-wonderful-time smile, but neither was it false or sarcastic. I leaned against the wall, just observing her. It was all a game, or at least she wanted to make it one so there was a winner and loser and she could prove she was the former. But that might have been my own pop psychology at work. One of the mindfulness exercises I had learned over the last year was to take myself out of my head and be fully present, observing what was physically in front of me. And what was in front of me, if I tuned out the noise and the context, was Izzy.

Objectively, she was still very, very beautiful. The teenage version of me would have been flattered that a girl like her would even notice me. But then again, that was the same teenager who put women on pedestals as something to attain, rather than get to know and understand. I had liked getting to know Katie, I thought, as Izzy remained standing triumphant in front of me. It was a pleasant unexpected highlight of a forgettable year. I did not need to feel admonished by Izzy for liking someone whom I had enjoyed getting to know.

'No. Not touched a nerve. Katie's been miserable for months about the whole Ethan thing. It's nice to know things are back on track, and she's feeling happier.'

Again, I smiled a small, sad smile, thinking of my friend and how grateful I was to have had her enter my life. I don't know why Izzy was that desperate to get a reaction, but it was New Year's Eve and a time for reflection, and I did not need to let her diminish my one positive of that year.

'I *was* about to use the shower before you came round. And I'm assuming Katie's dresses are in her bedroom rather than in here, so it might be best if you see yourself out when you're done.'

I took a step backward, out the door. Izzy remained glaring at me with that piercing stare of hers.

'I don't mean to be rude, but like you said, Katie isn't here and we're not exactly friends. I'm sure it will only take you one minute to find what you're looking for.'

The light in Katie's room was on when I got out of the shower. Her door was ajar and I caught sight of Izzy's shadow moving as I went upstairs. While in the shower, I tried my best to listen to the running water, think of descriptions of how it felt against my skin, look down at the muddy pool that was flowing into the plughole – all these things to be in the moment and not miles somewhere else on a barge watching Katie lie on her back while a skinny pretty-boy was naked on top of her thrusting away, making her cry out with pleasure. I did agree with Izzy on one thing – I too thought Katie was a birthdays and Christmas type of girl. Not intending to be disparaging, but I had built her up as the Disney Princess, a romantic ideal who only made love on her wedding night and was too busy thinking about ponies and unicorns to have her own sexual desires. It was like Vicky all over again. Did I even like Katie, or did I want this fantasy of chaste love? All the women I had claimed to love or care about, perhaps I didn't. The real pattern seemed to be me using them to create unrealistic ideals and not bother to get to know them as human beings.

Entering my room, I hoped Izzy did not stay much longer. I had meticulously planned my New Year's Eve so as to currently be lying across the sofa re-reading *Essays in Love*, treating myself to a hot chocolate while all the parties and fireworks displays around me kicked into full swing. However, as I opened my door, I saw two items that should not have been where they were. A white shirt lay on my bed, and next to it, a piece of notepaper.

OMG, you own a shirt! A grown man in his thirties who only owns one shirt… I'm sorry for storming into your house and being the Uber Bitch. I found wine in the cupboard. Please come downstairs and join me? Please.

There was a smiley face. She had used the word, *please*. Twice. And the word, sorry. I suddenly examined the note for traces of anthrax or similar poisons. I then looked down at my shirt.

P.S. Give the shirt a go, who knows, you might look quite handsome…

On the kitchen table were the bottle of wine and two glasses. I then heard my name called in a voice I didn't recognise.

'Scott, can you pour me a glass? It's a merlot I had bought when I came over a while back, so it's technically mine.'

The voice was Izzy's, but there was no sharpness or sneer. It wasn't condescending and didn't even have that public schoolgirl twang. What was left was a calm flat accent, like mine. She actually sounded older i.e. not like a spoilt brat, and I strangely didn't mind pouring wine for her.

'I'm just trying on a dress for tonight. I'll need you to tell me what you think.' Again, it was like walking into *The Twilight Zone*. Or a trap. I poured the wine, sat down, and took a sip.

'Does this look okay?'

I looked up. Izzy was in the doorway in a green dress with a wide black belt, which I vaguely recalled Katie wearing to work. But Katie would wear leggings under it as its hem would fall an inch above her knees. Izzy was bare-legged and taller, so, on her, the hem hardly touched her thighs.

'It's probably the nicest one she owns, and I want something that goes with my eyeshadow. What do you think about the length?'

I also remembered that Katie would wear a long-sleeved top underneath it too. Casually, she then twirled, showing me the back and then her side. It was certainly eye-catching. It was difficult not to stare at her long, toned legs.

'It's more a belt than a dress, isn't it? Shame, but judging from your expression, for the best. Can't have the boys popping their corks *before* midnight.'

She came back wearing the skirt that Katie had worn when she had sat drinking wine on my bed. I refrained from pointing out that it wasn't that much longer. Instead, I sat with my wine, trying not to feel unnerved by the sudden shift in dynamics.

'So,' she then said, sipping her wine. 'You're still the last man I've slept with. Make of that what you will.'

I didn't know what to make of it. She said it matter-of-factly like she was telling me a train had been cancelled.

'I had a boyfriend before you. Someone I met through the gallery. Total stud. Bit older than you. Very successful. And fucking amazing in bed.'

She smiled, a more natural, quite sweet smile, with a small laugh.

'Actually, tell a lie, we never did it in a bed. Our first time was at another gallery in Shoreditch. We'd been flirting and I told him I needed to get my coat. He went with me. Kissed me. And before I knew it we were in a quiet corner of the cloakroom, my dress around my midriff and him just fucking me senseless against the wall. The last time we had sex I told him I had to work late at my gallery and offered him a behind the scenes tour. It was fun. Quite naughty. It's quite liberating being completely undressed in the centre of your workplace having some man doing pretty much whatever he wants to you. Within reason, that is.'

She crossed her legs and sat side-on on her chair, sipping her wine with another self-satisfied smile which looked more like the Izzy I thought I knew. I kept listening, not sure where the story was going. I would have liked to believe it was her way of flirting with me, but I really didn't get that vibe. It was more like she had stopped seeing me as a man, and instead, I had become a sounding board or confessional.

'Oh, tell another lie. I kept my heels on. As I said, we never had sex in a bed. One reason being that his long-term girlfriend was tucked up in his. I guess, according to him, boning some skank he met through work is no more cheating than it is sport.'

She let her eyes kiss mine briefly and then gazed away.

'Shame though. He was a fun lay. I was also a little in love with him, so when he turned up again expecting to screw me in the storage vaults, I politely declined. Hence, slutty Izzy, whose friends are quick to condemn her for sleeping with quasi-married men, had her heart broken. And said friends never bothered to notice.'

Still sitting side-on, she drank from her glass again, this time for a little longer as my silence had become somewhat awkward.

'Do you still see him?' It wasn't that great a question, but I wasn't sure what to say.

'You could say that. Messages. Drunken phone calls. He came to our client Christmas party. I tried to ignore him but that didn't work. He knew the quiet corners of our gallery by then, and I was the drunk girl who gets felt up over the photocopier. Or in the refinement room, in our case. We didn't have sex but... well, let's just leave it there shall we?'

'Does Katie know any of this?'

She shook her head.

'Just the sex stories. Not the feelings bullshit. As I said, she assumed it was just sex, and I can't be bothered correcting her.'

'How come you're telling me?'

She gave a big elaborate shrug. She then put her glass down, smiled, and leaned over to me.

'Because it is exhausting being the Queen Bitch twenty-four-seven. Can I have just one night where I get drunk and pour my heart out to a total stranger?'

'Mine split up when I was thirteen.'

'Oh! *My* parents split when I was eighteen! First year of Oxford!' Izzy clapped her hands together, bouncing up excitedly. 'At last! Something we have in common.'

I was side-on on my chair, leaning with my back against the wall, a grin upon my face. Izzy reached over and poured the dregs of wine into our glasses.

'Right, there's one more.' She got up and went behind me into our larder cupboard.

'Don't you have to leave soon? What time's your party?'

'Scott, by the fact you've just asked that question says it all entirely. The party begins when I arrive and ends when the most gorgeous boy kisses me and begs me to go home with him.'

She came back with another bottle. It had been a strangely enjoyable evening. When she wasn't being herself – or at least the person she wanted people to think she was – Izzy was good fun. She was a lot more bubbly and animated than I had seen her. And she *could* smile without irony or malice. She might have considered smiling made her look less attractive, but it did give her a sweet, adorable quality, which I'm sure she would have been thrilled to hear me say. She began pouring the wine, but rather than going back around the table to her seat, she sat at the chair nearest to me. One that had successfully acted as neutral ground between us and had my foot resting against it.

'I also wouldn't mind a relatively mellow one. Duck in at midnight. Quick snog. Quickish sex with someone hopefully rich, handsome and single, and then catch the train tomorrow in a relatively more sober state so I can spend some quality time in my mother's greenhouse working on some pots I've got going.'

I was unable to keep a straight face.

'You like gardening?'

'What's so funny? Is it really surprising to imagine me getting my hands dirty and fiddling in the soil?'

'A little. Considering what I do for a living, and your earlier advice to me.'

'Well I do. I even take off a week a year just to help Mummy replanting the *phalaenopsis, alstroemeria and rosa.* What? Surprised I speak Latin? I do have a first from Oxford in Art History and Classics.'

'No, I'm surprised to hear a grown woman use the word

Mummy.'

She rolled her eyes.

'Oh, don't be an arsehole. I'm actually starting not to dislike you at the moment.'

She then reached for the bottle and topped up both our glasses slightly. 'How do you refer to your mother then?'

'I don't. We haven't spoken in about six years.'

'Ouch! And I'm meant to be the heartless one.'

I told Izzy about Orletta going off to find fame and fortune as an artist, and how, as our meetings became more sporadic due to her other commitments, we eventually drifted apart. It was a bit like referring to an old school friend. I briefly described what we had learned after Dad's funeral and how Ellie and I had let things drift, probably a bit afraid to sit down with her. To be fair to Izzy, she was a surprisingly good listener.

'I sold one of your mother's paintings once. One of my first sales. Katie mentioned you were related a few months back. Obviously, it's a common surname and you do not remotely look like the son of a successful artist. Successful binman or lorry driver, maybe.'

She casually sipped her wine as I felt my jaw drop.

'Hey!' I frowned. If anything, it was derogatory to binmen, who were always helping me out taking my garden waste from the allotments.

'Oh, you know what I mean. If I knew you were Orletta Roberts' son, I probably would have let you see me naked a lot earlier. Perhaps that night you tried to grope my best friend in that disgusting little club.' She shuddered, apparently at the thought of the indie clubs Joan and I would frequent.

'Mummy and I probably grew closer after the divorce. God, she hated Daddy. For years. So every holiday I had with him, she had to surpass it. Right up until the point where we were practically sisters going out to bars together at five-star resorts, us giggling

eyeing up very, very cute boys. In hindsight it was a little bit odd –
not us holidaying together, more that I wasn't exactly subtle about
my nocturnal activities while we were away. My therapist calls it
my acting-out phase and said Mummy's enabling of it was a
subconscious dig at Daddy: I was *definitely* not his little girl
anymore. Which is a charming way of calling me a ho and her my
pimp, don't you think?'

She poured more wine and gave this incredulous look.

'I actually see a therapist too.'

'There's a shocker.' She didn't even look up from pouring our
glasses. 'Artist's son, former aid worker, now gardener, who is
madly in love with his poor, tortured little flatmate, I can't imagine
what issues you would have to talk about.'

In a way, I was beginning to enjoy her cutting comments.
There was an honesty about how she saw things.

'Anyway, back to my story,' she grinned, sitting back in her
chair, one leg stretched out so that her bare foot was resting on my
shin.

'You and many others may be surprised to know that I lost my
virginity pretty late, comparatively. All-girls school, you see. I did
have a boyfriend when I was seventeen but it was more like having
a boyfriend for the sake of one. Don't misunderstand me, I wasn't a
prude or the other way inclined – I can see your male mind
working away.' She smirked and placed down her wine glass,
putting both her elbows on the table. 'I'd give the occasional
blowjob when I had to, just to stop him trying to hump me every
time we were alone. He would try to return the favour but literally
had no idea what he was doing – it was basically someone drooling
on your nether regions and then being intrusively probed. It wasn't
that I didn't want to have sex. More like I wasn't in a hurry to make
him my first.'

Izzy had this slightly faraway look as she turned her head and rested it on the palms of her hands.

'Meredith Mason's boyfriend, on the other hand. Now he was something I definitely would not have minded.'

She let out an audible purr and quickly took another sip of wine before turning her body to face me, giving me this seductive little smile.

'She was so annoying. This spoilt American bitch. Joined our school late but got made deputy head girl because she was so insufferable. Anyway, she was very quick to rub our noses in the fact she was dating a second year at Bath, or wherever, and had him come along to help us prefects set up for our leavers' ball. While she was barking orders to the other plebs, I gave him a bit of a look and let him follow me to a study room no one ever used. I was expecting just a bit of a make-out session but... Well, I'll let you fill in the blanks.'

The self-satisfied smile was back, but this time I noticed the backs of our fingers were touching.

'Was it worth the wait?' I asked. She didn't answer. She just gently swirled the last of her wine. I then lightly placed my fingers in hers. She turned, looked at me, and rolled her eyes, but still held my hand.

'What about Little Miss Perfect?'

'I don't know,' I said. 'She's made it clear nothing's going to happen, and she seems to be having a blast on that boat thing.'

Izzy's smile had gone as she stared at me more seriously. I suddenly felt sleazy. She had confided in me as a friend.

'So you don't have any feelings for her whatsoever?'

I smiled, lightly letting go of her fingers. But as if catching me in a lie, Izzy gripped them back and glared at me.

'I do. Probably very much so. To be completely honest.'

'Good.' She brought my hand to her lap.

'At least we then both know exactly what this is.'

We both leaned forward. I closed my eyes and let a wave of adulterous guilt be offset by the feeling of her mouth on mine.

It was different to the first time. Largely because there was far less commentary. Only a couple of words here and there – 'leave it,' she said when I was fiddling with her bra, 'sorry,' I said climbing on top of her in the dark, and 'a bit harder, I won't break.'

But also because we said *more*. After it was done, staring up at the skylight above the bed.

'Do you have the time?' she asked rather formally.

'Just gone quarter to.'

'So the cork *did* pop before midnight.'

I looked over, and she was smiling.

'Would you have preferred if I held out?'

'God no, I hate it when guys do that. Like they are earning some form of merit badge. I was just about done anyway.'

After a moment, either one triggered the other, but we both began to laugh. It was definitely the first time I heard her laugh.

'I've never been in bed this early on New Year's. Not sure what to do now. All initial objectives successfully completed.'

I glanced quickly at her and then smiled.

'Oh look, he *is* proud of himself! For the record, I wouldn't exactly call that having my brains fucked out. But I will give you your due, it was perfectly adequate. Not in the same league as Meredith Mason's boyfriend. God, I could hardly walk afterwards. Is it bad I have no idea what his name was? The boy who took my virginity?'

Surprisingly I felt Izzy wriggle and her head was then on my chest. We lay looking up at the blueish black sky and I felt her shiver. I offered to get her a t-shirt.

As I got out of bed, she sat up from under the covers, her hands to the side of her breasts.

'So what do you think, by the way? You didn't get to see them last time. Nothing to write home about, but they are what they are.'

I looked at her, confused as I got back into bed, and she put the t-shirt on.

'*No-tits Izz*, Meredith Mason and her little friends would call me. Witty, weren't they? Even these I developed late on. Probably part of the reason I enjoyed having sex with her boyfriend so much. He didn't seem to mind.'

'I would have imagined you were queen of your school.'

'Hardly. I was probably close to being nice once upon a time. God, I hated that place.'

Izzy wrapped her arm around me, and we were cuddling. I just lay there not wanting to move but unsure how we had ended up in this situation. This was not the same young woman who, on a bad day, could probably make me cry.

'They were just jealous. You're incredibly beautiful. You realise that, right?'

'Oh fuck off and stop talking,' she said looking up at me, actually annoyed before putting her head back on my chest. As she did we heard the first pop. Then a bang. And then the skylight started to glow orange and red as one firework flew into view.

'That's pretty,' she said, sounding surprised. She raised her head as another one exploded above us.

'I suppose we are close to the river. And there are the displays in the parks. Wow, there are a lot of them.'

Izzy joined me kneeling, looking out at the South London sky, towards the north. We said nothing. Izzy then looked at me, staring into my eyes like she was waiting for me to reply to a question.

'You realise this is a one-off? Like, it's just the moment and circumstance. I'm not going to suddenly start dating you tomorrow or become your fuck-buddy, you understand that?'

I nodded. Her head was tantalisingly tilted. Her mouth was so close to mine, and her hands had already pushed away the duvet.

'Good. Well, I'm not going to send you a written invitation if that's what you're waiting for?'

After months of continuous therapy and a reading list designed to dispel the myths of love and unbundle infatuation, it is difficult to look back at the romantic moments of my life and not consider them false notes or misplaced lust. I would have placed at number one my first night with Vicky. As Vicky and I sat on her sofa with our coffee, both of us in our smartest date clothes having just taken the taxi back to hers from the restaurant, I had still expected her to peck me on the cheek, hug me, call me a good friend and offer me the sofa on which to sleep. I wasn't quite prepared for her to kiss me or for her to gently unbutton my shirt.

There were other moments too, stored away in my memory, such as women I met on my travels when I had finally begun to get over Vicky and my one long-term relationship. But then, in that vein, probably leaping into the top three, would now be kneeling beneath a skylight with Izzy, kissing under the multi-coloured glows. The only issue was, as romantic as these memories were, I suddenly thought back to my number one memory. This was no longer my first night with Vicky. Instead, it was talking to a friend, curled up together on a sofa for warmth on an unpleasantly cold night at Loughborough Road. And how she had exhaustedly let her head drop onto my chest.

Izzy took me to a small café for brunch the next morning. It was both a light-hearted apology for jibes she had made while we sat in bed drinking coffee, and a bittersweet goodbye meal considering, as she put it, our paths were less likely to cross in the future.

'I suppose I should say thank you,' she said, sitting up with her coffee as I joined her under the covers. 'For making an effort last night. I wouldn't say it was a huge improvement, but we got there in the end.'

'That's quite the compliment. It's a relief you don't feel like you have to be nice to me.'

'I think we've established it's not necessary. Clicking my fingers will suffice.'

She partially suppressed another smile and gestured to the coffee, water, and toast I had fetched for her when we had woken up.

'It's not like we'll be seeing that much of each other going forward. Now that the happy couple have resolved their differences. Ethan will be back permanently in a few short months, and I'm assuming three would be a crowd here.'

Again another smile, this time less suppressed, and not very welcome. I was trying hard not to think about Katie and Ethan.

'What disappoints you more, not having sex with me again or not seeing her downstairs for tea and toast? See, I may not say nice things, but I'm not the arsehole in this scenario, am I?'

I looked at her, not exactly finding our pillow talk riveting. After Vicky, sleeping with someone new came as a temporary tonic to prolonged heartache. But what I was doing with Izzy, in the light of day, felt a little clinical. Perhaps my feelings for Katie were not as strong as I thought?

'You don't need to look so depressed. As I said, it wasn't too bad as sex goes. And you prevented me making a fool of myself at that party or worse, calling someone I shouldn't, drunk at three o'clock in the morning.'

She sat back up. I saw a slight frown come across her face.

'Are you still in contact?'

She merely shrugged. 'Now and again. If I'm feeling a bit... I don't know. Sex seems to help, though. Blows away a few cobwebs for a while. What about you and *Little Miss Wabbit Ears*? Going to be pining away still?'

Izzy laughed, beaming delightedly at me. She made a show of pouting and fluttering her eyelashes. She then rolled over on to me and took my wrist looking at my watch.

'To make up for hurting your feelings, I'll buy you brunch at this place Spoiler and I found. Would that make things all better?' Again the pout, but this time her body draped over me and her negligible weight pushed onto my chest. 'Or are you still annoyed with me?'

'A little,' I said, trying not to sound sulky.

'Good,' she smiled and then kissed me.

Outside the little French café, Izzy and I parted company on an amicable yet final note.

'Thank you for not being too much of an arsehole about this whole thing. I don't normally cry on people's shoulders, so this was quite liberating.' She smiled, zipping up her green leather jacket. 'You're not going to fall for me, right?' She then gave me a piercing frown, looking slightly concerned. I smiled back and said I would try not to. 'Good, because I'm also sorry about rubbing your nose in the whole Katie thing. We're an odd bunch, us Magdalen lot. Cliquey, incestuous, and completely absorbed in our own problems. You've had a lucky escape.' She then rubbed my arm like she was telling me it would be okay, and we hugged – a strangely prolonged hug. 'Well, goodbye then,' she said and spun around toward Brixton tube station, and as she faded into the horizon, I felt that all too familiar sinking sensation. I was left alone, and if Izzy were right, that would be something I would have to get used to once more.

CHAPTER 20

THE COLONY

I found myself spending entire days in the Jones' allotment and whole evenings sitting alone in my old tattered armchair back at Loughborough Road. I would occasionally glance down at my phone to see if Katie had responded to any of my messages. However, it was Ellie who called, lifting me out of that post-holidays gloom by bringing impending doom.

'Hey,' she said. I then heard a shriek in the background and Ellie tell Millie to leave her brother alone. 'Feeding time at the zoo over here.' I smiled, picturing Millie and Ed at Ellie's dining table, starting a food fight with each other.

'Maxwell's come back with a date to see Mum. Two weekends from now. He's coming along too, so it will be quite the little reunion.'

'I'll have to check my diary. I just got offered some work...'

'This was your f...!' She stopped herself and lowered her voice to a hiss. 'You're the one who said yes so readily. Whatever else you've got going on, leave it. I've not spoken to my mother in over four years, forgive me if I'm a little bit anxious and don't want a pr... Don't want you messing us about.'

'Okay, okay. Weekend after next, got it.'

'Apparently we can stay over. They will make a couple of spare rooms. Fu... that, I told him.'

I heard her mumble the word, as did Millie. On the other end of the line, Millie began shouting, 'Ummm! Mummy said a bad word!' I had just returned from the allotment when Ellie had called, so I started looking through my fridge, deciding what to have for dinner.

'We could split the driving, and I drive us back straight after.'

'Scott, that would be over six hours in a car with you. I don't think I could do that.'

She didn't sound like she was joking.

'Besides, they want us to stay for dinner – they have it all planned!'

It was a bit of a relief to hear the obvious sarcasm, as I heard more mumbling of children's voices.

'At least we're getting our money out of Maxwell with all the go-between stuff. If we asked our solicitor, I think it would bank-rupt me.'

'Yes, Scott, well done us for having our ex-uncle broker a conversation with our own mother because we're both too emotion-ally incapable.'

And that was what was bonding us. This newfound siblingship that went beyond our many petty resentments was based not on either mutual loathing or mutual animosity for the woman who had largely raised us but given up at the final hurdle, but on mutual fear. Neither of us hated her. That was not why we had stopped speaking to her. My reason went back to my last conversation with her. Mum's love for us was complimentary but different to Dad's, and I don't know if I was ready to be rejected again by someone who was meant to love me unconditionally.

At least the date was set. I would travel down to Brighton in the

early morning, and Ellie would pick me up from their local station
and drive us down to Devon. There was a pub doing bed and breakfast where we would stay, and perhaps by the end of the weekend
we would have all our problems resolved, become one happy
family, and be able to move forward with our lives. Or not.

'So, how's everything else then? Your latest career choice, flat
hunting, life with Miss Preppy Knickers?'

I hesitated before answering. It sounded like we were about to
chat. We didn't really chat. I heard Millie's and Ed's voices fade.

'The latest career choice might give me enough to pay my rent,
if these jobs Jane recommended me for come off. I'm *not* flat
hunting at the moment so I'm not sure where you got that from – '

'From the fact you live in a shit-hole with a girl you are obviously besotted with. Seriously, you really need to get your act
together.'

'And how's the music going, Ell? Done anything to get back in
the game?'

'Yeah, headlining the Albert Hall on Monday. Apparently you
can just ring up and they give you a slot.'

'See, it's not so easy, is it?'

I had opted for beans on toast and was pouring the baked beans
into a bowl. Perhaps I had gone too far. I admired Ellie for wanting
to go back into composing and playing again – *hugely* admired her.
I didn't mean to be belittling.

'I mean, you at least are talented. The only people that are
currently better at what you want to do are world-famous musicians. That's not a bad place to start.'

I heard a door open over the line and then what sounded like a
breeze. I could no longer hear Millie and Ed.

'Well, I guess we all have to do what we can. Neither of us have
got it bad. I wouldn't swap those little monsters for the Sydney
Opera House. But... yeah.' I heard a small laugh. 'I know it's meant

to be the other way around but I'd really like them to be proud of me. Give them that Albert Hall moment. See their moody bitch of a mother doing something that is not just making egg and chips.'

I took my dinner to the kitchen table, about to say goodbye to my sister when Ellie's tone changed.

'Scott? We're going to have to settle with her, aren't we? As much as I think Maxwell is a pompous windbag, we can't afford to keep forking out for solicitors – Mike and I are broke enough and you're not looking too flush yourself.'

'But it's our house, Ell. Remember what we said. What we can do with it. The solicitor's fees will pay for themselves when we win.'

'Just think about it.'

I knew she was right. For all our plans, there was not a clear way forward for us. We had had our Christmas there – we had had the Christmas Dad would have wanted, one that could perhaps allow us to let go. But part of me still wanted to fight on and keep hold of all those old memories. And also one new one. Mistletoe in the doorway.

I took my phone back out and went back to my messages to Katie. Still no responses. The Christmas break would almost be over. She must be coming home soon.

Are you back soon? I'm working up in north London for the next few days but am back on Sunday. Perhaps we can have dinner?

Looking at what had become a string of unanswered texts, I put my phone back down, feeling my latest attempt as futile as the others. However, this time before even cutting into my toast, my phone lit up. I saw her name and a response.

Hey sorry for the late replies, lots of traveling around. Yes back late on Sunday. If you're awake we can have a cup of tea or something.

It was something. At last, and at least.

That week I began my new project. Mr Jones had offered me the use of his tools to take to North London. 'You'll need a car, you know,' he said to me, arriving to survey my work on the allotment. 'Ideally a van, once you get a few more jobs. Won't be convenient lugging all this stuff around with you by bus. And God knows how you're gonna mow a lawn.'

He found it funny, as did I, in a way. I have to say, it had been a slow start to my career as a landscape gardener but it was *my* career. When I was a kid I loved playing football in the rain. I loved sliding in the mud, skidding through the turf. I preferred it to those sunny days of July when the ground was hard and baked. And I felt a similar excitement when gardening in January, in the cold and in the damp, embracing the elements. And back in North London, up in Oakwood, I found one of the reasons I had taken it up in the first place.

Jane's friend, Mrs Elsop, had what I would describe as grounds rather than a garden. Her large detached house went backed onto what could have been accurately described as a football pitch. She told me that her previous gardener had just stopped coming and it was now overgrown and an eyesore. It was non-flashy, had no flowers or plants bar weeds and wild shrubs, and therefore had so much potential. As I walked it with Mrs Elsop, ideas began to sprout. I suggested a kitchen garden in a patch that would catch the sun. I could get her lawn growing again for the start of the summer and I could plant bulbs and seeds and make use of the wet weather to get as much growing before March as I could.

It was ambitious. I would have imagined a *real* landscape gardener would have had a team of at least three, but being just me, and inexperienced at that, I was cheap, and that was my comparative advantage. So I got on with it and spent the week digging the outlines of what would be flowerbeds and the vegetable patches.

The hours that the garden needed meant I had to stay at Dad's like I had told Katie. As she was not going to get back until late Sunday evening, my plan was to work until the early afternoon and then shower at Dad's, stop at the supermarket for supplies, and then return to Loughborough Road to make Katie what would have looked like a spontaneous, effortless dinner. However, these plans were made redundant as on Sunday morning, instead of looking up to see Mrs Elsop bringing me a cup of tea, I saw a figure very much juxtaposed to my surroundings.

'Hey,' said Katie as I let my garden fork sink into the earth. I was slightly out of breath, having tried to reach some deeply embedded roots.

'The lady at your house gave me this address.'

'Ah, Jane.' The explanation made sense – kind of. Jane had come round that morning, but Katie was still in a very much alien London borough.

'Margery asked me to give you this.' Katie handed me one of two cups of tea she was holding. Rather than wonder why Katie was one hundred miles from where I had expected her to be, I instead looked at her, curiously wondering how she had managed to get onto first name terms with Mrs Elsop so quickly. I was suddenly conscious of how muddy my fingernails were as I took the tea, especially looking at how immaculate Katie looked in a shiny body warmer over a white sweater.

'This is a bit of a surprise.'

'My parents gave me a lift. We're heading to Stansted. I told you about those work trips? I've been asked to fly out a week early to do some meetings, but I wanted to see you before I left.'

I looked back at Mrs Elsop's house, imagining Katie's parents in a car waiting for her.

'They're driving you to Stansted from Wiltshire?' I thought it was a rather long round trip.

'No, they've been staying at the flat. They drove me up on Friday so they could do some London stuff with Joan and me for a couple of days.'

I found myself automatically folding my arms. I tried hard to un-scrunch my face.

'Oh. So you got my message about staying up here those nights?'

I put the cup up to my mouth to disguise my annoyance at her not telling me she was back. 'Listen, Izzy told me about you and her on New Year's...'

I felt my stomach churn. It was none of her business, but also I wanted it to be her business.

'It's cool. I'm not going to be all judgemental like before. She said she was having a shitty day, and you were really sweet, so I can't exactly deny two of my friends having a nice time together.'

Strangely, while Katie stood a little away from me on one of the less muddy patches, I felt disappointed. She seemed genuinely relaxed, close to being matter-of-fact, like me sleeping with her best friend again was no big deal.

'So, I'm likely to be away most of this month, and when I'm back... well, Ethan and I have decided to move back in together. His contract finishes in March now, so when I get home I'll be flat hunting and then moving out. I didn't want to tell you over text or email so...'

She shrugged her shoulders and gave me a frowny, quarter-smile.

'You drove all the way to Oakwood to tell me that?'

'It's kind of on the way. But that's not the point. Flats go super-quickly from what I remember last time we were looking, so I wanted to give you proper notice and do it face to face.'

Like a breakup, I thought. Again, I put the tea to my mouth and took a rather prolonged sip as Katie stood holding hers. All her clothes looked new – the body warmer sleek and shiny, her jeans a rich blue, her white sweater a lot more white than my white clothes ever looked. She looked so... proper. So complete, and ready for a big adventure.

'Maybe I can come with you,' I said. 'You can adopt me, and I can stay in a small box room.'

I tried to smile so she would smile too.

'I'm not sure what Ethan would say about having a lodger... It would depend on how much rent you were willing to pay.'

And there it was. Just a small smile.

'I'll miss you,' I said, for the first time feeling I could speak openly. 'I'm glad you've reconciled with Ethan, but I'll miss our talks and having someone to complain about Joan with.'

'Well there's always Izzy. My matchmaking skills weren't too far off the mark, were they?'

'I think we both know why that's not going to happen again.'

I knew it was hypocritical. I claimed to like Katie – to have feelings for her – but I still fancied Izzy and hardly hesitated when it came to spending the night with her. And if Izzy had said she wanted to make it a regular arrangement, would I still have spent my days moping around thinking about Katie? I honestly didn't know. I just knew that the moment Izzy and I had parted, I had begun to feel sad, and that feeling had just intensified.

She said goodbye, and we agreed not to hug as I would get mud all over her, so she walked back up the garden, and I just watched the shiny body warmer and those rich blue jeans enter the house and disappear.

. . .

'What are you doing?' yelled Ellie, leaning across the passenger seat to shout at me through the window.

'I need to stretch my back out,' I called from the station exit. I was standing with my back against one of the pillars doing an exercise I had been taught by a doctor years earlier when travelling. I had just arrived at Ellie's local station. It had just gone nine o'clock and it was freezing. I could see the condensation on my breath. Ellie then began beeping the horn.

'You look like shit,' she said after I had got in the car.

'Yeah, pulled my back digging a trench and I've not been sleeping that well recently either. Plus I was up at five to catch the train.'

'Wait till you have kids. That's – '

'That's when you'll know about backache and blah blah being tired.'

'Very funny, Scott. That's gonna make the day go a whole lot smoother.'

When we reached the main road my phone buzzed. It was a message from Mike.

Go easy on her today. She's not been looking forward to it. If you could do me a favour and drive back I'd owe you one.

'Who was that?'

'Izzy,' I lied. 'A friend of Katie's. She's being her envoy regarding flat stuff while she's away.'

'Oh.'

It was a more sympathetic noise made by my sister. We had been in the car together only two minutes and we had naturally settled into our passive-aggressive gripes. At least Mike knew us both well enough to foresee it playing out. I looked over at her as we waited at a roundabout and she inched forward. Her hair was slightly different. Blonder than usual, a bit like the colour it was when we were kids, and a bit sleeker. Compared to her, I did look like shit. She had on a blouse rather than one of her old sweaters, and wore trousers rather than jeans. I hadn't shaved for a few days, I still wore my old tattered jacket, and the most effort I had made was putting on a clean pair of jeans and not wearing my gardening trainers.

'Is she still moving out?'

'Looks like it. We've been exchanging messages – she was worried about leaving me in the lurch regarding notice. And about sorting out things like bills while she was working all hours on this trip of hers. I told her not to worry and we could play it by ear when she got back, so...' I shrugged to complete the sentence. 'Hence, Izzy also stepping in to help.'

'Very gentlemanly of you. Izzy's the friend of hers you keep sleeping with, right?'

Previously my sister and I would speak on the phone perhaps once every three months on average. In recent weeks it had become every other day. I don't think this was a sign of us getting any closer. More like it was through necessity and our mutual struggle to express our feelings to other people. We needed to talk about Orletta, to come up with a strategy, so instead I told her about Katie and Izzy and she told me about the kids, Mike's job and anything that wasn't our mother.

'Have you thought about dating someone who was single, or not closely associated with your flatmate? Or is that a deal-breaker? An agoraphobic's prerequisites and all that.'

The journey took three hours zig-zagging along the coast. Avoiding mentioning our mother, we turned our attention to other important subjects and philosophical debates, such as who had the worse taste in music and whether, if Ellie was driving and if it were her car, did I have any right to even look at the stereo?

'How's Mike's accounting classes going?'

'First exams next month,' she sighed.

'You don't sound too excited at that.'

We were only a couple of towns away, according to the map, and were in the land of green and yellow fields, which I could imagine being mowed by those giant harvesters you saw on television.

'Now it's less hypothetical it seems all the more unfair. He already has a skill. He's been playing guitars for twenty-five years, producing probably for the last twenty, and there's literally nothing he can't do. If he had taken up the cello, he would be good enough to play for the Royal Philharmonic, and we would be living in a posh flat in Notting Hill probably. But as it is, he's having to go join the ranks of those who never had the balls or imagination to follow their own dream and whose whole life ambition was to own an Audi and find someone to stick their dick into so they could stop jacking off into their hand.'

'Nice image, Ell.'

'And this Izzy girl? Still using her to relieve yourself of those pent-up fluids you were saving for Miss Preppy Knickers?'

I saw a small smile emerge across Ellie's face.

'Nothing's going on. The occasional message about Katie. That's it. We're just...' I was going to say we were just friends, but we weren't even that. I had obviously lied when I told Ellie that Mike's message was from Izzy, but we had maintained contact after our New Year's liaison.

Me: *I don't know if it's appropriate to say 'thanks for the other night', but it was good talking. That guy you were seeing is an idiot btw. You deserve a lot better.*

Izzy: *Ha yes definitely appropriate to thank me. You're quite the beneficiary from my lapses in judgement.*

Izzy: *Katie told me about her and Ethan finding their own place. I won't say I told you so. But, buck up? I probably shouldn't have been as blasé about it.*

Izzy: *Thank you, regards that not-so-single young man of mine.*

We wound our way through country roads, the sun high in the sky as we approached midday. There were signs for West May Artists' Colony guiding us away from what looked to be the village where our bed and breakfast was. We were then directed onto a narrow dirt track off the main road, with crop fields to our left and right. Ahead we saw what looked like working farm buildings – a horseshoe of them as we got closer with one side made up of a large barn and the others more modern structures, which reminded me of the new art labs they had built at Amberton. Just beyond, as the track wound around a stone wall, there were what looked like beach huts on a green lawn.

We pulled up and parked in front of one of the art lab-type buildings, next to an old muddy Jeep and an immaculately clean Range Rover. The ground was cream gravel and in the centre of the horseshoe was a very un-farm-like water feature – a large stone fountain with a tall sculpture of a woman who looked like she was emerging out of the waters beneath.

'Can you not park there? This is private property.' Ellie and I stepped out of the car as a voice shouted out of the barn. She had long – seriously long – red hair and an even longer dress that she seemed to be pulling up to not drag across the gravel.

'You are in the middle of my scene,' she called out again as we just stared at her. 'New and potential students should go up to the main house. And call in advance.'

'Who's this bitch?' Ellie turned to me.

'Why don't you ask her?'

'Who the fuck are you?' shouted Ellie.

The woman stopped in her tracks, glared at us, and then sped up over the gravel.

'I'd ask you to leave such language back wherever it is you have come from,' she hissed. 'West May is a place of calm study which you are ignorantly in the middle of.'

I would have assumed the woman was around Ellie's age – her sharp, authoritative tone had the quality of a headmistress and, on closer inspection, her dress was something out of the early Tudor dynasty. Before I could ask where to find our mother, Ellie reached into her handbag and brought out a small leather wallet in which she carried her cards.

'Metropolitan Police. Narcotics division.' Ellie put on a slightly deeper voice and quickly flashed the wallet open and closed. 'Are you Mrs Orletta Roberts?'

Our antagonist's eyes burst wide open. 'She's up at the house.' She pointed, a lot less assured, to the pathway we had been on and an offshoot we had driven past. 'They have an event today. This is just the Colony. We just paint here.'

'Well, don't go anywhere. I'm sure we'll have some questions for you too.'

Getting back in the car, Ellie threw me her wallet.

'Metropolitan Association of Libraries.' Metropolitan was in big letters over a black and white photo of Ellie. 'You realise that's an actual criminal offence. Impersonating a police officer.'

'Oh relax, Queen Matilda was the one actively engaged in role-play. Plus, did you see her face? She and the rest are probably running around trying to flush away their hippy supplies. Nice to see Mother breeds loyalty among her minions.'

After our false start, we drove up the aforementioned path coiling up a small hill behind the buildings. As we did, my view was of farmland as far as my eyes could see. There were also the occasional working and non-working farm buildings – one large tatty disused barn and one operating with a tractor and another of those large harvester-type machines at its entrance.

I wanted to ask Ellie how she was feeling as we approached

what could have been a National Trust country home. More cream gravel led to cream walls and pillars, but more immediately noticeable were the twenty or so cars competing for space on a not unsubstantial driveway.

'What the Hell is going on?' said Ellie as we crawled up to the front door – the only place to park. 'Is this the event... oh, for fuck's sake.'

As Ellie wrenched up the handbrake throwing me forward, I assumed the same childhood memories were coming back to her as they were to me. Galleries and her sycophants hanging on her every word as we were paraded as proof Orletta Roberts was not just a successful artist but also a doting mother, before being discarded to the side as said sycophants swallowed her up.

'How many bedrooms, do you reckon?' I tried to change the subject as we sat staring ahead.

'Oh, just the seven. But three are technically day rooms and rooms for her correspondence.'

I had forgotten that while this was my first time, it was not Ellie's, though from the way she was hunched over the steering wheel, angling her head up to stare at the upper floor, she seemed as hesitant to leave the car as I was.

'No wonder she wants the cash from Dad's. Butlers' salaries alone must be a fortune.'

We both stopped talking. The door to the house was already open, and from it emerged a woman with silvery blonde hair. She was older – obviously, yet it still surprised me – and elegant, wearing a stylish contemporary white blazer over a long flowing white skirt. A silver shawl around her neck gave her a celestial quality as she smiled this wonderful beaming smile that made me suddenly forget that the previous twenty years might have taken place.

Ellie was out of the car first as I scrambled to undo my seatbelt.

I did not hear what was said but saw them embracing, Orletta engulfing Ellie as my sister looked awkwardly rigid. She then let go of Ellie and turned to me. That smile, those eyes, no different to when I was thirteen.

'Mum,' I said weakly.

'Scotty.'

The last time I had heard that voice was on a bleak October day when I was twenty-nine years old. My heart was pounding so hard it felt like it was going to burst. I was on the train from London to Devon with the carriage to myself lying across the seats, my head resting against the cold fogged-up window. Beads of rain trickled down as we made our way toward the southwest.

At Paddington, the station crew was still clearing up the concourse from the night before and there were just a handful of early Saturday morning passengers waiting for the first train. I had self-consciously approached the ticket office knowing how much I would reek of alcohol and other substances, and was at that stage of intoxication where one part of my brain was thinking clearly but the rest of me was yet to catch up. I could hear my deep, drunk voice echo as I asked for a single ticket to Devon.

Having time to wait, I sat on one of the benches and hunched forward so I would not fall asleep. I then took out my phone, cleared my throat, hoping my voice would, this time, come out more normal, and called her.

'Mum, it's Scott. I know we never set a date but I have some time off and thought I should go get some fresh air.' I tried to keep my voice level and less wobbly as I left that first message on her voicemail. 'I'm actually at the train station now and should be down in Devon by midday. It would be good if I could stay a few days. Or I could book into a hotel. Either way, it would be good to see you.'

In the sixteen years since she had left for Devon and her artists' colony, this was the first time I had made the trip to visit her. Or been invited to visit her, I should say. I had seen her those months earlier for my birthday and left feeling we had turned a corner in our relationship. No other people were vying for her attention, and she was the one who suggested the visit. In the years after Mum left, when she would visit and regale us with tales of her new life, the Colony of hers became this mystical place where artists found themselves. At age thirteen, I got the impression that we would have to be older to visit so not to disturb the magical forces.

Years went by, Orletta's exhibitions became occasions I would dread and hence I would make the odd excuse not to see her. She would also take extended trips to the Continent, meaning she would be away for months at a time. Very subtly, the trips to London and her visits became fewer, as did the phone calls. As I told Izzy, it *was* a case of us drifting apart. But despite this, as I had left an impromptu house party with so much cocaine in my system hours earlier, all I could hear through the anxiety and paranoia was this small voice calling, *Mum.*

This particular night seemed to sum up everything in my life at the time. Money, drugs, emptiness, and me hoping I would find something in between those late and early hours that would make the rest of my life worthwhile.

We had finished in the club and my broker friend who had arranged the night – the charming, hugely popular, James – had invited us all to his flat for more drink and drugs. I had made excuses to forgo the wraps being passed back and forth at the club, contenting myself with a steady stream of alcohol. James was on very friendly terms with the club hostess who had shown us to his *usual table*, and soon we were paired up with a group of young women who all either knew James or our hostess.

As we piled back to James's, our host immediately made a

beeline for the bedrooms, his arm around the waist of the hostess, and waved the rest of us through to his palatial living room. At that stage everyone else was paired up or in small groups – one couple heavily making out in an armchair, the rest at the open planned kitchen doing lines off the island. Helping myself to a beer, I started examining James's CD collection for something to do and feel less awkward among people I largely did not know. The only other person who didn't seem to have someone to talk to was a girl standing by a lamp casually thumbing through James's bookshelves.

'You work with Jim?' she said when we were too close to ignore each other. I said I did and politely asked her how she knew our host.

'I don't really. Not very well, at least. I'm a friend of Sadie's. She's just...' She flicked her eyes to the bedrooms and rolled them.

I think it was love at first sight.

We sat down on the floor, our backs leaning against the sofa. She was pretty, softly spoken, and told me she worked in PR but her dream was to work in publishing. Something about her or the occasion made me think of Tiffany. If only I had stayed with Tiffany, I would not have been as lonely as I was. We ended up sharing my bottle of beer as we talked. When it was finished, she apologised for hogging it and went to the kitchen to fetch us another. When she came back, she held in one hand a newly opened beer and a small bag of white powder.

'They're still going strong over there, and who knows how long Sadie will be.' She poured an amount of the powder on the coffee table and then reached into her purse for a credit card and a banknote.

Slightly disappointed, I watched her gently snort a line in front of me. She then sipped the beer and handed me the note, dabbing her nostrils gently with her fingertip. I hesitated, thinking I should just pass it back and say I was happy to stick with the beer. But with it laid out on the table and the girl just sitting there waiting for me, I didn't want to do anything that would break a connection that had felt such a long time coming. I tentatively leaned over and inhaled.

I don't know for how long we talked. We finished the bag and a new one appeared. A doorbell rang, and the kitchen lot were distributing more wraps. Some people left, some people arrived, some went to the bedrooms, some fell asleep around us, but we kept our spot on the floor, drinking beer and making lines on the coffee table. It reached the point where I could hardly stop staring at her mouth, wondering when I should kiss her. Then it was no longer just the two of us.

Sadie, the hostess, appeared from behind us, wearing only a towel. She smiled down at the girl – whose name in hindsight I do not think I asked – and bent over to do a line. Her blonde hair draped over the edge of the towel, and she then started whispering animatedly to her friend. At first the girl seemed annoyed, and Sadie seemed to be pleading innocence before smiling and taking a swig of our beer. Sadie then gently brushed the hair away from the girl's ear and smiled again, reaching for the girl's wrist.

Holding hands, they walked around the sofa and towards the bedrooms, neither looking back at me. I waited for ten minutes, probably longer, but the girl never returned. I scraped together the remaining powder and finished it. I went into the kitchen where the crowd was still talking, drinking, and preparing lines. I opened another beer, drained it, and realised I was essentially alone. High and alone.

This had become my life. Nights out with strangers I called friends, getting drunk in a group, hoping to talk to someone who I could relate to who would save me from I-did-not-know-what. I left the flat. I was somewhere on the Thames and everything was silent and still. I then began running, as if I could run off the stimulants or run away from my weaknesses. I hated my life, and I hated myself, so I kept running and by the time I eventually found the main road, I wanted to run all the way back to somewhere where I felt safe again. When everything was going to be okay. And that's when I realised how much I missed my mum and how much I needed her to help fix whatever it was that was broken inside of me.

On the train to Devon, my phone then rang. It was Orletta calling me back.

'Scott? Scott, what is this about you visiting?' She sounded agitated, very unlike her usual calm, charming tone.

'That's not possible. It's just not. You should really have given me some warning.' Again, it was a voice I had not heard her use. It was shrill, annoyed, flustered. 'We have guests already. And then we're travelling and, oh! The Colony is already so busy!'

'I can stay in a hotel. I don't mind. When we last spoke, you said to visit any time I wanted.'

It was childish saying that last bit. There was then a moment of silence.

'Scott, it's just not a good time with all we have going on. I would not be able to give you my undivided attention.' Her voice was softer, but it also came with a deep sigh. Like it was what it was, and there was nothing she could do to change it.

'You haven't actually left yet, I take it?'

'No,' I lied, trying to stare out of the window but it was too fogged up.

'Good. Let's do this properly. Give me a few days, and we'll set an actual date once everything has calmed down.'

But it wasn't a few days. I waited for her to call. She never did.

The foyer or entrance hall – definitely not a hallway – reminded me of entering the Tate Britain or National Portrait Gallery. It was a spacious oval room covering the same square metres as my entire Loughborough Road flat, with stone-tiled floor and a circular table at its centre with an ornate vase of flowers. Thirty years ago, her house had a regular hallway whose walls had coat upon coat coming off pegs and muddy trainers strewn everywhere.

'We're gathered in the conservatory,' Orletta said, guiding us through the room and towards the light.

'We're?' mouthed Ellie to me as we were half-blinded by the sun shining into what appeared to be a long, glass function room. Men and women my mother's age stood drinking from champagne flutes, which were being poured by what looked like a team of caterers.

'I'm glad I wore my best trainers,' I mumbled to Ellie as we stopped following Orletta and just observed.

'It's like the fucking 90s.' As we stood there, I felt our hands touch. I don't think we had held hands since I was probably eight years old but I could tell she felt as overwhelmed as I did, being suddenly transported to our repressed teenage memories.

'There they are!' The typically ebullient Maxwell marched purposely over to us. I put my hand to my eyes to block the low January sun.

'Quite the little do, eh? Your ma has really pulled out all the stops.'

'Maxwell, what the f—- What the hell is going on?'

'Oh, wait a moment, my dear. Speeches.'

There was a tapping of a glass with a small knife. All eyes were toward the centre of the room and our mother. She was looking over at us, holding a glass of white wine.

'Everyone, may I please present our *special* guests. They've come all the way from London and, though I am completely biased, are here to make today and this occasion even more special. My daughter Eleanor and my son Scott.'

We were greeted with enthusiastic applause, which had me wanting to run for the exit. I turned to Ellie, who had a glass of wine in her hand. She then had a third of a glass.

'Go easy. You're the one who wanted to do the driving.'

'Piss off.'

Orletta was beaming and laughing with another of her guests. I could feel all these smiling eyes on me like I was the show-stopper to one of her exhibits.

'It was good for your ma to do this. To answer your earlier question, these are the Board, my dear. Of the West May Artists' Colony and Retreat. Quite a big thing in these parts.'

'I thought you said she wanted to see us? To come to some deal?'

'Plenty of time, my boy. I doubt this will take all day, and besides, you get to see your dear ma in her element. In my experience, such things are far more successful in reaching an accord than sitting around a table hashing out terms and conditions.'

Maxwell wandered away to speak to another grey-haired gentleman. When I looked towards Ellie she was gone too, leaving me by myself while the others were mingling. I felt a spectre, trying not to be seen and just observing. Ellie had gone to our mother, and our mother smiled brightly, introducing a reluctant Ellie to her fan club.

'Sparkling wine, sir?' said a voice awakening me. A girl in a smart outfit stood with a tray of champagne flutes.

'It's from a local vineyard. The soil is comparable to the Champagne region.'

'Do you work here?' I think it came out as an accusation rather than a question as I felt my face screw up, suddenly concerned that there was a significance at being told the provenance of the wine.

'Sometimes. Probably once a month, when Ms Roberts and the Colony hold events.'

I might have been imagining it, but she seemed to be staring at me rather intensely. I felt obligated to take one of the glasses.

'I used to study Orletta Roberts at university. She's a huge name around here, so I ask especially to work these occasions. You're her son?'

Again, she continued to stare, but the mention of my link to *the* Orletta Roberts had me looking back over in the direction of the woman in white who I had not seen in six years.

'Kind of.' I took a large sip of wine, still staring over at Ellie and Mum. 'I mean, yes, but you're probably more familiar with her work than I am.'

'You must be very proud,' she suddenly blurted out quickly. I felt myself again shoot the girl a look. She seemed so young and enthusiastic and so wholly ignorant about my mother or me.

'Not half as proud as my dad was when she abandoned him and their two children for all this bullshit.'

She gave me a polite quarter-smile and walked away far less cheery than when she had come over. I stared back at her, feeling a complete arsehole.

'You certainly seem to have a way with women.' Ellie was standing next to me again. I was about to say I should apologise when she handed me a fancy looking A5 piece of card. 'Maxwell was right. It's some special meeting. It says something about a presentation on the *future* of her little shithole.'

'I'd hardly call this a shithole.'

'She did something similar last time I was here. Wheeled me out for the opening of that barn-thing Queen Bitchface stormed out of.'

'When are we going to talk about the house?'

Ellie shrugged.

'*Why don't you ask her?*' she said, trying to mimic my voice from earlier. Despite the sarcasm, I was soon to have my opportunity as from across the room, I saw Orletta smile at us and then excuse herself.

'Right then, you two,' she beamed and held both our wrists. 'We're going to make sure everyone is sufficiently fed and watered and then take a short walk down to that little colony of ours so our friends can see our artists' works. I've been very much looking forward to introducing you to everyone – Ellie, Hans has spent twelve years with the New England Philharmonic Orchestra. And, Scott, you need to meet Millicent. She runs a hedge fund. Who knows, you could be her new rising star!'

'Mum, I'm a landscape gardener.'

'What are we doing here, Mum? Why invite us to this?'

'To talk, of course, Princess.' She stared at Ellie's hair and gently moved and dabbed the strands as she spoke. 'But it's been such a long time I felt a party would be appropriate. And I wanted to show you something which I hope will make everything a little clearer.' She then stood in between Ellie and me and linked arms with us. 'But first, please, tell me about those grandchildren of mine.'

While Orletta introduced Ellie to a tall Austrian man I took my opportunity to escape through the conservatory door. To give Orletta some credit, she had chosen a beautiful part of the world to leave us for. They had a large patio, which I imagined would be idyllic for summer drinks and barbecues, but, more so, beyond it was the view from the top of the hill, looking down on acre upon acre of rolling farmland. It was beautiful. Peaceful and serene.

I then caught sight of what was growing immediately in front of me. Their land led straight into rows of vines with little bunches of grapes descending the hill, and I scrambled down to examine them. They didn't look the healthiest of grapes. They were rather small and brown but still in these interesting compact little bunches that looked so satisfying and camouflaged between the leaves and vines.

'Our pet project,' said a man's voice behind me. At the top of the slope was Conrad, my mother's partner. It was the first time I had seen him that day as I could not recall him being with the others in the conservatory.

'I assumed this belonged to one of the farms.' I was still examining the vines and smiled politely at the man I had always found intimidating.

'Vanity project, I should say. Just this slope, but we've been cultivating for the last few years. With a little help, obviously.'

I let go of the grapes and stood up, feeling like I was trespassing.

'Please feel free to try. Those are chardonnay. The same grown in Champagne. The soil and weather here is very similar.'

It was an intensely sour taste. I didn't want to spit it out so reluctantly swallowed it down. I saw Conrad smile for the first time.

'Yes, not quite what you get at the supermarkets, but I've been reliably told it makes good wine. We're getting a few dozen cases out of this lot. Not a huge amount, but not a bad little experiment.'

'Does it... taste alright? Where do you do the fermenting?'

I was casually looking down the slope, counting the rows, wondering what it took to maintain and harvest a crop of grapes. I did know that English wine had become increasingly popular in recent years, but I assumed it was a little bit of a fad or gimmick.

'It does. Many French houses have been buying up land in this part of the world. Some neighbours of ours do the clever duties. Your mother and I are part of a cooperative – a group of small producers of which we are by far the smallest, and it all gets processed and stored at a facility a few miles away. Very civilised. I'll pour you a glass back at the house. We hold it back for special occasions rather than these types of dos.'

In over twenty years of Conrad being my mother's partner, I think this was our first conversation. We had spoken at Dad's a year earlier, but that was a business meeting rather than a conversation. This was the first time we had *chatted*, if Conrad could be described as the chatty kind.

I looked again at the rows of vines and felt this little thrill, like being back in the hills of Burundi when I had been taught the foundations of planting a crop.

'Could you make a living doing this?' It was more a hopeful question. I had this vision of me in my own little vineyard, away from everyone and everything, in the peace and quiet of just me and nature. *This one's like the wilderness...*

'It depends. Why? Can you see yourself giving up the City to come out here and work the land?'

Conrad chuckled as I climbed back up the hill, and we began walking back to the house. I tried to briefly explain that I had not worked in finance in a long time and that since I had given up international development, I would mainly be found clearing out allotments and other people's gardens.

'Ah, entrepreneur then?' Again Conrad laughed as we crossed the patio and the sound of mingling became louder. 'I began life trying to be a restaurateur, if you would believe. Complete disaster. But I saw it was a better deal to buy rather than lease the premises, and broke even by renting the flats above. Gradually I learned that the real money was in bricks and mortar rather than the businesses themselves. It doesn't come easily or quickly but the only way to learn is to go out there and do it. Keep your chin up.'

He patted me on the back and I found myself smiling for the first time that day. As we went back inside, I looked across the room for Orletta or Ellie, to see if there was any danger we could leave for the Colony, and get that part of the day over with. I saw Ellie by herself, staring at me, and walked over to join her.

'You two seem very pally.'

'He's alright. Why?'

'No reason. Just interesting how you give it all this about lawyers and Mum being the devil, and then you cosy up to stepdad over there hoping he might buy you a train set.'

Ellie was back to her sarcastic best, nonchalantly sipping her wine and glancing around the room while I felt the familiar sensation of resentment rise up. We hissed passive-aggressive insults under our breath at each other, and then Ellie walked away, saying, 'once a daddy's boy, always a daddy's boy.'

I guess it was too good to be true that our relationship had gone a whole month without reverting to pettiness and acrimony. As I saw her stand next to our mother and be introduced to a lady in a red dress, I felt overcome by her hypocrisy. *She spends the whole day at our mother's side and has the nerve to question my loyalties.*

Eventually, we did leave the house. The entire entourage in their coats and hats, descending a path down the hill, leading to the buildings we were ordered to not park in front of. Ellie was at the front with Orletta, and I was at the rear, again with Conrad, trying not to feel this sudden shame for in some way betraying Dad.

'I still feel a fraud at these occasions, no matter how many I have found myself at over the years. The uncouth businessman among the cultural elite.'

As we walked slowly, letting the rest meander ahead of us, I did wonder if this was a deliberate charm offensive put in play by Orletta to divide and conquer. After all, Conrad was a businessman, and perhaps he saw soft-hearted negotiation as the key to getting what they wanted. Alternatively, and from what my gut feeling was, he saw in me the only other person with who he did not have to hold a conversation about the virtues of the neo-classical versus Pre-Raphaelite movement.

'My late wife was the art lover. She would force me to accompany her to gallery after gallery, and I would impatiently look at my watch rather than the paintings, eager to leave and get to a telephone so I could hear news of whichever deal I was pushing through.'

The route had taken us through a field and was far more direct than that of driving, though I could not help wondering if the dozen or so sixty-somethings would struggle to make their way back up, especially with the sun due to set in a couple of hours.

'We moved here when we received the diagnosis. She wanted to spend whatever remaining time we had together out of the city and trying her hand at landscapes. After she passed away, I found myself visiting those same galleries where I had so clearly not been present. This time I could not help but be moved by a force I had learned to appreciate too late.'

Above us was what could have been a kestrel circling the clear blue winter's sky. The crunching of gravel accompanied the sound of Conrad's voice as we approached the Colony.

'All this somewhat began then. There I was, the businessman who knew nothing about art morosely in the company of art dealers, gallery owners and curators, trying to be close to someone I had lost. And then I met your mother. A rare thing among the rest: *talent*. And soon all this evolved. She wanted to be somewhere where she could solely paint, and escape the gallery set to somewhere she was not constantly surrounded by sycophants. So we formed *the Colony*, as it's come to be known. But not with some heavy sacrifices along the way.'

'Like my sister and me.'

It was not meant as a slight. I hope my quiet tone implied that. We were in the horseshoe courtyard, and Conrad stopped to put his hand on my shoulder.

'It's easy to have regrets. And it's easy to bear ill will. But from someone who knows, it does not bring you any peace of mind.'

Orletta led everyone into the art-block-type construction we had unforgivably 'photobombed' with our Volvo. The red-haired woman was at the entrance, and our mother was introducing her to Ellie. I saw her mouth an enthusiastic, *how do you do*, as if Ellie's threat of a drugs charge had not happened. We were in a long spacious room with light wood flooring, plenty of sunlight, and white walls. It was an ideal gallery space to display the vast collection of paintings, artwork, and sculptures before us. And then the *sycophants* gathered around Orletta, eagerly awaiting some form of announcement.

'Friends,' she beamed, her white clothes glowing in the light. 'I know many of you have become more than acquainted with these speeches of mine over the years, so I thought I would divert from tradition and be succinct. Which I am sure some of you will be pleased to hear.'

There was a light rumble of laughter among the bright smiling faces around me.

'Soon I will be leaving you in the capable hands of one of our most talented artists, Sylvia De Vale – ' There was warm enthusiastic applause as the red-haired woman stepped forward smiling. 'But before I do so, I would also like to say a huge thank you to two very special people who I am honoured to have here today with me...'

'Oh kill me now,' I heard Ellie's familiar whisper behind me.

'West May prides itself as being one big family and my only regret regarding what we have achieved together at our little colony, which has benefitted so many talented wonderful people over the years, is that we could not do more. Host more artists. Work with more people who see art as a sanctuary. Who need space to find themselves...'

'Like she found herself?'

'I thought you weren't talking to me?' I whispered back.

'It's not all about you, dickhead. It's all about *us* apparently.'

I had not noticed that my mother was standing in front of a small table. As she moved to the side, she revealed what I first thought was another sculpture. However, it turned out to be an architectural model.

'We are delighted to announce that the West May Art's Centre – our *Colony* – will see its first significant expansion since Conrad and I first converted those dusty old outbuildings into what we are standing in today. It will see a second gallery space, an extension to the artists' barn, and expanded quarters so we can welcome new friends – '

Another round of applause interrupted Orletta, this time even more enthusiastic.

'And none of this would have been possible without the generous support of my daughter Eleanor and my son Scott... Champagne? There should be more champagne going around. Do we all have a glass?'

And glasses were being passed around. In front of me was the girl from the house. She briefly turned in my direction to offer me a flute from her tray, but as I tried to smile apologetically, she simply ignored me.

'Please raise your glasses. To Eleanor and Scott.'

'Oh fuck off,' I heard both my sister and me mutter beneath our names being cheered.

My reunion with Ellie was short-lived. She was gone as soon as the cheering squad dispersed. Surprisingly I saw her back talking to Sylvia De Vale – or more accurately, Sylvia De Vale corner my sister – who seemed a lot less hostile, laughing delightedly with Ellie, her hand earnestly placed on her arm while Ellie seemed awkwardly forced to take the attention. There were a few people gathered around the model of the Colony. I approached feeling what I can only describe as numb. I wouldn't say we had been played or manipulated – there did seem to be a genuine look of pride as Orletta made her toast – but the result was that we had been played and manipulated. She had her legacy laid out on that little table with all the buildings beautifully crafted, and we had endorsed it by being present with all her cronies. I had two people come up to me and shake my hand, again telling me how proud I must be. I mumbled thank you and tried to step away feeling like I, ironically, was the only sane person in a house of fantasists.

It all seemed so calculated. We had been invited not to nego-tiate but to concede defeat, and our compensation was... what? The gratitude of some posh people we did not know. But I wasn't angry. Nor was I disappointed. Instead, I felt like I was about to let her down. What I had come to accept was Orletta's behaviour did not spring from any malice. More like a misplaced sense of joy. If she was happy, then everyone else surely must be happy. She seemed genuinely delighted to have us with her and so excited about her project, which would not happen. At least not immediately. Dad would not want his house sold so she could expand the cult for whom she left him. Surely she could see that?

Across the room, Ellie was now being given a tour by Sylvia De Vale. My sister's redheaded nemesis had her arm linked around her, and they were standing in front of a Jackson Pollock style canvas with splatterings of paint all over it. In front of me was an industrial metal sculpture of what could have been a horse about to gallop skyward.

'Do you remember when you were a boy, and you would love making up stories about monsters and heroes at every museum we took you to?'

Next to me, for once without an entourage, was my mother, quietly smiling, staring at the creation with me. I did not know whether it was a rhetorical question or I needed to scan my mind back to earlier childhood memories. I again mumbled something like, *kinda*.

'You were probably too young.' Like none of the last twenty years had happened, I then felt her arm link around mine, and for a brief second, her head was on my shoulder.

'You're all grown up.' She then looked at me, examining my face and then my hair. 'Obviously you were when I last saw you but more so now. An adult. Not a boy.'

I wasn't sure what to say. Instead, I just let this warm, soothing sensation wash over me as she again scanned my face as though I was a precious artefact and could not quite believe it was real. A small distant voice called out *why did you go?*

'We will talk. Soon,' she then whispered, putting her hand on mine. 'Once everyone has gone. I promise.'

I walked back up to the house with Conrad and Maxwell as the winter sun set over the hill.

'Charming young lady, that Sylvia. Charming! Had us all in absolute raptures. Quite the artist too by all accounts.'

I heard a low hum from Conrad as I saw his brow furrow.

'Yes, she is a favourite. Or at least she believes herself to be. There are some very talented young people here who perhaps go slightly under the radar because of Sylvia's... enthusiasm for the limelight.'

Everyone else had been driven back to the house, and when we arrived we were greeted by warmth and candlelight. This time we were corralled into a large dining room with a buffet laid out on its table. As I heard Maxwell regale the tale of our walk back up the hill as if we had been on an expedition in the Antarctic, I surveyed the rest of the room. Ellie was at my mother's side once more, sipping what looked like mulled wine, surrounded by the impeccably dressed hangers-on. Sylvia was laughing and beaming with two other guests across the room, and I began staring at the walls. Or what was on the walls. They were all works by my mother – when she was still my mother, and not *the Orletta Roberts*.

'Mulled wine, *sir*,' said the girl who had earlier offered me the sparkling wine. This time she had a tray of steaming Christmassy glasses and was distinctly curter, staring straight past me as she made the offer.

I looked over at Ellie, who was still sipping hers.

'Thanks. Actually, do you know how strong this is? My sister is meant to be driving, but I think she had a couple of glasses earlier and – '

'I don't know, *sir*,' the girl said politely, cutting off my rambling story. She looked around a little impatiently and gave me that same passive-aggressive quarter-smile.

'I'm sorry about earlier,' I said, taking a glass so she could go. 'I was a bit preoccupied. I haven't seen Orletta – Mum – I don't even know what to call her – in a long time, and I wasn't expecting quite so many people to have been invited to the reunion. It's still no excuse for taking it out on you when you were nice enough to talk to me.'

I sipped my drink, hoping the dark red liquid would mask what I knew would be my pink cheeks at having had to apologise to a stranger. I turned to focus on the painting so she could quickly leave. But she didn't.

'I guess successful families have their issues too,' she said in a softer voice. I saw she had on a kinder smile this time.

'Successful? Perhaps Orletta. You're talking to someone who had to pay for the weekly shop from the jar of change and coppers he'd been collecting the last year. *Costcutters* were thrilled.'

'I guess you're the *prodigal son* then,' she then beamed, with this warm youthful glow.

I laughed, immediately covering my mouth in fear I might spray wine either in her face or over the painting.

'She painted this when she lived with us. Before she was *successful*.' I was gazing back at the painting, suddenly remembering how it had sat on her easel in our conservatory. When it was her conservatory. I did not know if the girl was still listening. I was talking aloud, recalling a memory that had flickered to life in front of me.

'It's our local churchyard, but the scene as you come out of the church. I remember she would take us there for a walk, and she would stand at the top of the steps looking out. I'd ask what she was looking at, and she would say, 'Everything,' and smile at me like she knew something magical that we had not yet learned.'

It was autumn in the painting. The people were blurs, but the fallen leaves were vivid, as were the stone wall and headstones and the trees at the back.

'It's my favourite,' said the girl now standing next to me with her tray. 'She only exhibits these ones at the annual show in the town. It's probably one of the reasons I'm still a waitress. I get to spend once a month doing something related to my degree rather than doing admin at a solicitors or working at a vets.'

'Does my mother know she's got quite the fan?'

'God no!' she laughed. 'I think she'd take out a restraining order. I've never even spoken to her. Who knows what I'd say!'

I turned around, looking for Orletta. She was at the back of the room, still surrounded by her minions.

'I know exactly what you mean.'

Lydia, as she introduced herself, skilfully balanced her tray as we shook hands.

'I better get back to work. It was lovely chatting.'

She smiled, and I went back to gazing at my mother's painting, now a well-known artwork, exhibited to a community one hundred and fifty miles from where it was painted.

'Finished flirting?' said Ellie joining me.

'I wasn't. We were just looking at St Michael's.' I nodded to the painting.

'Who knows, if you made the trip sooner, you probably wouldn't have to have waited until you were thirty to lose your virginity.'

'Thirty-one, actually.'

'I'm being kind.'

We both then seemed to let the conversation tail off as we gazed at Mum's painting.

'I had forgotten about this one,' Ellie said quietly. 'It was her breakthrough piece. I thought she sold it.'

'Me too.' For some reason, I felt that icy cold sensation of someone proverbially walking over my grave.

When I next looked away from the painting, I saw some of our mother's guests with their coats on and goodbyes being said. Conrad was then at our side, telling us we would retreat to his study while those leaving left and the catering team set up for dinner.

'It's quieter in here. You can finally talk. Your mother's been wanting that for a very long time.'

Maxwell was already there waiting as we entered a full-sized drawing room rather than a study. At one end was a large desk with big leather chairs opposite, rather like the chairman's office at a large bank. At the other end of the room was a small lounge with four more leather chairs surrounding a circular glass table. Maxwell had taken his usual place perching on the desk and in his hand was another manila folder.

'We'll do all the goodbyes and be with you momentarily.'

Conrad left us with the perennially beaming Maxwell, who I'm sure would have been in his element with all the networking and the presence of southwest England's elite.

'Fun day. Good of Orletta and Conrad to do all this. Explain things properly.'

'Yes, such fun. Next time perhaps we could throw in a colonoscopy. Really get the party started.'

Maxwell smiled to himself, showing no sign of registering what Ellie had said.

'Listen, you chaps, before they come back, I should say it is very decent of your ma and Conners to sit down face to face with us like this. I know you believe you did the right thing getting that fancy solicitor of yours involved, but usually, once that happens, things get very tedious with letters exchanged and writs drawn up. I think you would agree this way is, if not better, decidedly cheaper.'

Ellie and I exchanged a look as we had gathered another chair to put in front of Maxwell, forming a crescent. I knew that if even a half-decent sum was discussed, Ellie would have us pull our claim on the house. A small part of me hoped it would happen. The fight would be over, Ellie would take the decision out of my hands and we would have closure. But what would I do then? My life would remain transient, and I would no longer have the only thing that anchored it.

The door of the study reopened. Orletta seemed to sparkle as she entered the room, the all-conquering heroine. The small child within me retreated back behind the sofa to watch her smile and glow.

'I'm so sorry, darlings, you've been so patient! A little bit of organising is still needed out there. We have a little soiree every Saturday for the artists, and obviously tonight's will be a little bigger with yourselves and our last few board members.'

Conrad followed my mother into the room. Maxwell was still beaming from the desk, and everyone else took a seat in the crescent. Apart from me. I had gravitated to the window at the side of the room. I was only a few feet away from Ellie, and I could see Maxwell fine. I found something soothing about the cool windowsill and cold emanating from the glass.

'Sylvia has kindly taken up the baton regards entertaining, and the agency girl is setting up the dining room. Such a pleasant girl, only a slip of a thing. They get younger and younger, don't they?'

'Young enough to give you a whole host of grandchildren if Casanova over there gets his way.' Ellie smirked mischievously at me.

'Oh don't talk such nonsense, Eleanor,' snapped Orletta, quite suddenly, quite jarringly. It definitely surprised Ellie as she stared back at our mother, a mix of shock and hurt in her eyes, who then distractedly flattened out her white trousers and, in the briefest of moments, let her serene smile return as she looked up at our family solicitor.

'Max. The floor is yours.'

'So, the business end of proceedings.' Maxwell opened the manila folder. Like Orletta, he smiled pleasantly as if this was all a formality before the real main event – another dinner party where he could work the room and network.

'Eleanor, Scott, your ma would like to make you the following offer regards your challenge to probate on your father's estate.'

The light from the house helped illuminate the darkness I was looking out into from the window. I could just about make out the vastness of the hills and fields. They had a beautiful house in that Devon countryside of theirs. Idyllic, picturesque, and with their own vineyard and artists' retreat thrown in. Mum had certainly gone up in the world since she had slummed it in middle-class suburbia raising us. Her conservatory dwarfed our conservatory. Conrad's study dwarfed Dad's. And now I was being handed a piece of paper that would swallow up our whole life into this already palatial estate, expanding that pretentious little *colony* at the expense of every happy memory I associated with my existence. As I stared into the night sky, my eyes firmly away from the room I was in, I thought about the apple tree in our garden and the swing Dad had built for us when we were small enough not to break it. I thought about the bookshelves in Dad's study. I thought about my Games Workshop pieces cluttered about my room and spilling out onto the landing, and then about Ellie's sheet music and music biographies. Mum left, but we didn't. She was the one who became Orletta Roberts and no longer our mother.

I had the piece of paper in my hand but did not look at it. By the feel of it – the thickness, its higher gsm weight, the not quite smooth texture – I could tell it was an official, formal offer and not just a number they had written on the back of an envelope.

'As you can see, it is very generous, all things considered.'

Still staring out of the window I heard someone rustling the paper. Of it being turned over multiple times.

'I think there's some kind of mistake. This is some sort of joke, surely?'

I quickly flicked my eyes across and saw Ellie staring perplexed at the paper as if she was near-sighted and it was advanced nuclear physics. I then saw the number she was struggling to comprehend.

'You can't honestly think this is an offer, let alone a generous one? Maxwell, I do understand that people once bought their first house for not more than this but things have moved on from the 1960s...'

'My dear, it is a substantial sum considering the circumstances and your rights under English law.'

'We are owed more than this! We've put in more than this. This is nonsense. It's... it's – '

'It's one percent of the value of the house,' I said, peering back out into the black. I could then see a small light in the middle distance moving steadily across the horizon. 'I guess two percent if the offer is to each of us. Which is probably the same as you'll end up paying the estate agent.'

'This is... ludicrous. Did you honestly think we were going to accept this?'

Ellie's voice was steadily rising and becoming slightly more high-pitched. I was used to her cutting sarcasm. Here, she sounded panicked. My sister was not one to panic.

'Eleanor,' said our mother, eventually, in her calm, soothing voice. 'I wanted you to come here today to see what could be achieved with this money. The good the money could do. If it was simply for my own gain, I would be more than happy for you both to split the house between you – '

'No you wouldn't!'

The light in the distance got a little brighter as it moved nearer. With my eyes adjusting to a dark not experienced in London, I began to make out the outlines of fields and the road cutting across the landscape.

'Eleanor.' Orletta's voice began to sound less patient. 'The expansion we intend to do here will not come cheap. Conrad has already been incredibly generous with his own money and his company's resources. This is simply a realistic, and not unsubstantial sum that represents the maximum that can be spared – oh darling, can't you see the good we can do? This will be your legacy. Yours and Scott's. You will have something here that your children will be proud of. Perhaps even their children. We will bring art and hope to the masses irrespective of people's income or situation.'

'Mum, with respect, you've never even met my children, so have no fucking idea what they will be proud of.'

The use of the F-bomb seemed to send the room into a silence as frosty as the cold radiating from the window. I then let my eyes adjust from what was outside the window to a reflection of the room. Ellie looked like she had been sitting forward in her chair and was now staring at the floor. Our mother was sitting back looking unmoved. Conrad had the same impatient expression he would wear when we would meet him at Mum's exhibitions. And Maxwell seemed to be studying his manila folder, oblivious to events around him. Eventually, the silence was broken, and I stared back out, trying to spot where the light went.

'Thank you, Eleanor,' said Orletta. 'I can see we have some ground to cover. Scott, you've been awfully quiet over there. Is there anything you would like to add? What do *you* wish to get out of this situation?'

I heard Ellie mumble something like, *like he's going to say anything, fucking waste of space.*

'I wish it could have been you, rather than Dad.' I said it into the dark, to those fields disappearing into the horizon.

It took me a moment to realise all eyes were on me. I turned back to the room. Ellie was giving me this wide-eyed glare. Maxwell's brow was intensely furrowed, looking between me and his folder like I had gone drastically off-script. Conrad looked both disappointed and yet reconciled. Orletta, however, stared at me with this small, slightly amused, untouchable smile. Like she had just realised who I was. I kept eye contact with her. I heard myself them mumble,

'If it had been the other way round, we wouldn't need to be here.'

I don't know if I felt I needed to justify myself or apologise or just fill the silence. I knew what I said was terrible, but all I could feel was that I meant it. Not in the way it came out, but in that I missed my dad and didn't want to be in that room.

I stared into those amused, patient, triumphant eyes of my mother.

'It's been a long day,' she said calmly, her smile still fixed. 'On top of that, you've both had a long journey. Perhaps we should come back to this in the morning.'

Maxwell heartily agreed and cited everyone's tiredness once more. Further excuses were made, and outside the room, Ellie and I seemed to gravitate to the front door. Our mother and Maxwell were elsewhere as it felt like the aftermath of an explosion, and I seemed to be walking with tinnitus in my ears. Ellie hugged Conrad – I do not recall seeing either of them do that before – and he shook my hand and gave me a nod.

'Jesus, Scott. Jesus.' She stomped through the gravel to the driver's side of the Volvo. She had turned the ignition before I belatedly realised I should get in or she'd leave without me.

She spun the car around, and suddenly we were speeding away from the house, the Volvo bouncing down the rough road.

'Ell you might want to slow down a bit.'

'What the fuck was that?'

We swung around a corner, and Ellie threw us onto a country road, perhaps leading to the village.

'Are you even okay to drive? *I've* not drunk anything since – '

'Seriously, you arsehole. What the fuck? You sit there saying nothing in your introverted little world, and then you tell *our* mother you wish she were dead! What are you, some kind of sociopath?'

She was going seriously fast. I could hardly see where the road ended and the stone walls began and I clung to the passenger door handle as the car ricocheted from side to side.

'She asked. I was just being honest.'

'No, Scott, that was not being honest. That was a negotiation with someone we haven't seen in years and who happens to be our only living parent. How could you say that?'

'You're the one who stopped seeing her too.'

'I was angry at her for not seeing Millie. I've never said I wanted her...'

The car flew round another corner. I don't think we were even on the correct side of the road.

'Seriously Ellie, slow down. SLOW DOWN!'

She was scaring me. I'd seen her angry before, I'd seen her pissed off, but I'd not seen her manic like this. Whichever road we were on was not built to take the speed we were doing as we continued to bounce and somehow avoid careering off into a ditch.

'What's wrong, Scott? It's alright to wish someone dead but driving a bit fast on a country lane turns you back into a mummy's boy? You've ruined everything. As usual.'

Our headlights hit a sign saying 'bend ahead', and I tried to warn her, but she yelled across me.

'We'll get nothing now. My kids will get nothing. She'll never talk to us again. You've effectively got your wish and included me in it. Thank you!'

Be it the fear, the high octane of having to cling to the car for dear life, but something inside of me then snapped.

'Oh my God, Ell, think of all the shit you said to Dad over the years. All the shit we had to put up with from you. I may have said I'd prefer if Mum and Dad swap places but you're the one who...'

'I what?' She turned her head to glare at me, challenging me to complete the sentence.

'WATCH OUT!'

'FUCK!'

CHAPTER 21

PAINT

It was lovely seeing her. It was that morning of my twenty-ninth birthday, I had barely had four hours of sleep and was still high on good indie music, my favourite lager, and a kiss from a stranger. I had celebrated my birthday the night before as I was due to have a proper birthday meal with Dad that evening. It had been a great night. Joan and Alison had organised it, and a dozen or so of my university friends had stayed out drinking and dancing. The stranger I had kissed was a girl I'd met in the smoking area outside, away from the speakers and heat of the dancefloor. It wasn't exactly a Shakespearean love story – she was about to leave and had said she wanted to make her ex-boyfriend jealous – but it was spontaneous and left me with an excitable buzz that I woke up with that morning.

And when I met my mother at the gallery, I still had that buzz, making me immune to my usual dread and awkwardness. And what was even more bizarre, so did she.

'Scott,' she called across the lobby. She beamed and walked over to hug me.

'Look how handsome you are,' she said, examining my face perhaps for signs of age or wear since we had last seen each other.

'Is it just us?'

'Of course! Who else were you expecting?' As she laughed, I did not want to explain that it was never just us. There were only two other people were in the Monmouth Square gallery lobby at that relatively early hour. Usually, the curator would be attached to Orletta's hip telling her who she next needed to speak to, and there would be numerous hangers-on awaiting a moment of Orletta Roberts' time.

'I stayed over at The Dorchester last night. Conrad is in the midst of one of his deals and needs to remain in Devon, so I thought why not make an early start and see my darling boy before it all gets hectic later.'

It felt like our first conversation in adulthood. The first time she seemed to put either Ellie or me at the top of her agenda as she squeezed my hands and kept staring at me, smiling like I had not seen her do in years.

She led me to the café, ordering enough coffee, juice and cake to keep us there the whole morning.

'So tell me about that very clever job of yours, are there any young ladies who have caught your eye?' She asked me questions that made the schoolboy inside me giggle and blush and seemed to have a rather optimistic opinion regarding my attractiveness to women. She then told me about her work and life in Devon.

'You have to come and stay with us,' she said, squeezing my hand once more. 'We have nine resident artists, and then there are the others who travel to join our little workshops. Oh, Scott, it is so peaceful. You would love it. I do not know how we have gone so long without you visiting.'

Her first meeting was at midday, and at five minutes to the hour, we walked back to the entrance.

'Promise me you will visit. Before the year is over,' she said as she hugged me. I promised and left the gallery having had the best day with my mother in a very long time.

'You were bloody lucky,' said the guy from the AA after towing the car out of the mud. 'Suspension seems fine. Brakes appear in working order – you might want to go easy on them though and take it to a garage for a quick once over – but, yeah this bog here pretty much saved you. Could have been very nasty otherwise.'

We were standing at a large gap in a stone wall, which Ellie and I had driven straight through, not noticing the sharp bend immediately in front of us.

'Can we drive it back to London?' I asked.

'Officially, I should say take it to the garage first. But,' he grinned, staring at the Volvo, a little browner and sadder than before, now back on the road with its headlights on, 'she's a tough old girl. Take it round the block and if she's handling well you should be fine. Just maybe do it in daylight and leave the Grand Prix driving to the experts.'

He smirked and handed over a clipboard to Ellie, who had hardly said a word since we came off the road. There had been a brief moment when I had thought we were both dead. I just remember our lights reflecting off a sign or something dazzling me, and then we seemed to shoot through the air into darkness and suddenly come to a standstill. Neither of us said anything for at least a minute. Ellie then groaned, 'shit' and I opened the door to put my foot in a foot of mud.

After, while we waited for the breakdown service, I surveyed the scene. We had pretty much carried straight on through what should have been a hairpin turn. Incredibly fortunately, the stone wall which previously had lined our journey had ended, leaving a runoff into an open field.

'It's been here a while,' said our AA man. 'Farmer leaves it open for access. Slope of the hill means it collects water so not much use for much else.'

I think something in our shell-shocked manner gained his sympathy as he offered to lead us into the village. Ellie had no objections to me driving.

Our bed and breakfast was a posh-looking pub with rooms. It had a very quaint Tudor look with its hanging baskets and then beams going across the ceiling as we entered. A young man in uniform stood at a small reception desk and smiled at the dishevelled strangers.

'The kitchen will be closing in ten minutes. If you're hungry you're welcome to go straight to the restaurant while I check you in and take your bags up.' I looked at Ellie, she nodded, and we wandered zombie-like straight through into the bar and were kindly placed in front of a roaring fire in a quiet corner of the pub.

Ellie was still silent and seemed transfixed by the menu, so I just scanned the room while we waited for our food. It was cosy and warmly lit – there was a light buzz of music in the background, and it had more of the feel of a fancy restaurant than a traditional country pub.

As the food arrived, Ellie picked up a chip, took the smallest bite, and seemed to chew it for an age staring into the fire. Her shoulders were hunched and she looked pale, though her eyes were a lot darker around the outside than I think I'd seen them.

'Fuck.' She said it in more of an exhale as she hunched further over, gazing into the fire.

'Fuck. Oh fuck. Oh fuck. What the hell was I doing? I could have killed us.'

She pushed her meal to the side and slumped, elbows on her knees, head in her hands.

'Seriously, we should both be dead. The last thing I saw was the wall and then...'

She was still staring out at the warm flames and crackling logs. I put down the chip I was eating, feeling it might be inappropriate to keep stuffing my face while my sister for once looked vulnerable.

'I was driving like a lunatic. What about Millie and Ed? What would they have done if something had happened? What about Mike? How would he cope?'

'You were angry. You're entitled to be angry after what I said.'

'So my response was to wrap us both around a tree at eighty miles an hour?'

We sat in our chairs listening to the fire. I could hear the light hum of the pub behind us, the glasses clinking, the low rumbling of faraway voices.

'I'm sorry about what I said. About you and Dad. That was a stupid, low blow.'

'True though.'

'He was more proud of you than he was of me.' I picked up my pint and another chip. I was suddenly starving but still didn't think it appropriate to tuck into my steak while trying to engage Ellie in a heart-to-heart.

'You made him happy. You gave him grandchildren. I made him worry. If anyone drove him to having a heart attack, it was me.'

Ellie still sat motionless while I hunched forward too. We'd never really talked about Dad *dying*. We talked about Dad and everything that came after but not the fact that he actually died and left us. That he had a heart attack and had to call an ambulance himself, or that it was a neighbour who let the paramedics in around the side and they apparently found him sitting in his chair in the conservatory fighting for what would be his last breath. We didn't talk about the fact he died alone, and surely if there was one thing we both owed him it was to have not let that have happened.

'Sorry about how I reacted. About what you said to Mum,' said Ellie, softly. 'It is as understandable as it is fucked up. Something you might want to discuss with that therapist of yours.'

'Fuck off, Ellie.' I surprised even myself at how defensive I got hearing my mental health brought into the conversation. The effect, though, was for Ellie to smile at me.

'We've made a mess of all this, haven't we?'

I don't think she was just referring to the trip to Devon.

'With Mum,' I reluctantly began. 'It felt like the last twenty years had not happened. She was that amazing, radiant woman who had once sat us on her bed and told us how wonderful we were. But if we were so wonderful why didn't she try harder with us? Keep us in her life? I wasn't saying I wished she was dead, I'm just not too thrilled with how the present has turned out and having to reconcile with someone who will reject us again once she gets the house.'

We ordered another round of drinks and eventually made a start on our steaks. We agreed not to take Orletta's offer and ask for some legal advice from someone less biased than Maxwell.

'I don't know about you, but I have no desire to have our house subsidise a bunch of Sylvia De Vales getting high in a circle painting bowls of fruit.' Ellie took a large sip of her red wine to wash down her last bite of steak.

We had turned our chairs away from the fire to eat. Ellie would occasionally glance over my shoulder, staring absently at the bar while talking. She at least looked a lot cheerier. She then smirked.

'So why didn't you ask for her number?'

'Whose?'

'Pretty young waitress from up at the house. The one who was giving you the puppy dog eyes of 'oh, your mother's my favourite artist, I feel wet just talking to you'.'

'Ellie,' I frowned. Even my most laddish of male friends did not have the vocabulary of my sister. It was part of her charm, in a way. When she would visit me in Exmouth Market she held legendary status among my friends for her turns of phrase.

'For one, she's a bit young. I think she's only just graduated. And two, I'm not really over Katie.'

'You were never really under Katie.' She burst out laughing, ignoring the fact that I was partly confiding in her my heartache.

'Well, after the whole Izzy thing, I just don't fancy being the type of guy who claims to like someone but then chases anyone else who shows him attention.'

'You Casanova, you!'

Ellie was almost in stitches, having to lean back in her chair as she laughed.

'One question for you. Since you arrived back in England, how many people have you slept with?'

This was not the type of conversation we tended to have.

'One,' I said a little defensively. 'Just Izzy. A couple of times.'

'And how long was it before her?'

I thought back, looking up to the ceiling, trying to recall when exactly it had been.

'Seriously, if you have to think about it that long I'm guessing it's not recent history.'

Here it came, some joke about being reclassified a virgin.

'That's not exactly the track record of a sleaze or chauvinist. You may like Katie, but she's with someone else.' Ellie shrugged her shoulders like it was just the way of the world. 'You are allowed to date other people. To sleep with other people. This isn't a Disney film, there isn't going to be a thunderbolt, and the girl of your dreams isn't going to appear suddenly in front of you, letting you carry her into the sunset. Best way to find someone to love, is date enough people to appreciate someone special when they arrive.'

I was a little bit taken aback by this sudden openness and advice with no trace of sarcasm.

'And, pretty young waitress is hardly a kid either. Very much a woman, from where I'm sitting.'

Ellie nodded to the bar. I turned around. The girl – Lydia – was standing there with another girl. As our eyes met, she quickly turned away, and her friend began laughing.

'So are you going to go over there or what?'

When I didn't, Ellie rolled her eyes and got up from the table.

'I'll get us another round then. See if liquid courage can get you to talk to a girl who has been staring at you for half an hour.'

I couldn't see what Ellie was doing or saying. She returned a good five minutes later with another pint and a glass of red wine.

'I forgot to order dessert,' she said, sitting down, this wide smile on her face. 'Off you go then, you can take your pint with you.' She shooed me away. I hesitated, then rose to my feet.

'Oh, and Scott? She's twenty-six. I think that's fine regards who's mature enough for who. See you in the morning.' She winked, sipped her wine, and turned her chair back to the fire.

As I approached Lydia, her friend smiled and wandered away. She had changed out of her waitressing uniform, put on more makeup, and her hair was down rather than up.

'Hi again,' I said, reaching the bar. She smiled back, looking as awkward as I did.

'I was telling your sister that I had wondered where you both had gone. I didn't realise you weren't staying for dinner.'

'Yeah, things didn't pan out as we hoped. Lovely pub, is this your local?'

I tried to move the conversation away from what would have

been matricide and car crashes – both figurative and literal. She again gave me this giggly smile.

'Kind of. This is where we go to *escape* the local. It's kind of for tourists or those who can afford the wine but the girls and I used to work here back in the day so we still get a staff discount. Plus, it's an excuse to wear something nice once in a while.'

I glanced down. She was wearing a smart black blouse and a black skirt, shorter than the skirt she had been wearing at the house.

'Your sister's quite forward.' Lydia's face went slightly pink as she grinned.

'What's she said?'

'Oh, nothing bad. Just that you'd had a fling recently that didn't work out and – ' She hesitated, going a little pinker. 'Nothing. She was just being kind. You're staying here, right? Rather than at West May?'

'Yes,' I said, slightly distracted by what Ellie might have said. I thought we should move off that topic and asked if I could buy her a drink. 'So you used to work here? You can probably give me the guided tour then.'

'What, of the bedrooms?' she laughed. 'Sorry, I'm not usually as bad at this,' Lydia said as her drink arrived.

'At what?'

'At talking.' She smiled again and tried to stop herself from laughing. 'To men.'

She had a beautiful smile, and I liked how she'd glance at me, seriously, just for a split second before beaming again or sipping her wine. It felt so strange having this conversation after the day I had had.

'We've actually come here for a bit of girl-only escapism. We occasionally chat to some tourists but normally we come here to avoid being hit on by locals – '

'Oh sorry, I didn't mean to – '

'No! You're not. It's just... I paint too, you see.'

My furrowed brow must have amused her as she laughed and turned pink once more.

'I waitress mainly so I can paint. Frustrated artist, you see. There are a few of us from uni who have a West May of our own. We gather every fortnight or so for weekends away, but unlike your mother's, ours is more what we envisioned the sixties to have been – drinking, smoking, free love.'

She bit her lip. Her cheeks were bright red, and she took a large gulp of cooling wine.

'It can all be a bit incestuous at times. What I'm trying to say, rather badly, is that it is nice talking to a single man for a change.'

Lydia pushed her brown hair away from in front of her face. She was gorgeous. She had this free, youthful exuberance that both felt infectious and seemed so excitedly hidden away in the softly lit pub.

'So you're not seeing anyone at the moment?'

Lydia shook her head. 'No one serious. Like I said, my circle of friends can be pretty tight-knit. In fact, the last time I had sex was with Emily and her boyfriend when we all got stoned together just before Christmas.'

She turned and flicked her head to the girls who had been at the bar with her. They were now at a table at the back, looking over at us, giggling. I had put my pint to my mouth and was taking a long drink, trying to force away the mental images of what I had just heard.

'Free love.' She rolled her eyes. 'I'm not usually this forward. Your sister said you were only staying one night. I told her I'm living in the village back with my parents while I save up to move to London, and... I don't know... She seemed to imply that I might not want to be backwards when coming forwards.'

Again, she smiled at me, both enthusiastically and innocently.

'I don't normally go home with guys I've just met. Or to their rooms. But if you're only staying the night we could just hang out?'

Ellie was still sitting by the fire making notes on her phone, her sticky toffee pudding finished, as I sat back down with a bottle of red wine and two fresh glasses.

'What are you doing?' She turned and looked back at the bar. Lydia was sitting at the back of the room with her friends. 'Seriously, Scott, how have you managed screw that up?'

'I didn't. I just told her that there was someone else, and it wouldn't really be fair on her. She said she understood. We swapped numbers. We may meet up if she comes to London for a gallery exhibit or something.'

'Scott,' Ellie said, glaring at me. 'There is no one else. You're allowed to have sex with other women. And she was going to have sex with you! Oh, Christ, it's like we're back at school and poor, sad Scott was blissfully unaware that there were girls who were interested in him, if he would only take his head out of his arse.'

'Well, I guess I'll just have to live with it.' I poured the glasses and passed one to an exasperated-looking Ellie. 'But for now, how often is it that I get to hang out and get drunk with my cool older sister?'

CHAPTER 22

SEMANTICS

I received a message from Camille asking me to meet her at *Coffee and Records* on Exmouth Market instead of coming to her office. They were only a short walk from each other, and I knew *Coffee and Records* well from my years living in the area. Its concept probably does not need explaining. The only element I could not say for certain was whether it was a small takeaway coffee bar that decided to fill the remaining space with records, or whether it had been a tiny independent record shop who then decided to sell high-end espressos and flat whites.

Either way, I arrived to see Camille at the counter staring up at the menu board.

'Decisions, decisions,' she said before ordering a Peruvian Americano.

'Or coffee, as we call it over here,' I smirked.

'That's enough of your cheek, or you'll be buying your own fancy-beans latte or whatever you're having.' I had my wallet out about to order when she said, 'this is on me, the least I could do dragging you down here so I can fulfil my caffeine addiction. Damn cafetière's stopped working.'

I ordered the same as her, and while we waited, Camille thumbed through the shelves of records.

'Scott, what I like about this place is they have taste.'

From the stacks she pulled out Bruce Springsteen's *Born to Run*.

'Nothing quite like The Boss to make a Cali gal feel at home.'

When our coffees were ready, Camille led the way out and said, 'how 'bout we go all *Good Will Hunting* and do our session in the fresh air? Make the most of the fact it's not pouring down for once in your fair city?'

We made our way down a narrow alleyway to Spa Fields, just behind Exmouth Market. It was a hidden away park, and at that time of day in winter, it was deserted. We sat on a bench facing the grass, and the warm coffee compensated the relatively mild chill.

'Normally, I don't like to stray too far from my office. Some of my more New Age colleagues in Cali would take their clients down to the beach and get them meditating to the sound of the surf, but sessions can rapidly go downhill if you make that breakthrough and your client starts bawling their eyes out in a public place. Not that I'm saying you're not allowed to bawl your eyes out – hey, do what you want to do. I more thought the change of setting might induce a catch-up session.'

And it did. Spa Fields was peaceful, and at midmorning it was secluded with no one around.

'Ellie has a call with our solicitors later. To talk about what our options are regarding Mum and the house. She's barred me from taking an active role in talking to anyone at the moment.' I made a light snort thinking back to the drive home and that compromise we made.

'You had no luck in Devon?'

I briefly brought Camille up to speed on the trip, including my last words to my mother before we left.

'We received a call in the morning from her partner, Conrad, saying that she was feeling under the weather and it was best we head home, and we pick things up the next week.'

'So you didn't hold back then?' Camille smiled.

Sitting hunched on the bench, I shrugged, watching some pigeons land opposite and start pecking the patches between the grass.

'I know you might not be feeling the best about yourself right now, but what you said was a minor breakthrough. I'm guessing that is the most honest conversation you've had with your mother in a long time?'

I sat staring out over the grass to the empty benches on the other side of the park. I felt I should have at least said something to my mother the next day to explain, but I still was not sure what that explanation would be. Or whether I was actually sorry. Because she showed no remorse either, for all the times she was not there and for now trying to take away all we had left – our house and memories.

'Scott, you spent the whole of last year deliberately avoiding one big thing – grieving for your father. It may be strange to hear this, but what you said might have been quite healthy, though perhaps you may want to consider how you vocalise further epiphanies.'

I noticed Camille watching me, giving me a moment to digest. She crossed her legs, and it looked like she was wearing black denim jeans under her long red coat.

'And what about Katie? And the situation with her friend? How are things working out there?'

I told Camille about Katie being away in Florence. I also told her about Lydia and how I could not stop thinking about Katie when talking to this beautiful girl.

'Oh my, you are in demand,' she laughed.

'Exception to the rule. It was only one kiss with Katie, and now she hardly even returns a message, considering I slept with her best *frenemy*. With Izzy, we were just in the same place not wanting to be alone on New Year's Eve. And with Lydia – she's more interested in who I'm related to – '

'Oh wow, this gets cheerier and cheerier! Scott, think back to how things were when you first came to see me. You've spent the last two months building relationships – something you were deliberately shying away from. As for this you-Katie-Izzy triangle, which may or may not be in play, people do have ex-partners and one-night stands. There are always pasts and shadows in the background. It comes with the territory these days. And also, women don't just sleep with men they are not attracted to purely because of who their parents are, or that they don't have a date for a party. That puts both you and them down. It may not come up in many Jane Austen novels, but you are allowed to let yourself go with the flow occasionally.'

Camille then hunched over to match my pose, holding her takeaway paper cup in the tips of her finger.

'Scott, you're a nice guy. You're a good-looking guy. Whatever happens or doesn't happen with these women, remember that you have qualities that make you very likeable to others, so you don't need to be surprised when that person you keep putting on a pedestal actually sees you at eye level.'

After the self-pity shaming from Camille, I returned to Dad's that afternoon, feeling it the appropriate setting to take Ellie's call after she got off the phone with our solicitors. It was also Jane's day reading through Dad's books and journals, and we sat in the kitchen as she put the kettle on.

'Thanks for continuing to do this,' I said. 'If it was left to Ellie and me, the whole place would be caked in dust.'

'It's my pleasure. George was always house-proud, and with me, it's more compulsion than any effort to give the place a once-over before I sit myself down and read through his collections.'

Jane poured the kettle into our old teapot and placed it in front of us.

'Margery has been very impressed with your work, dear. It seems to be coming along very well.'

'Early days.' I smiled as Jane poured the milk into each cup.

'I hope you didn't mind that I told that young lady your where-abouts. Since retiring I've always struggled with the art of keeping schtum. Decades of secret-keeping for Her Majesty makes you quite the chatterbox when the Official Secrets Act no longer dictates your every move.'

'Do they... *monitor* you? You know, make sure you're not divulging anything you shouldn't?'

Both Ellie and I had so many questions about Jane's life at MI5, which Dad forbade us from bringing up. He simply said it was not polite to ask a guest such a thing.

'Heavens no,' Jane laughed. 'You've been watching too many of these appalling thrillers they keep making. Real life is far more mundane. For one, both agencies have a front door at a not-so-secret address a stone's throw from a public underground station. And for another, while I may have signed the Official Secrets Act, I am hardly the holder of any juicy conspiracy theories. I was a bureau-cratic civil servant like any other.'

At that moment my phone rang. It was the call I had been awaiting from Ellie.

'Scott?' I heard her say. It might have been a bad line as she sounded like she was in the middle of a storm.

'Ellie? Where are you?'

'Walking down to nursery to pick up Millie. It's just started chucking it down and I'm already late.'

'Do you want to call me back?'

'No, I'll be quick. There's a way we can sort things out quickly and maybe even cheaply. They advised that if we want to avoid the courts and having our life savings sucked into the void of legal bull-shit-blah-blah, we do something called *adjudication*. Have you heard of it?'

'When someone *adjudicates* for you?'

'Yes I had gathered that for myself, thank you. I'm a piano teacher not a fucking idiot – sorry Ed-Ed – seriously, I really need to stop swearing in front of the kids.' I could hear Ed giggling as the sound of rain seemed to be diminishing.

'Listen, I'm getting close to the nursery so might have to call you back, but it's basically handing over all our arguments and documents to a third party and have them decide and let that be an end to it.'

'So, like a judge?'

'No. Or yes. I don't know. It means we don't go to court and someone sensible decides if Dad actually did mean to leave the house to Mum or us. The solicitor says it's probably our best option as probate law is technically with Mum, but just because Dad didn't sign those bloody divorce papers doesn't now give her the right to everything. If we can look through Dad's finances and show Mum received some form of settlement for the house when they split up, then that would work in our favour.'

'She did, though. We know she did. Remember that was half the reason why Maxwell was round so often when we were kids, trying to sort that out.'

'Yeah, but we were kids. What did we really know? The solicitor said to get our bank records – yours, mine, Dad's – going back as far as we can remember and prove she never paid us or Dad anything for maintenance or university. The solicitor was saying how because she was earning more than Dad that's important, especially as she was the one who walked out.'

I had stepped out of the kitchen while taking the call. I glanced back over my shoulder at Jane sipping her tea.

'I'll call you later and we can discuss,' Ellie said. 'The solicitor said it can be a bit of a lottery and once we submit our argument we don't get a second bite at it. But it will be over. One way or the other.'

She sounded out of breath and I assumed she must have reached the nursery as she hung up. Or she was as exhausted as I was by the whole process. I knew we were going to go for it, lottery or not, we couldn't afford to go through the courts, and negotiations had failed epically.

I could tell Jane had heard something of the conversation as I returned to the table.

'There are worse options, dear,' she said, placing her cup down. 'Adjudication has become popular, largely because this legal system of ours is up to its eyeballs, so something had to give.'

I told Jane about my mission to unearth Dad's bank statements and finances.

'I was going to spend some time here next week anyway while I was working on Mrs Elsop's. I'm assuming we need this stuff sooner rather than later though I have no idea where to start.'

'If you like, I don't mind casting my eye over your father's papers. Your generation probably wouldn't have a clue what to do if something originates away from that internet of yours.'

'You don't have to. You've been more than enough help already keeping this place habitable.'

'Nonsense, your father and I are from the same generation when it comes to storing old paperwork. I see you've collated most of his boxes already. Give me a week with what you have and perhaps we can see how much further along we are.'

Jane checked to see if the teapot was still warm and then topped up our cups, adding another spoon of sugar to hers and two to mine. It felt slightly disloyal to say she was a soothing, motherly presence considering we also had Auntie Pam. But with Auntie Pam's globetrotting antics, we hardly saw her, and, besides, Ellie and I were far too intimidated by Auntie Pam to ever refer to her as *motherly*.

'You've enlisted Miss Marple?' said Ellie, over the phone, as I let myself back into Loughborough Road. I had it to my ear as I placed Mr Jones' tools on the newspaper I had left for them by the front door. I was panting for breath and mentally chastising myself for not owning a car to making working on the other side of London less of a time-consuming, arduous pain on public transport.

'Jane offered. And it used to be her day job.'

'So to make up for the fact we don't have the cash to argue our case in court, we've brought in a retired government spy to do our admin?'

'I'm going back to help. Jane just seemed to know what she was doing. As opposed to me...'

Kicking off my shoes, I climbed the familiar wooden stairs, noticing one floorboard was creaking and sinking more than the others. I thought about messaging Joan but realised that was a waste of both our time. I made my way directly to the bathroom and put the phone on speaker, placing it on the sink while I changed out of my mud-stained clothes.

'When's Miss Preppy Knickers coming back?'

'Next weekend,' I said, letting the water from the shower warm-up and then staring at myself in front of the mirror. Again, I had somehow managed to get mud into my hair. I wondered if, if Katie was single, would she overlook the state of me. I didn't know what

I'd say to her when she got back. Part of me just wanted to see her again, and overwhelm her with as much platonic positivity I could muster so that we would inevitably go back to being friends.

'How long before she's off properly?'

'No idea. Maybe a couple of months.'

'So, are you two just going to sit around in awkwardness pretending nothing's going on? Or are you at least going to try to get your life together and get out of that shithole?'

'Nice pep talk, Ell. Thanks, cheered me up no end.'

'Scott, if Mum agrees and we're able to sort out the house in the next few months, you've got no more excuses for all this dossing around.'

'Just remember, Ell, we made a pact. You get back out there with the music, and I'll... well, I'll do something. Maybe.'

'A pact means one of us actually does something, not use each other's uselessness to make excuses,' she mumbled, finishing our conversation on a positive note.

I checked the water temperature and was about to remove the rest of my clothes when my phone rang again. Expecting Ellie, I was surprised to see Izzy's name flashing back at me.

'Hello, handsome,' said a voice I didn't initially recognise. It was nicer, slightly more mellow, and definitely sexier than what I would have expected from when the caller usually addressed me.

'You are an arsehole, you know that? A complete arsehole. Terminal, in fact.' It was definitely Izzy.

'You've called to tell me that?' I could hear some low-level activity in the background, the low rumble of conversation, and plates and glasses clinking. It was not loud enough for a bar so I presumed she was at a restaurant, though I had no idea why she was calling me from it. Perhaps she had misdialled and referred to every male she knew as an arsehole? It was not unlikely.

'I called to say – firstly – you are an arsehole for not telling me you'd been to reconcile with your mummy. And – secondly – that I'm bored and want entertaining.'

I was reminded of our first conversation when her responses were barely one word. It now sounded like we were old friends, and she seemed to be flirting with me.

'I'm on a date and he's taken me to this to-die-for place with the most amazing wine, but the problem is he's turned out to be a complete dullard.'

'You've called me to tell me you're on a date?' I turned off the shower and saw my face in the mirror crease up into a what-the-fuck expression.

'To give him his credit, he does know his wine. And he does know how to treat a girl. Unlike some.'

'Is that why you're on the phone to me rather than talking to him?' I smirked, picturing Izzy at a fancy bar with some young toff in an expensive suit.

'He's in the little boys' room if you must know. He's been plying me with alcohol the whole night hoping I'll be drunk enough to find his knowledge of Chippendale sideboards interesting. Mmmm, great wine. Not great enough to offset the dullness.'

'I'm surprised to hear from you,' I smiled and had a quick glance out of our bathroom window as if making sure there were no eavesdroppers to our conversation. 'I was going to call after New Year's but – '

'But you're an arsehole. And to give *you* credit you did fulfil your purpose. Now, I need something from you. What are you doing, by the way?'

I put my t-shirt back on as the only way to make the conversation even weirder was to have it semi-naked.

'Nothing. Just house stuff.'

'My, what an exciting life you must live. Spoiler's away and I need you to fill a role she normally plays.' The flirtiness was suddenly gone. I imagined her with her game face on. She then began whispering.

'It's pretty simple. I just need you to talk. About anything in your sad little life. Like one of those gardens of yours. Ready? Okay. Oh, babe! I'm so sorry!'

'Gardens of mine? Izzy? What the – '

'She must be feeling rotten.'

'Who are you talking – '

'It's my gay best friend. Our friend's partner's just dumped her. She's in bits, the poor thing!'

'I'm your what? That's quite flattering, to be fair – '

'Oh shush, babe, I'm on my way to relieve you. He's over there with her, but he's got a date, you see, sorry I really should go. Babe, I'm on my way. See you soon.'

'Izzy, this is ridiculous even for you – '

She hung up and I was left half bemused, half impressed. My job was apparently done. I waited for a minute in case she was going to call back and then turned the shower back on. It was a strange diversion, though I could not help smiling as I took off my t-shirt once more. It was flattering to be thought of, even as an excuse. With Katie moving out, I was soon to be as anonymous as I had been when I entered the flat. So it was nice to be thought of as, well, a gay best friend, I guess.

I was treating myself to a second glass of wine, hoping the mela-tonin would give me a good night's sleep, when the doorbell rang for the first time. By the time the ninth ring had sounded, I realised the wine might have been stronger than I thought, as I felt a little light-headed, having to run downstairs barefoot in my pyjamas to see what the emergency was.

'Izzy? What are you doing here?'

There on the doorstep was the girl I had been having a quasi-flirtatious conversation with half an hour earlier. Though, I say a girl, screen actress or model would be more apt. She stood there with this sharp accusatory smile in a short frilly black dress that sprang out just below her hips in an obtuse triangle – a sexy obtuse triangle, that is. Her lips were blood red, and she could quite easily have been on the red carpet of a Hollywood premiere rather than a back street in South London.

'I told you. I'd been plied with wine and was too drunk to guarantee I would not end up letting that poor sweet dullard have his wicked way with me.'

She beamed and then kissed me on the mouth before gliding past and walking inside. Her lips tasted sweet. Like expensive wine.

'I mean, what are you doing *here*?'

She was rubbing the goosebumps on her arms as I closed the door.

'Maths,' she shrugged and then walked up in what I noticed were the same heels that had pierced my side a month earlier. I saw her stumble slightly as she reached the landing. Perhaps it was the ridiculously high heels. Perhaps not.

'Maths?'

'I told you. It was dullard's and my first date. Can't get drunk and do something desperately slutty on the first date.'

She continued into the kitchen and spun around in the middle of the room smiling at me, with this strange slightly wonky intense smile that – while making her no way less attractive – scared me by its intenseness.

'Us, on the other hand, this would be our fourth. Perhaps, if I'm generous, our fifth date. Nothing wrong with doing something slutty on a fifth date, is there?'

'Izzy, I was actually about to go to bed...' Rather than fully comprehending what she was saying, I was still a little unnerved by her smile. 'And, you kind of made it clear you wouldn't be interested in me – '

I cut myself off, still staring at this completely different person in my living room. My first thought was that this was some form of trap. It was her elaborate game to prove to Katie what a creep I was and then humiliate me – Katie was on some other end of a hidden camera, though there wasn't an obvious place on her she could conceal it.

'And I thought you said – '

'Scott!' she interrupted me, still beaming. She slowly walked forward and put her arms around my shoulders. 'What would you prefer? We could stand here arguing about semantics. Or you could put your cock in my mouth.'

At school, being born towards the end of the summer made me feel a bit of a late developer growing up. It wasn't just being one of the last ones to be legally served in pubs or be allowed into clubs – obviously, everyone was drinking and smoking well before the respective legal ages. There was something in being almost a year younger than all the cool kids which kept me a little in my shell, and less likely to develop my own *coming of age* narrative.

When it came to women, I have always felt at the younger end of my peer group even if this peer group could now be classified as twenty-two to mid-forties. And associating myself as the fresh-faced young man who was naïve with women resulted in a self-fulfilling prophesy: I worshipped them, I put them on pedestals, I did everything but consider them as normal human beings with the same flaws, insecurities, and the same needs as me.

So it was certainly not the norm for attractive women – two in a week – to seek me out and ask to see my bedroom. And for all the pretence of believing Izzy to be shallow, arrogant, dismissive, and rude, it was me who put her on a pedestal based on her looks.

'You should see your face!' Izzy then laughed, her arms still on my shoulders. 'You know you aren't bad-looking. There's something quite sexy about this lost-boy innocence.' She stared at me and then placed another quick kiss on my mouth, kind of childlike, like she was doing it to see what my reaction would be. She then stepped away. I assumed this was her drunk, but then she did a perfect pirouette in front of me. It was a full three hundred and sixty degree spin in high heels, with complete control and more than a touch of grace.

'After all, I did say I was coming over to relieve you.' She gave me an over-elaborate wink and then flung herself down onto the dining chair smirking. She picked up the bottle of wine, topped up my glass, and drank as if it was her own.

'Oh that's awful,' she said, pulling a face. 'I should give you dullard's number. Perhaps he could teach you a thing or two about wine.' The lack of vintage did not stop her from taking another sip.

'Scott, I miss Katikins! And it's your fault, so the least you can do is drink with me and cheer me up. I promise I'll won't keep you up much past your bedtime.' She then slid the wine glass towards me.

'Oh, and nice *PJs*! I saw something similar when I was baby shopping for my cousin's daughter. Very sexy. Oh, and you might want to make sure that you don't have an erection when you try to look all serious like I'm such an inconvenience.'

'You're very chatty,' I said, reluctantly sitting down and making sure the table concealed any outline emerging at the front of my pyjama bottoms.

'That's probably the line of coke I did before the date.'

We had a strange conversation. Izzy called me a hypocrite for asking why she was doing cocaine, especially before a date. 'I am allowed. I don't do it often and it's been a bit of a shit week. It's not like I've let the occasional line fuck up my life like it did yours.' I replied, 'Well then, I know it doesn't help. Either short term or in the long run.' 'Were you always this boring and judgemental?' 'I'd like to think we've become friends and think you might be upset about something.' 'You are such a fucking arsehole,' she then said, both glaring at me and running her fingers over the back of my hand, which was on the base of the wine glass we were sharing.

'Do you have any orange juice, then? It's meant to neutralise the effects. Acid combats the alkaline apparently.'

I did have orange juice and got up to get it from the fridge. When I turned around, she was gone.

One of my blues albums began playing at a deafening volume from my room above me.

Quickly ascending the stairs, I was apprehensive of what she was doing in my room. I imagined record sleeves and easily-scratched vinyl thrown onto my bed. She also genuinely seemed like she needed to talk, at least until the cocaine was out of her system.

As I walked in, my lamp was on low and Izzy was standing in front of the bed staring at me with that same strange-looking, piercing smile. She lowered the volume.

'Let's play a game,' she said, walking over to me. In front of me, she again put her arms on my shoulders, smiling. She then dropped them and raised my pyjama top up my stomach.

'Izzy, I don't think this is a good idea.' Rather than taking notice, she mock-pouted and then kissed me.

'Be a sport. Like I said, it's only a game.' This time felt the tip of her tongue touch mine. She started kissing my neck. She lifted my top further till it was also at my armpits.

'Izzy, I want to but – '

She made her typical pouty face and then mimicked my voice,

'*Izzy, this is bad. What would poor Katikins say?*' I half raised my arms and then stopped abruptly.

'Scott, be a good little boy. Just one game and I'll go home like a nice girl.' I then felt the top yanked up over my raised elbows. It was an old top and was narrow around the neck, meaning it wasn't the easiest to take off at the best of times. Now it was hooked under my chin and stretched over my face like I was an old-fashioned bank robber with a stocking as my disguise. She then seemed to stretch it further and hook it around my elbows, somehow immobilising my arms above my head. I couldn't see a thing. I just heard her laughing as I stood like I had just surrendered to armed police, unable to free myself with my shoulders locked.

'Oh, hello. Someone's enjoying this more than he's letting on.' She was still giggling, and I felt the tip of her finger tap the part of me where all my blood had been involuntarily flowing.

'Izzy, stop messing around. This isn't funny.' I felt suddenly claustrophobic, anxious hearing her laugh like this was the joke she had planned all along. A weird game of dominance and very much her style.

I then felt my pyjama bottoms yanked down. My hands were still stuck above my head, and I anticipated her laughing more at the school ground *pantsing*. I felt their cord tighten and tied so I couldn't shift my legs.

'Seriously?' I muttered. In the darkness, I pictured her getting out her phone and taking a video of me in that ridiculous position, then blackmailing me with it the rest of the night. But then she stopped laughing. I first felt her hand. I then felt something that was definitely not laughter.

CHAPTER 23

SEX DRESS

'Well, that wasn't humiliating at all,' Izzy eventually said, her hand covering her eyes as we lay under the covers. I'd forgotten to close the blind, so early morning daylight shone brightly on both of us. 'Thanks for not being a complete, *utter* arsehole about it. Much appreciated.'

We'd both been awake for some time. I knew that because of several factors: the sighing; her pinching the bridge of her nose and then elaborately throwing her arms down; the kick to my shin as she turned her back on me; and the fact she had rolled on top of me like I wasn't there to drink the whole glass of orange juice I had brought her the previous night.

'You weren't exactly yourself,' I mumbled, half embarrassed, half annoyed with her. I was suddenly very conscious about how naked we both were under my duvet.

'So, what? You thought you'd be taking advantage of a drunk slut who throws herself at arseholes when she's high?'

Both our voices were still low despite the content. I hadn't slept much, and Izzy sounded hungover.

'It all seemed a little bit sudden, that's all – your interest in me. We'd hardly said anything since New Year's and – '

'Ahem, there's no interest, Scott, last night was just...' She covered her eyes and shook her head. 'And I think you being stalkerishly obsessed with my best friend may have something to do with our lack of chat. Failed to mention your little eavesdropping session, didn't you?'

She rolled onto her side and gave me a piercing stare.

'Not that it matters.' She then rolled back, seemingly content her blow had landed. 'She seems just as obsessed about not hurting your feelings, if that's what last night was about? A belated show of worthiness?'

On the floor next to the bed lay Izzy's dress, my pyjamas, and the remains of my floor lamp. With Izzy still glaring at me, I thought back to what had been our latest 'night of passion'.

Naively, it had first taken me a moment to realise what was happening, as I still struggled with the straitjacket Izzy had created out of my top.

Puritanical, perhaps, but with my t-shirt blindfolding me, the sensation I was feeling caused a face to pop into my head, and it was not Izzy's. *What are you going to tell Katie?* said a voice somewhere. Suddenly freaked out and guilty, I tried to lower my arms. I have no idea how Izzy managed to create such a tight bond and I couldn't move them. I tried to slowly back away, but the cord to my pyjama bottoms still tied my legs together. I then felt a new sensation, one I'd not felt before, slightly lower and beneath where it had been. I thrust myself away. Or at least I tried to.

'What the fuck, arsehole?' I heard Izzy jibe.

I tripped. I first wobbled backward and then swung myself forward to counterbalance. As she swore at me, I tried to jump away and turn my back, beginning to panic from sensory deprivation and the inability to free my arms. I then stumbled, careering toward the only light in the room.

There was a loud snap, then a pop. 'What the fuck are you doing?' came Izzy's shrill voice as the light went out and I free-fell to the floor. The crackle of electricity then followed as I lay on the broken pieces of metal and glass.

On the floor, in the rubble, I finally threw off my top and then tried to pull up the bottoms, but I couldn't – Izzy had tied a tight double knot in the chord, so I kicked them off too. I lay on the floor completely naked, letting my eyes adjust to the dark.

'Izzy, I don't think this is a good idea.' I suppose my words would have had more potency had they been less monotone and I not been prostrate at her feet staring up at the ceiling wheezing. I felt a toe prod me. Twice.

'For fuck sake.' At some stage during the experience, Izzy must have undressed. She was naked, and furious, and I then saw her legs flip onto the bed. When I eventually got to my feet – it took at least a few minutes – Izzy was under the covers with her back to me.

'You can get in. I'm not going to bloody pounce on you,' she mumbled, now sounding sleepy.

I delicately placed myself at the edge of the mattress.

'Hand,' she then ordered. Before I could do anything, she reached behind her and grabbed mine, bringing it to her waist. 'Just hold me,' came a softer voice.

Izzy rolled back over, bringing our conversation to an end. Without another word I collected some clothes and left her. In the kitchen, I put on coffee, set the table for two, and raided the fridge to make scrambled eggs.

'Expecting company?'

'Just you. I haven't had a chance to do much of a shop recently but what I do have is a lot of breakfast things.' I had my back to her, gently stirring the eggs. 'I've poured you some orange juice and the coffee's on the table.'

'I'm going. I've already ordered a cab.'

'Shame. There's toast too. I've already buttered it so you can take it with you.'

I was still deliberately facing away from her, cooking the eggs. I transferred them onto a serving plate, and as I turned around, I saw I had an irritated-looking breakfast companion resentfully pouring herself coffee.

'I didn't eat anything last night,' she mumbled and took a small bite of toast.

'Just the excellent wine?' I tried not to grin.

'I don't normally eat breakfast.' She prodded at the eggs with the tip of her fork before scraping a small amount onto her toast.

'I was drinking neat gin by myself when we first had sex. If you could call it that. You didn't seem to have any issues taking advantage of a drunk girl then.'

I put my knife and fork down. Apparently she did not do small talk either.

'I was drunk too. And you seemed like you could more than handle the gin. Last night seemed different, that's all.'

'I'm not saying I'm not relieved and completely over the moon not to have had sex with you, but I think I might have preferred that ignominy to the knight in shining armour routine, saving me from myself.'

I smiled. The Izzy I had come to know was back, and there was something very reassuring about it. Izzy then glared at me.

'If it was a straight choice between Spoiler and me, both single, both wanting you, who would you choose?'

'I... I don't know you that well enough,' I sighed. Izzy was staring, open-mouthed.

'And *I'm* meant to be the brutal one! I had you at least sitting on the fence. Good to know where I stand, Scott.'

'You said it was a hypothetical.'

'Interesting though that you've slept with me a selection of times and not even slipped your hand beneath Spoiler's chastity belt, but apparently, you don't know *me* well enough.'

'You *don't* want me, though, Izzy,' I smiled. 'You don't even like me. You've made that quite clear. You just seem to come round when you need...'

'Need what?' She stared at me sharply. Her mouth curved into what could have been mistaken for a smile had her nostrils not been flaring.

'Someone to listen to you,' I mumbled. I was beginning to think breakfast had been a bad idea. And her description of me wanting to be her knight in shining armour was, embarrassingly, not off the mark. It was like I could not solve my own problems, so I had hoped a plate of scrambled eggs would fix hers. Like they were trivial.

Izzy went back to nibbling a small amount of egg off her slice of toast. She did, however, gulp down most of the orange juice.

'I need to go home and change before work. I can't go in like this.'

She glanced down at her black dress.

'You look fine. Surely you're allowed to wear a dress two days in a row?'

'Scott, it's a sex dress. You wear it on nights you want to have sex. Wearing it into work means you're coming in after a one-night stand.'

We ate the rest of breakfast largely in silence – the majority of sounds were either sighs or the breakfast things being moved around the table. Izzy then turned over her phone and put down her toast. For a second I thought she was about to leave.

'That guy I told you about, at New Year's? I saw him last week. Nothing happened between us. He was with his girlfriend.'

She was leaning against the wall, her arm draped along the back of the chair.

'I can already imagine what my therapist would say. *Izzy sees well-known heartbreaker. Izzy tries to convince herself she can be happy with dullard instead. Izzy then goes and drops her knickers for some pleb she's already drunk-screwed twice.* Shit, I really have to stop calling Otto a dullard. He was more relieved than disappointed when I said I had to leave.'

'But it's okay to call me a pleb?' I smiled, hoping it might cheer her up.

'A pleb who's my go-to fuck-buddy when drunk. Or at least he was until he turned me down.'

We had both moved on to our coffees. The atmosphere in the room felt delicate, though considerably less tense than it could have been.

'Do you need a fuck-buddy?' I found myself asking, looking at Izzy. Her dark hair draping down past her shoulders, those intimidatingly sharp cheekbones, and fierce, sexy eyes surely meant she would be immune to the insecurities as the rest of us? I was slowly learning it did not.

'You've got everything going for you. I guess what held me back yesterday was that there was no need for you to be here.'

I wasn't sure if I was rationalising the situation to Izzy or to myself as I continued to look at her. 'I knew that neither of us would get that feeling of *wow, I want to spend my life with this person.*'

'And you get that feeling with my best friend?' It was a challenge rather than a question as she sent me a piercing stare.

'I just didn't expect to feel so guilty when I last saw her. Even though I knew she was back with Ethan.'

'So your strategy is abstinence? Interesting. For your whole life or just until you meet Miss Wow?'

I knew she was ridiculing me but I didn't mind. If anything it was refreshing just talking to someone. Even Izzy.

'She's only here for another couple of months, max. I'd rather enjoy them. Even just as friends.'

'Interesting.' She sipped her coffee again. 'Men and women being friends and not having sex. Is that possible? Where's the fun in that?'

A trace of a smile flashed over the rim of her coffee mug.

'Who knows. I'm not exactly an expert. But I'm up for it if you are?'

I had fallen out of the habit of checking my emails, not having an office-based job. But having a fledgling business that can't afford an app or website meant I did at least have to log on once a week to see if I had any responses from my gardening leaflets. So while Izzy was in Katie's room changing out of her *sex dress,* I fired up my old laptop.

'This is alright, isn't it? Librarian enough to counter the amount of leg I'm showing off?' Izzy had changed into one of Katie's work dresses – a black and white corduroy dress that, only later I realised, made her look like she was going to a fancy dress party as a clichéd, *sexy librarian.* She even picked up a pencil from the table and used it to tie her hair up. 'I only need the glasses,' she said as I guiltily closed my laptop, hoping my face didn't betray what I was looking at. Only when the coast was clear and her Uber had left the street did I rush back upstairs and return to the screen that I wanted to read in total privacy.

Hey stranger. Conferences have gone really well, thanks. Lots of discussions on Florentine art and I have duly kept my mouth tightly shut, just nodding sagely so people won't know what a fraud I am. Arrived in Copenhagen a couple of days ago. It's lovely here! So wintery but a nice cold compared to the bone-chilling ones we get. I actually got very drunk last night at a work dinner in this amazing restaurant and ended up boring some elderly professor rigid about all I knew on the Pre-Raphaelite Brotherhood. Had such a hangover this morning.

Sorry for the lack of replies to your messages. Things have been so hectic, a bit overwhelming if I'm being honest. Even tonight I've had to go to another reception and have been force-fed more wine. Oh it's a hard life, I know! Anyway. Just wanted to say I miss our chats and sorry we didn't have more time to hang out before I left. I'll be back Saturday afternoon, perhaps we can have a cup of tea and catch up then? Take care.

I felt the universe was finally with me. Like in Old Testament bible stories, I had been sent a test, and this was my reward for not succumbing to temptation. I then had a panic that Katie had sent the email days earlier, so I checked the timestamp. It was five minutes past midnight that morning. Just after Izzy's and my fumble had resulted in me lying in the sad remnants of my lamp and my dignity. I then looked back at the time. It was late, and she had been drinking wine, and she was thinking about me enough to write. I knew I should not read any subtext into the email. Or let it give me false hope that she did think about me when she was alone, like I did her. But it was too late. That false hope was bubbling away ready to erupt.

CHAPTER 24

NOTICE

Ellie was driving up to meet me at Dad's house. She informed me that Mike had finished a series of session projects that had him losing most of the previous weekends, so he would have the Friday off and spend it with the kids. 'Our equivalent of giving me a spa day,' she had said over the phone.

'Your ma has agreed to adjudication,' said a less enthusiastic Maxwell, also over the phone, the day before, and was the reason why I was making my way back to Wood Green the day before Katie was due back. Maxwell said he would come over and drop off some of the paperwork we had to sign. 'If you'd come to me first, I would have advocated you first go through the negotiation and arbitration routes...'

We had also asked Jane to join us to go through Dad's paperwork, and she could let us know what she had found in all those boxes of jumbled statements and invoices. After everyone else had gone home, I then planned to spend the evening familiarising myself further with all the forms and papers and try to be of more use than I had so far been in proceedings. I would stay the night and then return to Loughborough Road in the morning, having already cleaned the flat both to the best of my abilities and to what was possible considering what it was.

Arriving at Dad's, I could hear the sound of the piano. The keys were crashing down quickly and a wall of sound was building up as I let myself in. I entered the living room and silently joined the already present audience of two; Maxwell and Jane. Ellie was sitting at her stool and continued undeterred, ascending the scales, driving the volume. Her hands were positively flying through the keys. The notes were both thunderous and deliberate – a melody controlling a storm. It built and built and then, just like a giant wave, suddenly broke and crashed to the shore. Suddenly came something calming – soft and beautiful and perfectly controlled. As the dust settled, I was transfixed, in awe at what I had witnessed.

Jane, Maxwell, and I applauded as Ellie took her hands off the piano.

'My final piece from university. The way it should have sounded if I wasn't doing whatever it was I was doing instead of practising.'

'Dear, that was wonderful. You should be very proud of yourself.'

'Well, I guess that's what happens when you only get five hours of sleep a night raging away on an electric piano while the kids are in bed.'

'Five hours is plenty. Margaret Thatcher thrived on just the four, it is said.'

Ellie closed the lid of the piano and looked up at me. Before she could say anything Jane addressed me.

'Eleanor's been telling us she has an interview.'

'Not an interview. Just a meeting.' My sister got up from the stool and joined the rest at the sofa and chairs. 'Small amateur orchestral group in Worthing. One of the yummy mummies plays the viola and told me they were looking.'

She didn't look overly enthusiastic, but then again, this was Ellie, Queen of Sarcasm. On the other hand, I was surprised and a bit daunted by the fact that she had done something already. I tried to give her an impressed look, which she ignored and instead turned to Maxwell. 'So, she's agreed then?'

'Well, from a purely legal standpoint she would be a fool not to.' The tea set was arranged on the coffee table and Maxwell had a cup and saucer in his hand. He looked rather vexed.

'My girl, I wish you would have talked to me before doing this. I would have at least like the opportunity of talking some sense into you.'

'Maxwell! We followed your advice last time and ended up with an offer that pretty much equated to nothing and a plaque in our names over a barn conversion.'

Apart from Jane, we had all shuffled forward in our respective seats. Jane and Ellie were on the sofa, and Maxwell and I took up the armchairs, looking very much the circle of conspirators.

'My dear,' Maxwell sighed but straightened his back, looking more business-like. 'The reason why I myself had not suggested adjudication is that it has every means of taking the power completely out of both yours and your ma's hands. For every winner there is a loser, and something your solicitor may have failed to divulge is, practically speaking, it is no less hard work than proceeding through the courts.'

'But, Maxwell, you're the one who advised us *against* going through the courts,' I tried to counter, mainly to appear of use. '*Jandice and Jandice*, and that. It would cost a fortune. This solves things quickly and gets it done.' Maxwell gave me a tired look, like I was being the opposite of use.

'Scott –' another sigh – 'the original intention of adjudication was that the process would be fairly informal. Something for the everyman. However, as with most of our legal shortcuts, it has developed into a formal process involving detailed submissions, witness statements, and often even expert reports. There is no wise King Solomon on the other side who will judge sagely and fairly. In my humble opinion, the system is as bureaucratic as any other and prone to far greater misunderstanding by whoever is charged with adjudicating your outcome.'

Unlike me, Ellie looked unmoved as Maxwell tore our choice down. She just sat listening like she was waiting for him to move on to the ins and outs of what came next.

'If you had come to me, I would have asked you first to consider negotiation and then arbitration. Our meeting with your ma...' I'm sure there was a sideways glance in my direction. 'It perhaps could have gone smoother, but it was only step one. Slow and steady wins the race. We could have gone back to the negotiating table, we could have brought in a third party to arbitrate, all while *building* bridges, not tearing them down – '

'Maxwell, we see what you are saying. But every morning I wake up and get two small children dressed and fed, take them to nursery, go to work, collect them, find some time to try to plan my future and then curl up on the sofa with my husband discussing who is more permanently exhausted. For me, slow and steady doesn't win a thing. All this is time spent away from my husband and children, and if I can get anything out of this for them, that is the only thing I give a shit about.'

I'm sure I saw a slight wince from Maxwell again as Ellie swore, but she calmly put her teacup down and stared up at him, resolute and steady.

'So why don't you tell us what my idiot brother and I can do to get things moving, and in your humble opinion, come out of this with something more than nothing?'

And as if calm assertiveness was the primary language that Maxwell understood, he briefly detached from Ellie's stare to peer down at his cup. He then chortled to himself before smiling and looking back up at us.

'Very well, my dear. Very, *very* good point.'

Commencement, Notice of Adjudication, Appointment, Referral Notices. To give Maxwell his due, he did know the law backwards and forwards and had no qualms about offering up a tutorial. Our solicitor had briefly told Ellie and me what to expect, but as more tea was poured and biscuit selections opened, we were given the full virtual tour of what we had embarked upon. If I was completely honest, Ellie's downplaying of my role did slightly irk me, considering it was my idea to bring in a solicitor in the first place. But then again, if Ellie had started praising me for my efforts, I would have known something to be drastically wrong.

I was also quite proud of myself for enlisting Jane, despite my sister's lack of enthusiasm. With Jane in the room, it felt we had the grown-up we needed to prevent the combination of Ellie and me reverting to childish, impulsive ways. She sat and listened with us, but I could not help feeling she had heard what Maxwell had to say before. Jane would casually comment, 'and the adjudicator will abide with the standard 28-day period?' and 'and you both need to wait until said adjudicator is appointed before you discuss fees, so bear in mind you'll still have some negotiation to do.' I suddenly felt for the first time in the process we were not be totally out of our depth.

Maxwell left us with a document called the *Notice of Adjudication*. He said it kicked off the process, and from that, our adjudicator would be appointed. This then gave us seven days before something termed the Referral Notice would be served. 'Now, listen carefully,' Maxwell said, sitting so forward in his armchair he was virtually squatting. 'This sets out your whole case. Everything you want to say – your argument in detail, the evidence backing up your argument, any supporting documents or expert reports – must be submitted here and here only. As Jane has already divulged, all will then be decided in just twenty-eight days.' Maxwell then triumphantly held up the Notice.

'So, in total the process takes just thirty-five days, and bosh! All is decided! How's that for a turnaround?' Maxwell then gave us a very much villainous grin. 'Now tell me, what could possibly go wrong in trying to resolve within just thirty-five days a matter that has so far taken all parties one full year to even arrive at the negotiating table?'

I guess I could not begrudge Maxwell one I-told-you-so moment. Preferably there would not be another one after this was all over. As we walked him to the door, he did however show some sympathy. 'My boy, my girl, you still have time to think this through – and I am not talking about backtracking before you accuse me of further one-sidedness. Get your Referral Notice done, dusted, and one hundred percent refined before submitting your Notice of Adjudication. Do not leave out a thing. Seven days is hardly any time at all, and you can be assured old Conrad's lawyers will do your mother's as a courtesy, meaning a lot of associates spending a lot more hours than your solicitor who will give it a once-over if that. Use Jane – that lady puts us all to shame with her knowledge of the workings of the world – and for Christ sake, use me! No matter what you believe, I loved your pa, and I love you both as you were my own. I won't have you going into this unsightly thing underprepared or underrepresented.'

He then did something rather bizarre. He hugged us both. Ellie had the same what-is-he-doing expression as I am sure I did as he squeezed each of us in turn. Three non-huggers hugging. He might have been sincere about his offer to help.

By the time Ellie and I finished giving each other a what-the-hell-was-that-about look, Jane was at the dining table where four dusty old cardboard boxes had been left by me weeks earlier.

'Listen, dears. Eleanor, I know you have to get back to your young family of yours, so I will keep this quick.'

From one box, she took out a bunch of papers.

'He does raise an excellent point regarding this whole process,' Jane said, I assumed referring to Maxwell as she took out another stack and then another, arranging them side by side. 'From the current legal standpoint, your mother is the incumbent. Probate should side with her. Therefore, our job is to lay out the argument that our case should be considered an exception to the rule. In evidence as well as for fairness.'

Like watching a science demonstration, Ellie and I stood at the piano while Jane conducted her presentation. First, she passed us a series of old letters. They were bank statements.

'As I told Scott, your father and I are the generation who would keep such records well stored, fully aware of the faff and bureau-cracy involved at not doing so. Hence, please look at the name on the account and the dates.' Jane stepped over to place her finger where we should be looking. All the statements were from the 90s, before and after when Mum had stopped living with us.

'Exhibit A, so to speak, your parents' joint account becomes your father's account solely.' We could see the names of the account change. 'Exhibit B.' Jane then took some of the statements from us and drew our attention to some of the itemised transac-tions. 'Some hefty sums being paid from this account to another, this time in your mother's name. You can argue in that Referral Notice of yours that even if your father did not confirm definite legal termination of his marriage, he definitely demonstrated sepa-ration of financial assets. This in itself should be enough to open the door regarding whether your mother will be financially compensated twice if she were then to receive the house.'

Jane brought out copies of the house deed with just Dad's name on and then copies of council tax declarations.

'You will be painting a picture to the adjudicator. Explaining to them that this is not a straightforward case of probate and that your mother was absent from George's affairs.'

I then felt a cold tingle seeing our evidence laid out in front of us. I don't know if I expected vindication at being presented what could have been a winning position, but what I did feel was a cold sweat coming on. It all seemed so clean. Orletta had disappeared from our lives without a trace.

'So we can package this all up and write an argument about how she had nothing to do with the house or Dad?'

Ellie wasn't saying anything. I assumed she had a similar feeling to me, more so considering she was less openly detached about our mother, and there was still part of her who was that sixteen-year-old girl crying into her arms.

'She's also a relatively wealthy woman. I do not know how lucrative the world of art is, but you could very well use those statements to illustrate a lack of financial support going the other way –'

'It was all being sunk into that cult of hers,' finally mumbled Ellie, taking the bank statements from me. Jane then frowned. She reached back into one of the boxes and brought out another set of letters.

'We should leave it there. After all, it is best to state your case with as much clarity as you can muster and not rely too much on challenging the other person's actions. However...' She handed us over the series of what, on closer sight, were invoices.

'These papers tell a slightly different, more ambiguous story.'

Jane's frown scrunched up further as Ellie and I shared and shuffled through the invoices between us.

'Medical bills?' said Ellie. 'For what? Dad used the NHS for everything. I'll testify to the amount I've heard about Dr Randel prescribing him whatever over the years.'

I too remembered those conversations – Dad and his various ailments and his chats with Dr Randel. We knew about his blood pressure, but Dad was super careful. In this day and age, he should have surely lived until he was at least ninety, right? I started hurriedly reading through the invoices, suddenly hoping to make more sense of Dad's passing, like there was something we did not know. Something we should have known.

'These aren't even his,' Ellie then said, a little indignantly, first staring at me and then at Jane.

'They're Mum's. *Mrs Orletta Roberts.*' She pointed to the billing items, which, for all the invoices, clearly stated our mother's name. 'What have these got to do about anything?'

'Cross-reference these with your father's bank statements. You see, he paid them. They start the year after your parents separated and carry on for over a decade, up until five years ago. The invoices show a split payment. Each for half the respective treatment.'

Jane paused and let us further examine the numbers and the dates. Ellie and I passed page after page between each other.

'Like I said, it shouldn't affect your case – '

'Oh bollocks to the case. These are for thousands,' said Ellie, her voice a little higher than normal and still staring at the invoices. 'In one year alone there's ten grand. That's just Dad's share.'

'This one's for three thousand in just one go,' I added.

'She was never ill, though. She was always too busy to be ill. She would be exhibiting here, travelling there. If she was ill we would know.'

'Maybe it was diabetes or something medication-related.'

'It's not diabetes, dickhead, she'd have that off the NHS. It's not the fucking Dark Ages.'

'I said *something* medication related. I know as much as you bloody know.'

'Children, please.'

Jane nipped the bickering in the bud. Ellie's voice was becoming strained and mine becoming sulky as she snatched the papers away from me and I tried to claim them back.

'I was in two minds even to mention these – in some ways despite demonstrating more financial compensation by your father it rather goes against our assertion that their assets were completely independent after their separation. But... well, George rarely spoke of your mother to me except in a nostalgic manner.'

I leaned against the piano as Ellie wandered away with her share of the paperwork, trying to detect as many clues as possible from pages with very similar entries.

'Do we know what type of hospital this is?'

'They are from a standard medical services company. No details of the hospital or the treatment.'

Jane did not have to say what we already knew.

'We can't just ask her. *Mum, we think you might have been seriously ill over the last twenty years. Do you mind telling us what's been wrong with you?* Especially as *you've* already said it was your preferred outcome.'

'We don't know she was ill,' I said, trying to ignore Ellie.

'Because healthy people spend a fortune on medical bills. It's not likely to be an ingrowing toenail.'

'I mean, the frequency, the fact it was not one huge sum but a lot of medium sums, it doesn't sound like... I have no idea. But you saw her, Ell. We both did over the years. She never seemed lacking in energy and, if it was serious, Dad would have told us.'

I was convinced of that last bit – my only certainty. Dad had passed away in a lot more mystery than he had ever lived his life, but there was no time at all that I believed he was hiding something.

Ellie dropped the papers back down on the dining table. She sat back at the piano, looking deflated. 'What type of parents don't tell their children when one of them is ill? What type of children don't even notice?'

Jane and I convinced Ellie there was nothing to be gained by her staying and that she should drive back to Brighton to spend time with her own family. I then took Jane out for dinner at the Argyll Arms. Once a Beefeater, then a Harvester, briefly a Weather-spoon's, and now a gastropub, it seemed to represent the changing eras of Wood Green High Street.

'She doesn't mean it, you know.'

I stared back at Jane over my Herefordshire burger with locally sourced mustard and Dalston-brewed-beer-battered chips – a greater mouthful to say than it was to eat.

'We're always rattiest with those we're closest to.'

'I know,' I said, dunking a chip into the homemade ketchup.

'It's all a bit much for her what with how she worshipped your mother.'

'I get it. I just feel a bit useless at times. Like, you've done all the research from boxes I should have looked in months ago.'

'You're doing what you can. Things are moving quickly now, and do not be afraid to ask other people for help.'

I had lost my appetite and regretted choosing the burger as it was ungraceful to pick at. A few weeks ago, I had wished for my mother's early demise, and it turned out it could have come true.

'It just seems to matter less now. If she was ill and we weren't around. And now we're fighting her for an inheritance. It proves

Maxwell right – that we look like spoilt brats who could not get their own way.'

I slumped in the wooden chair, wondering if Ellie was feeling the same on her drive back. Jane sighed in a calm, motherly manner.

'I can tell you one thing from my many years on this planet. There is no manual or correct decision-making process to all this. This may not be the easiest time for you and your sister, but it has had you in the same room together. And, that would have delighted your father. Believe me, he would not stop bending my ear about you both, and if there was one thing he did confide in me, it was how you both were the world to him. Seeing you together getting on well, despite all the upheavals from your childhood, was his greatest pleasure. Who knows, perhaps this was his hope all along. Without a will, you would be forced to sit down and thrash things out. He was never one without a plan, was George.'

I had thought we were finished second-guessing Dad's motives, but apparently not. Maxwell had left me instructions of how I needed to lay out our case, and Jane had spent part of dinner talking me through a legal argument. 'Also,' Jane had said, 'do not feel too invested not to backtrack if needs be. If you want to take some time and talk further with your mother – to ask about those medical bills – perhaps that would give more peace of mind than even settling on the house.'

But Ellie was also right – we could not simply just ask our mother after all that had gone before. But there was someone who might know. Someone who had been uncharacteristically quiet on the subject of our mother and someone even Dad would not have dared keep in the dark about something important.

. . .

The thing about Auntie Pam is that she gets in touch with you, not the other way around. Even before Christmas, Ellie blew her top trying to contact her and invite her to lunch. 'What type of person doesn't have a mobile phone in this day and age? How am I supposed to WhatsApp her if there's no means to send her a bloody message?'

'Is Auntie Pam really the type of person who would ever use WhatsApp?'

Instead, our aunt had left us a series of clues as to her whereabouts, the first being another landline number for someone called Jean-Luc at the Royal Society. Unsure if it was a work or home phone number, I dialled it hoping I could at least leave a message asking where to find my aunt. To my slight panic, a man's voice answered within three rings and I had to explain to a gravelly sounding stranger the cryptic nature of my mission.

'You are Scott!' he cheered loudly down the phone in a French-sounding accent. 'I have been waiting months for your call! Your auntie told me I should *command* her itinerary.'

He had such a powerful laugh that I had to remove the phone from my ear, and he seemed to find great joy in the use of the word command.

'I was Pamela's private answering service before she retired. 'If you need me call Jean-Luc, he knows how to get hold of me'.' Again, the booming laugh. I quickly apologised for the inconvenience and interrupting his evening.

'It is no bother. I used to call her *Madame Ministre*, she was such the top dog. We miss her very much at the Society.'

Jean-Luc passed on the name of the hotel where her expedition was staying. They had left Amman three days ago and were at a town halfway to Petra. As I finished the call, I thought about calling Ellie next. I wanted to keep this a solo mission and prove to her I could do something useful and get to the bottom of this mystery.

But it didn't feel right interrogating Auntie Pam on my own. We were still meant to be a team, and it was also clear how personally she had taken the news about Orletta. If there was someone who deserved to be the one asking the questions, it was her.

So I waited until the morning.

'Urrrrgh...' was all I heard when I mentioned calling Auntie Pam. A long groan that overwrote what had been a more optimistic tone when she had answered the phone. She had initially told me she had a good evening with the kids and had then sat on the sofa with Mike watching a film and trying to take her mind off the whole medical bills business.

'We could Skype her? Together. Now.'

'Now?'

'According to this Jean-Luc guy, they keep moving about so it could be a different hotel tomorrow or later.'

We had tried Skype with Auntie Pam once before. And it was a total pain. I assumed Auntie Pam would have retired before video calls were the primary mode of contact when abroad. Or else she ignored the fact it existed and left the technology to Jean-Luc and her team. When I was in the Middle East, Dad arranged a family Skype call including Auntie Pam's landline. It was probably one step too advanced for all concerned as the entire call was spent yelling out questions about technology. 'Scott, I can't see you, can you see us?' asked Ellie. 'Eleanor, what the devil are you doing in Lebanon?' 'She's not Pamela. I've added your number to this call thingy. It's like a teleconference.' 'Having to teleconference one's own family now, are we, George? Times do move on.' 'We can see you! Wave to Uncle Scott, Mill-Mills.' 'What on earth is your daughter on about? How can we see young Scott if he's in the Middle East and we're on a teleconference?' And so on. So I waited for Ellie to fire up her laptop and told her just to press the mute button when she felt like screaming.

'Scott dear, splendid to hear from you. What can the matter be?' Auntie Pam did have a way of getting the conversation straight to the point.

'Auntie Pam, we'd like to ask you some questions about Dad's –
'

'Eleanor? Are you there too? Come closer to the phone. You sound a little echoey.'

'I'm in Brighton. And we're calling over the internet – '

'Scott said you were calling from your father's?'

'I am. I'm here with Dad's things – ' I instantly wished I hadn't tried to explain as the conversation seemed to turn a corner and go down a detour. Auntie Pam exclaimed how preposterous it was that we were in two different places calling her in a foreign country and then lectured us for the phone bill we would be racking up. While this was happening, I received a separate message from Ellie: *4 FUUUUUUCCCCCCKKKSSS SAAAAAKE!!!*

Eventually, I managed to get us back on track, taking the lead as I could see Ellie's Skype was now on mute.

'Auntie Pam, it's about Dad's estate. There's been a lot of money going out on medical bills. But not for him. They're all invoiced for our mum. Do you know anything about this?'

Auntie Pam didn't say anything. I could tell she was still on the line as I could hear the tinny echo of a public address system and a prayer in Arabic being sung – the call to prayer, I knew it to be.

'Auntie Pam?'

'Scott, I know you mean well, but I do not appreciate the ambush here while I am working. Surely this could be asked once I am home.'

'Ambush? Auntie Pam, we're just asking a question,' said Ellie cutting in.

'It is not a pertinent one. And why would you assume I hold any answers? Your father had his own motives for his actions. God help me if I could understand them at the time.'

'So you do *know*?' I said. 'You know he *acted*? That something did happen?'

Again the prayer rung out in the background and I could imagine Auntie Pam's hotel looking out over an arid landscape with ancient white stone buildings, similar to photos she had shown us of her trips when we were kids.

'Because it was a shock and a little confusing for both Ellie and me. Like, if Mum was ill, or is still ill, it doesn't really say a lot about us. And we can't ask her because of the house, and you've been so quiet regarding what we should do... Without Dad here you're really the only person we have left...'

I cut myself off. I was rambling and laying it on a bit thick to someone who saw sentimentality the same as frivolity. With no reply and the call to prayer now at an end, I checked the Skype app on my phone screen. Ellie was still on mute, and we still had Auntie Pam on the line.

'Hello?'

'I can hear you loud and clear, Scott.' Another pause. If I was beginning to find the conversation frustrating, I would have liked to be a fly on the wall in Brighton.

'Oh very well,' then came an equally frustrated sounding voice. 'But not over the telephone or whatever this is you are dialling me on. If we've waited this long another two weeks until I return will not hurt you. I'll be in touch regarding arrangements.'

'Auntie Pam, we'd really appreciate it if you could at least...' No sooner had Ellie unmuted herself than Auntie Pam hung up.

'Auntie Pam? Auntie Pam!'

'She's gone, Ell.'

'What a fucking bitch.'

CHAPTER 25

HOMECOMING

Neither Ellie nor I were delighted, but the call did have us breathing slightly easier. Despite Auntie Pam saying very little, it was what she did not say that I think both gave Ellie and me an inkling of relief. She was annoyed, frustrated and a little angry. It might have been the reaction of someone keeping a secret but not of a person who knew something of life and death. Or at least that was my hunch. If our mother were ill, I would have expected her to be more solemn under questioning. Instead, Auntie Pam gave the impression that we'd found out something we were not meant to know, and she had hoped to wash her hands of it.

'Maybe they're not medical bills. Maybe it's a shell company or a holding company that Dad's been paying into for tax purposes.'

'Dad's a tax dodger?'

Ellie's tone was rightly dubious as we carried on our conversation while I locked up the house and began my walk to Wood Green station.

'Well, medical insurance comes with a tax break. And so does putting assets in the name of your spouse,' I remembered from my financial exams.

'Very plausible. I should have suspected as much when he asked me to be the signatory on his Cayman Islands bank account. Come to think about it, that gold bullion I found under the floorboards was a bit suspicious.'

She wasn't even making an effort to be sarcastic.

We could wait until she got back from Jordan. That was not too much of an issue, just another inconvenience in the whole stop-start process. But, it would probably also take us two weeks to get the Notices, which I had spent the night writing, into a decent enough shape that an adjudicator would consider, that is, if Maxwell kept his word and helped us.

'I'll take the train up again next week. I have to be in town anyway, and I wouldn't mind having a look over things again. In the meantime, dickhead, please stop watching Netflix, gangster films or anything with a money laundering subplot.'

With that arranged and affirmed, I finally made it onto the tube with just a few hours to mentally prepare myself for seeing the woman I had an almighty crush on and with whom had an undeniable habit of screwing things up.

When I arrived at Loughborough Road, the door was wide open. I heard voices upstairs. They sounded like Joan and Alison's. There seemed to be some activity going on as I walked up the stairs, wondering what on earth people were doing in my flat at barely eleven o'clock on a Saturday morning.

'If we could put the plates and cutlery at the bottom of the crates, we can use the tea towels as cushioning,' said a voice I had not expected to hear for another couple of hours at least.

I was on the landing, and all the commotion was coming from the kitchen.

'I don't know why you don't just get rid of this tat and buy everything new, now that Ethan is head arse-kisser at *Nobhead and Nobhead.*'

'*Noble and Noble.* And *I* want to keep this tat, Joan.'

Even our flat had not seen such a state of mess and chaos. Half-empty and empty packing boxes were strewn on the landing resembling the morning we first moved in. A suitcase was open in Katie's doorway with a tower of clothes piled on top, not even a remote chance of it closing.

As I entered the kitchen, my three friends were all in one room with crates in their hands. All our cupboards and drawers were open as if I had interrupted a burglary.

'Scott!' Alison was the first to notice me and put down her crate to hug me.

'It's about time,' said Joan. 'She's had us at it for hours.'

Katie stood silent, the furthest from me. Her eyes had shot wide open.

'It looks like you're moving out,' I joked weakly.

'Yeah, and leaving me and you both in the lurch,' Joan said while dragging a large box of tinned and dried food out of the pantry.

'We're good in here if you both were to start on the bedroom?' Alison looked from Katie to me, picking up one of the throws from off the sofa and folding it. Katie was still staring at me.

'Okay,' she then said and navigated her way past the crates, giving me this awkward-looking smile.

As we left the room, I heard Joan say to Alison, 'I guess she's not told him.'

Katie's room looked like a bomb had hit it. Clothes were everywhere, the duvet and bed had been stripped, even her lamp lay disassembled on the floor.

'I didn't think you'd be back so soon,' I said quietly, wandering around the bed to the other side of the room.

'I took the earliest flight in the end.' She picked up some of her clothes, began folding them and then dropped them down.

'A friend of Ethan's is subletting his flat and it's ideal for us. It's also an amazing bargain. But he needs it taken this weekend, so hence the rush. I was hoping to tell you all this in person when I arrived, but you were...'

She seemed to leave this open for me to state my whereabouts.

'I thought Ethan wasn't back until April.'

'That's still the plan, but this is a really good deal. And as Joan has been screwing us both over on rent since we moved in, I called him and said I needed to move out early. You know the mortgage is only a third of what we've been paying combined?'

I was completely ambivalent to that news. I stood trying to keep a passive face and process how different the current scene was to what I had played out in my head over the previous weeks.

'And I can't do the move tomorrow because I have to go into work for an event. And then I'm doing debriefings from the trip all next week...'

She took a deep breath and then put her hands to her face. She looked tired and exasperated and my chance to say anything to her had realistically evaporated. It was now a case of parting on good terms. That was all I could hope for. All I could now do was push my face into a smile and look happy for her and less completely deflated.

'So...' I took a large breath. 'How can I help?'

With less time to organise than when she had moved in, Katie had said she had opted for a *man with a van* who was on his way. We made steady progress, and boxes had migrated downstairs to go in said van when it arrived. Alison and I were at the kitchen counter wrapping Katie's glasses in newspaper.

'Joany, is there anything in this house you actually own? At the moment you've left Scott with one plate, a bowl and a water glass.'

After an initial spell of packing, Joan had spent a lot of time creating space to bring the sofa and fridge forward so he could lie on the floor behind it and start unplugging and untangling wires that had connected up his old hi-fi. With Katie's throws packed away, the sofa was left exposed with yellow foam protruding from tears in the worn black leather.

'Yeah, I need to talk to you about that, mate,' he said, I assumed to me, still behind the sofa messing about with wires.

'I don't know if I can be arsed with the landlord stuff anymore. Boiler nonsense, repairs, furniture, and that.'

'It was one repair, Joan,' Katie said, coming back in with another empty box to scoop up what was left in the room. 'All you had to do was call someone. Or let me call them. Not exactly taxing.'

'Still, I don't want people whining at me at all hours.'

Katie then put down her box and stood staring incredulously at Joan's protruding body, her hands on her hips.

'It's not exactly whining when you're politely asking someone to do something that is their obligation.'

'Whatever,' he said, Katie's complaint hardly seeming to register as he threw a speaker wire up over the top of the sofa. I was going to ask if he needed a hand, but it then dawned on me that the stereo was not even Katie's, so I wasn't sure why he was removing his property too.

'I was talking to Alison's dad the other day, and he was saying it was probably a good time to sell.' He wriggled on the floor, and I could still only just about see him.

'He's done up a few houses over the years, and he's given me a couple of numbers of people who could do a relatively cheap job plastering the walls and sanding down the floorboards. He reckons with a couple of cosmetic touches this'll go for a mint.'

'When did all this happen?' Alison joined Katie side by side, her hands on hips too, staring down at Joan.

'Christmas. I'd been too busy to do anything about it until now.'

'What do you mean until now?' Katie glared down.

'I mean, as you're moving out, I might as well get on with it. Ali's dad said his guys are free next week, so, mate, if you could also sort yourself out somewhere new too, I'd be grateful.'

I guess what I do notice about myself over the years is that I'm a bit of a processor rather than a reactor. Joan was finally sorting his flat out – that was surely positive news as it was long overdue. Joan was also implying I needed to move out, perhaps within the next two days – less good news. Luckily I could process away to my heart's content because I had two reactors in front of me who definitely did not share Joan's optimism about the situation.

'You're evicting Scott? Because I'm moving out? Where's he going to live? Where's he going to store his work tools?'

Joan shuffled up onto his knees so I could see him. 'Mate, can you pass me that screwdriver?'

'Joan!'

He shrugged and shot Katie a scowl back. 'How should I know?'

'To be fair, I should be putting them back in the Jones's shed every night but – '

'You capitalist bastard,' suddenly shot Alison, open-mouthed. 'This isn't bloody *Property Ladder*. Houses aren't assets flipped by the middle classes so they can price out normal, hardworking people. This is everything we despise!'

'Scott has rights, *brother of mine*. He could sue you. He should sue you.'

Just the word *sue* had triggered a headache. Had I not taken

legal action against enough of my loved ones so far that year? Joan
got to his feet, looking neither amused at nor ashamed of the accusations thrown at him.

'Listen.' He stared at Alison. 'I know you think you're a socialist
but you're happy to buy clothes from Topshop, have girly shopping
trips to department stores and spend four quid every morning on a
branded Starbucks latte. Hardly what Karl Marx envisioned when
he was writing the manifesto.'

Alison visibly took an intake of air and glared, but before she
could respond Joan had already turned to Katie.

'And let's not talk about rights from the person who is now
fucking off to take up some wanky banker's flat in Brixton because
her polyamorous boyfriend has finally had his fill of getting his end
away with Tess Philips every – '

'Mate,' I said, stepping forward probably too late. Katie was
glaring even harder. Her eyes went big and her jaw appeared to be
trembling as she stared at him.

'Plus,' Joan said, in a lower voice. 'Village gossip back home is
she's moving back too. Coincidence, I'm sure.'

Alison luckily saw it happening first and wrapped her arms
around Katie's waist. Part of me was tempted to unlock Ali's arms
so Katie could have a free run at Joan – her arms were flailing
around as Joan stood naively bemused – but then Ali suddenly let
go. I briefly saw her mimic a classic Joan shrug and a livid Katie was
allowed to stumble forward, her arm swung back either in a punch
or almighty slap. As Joan then flinched for impact Katie hesitated.
Her face was screwed up in concentration and then rather than
unleash a right hook she shoved him hard in the chest.

I say hard. Joan is the same height as me, a skinnier build
perhaps, but at almost a considerable height and size disadvantage
Katie's shoves had him looking more confused than at risk of his
life. -After shove number three, each accompanied by a light tennis

player's grunt, she resorted to a double palmed slap making Joan's chest sound like a set of bongos. Alison and I stared at each other uneasy. I think we would have preferred a fight to have broken out rather than watching this prolonged awkward scene. I decided to step forward and hold Katie back. But not by grabbing hold of her. Instead, it seemed more appropriate not to touch her, so I hooked her away from him by pinching hold of a belt loop on her jeans. It was, however, effective as I didn't have to step in between them and her jeans were high enough for the loop to be central lower back. She did, unfortunately, look like a toddler on a leash. With a last flailing slap, she stopped.

'Oh, screw you, Joan, you're not worth it.'

She then turned and grabbed up a set of keys that were on the dining table.

'Where are you going?' Joan called after her, still looking bemused. We heard her feet descend the stairs, and the front door slammed.

'The van will be here in five. She'd better be back to load this crap up.'

'If she's anything like me, she's gonna leave it to the man who needs this place spotless because he can take advantage of the capitalist system.'

Alison grabbed her coat from the back of a chair.

'But what does a fake socialist like me know!'

'You're going to leave Scott and me to clear all this by ourselves?' he called to her as she left the room.

'Actually, I'm off too, mate.' I suddenly rushed past Joan, past Alison, and was out of the flat looking left and right for where Katie went.

. . .

I just caught a glimpse of her black coat turning the corner at the far end of the street. She was heading in the opposite direction to the pub Joan and I had previously tracked her to. I eventually caught up with her on Stockwell Crescent, grateful I had not flipped arse over tit the two times I had skidded on a January frost-lined paving stone.

She ignored me as I called her name, and I had to run up and get in front of her. We were in front of one of the area's posh houses with a small front garden, cream front, and a set of stone steps leading up to an ornate glossy back door.

'Joan told me Eliot Alms lives there,' I panted. 'The author. Not the comedian who does all those panel shows. I think he's at number thirteen.'

'Scott, I don't want to be rude, but I am honestly not looking for a guide to the local area.'

I was surprised that I was still panting and suddenly had to hunch down to catch my breath. The amount of outdoor work and running I do, I assumed would have made sprinting three and a half streets around the Camberwell-Stockwell borders a piece of cake. Katie began to look agitated while I got my breath back.

'I know. But getting pissed off at Joan for being Joan is like getting pissed off at a dog for urinating on a lamp post. It's what he does.'

'I'm not pissed off at him!' she hissed, like someone who was now pissed off at me for invading her personal space. 'I'm sick of him and sick of his opinions on parts of my life that are nothing to do with him!'

She flung her hand to her brow and took a deep breath. She closed her eyes and suddenly looked like she was about to fall asleep standing up. I remembered that she had begun that day still in Denmark.

'And why are you defending him? He's evicting you and it's me and Ali who are fighting your battles for you!'

'You sound like my sister,' I smiled, misjudging that it would lighten the mood.

'It's because he's the one who did me a favour in the first place. I had spent so long living out of a rucksack in between Airbnbs that my head had started to spin.'

She did have a valid point, and in truth, I wasn't too sure why I was more relieved than unhappy at being kicked out of a flat I had come to regard as home. But looking into her fierce brown eyes, despite the glare or perhaps because of it, I was reminded how much I was going to miss seeing that face. How much I would miss being in this proximity to her and talking to her whenever I wanted.

'And besides, with your stuff packed away it already has somewhat of the abandoned drug den vibe.'

Despite her assertions to the contrary, she still looked pissed off. Her hands were still on her hips, and her face seemed to rest into a scowl. I was starting to feel a bit self-conscious, having this head-on conversation on the neighbourhood's poshest street with its immaculate townhouses staring down on us disapprovingly for disturbing the peace.

'Do you want to get a coffee? There's a café on Love Walk that does a really good chocolate twist. We could take it to Ruskin Park, hang out there for a bit? Ali's forcing Joan to pack up the van by himself so hopefully it will teach him a lesson and give me a chance to ask you about your trip.'

CHAPTER 26

RUSKIN PARK

They would close Ruskin Park at sunset during the winter, so with my days taken up either at the Jones's allotment or Mrs Elsop's garden, I had not had the same opportunities to wander or sit at the community gardens as I had done during the summer. In my opinion, it looked even more beautiful in January. It was more or less empty, bar an occasional dog walker or couple in thick jackets circling its perimeter, and the grass had been allowed to grow and looked lush green and wet. When it came to the other London parks, come one relatively warm day, you would not be able to find an unoccupied patch of grass for the amount of twenty or thirty-somethings that would descend with their bottles of prosecco, Frisbees and sound systems.

In Ruskin, kids were still allowed to play football, rather than hipsters colonising it with mini barbecues and hacky sack circles. But there was also a labyrinth of trees, hedges, and gardens where you could just wander unseen and even find yourself on a bench in the middle, discovering our *Friends of Ruskin Park* Community Garden. It was the perfect place to mend a broken heart. Unless it was where you chose to have your heart broken.

With our coffees, Katie and I proceeded to circle the duck pond and then take a path through the trees. Katie reluctantly told me about her trip. I say reluctantly because it seemed like she had such a wonderful time seeing art and sculptures she had only read about during her degree and having dinners with such high profile colleagues that her glum demeanour somewhat took the gloss off it. Why do we do it to ourselves? Let a comment from another person ruin something that should otherwise be an untouchable happy moment.

'Yeah, and Copenhagen was alright. They took us on a night tour last night, and we drank warm cider in the frosty air lit up by the lights of the city.'

'Sounds better than just alright,' I laughed. She didn't laugh back.

We walked through the passage of hedges that flanked the community garden. There was a small clearing just behind with a bench overlooking the grass and trees. We sat down, and suddenly there was a lull in the conversation as we just held our takeaway cups looking into the distance. I found myself awkwardly catching glimpses of her. She looked drained. Glum and tired. And still really pretty.

'He didn't mean it,' I said.

'It doesn't matter. Some support would just be nice for a change.'

'Well...'

'Well what?' She turned and looked at me with the same scowl she had on at Stockwell Crescent.

'He said it in the worst way possible, but he did have a point.'

I didn't know if I was attempting to defend Joan or shunt Katie out of her self-pity, but there was something that sat uneasy with me. Perhaps I owed it to Katie not to spend our last conversation as flatmates lying to her?

'It is a bit sudden, moving back in with Ethan after some of our conversations before Christmas.'

Or perhaps I was pissed off at her and fancied being an arsehole and twisting the knife further?

Katie stared at me, now wide-eyed and mouth opened in disbelief. She then smiled the type of smile I would have associated with Izzy.

'Really? You think that, do you? Well, lovely to hear where your loyalties lie. I'm going to miss these little chats of ours.'

The smile crashed into another scowl, and Katie crossed her legs and swung her head away from me. I could have taken this as a hint that she did not appreciate my opinion, but the words *our little chats* stung.

'Is that why you're running out the door at the first opportunity?'

She turned back and gave me a what-the-hell-are-you-talking-about frown.

'You didn't have to move out today. You could have done it next weekend. Like, Joan's a dick, but he wouldn't screw you over if you wanted to keep your room here and still take on the new place.'

'Is that so?' she snorted.

'And even if things are going well with Ethan, you only spent a week with him after Christmas, is cheap rent in a new flat really the best reason to – '

'Scott?' she said suddenly. 'Fuck off.'

She took a long drink of coffee, apparently draining the cup. She then uncrossed her legs and got up.

'I think that's the first time you've sworn at me.'

'I hadn't wanted to tell you to go fuck yourself until now.'

It sounded strange coming out of her mouth. In her voice, it sounded too well-spoken to be an insult. She started to walk away, and I jumped to my feet.

'I don't want you to go.'

She had only gone about five yards, but I yelled the words nonetheless.

'I told you I was moving out,' she turned back to say. 'I even did that face to face, crossed half of bloody London to do it. You can't accuse me of being unfair or rushing into this. He's my bloody boyfriend, after all.'

'He doesn't have to be.' Her brow furrowed as I said the words.

'You were going to put things on hold. You *had* put things on hold. You kissed me!'

As she stared hard at me, realisation seemed to suddenly dawn on Katie as the scowl-slash-frown that colonised her face softened into something closer to embarrassment.

'Listen, Scott, about that kiss – '

'This is not about the kiss. This is about the fact that I like you, I have feelings for you, and maybe... I'm falling in love with you.'

There was still that five yards of damp grass between us. I saw a squirrel dart across the clearing behind her and shoot up a tree. I felt my eyes staring at her a little wider, slightly terrified by what I had done and what would come next. I had known all the way throughout that day such a declaration would be fruitless. The best I could expect was a sympathetic acknowledgement. Instead, she began to laugh.

'You love me? You're kidding, right?'

'No!' It was now my turn to scowl.

'So you're asking me to break up with the boyfriend I've been with for seven years – who I am about to move back in with – and what? What are we supposed to do?'

She gave this big fling of the arms and started staring around her like she could not believe what she was hearing. I suddenly felt like I needed to be still. Really still and focus my face into a frown as I had said too much, I looked an idiot, and could feel the same sensation the day I had waited for Ellie drinking three hot chocolates at Exmouth Market.

'Scott?' came a softer voice. 'I'm sorry about Christmas.' She was still the same distance away, but there was something more sympathetic about her stance. 'You were so nice. And so welcoming. And I was so relieved to have one day away from my own drama. I encouraged you when I was feeling a bit lonely and completely lost, and I'm so sorry if I led you on. But I love Ethan.'

I was finding it difficult to do much more than just stare back at her. Katie looked more inconvenienced than pissed off now, her eyes trying to remain on me to compute I had understood what she was saying, but with every breeze and noise she would do a sideways glance. This was not how I planned the day and how I would have wanted to have the conversation. But thanks to my impromptu questioning and declaration, I would likely never see her again. So if I had anything more to say, it would forever otherwise remain unsaid.

'I know this isn't the best timing,' I offered weakly. 'But for me, it started well before Christmas.' I took a step towards her and saw the faintest glimpse of panic flash across Katie's face. I took another half step just so I didn't need to shout. 'I come home every evening excited and relieved to see your light on. I'd get to spend the evening just talking to you, and it somehow felt all I've ever wanted.'

To this declaration, Katie put the palm of her hand to her head. She closed her eyes and let out a deep sigh.

'Scott, you've been sleeping with my best friend.'

Before I could respond, I heard the name 'Elsa!' called from the hedges behind me. A small dog, maybe a Jack Russell, ran up to us and stared up at Katie with a big smile on its face, wagging its tail. The voice shouted Elsa! again as the dog jumped up and put its front paws on Katie's shin. Like a police officer trying to placate a mad gunman, she slowly crouched down, not taking her eyes off me, to stroke the dog. It must have been for more than a minute that Elsa darted back and forth like she had joined some happy game between the two strangers standing silently in the middle of the clearing.

When Elsa eventually found her way back to her owner, Katie was already looking at her watch, her thoughts likely on her new flat, the van, and all her belongings entrusted to someone she did not trust.

'Scott, it's not just Izzy. Or Ethan. The idea of you and me is... well... weird.'

She gave this shrug-like gesture, an apologetic it-is-what-it-is expression.

'Yes, even if I was not still with Ethan, you having slept with Izzy, not just as a one-off, would be a pretty major impediment.' She narrowed her eyes as if examining hard that I was fully comprehending what she was saying. 'But it's not just that. We are meant to be friends. There shouldn't be this grey area. I told you all those things about Ethan as a friend. Not to make you feel I needed rescuing... It's just *weird* us now having this conversation. Plus, you're my brother's best friend. Probably his only friend. We're close partly because I see you as the surrogate older brother I would have actually wanted... see, it's weird!'

I had let out a small laugh as she described me as a replacement Joan.

'And what's also weird is that despite me knowing what huge courage it must have taken for you to say what you've said, I'm feeling so, *so* pissed off with you right now for doing it. If you want me to be honest, that's how I'm feeling. That you thought now was the right time to do this.'

Silently, we agreed to differ. I agreed to stand fixed to my spot and mumble something like *okay*. And she agreed that she would stop ripping my heart out and walk away across the clearing and disappear through the tree-lined path beyond.

CHAPTER 27

THE DEPRESSED PERSON

It's impossible to describe depression when you're no longer in it, to quote myself. What I meant was when you're out of depression, you're out of it – you're no longer one of *the Depressed* – and hence it's so contradictory to describe. The feelings and emotions you were going through would only make sense to someone else who can see the rationale behind what causes you to act so entirely irrationally. Therefore the first thing to note about falling into depression is the fear that comes over you stemming from a complete lack of confidence.

I only ate cereal the first day after Katie left as I was too paranoid to leave the house, not wanting to face anyone. Even venturing to Tesco Express would have me passing people on the street and just the very thought of their presence made me feel so anxious I retreated to my duvet. It was like they were all judging me, looking at me, seeing me for who I was and what I had done.

I postponed Mrs Elsop and the allotment, citing flu symptoms. I exchanged messages with Ellie about the house, Auntie Pam, and the Referral Notice and got told I was a lazy dickhead for not going

back to the house to send her more information about the company
that did the medical invoices.

Joan's builders and decorators arrived, and I could sense them
laughing at me – they somehow knew of the events of Ruskin Park
and that Katie was out of my league. Every smile and attempt to
make conversation was their way of subtly saying, 'what the fuck
did you think was going to happen?' So I stayed in my room and
could hear them whispering about me through the floorboards –
about the loser in the attic. Even long after they had left for the day.

'He didn't tell us he'd have someone still living here,' was what
Frank, the heavyset leader of the bunch, actually said. 'We're pretty
much stripping this entire floor and we told him he needs a new
bathroom doing as no one is going to spend the money he wants for
this place on those fittings. Luckily for him, we've got a decent one
returned to us. Not exactly cheap, but if he wants the job done
quickly, it is what it is.'

Not even the thought of Joan quite obviously being ripped off
had me registering a smile, and I was given a bucket for each time I
needed the toilet. All this probably sounds like I was just feeling
sorry for myself. And I was, I won't deny that – self-pity all the way,
baby. But that is what, I feel, makes mental health still a taboo even
though now you've got the whole world advocating how it isn't.
Because from the outside *these symptoms* look like I'm just having a
sulk and am being a little tedious, so talking about it to a trained
professional would surely be self-involved rather than appropriate.
Oh, she's just going through a breakup, compared to; *oh, she's having
a breakdown.* As an outsider, how do you tell the difference? As an
insider, how do you know, yourself? The answer in most cases is:
too late.

What I did know while spending days with no heating or
running water wrapped in my cloud of a duvet was a lot of the
wounds I was feeling were being self-inflicted. With Sarah my

internal monologue was the killer. *What made you think a girl like her could ever like you? You are not enough for her, you are useless, you are worthless, you have nothing to offer, if she's seen through you what hope do you have with someone else?* Who would have known my subconscious would turn out to be such a bullying prick?

I guess from an outsider's perspective perhaps you should try locking yourself away in a small concrete cell and have a group of people acting as your jailers constantly shouting those accusations at you for five days straight. Doesn't sound much fun, does it? With Sarah, that voice didn't shut up for five months.

'I like the bed hair,' smiled Camille, not too sarcastically.

With the builders in situ even over the weekend, I was eventually forced out of the house. I had initially postponed our appointment during the week following my run-in with Katie. I don't know if Camille sensed something was wrong, or it was her trying to balance her calendar, but she asked if I could come in the next week. So I arrived, with a small bag, as I had just spent the early hours of the morning having a long, unpleasant bucket shower – a different bucket from what I was pissing and crapping in – and thought enough was enough. If I were to continue hiding away from the world, it should be at Dad's where washing facilities and a toilet were present.

'Hmmm, normally if they're doing a bathroom they reinstall your toilet straight away,' Camille said, coming back from her desk with our coffees. Thinking about it, it seemed Joan was not the only one the builders were taking for a ride.

'Are you disappointed by what she said?' Camille said, immediately bringing up Katie and Ruskin Park. I gave her a puzzled look as I thought that was obvious.

'I knew what the result would be. I just didn't expect her to be such a... dick about it.'

I winced. I felt name-calling unfair, but I had done it in lieu of a more elegant answer. Camille smiled.

'You're beginning to sound like me. What makes her *a dick*?'

'She's not. Or she wasn't. To be fair to her, she took me seriously when other girls would have probably cringed. But then she got pissed off like she had expected better from me. Which then made me feel like shit because I had let her down.'

'But letting her down isn't your responsibility, Scott. Remember that critical side of you that manifested itself with Sarah? The voice saying you've not done this, you've not done that. Scott, you've done the best you can and that voice needs to shut the fuck up for once.'

Camille sat forward and looked focus – mean even. Like a heavyweight boxer staring down her opponent, perhaps staring down my critical side.

'Scott, I know it must hurt. *You* know it must hurt. If this was happening to a friend of yours, if this was you aged twelve or sixteen, what would the *you* present in this room now say to him?'

'Don't worry about it?' I offered, unsure where Camille was going.

'And? More realistically. Imagine yourself now aged six. Picture young Scott sitting where you are and how sad he feels. Are you really going to just say 'don't worry about it' and walk away? Imagine this is his first broken heart. What do you want to say to him?'

I reluctantly closed my eyes and reimagined one of our holidays when I was a child. I was chasing after Ellie, and Dad and Mum were laughing and giggling on some picturesque patch of green overlooking a calm beautiful coastline. I took that version of me and placed him in my old bedroom, on the bed looking so small and sad.

'It will be okay,' I said again. 'That she is just a kid too so what does she know. Just because she feels that way does not make him any less special or... less loveable.'

I suddenly felt a different type of sadness. And a huge pang of shame. A sadness for that little boy and how alone he was and how much I wanted to give him a cuddle.

'I'd tell him he was fine – great even – just as he was, and one day he'll find someone who loved him just for being him, and who would feel as excited and happy to spend time with him as he was to spend time with her.'

I imagined myself sitting on the bed telling myself that and wondered what happened to that boy and why no one told him this before. I then thought about all the name-calling and bullying I had done to that boy over the years – for calling him a geek for playing World of Warcraft and chastising him for not being *cooler* and more charismatic in front of women. I was the dick, not him.

'And what would you tell those critical voices?'

'I'd tell them to get lost.' My voice was a lot less self-pitying. I was suddenly angry at those voices, those ugly bullying pricks picking on a kid. Fuck them, was what I wanted to say.

CHAPTER 28

AUDITORIUM

I don't know if I felt any better after my session with Camille, or any stronger or energised, but as I got on the tube heading for Wood Green I at least felt more protective of that side of me who wanted to hide away under a duvet. And I needed that protection because I was about to face another woman who I had pissed off.

During my duvet week I had received a series of messages and voicemails. Maxwell had responded about the notices, giving me some reluctant waffling feedback about it being a 'dutiful attempt' but I still needed to work on my evidence layout, and my legal argument was a pile of shit – I am paraphrasing, of course. He said he would drop the notices back at the house with notes so I could have another go. He also left a similar message with Ellie, who left me a somewhat different message,

Where the fuck are you and why aren't you doing anything? You're the one who said you'd sort it.

I did eventually reply to her, saying I'd been feeling under the weather. She then made the suggestion – no, the order – that I meet her at the house and we go over Maxwell's notes together so I wouldn't fuck it up again – I am not paraphrasing this time.

On my way to the house from the tube station, I tried to get this new protective side to ignite my angry side so I didn't get steam-rolled by whatever sarcasm and thinly veiled abuse Ellie had planned for me. She had told me she was going to drop the kids off at nursery – Ed having just started one day a week – and be on the first off-peak train. I put my key in the lock and braced for impact.

'Hey!' she said, surprising me. Ellie had been standing hunched over the dining table when I entered the living room. She was smiling. No, not just smiling – beaming. This weird fixed smile that I'd seen her use at her children's christenings when people we didn't know came up to her telling her how proud she must be. There was something seriously wrong.

'I was just leaving you a note.' She had on her black parka with the fur hood – the one she wore when she just started out in music journalism. She was staring at me like someone had a gun aimed at her, and I stared back to see if I could work out what covert message she really was trying to relay.

'How are you?'

She never asked that question. I slowly put my bag down.

'Alright. Sorry I'm late. I had a thing to go to. Were you about to leave?'

'I've got a thing in town but it's not for a while still.'

'Look at us with things to do. Anyone would think we're normal people.'

'Tea?'

I followed her to the kitchen, my heart beating as if this was the quiet scene from a horror film. This was not normal unless she was trying a new branch of sarcasm that had her delay the impact of her blow for maximum effect. But even switching on the kettle and getting out the mugs, she seemed almost chirpy.

'How was your week?' she asked over her shoulder, arranging the tea things.

'Alright, I guess. Still a bit flu-like.'

'Your friend Joan called us,' she then said calmly, still with her back turned so she couldn't see my face twist.

'Joan? How does he have your number?'

For the briefest of moments my mind shot back a decade to the days of Exmouth Market when Ellie would get drunk with my friends and me. They'd not swapped numbers then, surely? They'd not done anything else... My eyes sprang wide open in terror.

'He called Mike. He got his number at Mike's last gig to do promotions in exchange for free tickets or something. It doesn't matter,' she said firmly, letting a moment of silence go by while the kettle boiled. Still with her back turned, she said,

'He said you and Katie had some big falling out or something. He said she was pretty upset.'

I heard myself groan. She'd told people. And now I was being accused of being some weird obsessive who needs the girl's brother warning me off.

'Did you tell her how you feel about her?'

'No!' I replied resentfully. 'Okay, perhaps a little.'

I saw Ellie stirring the tea and carefully remove the tea bags. I was still hovering, too on the defensive to take a seat.

'He also says you're living in a building site. That the builders have told him you've locked yourself in your room and not left it in a week.'

'So he's called you to evict me?'

The whole world seemed to know my business, and my duvet at Loughborough Road was now a goldfish bowl. I was about to tell Ellie that Joan didn't know what he was talking about. He was a slumlord, and all he could now see were pound signs, and I was more than happy to tell him where to stick his room – as long as I could get my deposit back.

Ellie turned around with the mugs. She placed them down on

the kitchen table and before I knew what was happening I was being hugged. A silent, long hug.

I've said many times that we were not huggers. Brief embraces were largely all we had stretched to over the years to show others we had a human side. But this was the first time since we were kids I could recall her putting her arms around me and squeezing me. I was unsure whether to engage back but as she held me, something inside felt like it had started to break. Despite a week in bed I suddenly felt tired to the point of collapse and did not want her to let me go.

'He's a shit friend. And I'm a shit sister,' she said, still hugging me. 'But we're not that shit or that selfish you can't just be yourself around us. You don't have to hide away and scare the builders.'

She eventually released me and looked as awkward and embarrassed as I felt.

'Oh Jesus, I'm late.' She put down her mug, splashing it on the table, and started scrambling around in her pockets.

'I've got this stupid bloody thing at Guildhall. I'm speaking to an old professor of Mike's.' She began putting on her coat and checked her watch again.

'Listen, do you have anything planned today? We've not had a chance to talk about Maxwell's notes, so perhaps you can come with me?'

I didn't know if Ellie had invited me because she deemed I needed further adult supervision rather than to talk about Maxwell's notes, but we travelled together into town regardless.

'I've not told Mike I'm doing this so don't let anything slip – he's picking me up later.' We exited Barbican tube station and I scurried to keep up with her, until we reached the entrance of the Barbican theatre.

'I thought we were going to Guildhall?'

'The Guildhall music department is in the Barbican.'

We pushed through these insanely heavy metal and glass doors and were in a cavern of vast indoor open space. The ceiling stretched up to the heavens and there were colourful fabric chairs and sofas with people sitting with MacBooks everywhere like it was a dystopian open-plan workspace.

'The music department's less grand and mad,' Ellie said as I followed her past a coffee shop and away from the crowds. 'Keep up.'

We eventually found ourselves sitting in a corridor outside a series of offices or tutor rooms.

'It's like being back at school,' I said. 'Being summoned to see the Head.'

'When did you ever get summoned to see the Head, you swot? What, did you forget to do all of your extra credit maths homework once?'

As I laughed, it felt comforting to drop back into a memory of simpler times. Behind us was a wall of glass looking out onto a courtyard. There were a couple of empty benches and a few green plants and small trees trying to balance out the grey paving stones. I appreciated Ellie bringing me along and giving me the distraction of a change of scenery, but I had no idea why we were there. Roaming the halls were students who looked no older than teenagers carrying cases for their violins or clarinets, bypassed by quickstepping adults purposefully moving from room to room with an aura of self-importance that I would associate with the world of academia.

Ellie started crossing and then uncrossing her legs like she had some itch she found impossible to sate. She sat forward, hunched over, sat back, sighed, frowned.

'You alright?'

'This was such a stupid idea. Mike's going to kill me.' She flung herself back, crossed her legs once more, and shook her head, looking thoroughly annoyed.

'There's a chance of a job here,' she finally said. 'I saw it in the papers when I was daydreaming about what *I* could do. It's lecturing contemporary music and specifically looking for someone with production experience – the Guildhall and the other poncey London music colleges finally acknowledging a world exists beyond the nineteenth century. And Mike pretty much said the same when I told him he should apply. He laughed and said technical colleges have already been teaching production for donkey's years and if Guildhall wanted to do something actually *contemporary* they needed to do what the techs weren't doing: *merging* it all together.'

The door next to the one we were waiting for opened. Out walked a tall skinny girl who had to duck when coming through the doorframe. She was followed by an older, shorter woman with curly black hair and horn-rimmed glasses. They spoke what sounded like German and walked away down the corridor.

'He was still laughing it off, but we ended up opening a bottle of wine while he described how technology was now there to bring musicians together anywhere in the world. You didn't need people to be in one studio. Instead, you could play live down video calls and pretty much live mix. Guildhall could then have their classical students working with contemporary musicians at the technical colleges or recording studios, and move away from all these endless strings samples and computer-generated orchestras and have real-life collaborations instead.'

I could imagine Mike advocating this case. For someone who was looking to leave music for the high-flying world of accountancy, he seemed to genuinely love what he did more than anyone I had met across the range of occupations I had taken up. In banking, you did what you did and waited for bonus day. In aid work, everyone was as disillusioned as each other. But *The Musician* was a purist. He loved his family and he loved his work. Why couldn't he have both?

'So I told Mike he should then apply and tell them all this. He's an ex-student, he has a degree, he's completely qualified! But he just laughed again saying he's got no teaching experience and they wouldn't even read his CV. So...' Ellie looked at the closed door and nodded. 'So, I'm doing it for him.'

The door we were waiting for then opened, and out walked a grey-haired man with a short stubbly beard wearing a thick cardigan.

'Ellie,' he beamed as she jumped out of her seat. 'Lovely to see you again.' The two embraced as I got to my feet too.

'How's young Mike? How are the kids?'

There seemed to be a familiarity between them that Ellie had not yet told me.

'This is my brother, Scott. He's come along to keep me company. Day out in London and that. Scott, this is Professor Hains, Mike's old mentor.'

'Emphasis on old,' he laughed, shaking my hand. 'And please call me Richard.'

'Richard is also a family friend and basically runs the show around here.'

'Not true! At least about running the show, but I do feel honoured that Mike's kept in touch. And speaking of running the show, I've asked Josephine to join us.'

Stepping out of the office behind the professor came a woman dressed all in black, her top and trousers emphasising how lithe of figure she was. She must have been around my age, if not younger, and her tied-back, sleek blonde hair was a sharp noticeable contrast to the rest of her outfit, including a black-framed set of glasses. She shook hands with Ellie, with a nod rather than a word.

'Josephine heads up our contemporary music department and leads the majority of our more challenging collaborations. Scott, will you be joining us too?' I quickly responded that I'd just come along for the ride and would wait here.

'In that case you might want to go straight to Auditorium C, down the hall to the right.' Professor Hains pointed me in the direction. 'Your sister's promised to play me one of her new pieces so I've taken the liberty of booking it out. Perk of the job!' He had an infectious, energetic grin, and I could perhaps see from where Mike's love for music stemmed. 'The seats are a lot more comfortable, and just between you and me, I find it the perfect place to have a coffee and read the paper.'

As the professor and his colleague both turned to re-enter the room they missed the look of pure terror and confusion that shot across Ellie's face.

'You're playing?' I mouthed. Ellie's response was to screw her face and mouth back, 'what the fuck?'

I bought myself a hot chocolate. It was my first in months, and I was glad I did as Auditorium C, with its drama-studio low lighting and cinema seats, provided the perfect atmosphere for comfort drinking and wallowing. I chose a seat in the bleachers looking down on the room, hoping being high up would somehow keep any demons at bay. There was a small stage at the front and on it was a black grand piano, its lid open and ready to be played. I didn't need the newspaper – I was more than happy to replay my own misery inside my head.

Katie and I had kissed only once. We had been friends barely two months in total – we had almost spent just as much time ignoring and avoiding each other. The maths, therefore, did not make sense. I should not be this heartbroken about her. To feel like

I felt would make me somewhat weak – prone to attachments, easily obsessed, un-resilient, and any other undiagnosed psychological defects you wanted to throw at me. But how did acknowledging any of this help?

Camille's last words to me that morning were: 'Would you say any of that to that small version of yourself who is feeling hurt and sad? No. So why scream it now?'

Eventually, I was interrupted by the auditorium door opening and Professor Hains and Josephine entering. While Professor Hains gave me another beaming smile, his counterpart had her head buried in a notepad in which she was busy jotting away.

'Your sister's just using the facilities,' he called up to me, taking a seat in the front row. He then turned around to continue the conversation. 'Truth be told, I've known Ellie longer than I've known Mike. In fact, she's the one that got away.'

While the professor was engaging me, his arm draped over the back of the chair, his colleague was still keenly writing.

'I interviewed her, twice, for the undergraduate and then the postgraduate programme. Turned me down twice, unfortunately.' He chuckled again and shook his head like it indeed was on his list of life regrets. 'She does occasionally indulge me with a recital when I drag the two of them up to Norwood for dinner. Unique talent, I've been singing her praises to Josephine ever since we set up this little meet.'

Josephine was still scribbling away and did not even look up when Ellie walked in. She gave her audience a raised eyebrow look of 'alright' and then took her seat in front of the grand piano.

An ability Ellie had, and I would associate it as the difference between the professional and the intermediate, is to make her music sound like two people were playing simultaneously. What I mean is when all eyes descended upon her, two pieces were playing in harmony. One was powerful with aggressive overtones, and then the other, waiting in the wings, shy at first, and then ascending through, light and beautiful, the two somehow forming the perfect duet. Angry and loud, soft and melancholic. There was a sense of sadness but such a fluidity about her playing I had no time to realise I was sad. I was simply swept up.

I could see only the backs of her assessors' heads so I had no idea if they were as moved as me. I had not heard Ellie play this piece before, and though I knew little about the technicalities of classical music, what I did notice was that Ellie, despite the intervening years, was better now than when she was considered a musical prodigy. On that lonely stage, the little spotlights shining off the grand and her brownie blonde hair, she was not the angry young woman who would either hit the keys with such force you feared for your eardrums or the girl who would play with a nonchalance which, while impressive, did make you wonder if her heart was really in it. Instead, amidst the waves and flows was a control. A determination I could see in her posture – more upright and less slouched than that girl of sixteen or seventeen I once knew.

And then there was the music itself. The transformations and emotions which I do not think my kid sister would have known how to convey. Anger had made way for sadness, but as she suddenly flew through the keys with rapid speed, out of nowhere I could feel hope and joy, and suddenly my life did not seem as it was. I was sad, but I was grateful to be sad. There was something inside me that was a gift. That as the music played, I was living it, and with each melancholic note there would also be joy, and it was notes of melancholy which made the joy that little bit sweeter.

I felt the tears roll down my cheeks as the piece gathered and gathered momentum, pushing its peak higher and higher to the point I couldn't breathe. And there it stopped, suddenly but just for a second, and with an unexpected subtlety, smoothly shifting down through the gears, bringing me back to the auditorium as Ellie set down the last note.

I was not sure that applauding was the done thing. But I did so anyway. I wanted to jump to my feet and give my sister a standing ovation. The others gave little away from their seats down at the front. It did sound strange – my one-man clapping – until Professor Hains eventually joined me, perhaps realising this was not a formal interview, and he was allowed to show appreciation.

'Ellie, thank you for that. Can you tell me where you found your inspiration for that piece?'

Josephine had not joined in our applause. Instead, I could just about see her sitting forward and placing the tip of her pen to her lip as she questioned my sister. I had half-expected Ellie to shrug and say *dunno* like she would when asked almost anything back in the day.

'A lot of what I write these days is an accumulation rather than a Eureka moment.' Her voice was thoughtful. Again, uncharacteristically calm and poised. 'I have found becoming a mother had transformed what was an impulsiveness in my early work into something more... *life-affirming*. I have realised I am still on a journey and will be for two glorious more decades, and can relate to those around me – other parents, grandparents, our *Audience*.'

She was definitely using her posh voice. The one she uses with Auntie Pam to disguise when she's taking the piss. She also had this subtle look of confidence as she engaged with Josephine from her stage. Like she was Elton John doing a Q&A with adoring fans.

'And you graduated from Bristol? At bachelor's level? Before pursuing a career in journalism?'

Ellie hesitated. I had not fully grasped the importance of this performance at first. Rather like a pushy recruitment consultant plugging a job that you're not altogether interested in, saying, 'just go in for a chat.' It is never just a chat.

'Yes, studying under Ugo Nemongoma, who at the time was resident lecturer, lecturing contemporary composition from Yale. Very few other colleges were quite as advanced on contemporary composition back then. So I ended up turning down offers from the Royal College and Royal Academy, and, yes, I moved into rock journalism straight after to fund my freelance composing, which is how I met my husband and, obviously, Professor Hains.'

From my seat in the gods, I could just about see the tell-tale smirk of someone who knows they have crushed it. I also noticed from up there that Josephine made a note in her pad with each answer.

'*Life-affirming? Journey?*' I could hardly contain my excitement as the metal and glass doors of the Barbican flew open before us.

'The more bollocks you spout, the less bullshit questions they come back with usually. Throw in the mother card and it has someone like her scrambling into uncharted territory.'

'Nice answer on Bristol.' We were almost skipping back to the tube station, a far cry from the anxious shuffle that was our first leg.

'Bar Richard, the majority of them are complete snobs. Bristol actually has better facilities. Fuck, you've seen Guildhall now. It might be joined to the Barbican, but no one's touched those rooms in fifty years – no exaggeration. It looked dated even back in the 90s when I was given a tour. And the students were just as capable, if not more with the overseas guys who came over – Suki Jimamoto and Tari Gibbs play for the New York Symphony, you know. I should have told that to Little Miss Look-How-Pert-My-Tits-Are.' Ellie put on a high-pitched voice and wiggled her chest, not noticing the look she received from the attendant at the ticket barriers of Barbican station.

'Can't say I noticed,' I smiled, casting my mind back to Josephine's black top and alluringly dismissive nature.

When we were on the more familiar ground of the northbound Piccadilly line, Ellie told me that Dr Josephine Kim was a creative director at Guildhall and, according to Professor Hains, she worked closely with television and film production studios, including the BBC.

"Oh it's such a tough game to get into. If I had a penny for every want-to-be musician who thinks they can compose..." Ellie fell back into her high-pitched posh mimic of Josephine's voice. 'We weren't even meant to be talking about me. I think Richard thought he was doing Mike a favour pitching my composing to the snotty-nosed bitch. Definitely the Royal College type.'

'It went pretty well, though. Better than well.'

We had just seen two seats together and moved across the tube carriage to take them.

'I'm too knackered to think about it. Richard likes Mike's ideas, but it's Pert-Tits' show, apparently. But she's also too high and mighty with all the time she spends deciding what will make stage and screen, so who knows.'

'I guess all you have to do now is tell Mike that you've gone behind his back and effectively interviewed for a job on his behalf.'

It was a little bit harsh, but I knew Ellie could take it. If I wasn't feeling as positive as I was in that moment, I wouldn't have ribbed her. However, it did turn out to be closer to the bone than I intended.

'It was a throwaway comment.' Mike looked genuinely annoyed when he met us back at the house. At least Mike's version of annoyed: a deep sigh and slightly confused expression at not understanding why Ellie had done what she had done.

'No it wasn't. It was an idea. A bloody good idea. A commercial idea and they loved it!'

It wasn't exactly an argument, but as the three of us sat down in the living room, I did feel an invader to what should have been a private moment. Ellie defended her stance and even went on the offensive, telling Mike he needed to stop being so hesitant and had to put it all down in writing before Josephine Kim stole the idea for herself.

'You could have at least looped me in,' I heard Mike say as I left the room on the pretence of checking the mail.

Jane had stacked post and bills in the letter rack by the front door. I could just about hear Ellie giving an enthusiastic pitch of how Mike should see this as an opportunity as I flicked through them. I stopped at a handwritten envelope unexpectedly addressed to me.

Inside was a smart-looking card. An invitation. From Vicky, my first love.

CHAPTER 29

MIDDLE ENGLAND

A week of moping set me behind in my work. The next week forced me to rise early and dig trenches in the dark to get Mrs Elsop's back on track if it was to look like anything resembling a real garden come spring. If hiding away under my duvet had failed to take my mind off Katie, perhaps continuous physical labour would.

I did that all week, and then on Sunday afternoon, I was on a train to Cambridgeshire, dressed in my only suit, even wearing a tie and footwear not designed by Adidas or New Balance. Even a short distance outside London, it was wonderful to see the rolling fields of green and yellow under a fairly blue sky.

The address was a village just before the world-famous university city. Stepping off the train, I was in Middle England. I was at a small, quaint station which, apart from a couple of overhead signs, had all the characteristics of an Agatha Christie novel. Wooden benches lined the platform, and as I exited, I saw its ticket office – a wooden booth with a closed sign dangling at the window.

There was no town centre or main road. Instead, a refreshingly quiet walk up a country lane and only a line of Range Rovers would break the mystique of in which era I was. The lane then turned into scattered cottages, and I was soon at my destination, a large detached house with balloons fixed to the front door. It was then I decided to go back home.

It had been a mistake and was clearly a token invitation. 'Let's not leave it so long next time,' Vicky had said as we said goodbye after the wake – over a year ago. 'Yes, and perhaps something in more cheerful circumstances,' was my reply. Now I was standing on her doorstep, at her daughter's christening, with a small wrapped present in one hand and a bottle of wine in the other. What about this had made me think it was a good idea?

I blamed Camille entirely for this lapse in judgement. All those sessions encouraging me that I needed to face adversity, handle anxiety – notice, acknowledge, and find a peace to move on – lay as the underlying behaviour manipulators.

I was about to leave the present anonymously on the doorstep when I heard a tapping. To the window to my right was Vicky, smiling, waving, and with a baby on her shoulder.

'You made it!' she smiled, opening the door. She looked amazing. Positively glowing. Her smile was bright, as was her blonde hair, as was her white and blue dress. Vicky then carefully turned her child around to see me.

'Mary, this is my oldest friend, Scott.'

As she led me through a massive open-plan downstairs – it looked like something from a design magazine with everything so immaculate and literally shiny – Vicky explained that the christening proper had taken place that morning at a church in the next village.

'It was going to be such a faff asking people to show up at half-past ten on a Sunday morning and then come all the way back here. We thought we'd keep it to just us and the grandparents and then have everyone rock up to something fun at a more decent time.'

We were heading towards a set of French doors and the garden where a marquee was erected.

'Plus, we felt frauds. We've had nine months to do this but prioritised renovating this place over the spiritual wellbeing of our child.' I took another look back at the room before stepping outside and, yes, the spaciousness, smooth walls, and untouched surfaces all sung out expensive ambitious refurb.

Opening the doors, we stepped out onto the patio. If I had thought the inside was massive I had no words for their garden. The marquee might have been the size for a wedding venue, but it took up just a fraction of the space as the grounds stretched all the way down to what appeared to be their own woods at the bottom.

'I know, a garden party on the first day of February! Martin's idea. He says if we wait for spring Mary would practically be a toddler. *Plus* we do have heaters, and at least it's brightening up!'

Her optimism reminded me of our teenage years and how she had led me by the hand through our adolescence, encouraging me to go with her to parties and festivals, saying how much I would enjoy myself if I just gave them a chance. I rarely did enjoy myself, but I appreciated her misplaced faith in me. Vicky told me that she needed to change Mary, but she waved over to a thickly bearded man inside the marquee before leaving me. He bounded over and was wearing a highly noticeable tweed suit and flat cap.

'Hello! You must be Scott, from Vicky's Wood Green days.'

The world's biggest hipster was shaking my hand eagerly. In his other hand was a pewter tankard.

'We've met before, briefly. Years ago. Tom O'Neil's birthday.'

'Really?' He looked genuinely perplexed at the oversight. 'Ah! Yes! What's Tom doing now? Hey, you don't have a drink. Come with me.'

It was unnerving how unnerved Hipster Martin was. And it slightly pissed me off. I was meant to be the elephant in the room.

Vicky's ex-fiancé, the former love. Not her mate from Wood Green. I just about realised that Martin was telling me something about microbreweries doing eighteen or so versions of some craft beer when we reached a makeshift bar at the end of the marquee. As he poured me the beer he recommended with a ratio of malt to wheat that was meant to be significant, I struggled to take in what a cliché Vicky had ended up with. And the fact that I kind of liked him.

'Are you a craft man, Scott?'

'Normally lager. But it makes a nice change.'

'That's the spirit!' He thumped me on the arm. He was quite a bit shorter than me, which I think helped my incredibly feeble ego – he might be rich, have my dream house, my dream woman, my dream life, but at least I was taller. That was what truly mattered.

I know I am a broken record regarding the hipster thing. What I don't get is the fact that it was quirky at the time – *hip* even – but it has now been done to death. You can make wine from mangos – we get it. Beards are fashionable again – yes, you're a rebel, or at least you would be if everyone else wasn't dressing exactly the same. But Martin did seem to have a genuine love and enjoyment for it all, and he was so comfortable in his own skin. So what did it matter that I deemed he was not unique or if he was. There was a lesson I could learn there, and I could see why Vicky had married him.

'So if you know Tom O'Neil then you must know Jon-Boy, no?'

I shook my head. I was warming to Martin, but I did not fancy a game of which person he knew that I knew.

'Oh, I could have sworn they were as thick as thieves. What about Alison? Ali, Vicky calls her.' And saying her name, he waved across the room to a pair of traitors I would have hoped at least had the decency to hide from view as I had entered the marquee.

'You have to be fucking kidding me.'

. . .

With my drink poured, Martin left me to rejoin his bearded friends, and I made my way to have words with my soon-to-be ex-best friends.

'So, how long has this been going on, you two-faced bastard?' I said to Joan with the self-righteousness of a lover who had just spotted his partner with another. At least they *had* had the decency to hide from my view as I found them both huddling behind a pillar.

'Someone been taking their melodrama pills?' he said, sipping a bottle of beer casually, averting eye contact with me.

'You told me you lost touch with Vicky years ago.'

'We did!' said Alison with a huge, fixed smile like she was summoning every ounce of positivity she had so that I would not make a scene. 'We just kind of got back *in* touch. At parties... And weddings?'

'You went to her wedding?' I knew my horrified, jaw-dropped glower was hardly reversing Joan's initial assertion.

'Well, you were out of the country at the time, and it didn't seem the thing to write an email about – 'hey mate, know you're in a war zone right now but guess who we ran into.' Plus, she's Ali's friend more than mine.'

Alison spun around, her big smile flipping into an even bigger scowl before returning to me.

'We were worried you'd take it to heart. That you'd think we were taking her side – not that there are sides to be taken, we were all friends back then. Me and Vicky. *Joan* and Vicky.' She swung her elbow into Joan's ribs which temporarily had him grimacing.

'Yeah,' he groaned. 'You have to admit you didn't exactly take it well when she, you know. Telling you seemed a bit, you know... harsh.'

I wanted to be still livid at them both. I wanted to maintain my narrowed-eyed scowl and see them squirm uncomfortably, especially Joan. But Joan's defence was like an arrow to my chest. He wasn't exactly squirming, but he did look embarrassed, and I do not think he was embarrassed for himself. He was there when I was making an ass of myself drinking every other night, chatting up girls who were obviously not interested, and disappearing off to toilet cubicles to partake in my newfound powder-related hobby. I know our friendship does not seem the most, well, *friendly* at times, but there were so many times back then I found myself waking up on his sofa hungover and unable to remember how I had got there. Don't get me wrong, he acts like an arsehole and still took the piss out of me at every available opportunity, but he never judged, and a lot of the things he did do were a lot kinder than anyone else had done for me in my friendship group.

My cheeks began to feel warm as Joan's embarrassment transferred to me. 'Well, you could have said something,' I mumbled quickly and then looked away taking an overly long swig of my beer.

'You guys taking the train back then?' I said, trying unsubtly to change the subject.

After a far more civilised catch up with Joan and Alison – we deliberately skirted the more controversial subjects of Vicky, Martin, Katie, the flat at Loughborough and him having called my sister – I decided to wander the garden by myself, part of me at least wanting to feel superior for being a better, more creative gardener than Martin even though his was rather impressive.

Vicky was right, and the day had brightened up. It was still a good day to be wearing the layers of shirt and jacket, but it allowed a mob of small children to run up and down the long lawn away from the marquee heaters. I guessed a little blonde girl who kept running up to Martin was Vicky's eldest. In a way, I was watching what my life could have looked like: the big house, big garden, a shiny-haired daughter running up to me demanding I pick her up and swing her about. Five years ago, such a sight would have crippled me. Eight years ago I think I would have completely imploded. Now all these years on, it just made me feel this sad but soulful pain. It was bittersweet, rather than simply bitter.

'I'm glad you came.' I heard Vicky's voice next to me, on the sidelines of the children's game.

'Sorry I didn't reply. The invitation had found its way into a pile of mail I have been lax at checking.'

'I wasn't sure where to send it. I hoped it would get forwarded to you if you had sold the house already.'

I let out a spontaneous laugh.

'That's become a long, arduous story.'

'Well, I do have time. The only stories I get to hear now involve a nosey blonde chick and three justifiably put-out bears.'

I gave another involuntary snort, still looking at Martin and their daughter playing a game with the others. 'What's the time, Mr Wolf?' was being shouted out by Martin as he and the others sneaked up on the little girl, who then spun around and began chasing them.

'Nah, this is a better story,' I smiled. 'This is lovely, Vic. Really lovely. You've done so well for yourself.'

'Remind me of that at three a.m. when Mary's screaming the house down.'

'Well, lucky this place is detached so you don't have to worry about the neighbours.'

She slapped my arm lightly. It was funny, it all felt so comfortable.

'I meant what I said. About you being my oldest friend. I've missed that.'

We still gazed over at the running, squealing children, both of us keeping up the Englishness of acting like we were discussing the weather.

'Thanks,' I said quietly. 'I guess I have too. I was too busy thinking about everything else I forgot that bit.'

'Everyone does to some extent.' I then felt an arm wrap around mine.

'I know I said it at the funeral, but I am sorry. I didn't mean – '

'Vicky, you have nothing to apologise for.' I turned to face her and found I was smiling. I then gestured around us to the marquee and the kids running around. 'All this should not come with an apology. Not to anyone. It's far too special for any regrets.'

'But I do have one.' Vicky then had this strange expression, like she was sizing me up.

'I was really angry for a while after we broke up. Angry at *you*.'

This, I did not expect her to say. I felt myself frowning, wondering if I had misheard her.

'This is going to sound so entitled, but I was angry at you for not letting me have my cake and eat it. That we couldn't go back to the way it was. Back to being friends. I couldn't call you up to go for a walk or tell you about my bad days at work. When I needed a shoulder to cry on. I forgot how much I loved you for that. For being my best friend.'

It felt a bit weird hearing those words from her, and seeing her eyes slightly glisten as I too found my focus impaired by moisture. The kids were playing a new game with Martin and the other dads. The dads seemed to be pretending to be sleeping and when the kids ran close would transform into monsters. Again, Vicky and I looked on side by side, pretending not to have had a heart-to-heart. Anything I could have responded with would have been a cliché so we just stood watching the game. I've never denied not missing her, but until recently I had forgotten about our friendship. That she was my oldest friend too. I wasn't sure if I would ever completely stop loving her as my first real love but did feel relieved at just being able to talk to her again. So I reached over and squeezed her hand.

'Come on, let's join them.' Together, we ran into the throng, waving our arms and making big monster faces at the kids.

Joan, Alison, and I filed out of Vicky and Martin's front door late that evening to catch the last train back to London. We were the last to leave, having turned the christening into more of a piss-up. Infuriatingly, pretentiously but also satisfyingly, hipster Martin even knew a thing or two about wine, and we had huddled around a heater in the crisp winter air sipping from various different bottles.

'It was *so* good to see you,' said Vicky with red pinot lips, squeezing the life out of me with a bear hug. 'Next time, perhaps feel free to bring someone? Or will that be too strange?'

It felt very much like we had wound the clock back fifteen years and the four of us, plus Martin, were outside our student union at the end of the night saying how much we loved each other.

'That side of things is currently a disaster.'

It was probably the copious amount of wine that had been shared, but Vicky looked genuinely disappointed and clutched my forearm.

'There's always time to – I don't know – say you're sorry or buy her flowers. No. Don't do that. Don't listen to any advice I give after two or more glasses of wine. But it's her loss, you realise that, right?'

I nodded more as a thank you than in agreement, and in true student union spirit, I had Joan's arm around my neck, putting me in a headlock dragging me away so we would not miss the train. Freeing myself on their driveway, I turned back for one last word.

'Vicky,' I called as she stood at the front door. 'I'm really happy for you.' And to my surprise, I really meant it.

CHAPTER 30

TURNER

On the train back to London, Joan had drunkenly promised me I could move back into Loughborough Road once the refurbishments were done. 'I'll even keep the rent the same, even though it will be nicer and just be you.'

'He's only saying that because my dad neglected to tell him it could take months to sell, and he'd be having to pay the mortgage,' smirked Ali.

'I could put it on Airbnb.'

'Yeah, right. While you're doing house viewings. Those white walls aren't going to look so white once you've had six Aussie back-packers couch surfing in your living room.'

I would probably take him up on his offer. What other choice did I have? The next week would bring the return of Auntie Pam, and hence there would be nothing else stopping us submitting our adjudication notices. But with a wine hangover, I found myself in Dad's study with a pen and his notepaper and took up the advice I'd been given the night before.

I'm sorry, I began. *I should not have put you in the situation I put you in... I should have been more supportive about you and Ethan... I realise how much I miss you as a friend...*

It was a little bit mushy, in all honesty. I kind of got caught up in the moment of going back to paper and pen rather than posting an Instagram video or whatever you were meant to do in the current age. I just remembered how I felt when Vicky and I had discussed our lost friendship, so I told Katie how I missed laughing with her while sitting around Loughborough Road in the freezing cold.

As simply as I could, I finished the letter by saying that I missed her and my life felt poorer without her. I placed it in an envelope and put that within a small bundle of mail for Katie I had brought with me from Loughborough Road. Alison had offered to pass it on for me – Joan could not be trusted for such a mission. And with that, I just had to wait, hoping she would read it and not detest me anymore.

However, I did not have much time to go back to brooding about Katie. Not only was Mrs Elsop's garden in the critical phase of having its new plants and shrubs delivered, but Mr Jones also wanted me in South London to discuss how we were going to win the blue rosette for best allotment. And just to add a little bit of spice to the mix, I also had to play go-between for the inevitable Ellie-Auntie Pam family feud.

'What do you mean she wants me to pick her up at the airport?' shouted Ellie at me down Dad's house phone. I had taken to using Dad's landline as Auntie Pam was determined not to call my mobile from abroad. This meant that I had to wait in on evenings for her to call at prearranged times.

'Why can't she get a taxi?'

'Because she's a seventy-year-old woman who is having to fly into Gatwick. And she wants to spend time with you and the kids. So she'll be spending the night at yours too.'

'She's what?'

I'm not going to lie. I was delighted by these events, and the sound of panic and pure belligerence in Ellie's voice did make me feel more at peace with the world. The plan was set and Auntie Pam would travel with Ellie and Mike to Dad's, where we would have our long-awaited conversation. I just had to keep fielding the phone calls in the meantime and wait for the house phone to ring so I could receive an updated itinerary from Auntie Pam.

And on Saturday morning, as I was waiting in just in case she should call, the house phone cordially rang.

'Good morning, the Roberts' residence,' I said in my most appropriate telephone voice so that Auntie Pam would not criticise my manners. The only problem was, it wasn't Auntie Pam.

'Hello?' said a soft, faraway voice from the 90s. I felt my heart literally skip a beat. 'Scott? Scott, it's... it's Mum.'

Perhaps she did not know how to refer to herself either after all that had passed.

'Hi,' I said, off guard like it was someone calling from the gas board. I felt a rush of panic. I suddenly thought back to what I had said the last time we spoke.

'Scott, can you meet me? I'm in central London today. Now. It's nothing urgent, but I would like to see you. It won't take long.'

Her tone made it impossible to tell her it was inconvenient – so soft, not reproachful or summoning. Very much not what I deserved.

I think it was the lack of time that prevented me from dwelling or overanalysing. I had to leave immediately and make my way from Wood Green to Russell Square. There I had to find the Fulsham Gallery. And arriving at the stone steps leading up to its entrance, I tried to clear my mind and keep moving forward and not think about what on earth we would say to each other.

She told me to meet her in the Turner room. Inside the gallery were the tall ceilings and red-carpeted stairways I would associate with a period house. When I found the room, there was no sign of Orletta but on a plain white wall, I discovered why the room was given its name. A work titled *Peace* hung in prime view painted by arguably the greatest British artist of the nineteenth century.

It was not a massive overbearing canvas that bored down on you. Instead, it was a compact square with a single ship sailing into a light that poured from the paint. This contrast between light and dark was mesmerising. I stood, allowing myself to feel the awe it was there to aspire.

I then saw her. There was a small doorway at the end of the room, it looked more like a fire exit than a public entrance, and she was just there watching me for I did not know how long. Seeing me notice her, she gave me this delicate half-smile. I felt myself brace for impact.

'This room felt appropriate. Neutral ground. And common ground.' There was no hug or greeting. She came up to me and began staring with me at the Turner.

'You had very refined taste as a child. Other children would want to visit the science museum, but you would be placated sitting in front of the Great Briton who stopped us fixating on horses.'

It was unnerving how peaceful it was. My mother and I stood together as we had done twenty-five years before, allowing the brilliant sun and sky to shine out of the canvas, and the sails and water hold our attention. Yet it was unmistakably clear that we were guests in its company. We just stared, silently, *Peace* superseding the awkwardness.

'You do not like me much,' she then said. Again, not a rebuke, but with a smile in her voice which shocked me even more. My eyes flicked right and I saw a little upward curve to her mouth.

'No! I mean, I do...' I stumbled. I wanted to deny the accusation, a cold sweat materialising as we touched on my shame. But I also could not wholeheartedly argue the opposite.

'I don't really know you,' I ended up just mumbling.

And that pretty much said it all, as she continued to gaze at *Peace* with her half-smile, and I stared forward, trying to hide my disappointment at not being able to muster the human emotions to talk to my own mother.

'That's it,' she said as she turned to me. 'That's all I wanted to ask.' She smiled at me with this warm, kind smile as if she was telling me how proud she was of me.

'I better get back, I'm an honorary board member and we're having a terribly dull meeting.' I felt my hand being squeezed. 'It was lovely to see you, Scott.'

My mother, Orletta Roberts, or Orletta Roberts, my mother – I could not tell which at that moment – turned to walk back to that fire exit door as I remained frozen.

'I didn't mean what I said,' I called after her. She turned and looked at me with the most amazing patient, non-judgemental look, again putting me completely on the back foot.

'I didn't mean what I said in Devon. Obviously, I didn't mean it.' I lowered my voice and stepped a yard closer so those staring at the paintings around us would be less inclined to eavesdrop. 'But *this. This* being the whole extent of our relationship. How often we see each other. It is not down to me. You see that, don't you? Mum?'

I felt the last word hang as she continued to look at me, just as she did when she had called me handsome in Devon. She then tilted her head and gave me a fuller smile, perhaps her way of telling me she understood, or telling me that I would not understand. But she said nothing more and left the room.

·   ·   ·

'What do you mean it didn't come up? How could you not talk about the house?'

Ellie wanted answers and wasn't overly happy by the impromptu meeting.

'She just said she was in town. It's not like I could say no.'

At least I had Ellie at an arm's length by relaying events over the phone while walking to my next meeting.

'Was she angry? Was she upset? What the hell were you doing going by yourself after last time?'

I knew she wouldn't be pleased, hence why I was making the call on the move through the crowded frosty streets of Oxford Circus, dodging other pedestrians, making my way down to Green Park.

'I think that was the point. Just me and her after last time.'

And that was pretty much all the information I had to pass on as despite being a first-hand witness, I had little idea of what actually took place. The only thing I did know was that I had come away feeling both relieved and a little sad. When I had called out to her, I hope she might come back. I hoped she might have stayed with me a little longer. She remembered our visits to see the Turner collection and that meant something to me. But I had little time to dwell as I was almost at my destination, and I could see my unlikely date coming in the opposite direction.

'Cheer up. People would think you were the one doing me the favour,' said Izzy, smiling that confident, slightly wicked smile of hers.

'I guess I'm not used to being summoned.'

'We both know that's a lie, sweetie.' She leant forward and placed her cheek next to mine twice. 'Look at us both with our . clothes still on. Shall we?'

She had asked me to meet her for coffee. She gave me a time

and a place and little else, so I followed her into the fancy-looking coffee shop on St James's Street.

'I was going to tell you all about my day and having to spend my precious Saturday overhauling an awful display put together by my cretin underling. But I wouldn't have your full attention, would I?'

'Just some unexpected family stuff.'

Izzy raised her hand, and a young smiling waiter came over to take our order.

'My gallery is a short walk from here. We occasionally take the odd client for lunch, you know, the ones we want to keep sweet but not sweet enough to buy champagne for at *James's Place*.' From my walk, I knew she meant the expensive-looking wine bar next door.

'You do have my full attention,' I said, and smiled feeling a little more at ease knowing coffee was on its way. 'It is good to see you. How have you been since...?'

'Since you ruthlessly refused my advances? Ha!' It was a strange laugh. She seemed to glow a little pink. 'Yes, well, best not dwell. Let's just say I still think you're an arsehole, but at least one I might be able to trust.'

She sighed and then slumped slightly. Her immaculate posture dropped to become elbows on the table.

'And how are things with...' I don't think she told me his name.

'Over,' she exhaled. 'He's not going to leave her, and I need to have more respect for myself than throwing myself at him every time he fancies a quick fuck. Or jumping into bed with anyone with a relatively adequate penis and is grateful to get laid. No offence.'

'None taken. Glad you found it *relatively* adequate.'

'Don't smile. Thanks to you, I've given up sex for the time being. You are essentially my rock bottom.'

I laughed and told her she was welcome. I have to say, there was something different about Izzy. Or perhaps it was something about me. Either way, I felt more comfortable in her presence.

'She's well. That's the question you want to ask, isn't it?' She stared at me again with that same smile. 'You obviously didn't think I'd invited you here to seduce you again? I honestly don't think there's enough alcohol in the world for me to tread that path for a fourth time, so let's address the elephant in the room, shall we? You're quite the letter writer, I hear.'

I felt my heart plummet into my ankles. Katie had shown someone else my letter. I was like a schoolboy with a pitiful crush on the head girl, and now the whole school had found out. My shoulders dropped, and I exhaled one long, defeated breath.

'I was just trying to say sorry. It's not a big deal. She doesn't have to worry about me doing – '

'She's broken up with Ethan,' Izzy interrupted casually. 'Well, they're having an extended break, and him moving in is now indefinitely off the cards. Apparently, you also have a way with words which I'm not overly happy about. Calling her an idiot for staying with him, very nice, Scott.'

She looked more serious as she sipped her coffee. I was now confused regarding the reason for our meeting. Was I being accused of harassing Katie into ending her seven-year relationship? Surely nothing I could have said would have that influence.

'Izzy, I don't know what she told you, but – '

'This is how it works between her and me. I'm occasionally a little mean, she puts up with it until I overstep the mark, she gets pissed off, I flutter my eyelashes and tell her I really do love her, and we're all sweetness and light again. I don't like other people upsetting her. I won't accept it.'

'I didn't mean to upset her – '

'Oh my God, I'm not talking about you! I've asked you here to discuss how we both will fix this mess and have *Miss Disney*

Princess stop moping about like she's lost the family pet. Personally, I would have stuck it out with Ethan and done the whole play-him-at-his-own-game thing. She's already snogged some cretin, might as well let said cretin unfasten that chastity belt.'

Izzy smirked, picking back up her coffee cup.

'Tell you what, why don't I write you a reference? It wouldn't exactly be five stars, but you did get the job done, and perhaps that's what she needs to snap out of it and come to her senses.'

She continued to stare at me with big eyes as if daring me to be shocked. I wasn't going to rise to it.

'When did it happen?'

'Pretty much the week after she moved out of that hovel you shared. Didn't surprise me. The reconciliation was a little bit too good to be true. I absolutely adore Ethan, but she did make herself a doormat.'

The waiter came over and cleared the table next to us. He smiled a flirtatious smile at Izzy, who just rolled her eyes.

'I don't want to encourage him,' she said after he left. 'Don't get me wrong, I'd definitely sleep with him. It's just a question of timing. After all, I don't want the inconvenience of having to change coffee shops if it makes him think too much of himself.'

'Thanks for letting me know.'

'My pleasure!' She then beamed with I assumed all the irony and sarcasm she could muster, grabbing my hand. 'Seriously though, I'm not altogether having a terrible time. It's nice talking to a boy for a change. You know, I have had a lot of boyfriends but not actually one boy-*friend*. All-girls school and that. This is fun!'

'And that's why you've asked me here?'

'Of course not!' It was like Izzy was drunk. She was so giddy and merry, laughing at her own jokes and theatrically making fun of me. 'Well, yes, kind of. With Spoiler all wrapped up wallowing, it would be insensitive to bang on to her about my life or dilemmas. Dullard and I have had a second date and, well, it was quite nice.'

Izzy stared to the side and smiled as a flash of pink lit up her cheeks.

'Dull. Definitely still dull. Terribly, terribly dull in a very, very sweet way. And so naïve! In fact, Otto is so dull and naïve he can't see what a complete bitch he is being so lovely to.'

Izzy sighed and screwed her face into a frown. She then sat up straight, more business-like.

'Anyway, your job is to prevent me screwing this up. I take it you have no meaningful plans this Thursday?'

CHAPTER 31

DÉJÀ VU

What should you do if after not speaking to your mother for years, you explain to her that you would have preferred your other parent to have outlived her, and then your next conversation cordially lasted four sentences, and you refused to deny the accusation of disliking her? It's not one hundred percent a no-brainer, is it?

Or perhaps it was. For the first time since standing at a London railway station in the early hours of the morning, high as a kite, I picked up the phone to call my mother. It went straight to voicemail. *I just called to see that you had got home safely*, is all I could think of saying. Anything else would have probably been too much considering I was still taking her to court – or at least adjudication. And considering I had effectively told her that my disdain for her was also her fault. Part of me wanted to apologise for everything that had transpired between us, but when she had asked me that question in the gallery, and as she had walked away, I think that was the most honest I had ever been with her. And until she apologised for all those years of being Orletta Roberts, then I couldn't just tell her I loved her and wanted to start over with a blank slate.

And, no surprises, she didn't return my bloody message.

. . .

After our initial conversation about our mother's surprise visit, Ellie did not seem to have much inclination or time to dwell on its meaning either. Over the next week, I relayed six messages to her regarding Auntie Pam's arrival in the country. For me, after receiving my last call from Auntie Pam – who told me she was at the airport and everything was going according to plan – I was then free to take on my next convoluted mission.

When Izzy had communicated the favour that she wanted from me, she had also offered up the incentive, 'well, what else have you got to do in your boring little life?' This was true. Though, while I was beginning to enjoy aspects of said boring life such as seeing neglected landscapes transform into something more promising, there were just so many nights I could spend reading old graphic novels on my childhood bed.

The plan was for me to act as Izzy's chaperon. Her gallery was hosting an event at their premises just down the road from the St James Street café, and there was a chance Izzy's ex would show up. 'We both know how it will go,' she said, her elbows on the café table, her hands twirling a sugar dispenser. 'I will ignore him, he will see it as a challenge, and before we know it, we'll both be in the storeroom boning away. But not this time!' Unexpectedly, she swung her fist down onto the table like a gavel. She smirked glee-fully as I looked around us. 'You are to be my wingman and remind me that I owe it to Dullard, if not to myself, to keep my desires at bay.'

In my defence, I was initially sceptical, especially considering what happened when I last helped her out in a dating situation, and it did seem a lot of effort for her to make. 'Like I said, I can't exactly ask Katie. Misery guts will kill the mood of the entire event. You will have to do.' And, in hindsight, that should have been a clue.

. . .

Izzy's gallery was one of those long white spaces on a Mayfair side street. I would walk past such places in my banking days and see a few pieces hanging sparsely across the walls and one solitary person clicking away at a Mac. However, this evening it was full of designer clothes tailor-fitted to very elegant-looking people holding champagne glasses. I cast a look around for Izzy as I stood awkwardly one yard inside the entrance, feeling I should at least offer up an explanation for my presence. However, it did not take long for me to catch someone's eye.

'Can I help you?' came Izzy's voice from another woman's mouth. She was stout, most probably in her late forties, and looked both curious and alarmed as she made her way to intercept me.

I stammered, saying that I was Izzy's guest.

'Oh, *Isabella*,' the lady sneered. 'She's not here this evening. She called in sick, something about a migraine. Are you a client?' It was not a question but a steady interrogation, causing my tongue to feel swollen as I braced myself for the humiliation of being kicked out of somewhere I didn't want to be at in the first place. I then felt a hand upon my shoulder.

'Scott!' said a friendly but unfamiliar Italian accent. A young man in a crisp black suit and sporting a short, cropped beard was beaming at me like we were long-lost friends. I nodded suspiciously.

'Clarisse, this is Scott. I promised Isabella I would show him the Killian collection. Scott, please, come with me. Isabella tells me you are looking for a contemporary, stylistic piece.'

I was led away from the suspicious-looking Clarisse, through the clusters of champagne drinkers, to another room.

'Lorenzo,' the young man shook my hand and then laughed. 'Do not look so scared! She is like that with us all. This is Clarisse's gallery – she is queen, Isabella is princess, and you and I mere peasants. Come, there is someone I have been told you should meet. Ordered, in fact!' He laughed again, a full-bellied laugh, appearing a lot more comfortable with the situation than I was.

It was then I saw her. She was staring at me wide-eyed before masking her face with her hand. For a split second, I didn't recognise her. Or at least I didn't recognise her as my former flatmate. I did, however, immediately recognised the dress. It was the same one that Izzy had worn the night she turned up to Loughborough Road after her date with the dullard. But Katie's hair was different. Drastically different. It was shorter and lighter – a wavey, layered auburn bob. Combined with the short dress, the effect was striking. If it had not been for the all-too-familiar glare she was giving me, I would have had no idea who she was and just stared at the beautiful woman standing by herself.

'*Ciao*! *Bella* Katie!' Lorenzo then beamed with his arms outstretched and approached Katie, kissing her on each cheek. As our eyes met, I sensed her gritting her teeth, and I wanted some hole to bury myself in, knowing she had not remotely forgiven me for Ruskin Park.

'You know Scott, no?' While Lorenzo was now grinning at some in-joke only he was privy to, Katie looked decidedly unamused and turned her head away from me. I was still trying to get to terms with her new look. I had always found Katie beautiful, but there was something quite breathtaking about her, dressed in what Izzy had termed her *sex dress*. I then felt guilty for not looking adequately chastened.

'Katie, Isabella just messaged me – she is sick. She will not make it. But she has told me that Scott will be your chaperone. He is *Mr Art!* Isabella tells me.' Still smiling away, his arm was then around Katie's shoulder. 'Katie is my wing-woman tonight in Isabella's absence. We will go to the club and I will find her a nice boy and she will find me a not-so-nice girl. Drink, drink, I see you both later.' With one more pat on my shoulder, he laughed again and left us.

I did not need to say anything at first. Katie had her hand to her forehead, pinching her eyelids. I felt the déjà vu sensation of pre-Christmas at the museum. But this time, I also felt the injustice of it being forced upon me. Not that I am saying I did not owe her an apology. I just didn't want her to think ambushing her at events was my go-to M.O.

Katie then turned away from me. She lowered her hand and began staring at a small painting on the immaculate white wall. I had to stop myself staring hard at her – she looked so different with her new hair, and even the way she held her champagne close to her chest had me staring at her figure, which I am adamant I had never done while we lived together.

'I used to go to these sort of things all the time when Izzy first started working here,' said Katie, not taking her eyes off the underwhelming series of dots on a white canvas. 'Lorenzo's very sweet. Very young, very boyish. He's become a younger brother to both Izzy and me, the number of years they've been working together. Her, him, and Clarisse – who is Izzy's idol and openly shows disdain for anyone who doesn't earn at least six figures or drive a sports car. Though, I never saw *you* as a lover of contemporary art.'

She put her champagne flute to her mouth, still not looking directly at me.

'I think I've had my fill of galleries, to be honest.' I thought back to the Turner room and wondered where I felt less at ease. We were side by side, perhaps looking like we were giving a critique.

'What did she tell you?' Katie then asked, still staring intently at the painting.

'Something about being her wingman and stopping her succumbing to temptation.'

'Mine was the reverse. I should dress up and get drunk with her on enough champagne to let my inhibitions go, *for once in my life*. According to Izzy, the best thing for a breakup is rebound sex with pretty, well-groomed men.'

I was tired of gazing at paintings while trying to have a conversation, so I just spun back around to face her.

'She told me about you and Ethan – '

'Great! Good news travels so quickly among one's so-called friendship group.'

'I'm as comfortable about being here as you are,' I whispered, staring back at the painting as this wave of heat smacked me in the face.

'Well, I guess neither of us *has* to be here considering it's all been such an amateurish setup.'

It was the first open sight of irritation. Around us, the laughter was getting louder. I glanced and the gallery space was filling up. The lady who stopped me at the door – Clarisse – was now smiling and cackling with a group of more smartly dressed art lovers. I then leaned my head closer to Katie's and whispered again,

'I miss spending time together.' My voice was low so as not to attract more attention and recreate another Ruskin Park moment. 'What I said that day, I don't know why I said it. I guess I knew once we stopped living together, we'd just drift apart, and it freaked me out.'

Katie's response to this was to remain as she was. Her feet did shift slightly as she seemed to contemplate the painting more.

'So you don't have feelings about me?' she said and looked at me, calmly, mildly curious. 'So, if anything were to happen with us, like tonight, you would see it purely as a one-off – like with you and Izzy – no awkwardness after?'

She looked at me deliberately passively. As if she had asked which I preferred, tea or coffee.

'Maybe,' I said, a tad annoyed, sticking my chest out like we were teenagers and she was goading me regarding if I had ever smoked weed – which I never had.

'Okay.' Katie finished the last of her champagne. She then looked around us, just as controlled and steadily as when she was studying me. 'Follow me.'

We went through a door marked private, past a set of offices, and to a door marked storeroom. 'This is where Izzy normally goes at these sort of things,' Katie said, not looking back at me. Inside was dark, and Katie had not turned on the light switch before the door closed on us. I stood silently in the dark, waiting for whatever game of chicken we were playing to end, for us to have either a normal conversation or an argument. Instead, I felt her hands on my hip. My déjà vu moment from the pre-Christmas museum then turned into another déjà vu moment entirely. I was back at Christmas Day, under the mistletoe, with my eyes closed, surprised and in awe, as I felt her kiss me.

It was like all the pent-up frustrations of the last month were flowing out of me as I kissed her back like I can't recall kissing anyone for years. Perhaps it was sensory deprivation but all I could think of was how much I wanted her. I felt the fabric of her dress – her hips beneath it – and wanted ever so much to raise it over her head and take my own clothes off too. But then, the kissing stopped.

'I can't do this,' she whispered.

We had found a quiet spot sitting on a fire escape in an alleyway behind the gallery. I had just returned from the main event with two full glasses of champagne and handed one to a depressed looking Katie, hunched on the steps.

'That was unfair of me,' she sighed, taking the glass.

'I was using you to get back at Izzy. And Ethan.' She then screwed up her face and looked at me. 'And *you* come to mention it.'

'You were using *me* to get back at *me*?' I frowned, sitting down on the cold metal stairs. I was still feeling the effects of an array of hormones rushing through me as if I was a teenager. I had just kissed – or been kissed by – the girl I had set my heart on, however unlikely as that was. She had stopped and looked thoroughly miserable at the experience, which both changed the mood yet still left its mark on me. Looking at Katie, as with Izzy, it seemed like I too was her rock bottom.

'With Izzy,' she seemed to grit her teeth, 'I think I've taken all I can of this *get-under-someone-to get-over-someone* goading, implicitly saying there's something wrong with me for not being up for an open relationship and how constantly prudish I am. Looks like she was right! I can't even snog someone while newly single without feeling I'm cheating on Ethan!'

Her body sank, her chest resting on her knees.

'And with me?' I said, unable to resist a quick smirk. She then sprang up, depression turning to accusation.

'And you! This whole *leave Ethan for me, you fucking idiot* declaration. I know it was cruel, but hey, if everyone else is so up for casual sex, why can't I?'

She rolled her eyes, exasperated. I was still trying to get my body temperature under control after those two minutes in the storeroom.

'Because it's not you. Unfortunately for me.' I smiled. We both sipped our champagne. I could hear music coming from the gallery as we sat overlooking the bins of fellow businesses lined up down the alley. Katie seemed to be making a conscious effort to stretch Izzy's short dress as far as it could go over her knees.

'This is humiliating. You acknowledge that, right?' she then said, still looking just as pissed off as she was that day at Ruskin Park. 'Both for me and I assume for you. It's like the world's biggest hypocrite, whose personal life has been a self-styled train wreck ever since I have known her, is now telling us both to get our heads out of our arses. You understand why I'm annoyed, right?'

'A little, perhaps.'

'Okay. Then perhaps you'll understand that I resent having to apologise to someone who I should have apologised to ages ago – on my own terms – without my so-called best friend having to intervene and force me?'

The question was rhetorical. I could have replied but Katie then looked away, back into the stillness of the alley. When she next spoke, her voice was softer.

'I liked your letter.'

'Well, calling you an idiot in public wasn't exactly my finest hour.' I gave her the briefest of smiles. 'I seem to be not very good at not screwing things up with you.'

'Or I with you.' She gave a tired, groan of a laugh. 'I liked kissing you. More than I should have at the time. Considering Ethan. Considering the weirdness.'

I couldn't help a louder, more genuine blurt of laughter. I cradled my champagne, hunched too, listening to her, while staring blankly at the bins.

'We were meant to go dancing tonight. Izzy told me – ordered me – to wear this dress, and we were going to drink enough free champagne until our heads spun and then follow her gallery lot to some club where I would finally stop being a stick-in-the-mud and let myself go.'

'You can still go dancing. Lorenzo seems fun. Certainly outgoing.'

'Yes, very. But then you walked in and reminded me that rather than let some gorgeous, wealthy young man rock my world in the sack, I would rather be at home in my dressing-gown drinking warm cocoa and watching trash television shows on my laptop.'

Katie put her glass down to the side and then slumped further, her head on her knees.

'It also means I should be more honest. Both with myself and with you.'

She sat up, pushed her light auburn bob from obscuring her face and turned to look me in the eye.

'I like you, Scott. It is seriously weird, but I do. And part of me being so pissed off that day at the park was because you wanted me to do something that part of me really wanted to do. But that's the whole thing. Part of me also wanted my relationship with Ethan to go back to normal and forget this whole stupid year had ever happened.'

I was beginning to lose feeling in my fingers, holding the champagne in the cold air. But I didn't want to move, knowing this moment would never come round again.

'And part of me also wants to grab Izzy and scream that open relationships are not normal. Having to pretend to be up for a threesome with female college friends just to make you more desirable to some pervy guy is *not* normal. So not wanting to have sex with *anyone* right now does not make me a prude.' Her eyes shot to the heavens and she flung her head back, looking like she wanted to explode. She then let out a deep sigh and looked at me slightly more hesitantly.

'This is where I say it's me, not you.'

Katie looked so apologetic. After the Ruskin Park incident, I took some consolation in that it was difficult for my heart to break when it was already broken.

'I want you to know that I do like you. I have feelings for you. But, all I want to do is put on my most hideous pyjamas and eat my own body weight in ice cream. And I don't think that's going to change for at least the foreseeable future.'

'I think that's the nicest brush off anyone's ever given me.' I half-smiled, and she gave me a friendly shove.

'I meant what I wrote about missing you. I feel a bit lost, to tell the truth, not having you to talk to when I come home.'

Both our hands had fallen to our sides and were touching. She then squeezed mine.

'*Rock your world in the sack?*' I found myself smiling.

'See!' She shot me her first natural smile of the night. 'I don't even know what they call it anymore.'

It felt like a last ode to Loughborough Road. We sat on the fire escape, slowly drinking the now flat champagne, in the neo-romantic setting of bins and litter. But at least we were finally able to talk to each other, just like we did before. Largely about her and Ethan.

'We're arguing about the flat. He says he was the one who found it, so he should get to keep it. Eight years in a relationship and that is his only sticking point.'

'It's probably more than just that,' I tried to offer my worldly advice, a little more cautiously than I had done on previous occasions. 'If you're arguing about the flat that kind of keeps you together. I think they call it transference.'

Despite my months of therapy, I was not exactly sure I had done justice to the term. She laughed an ironic-sounding laugh.

'A bit like how I'm mad at both you and Izzy for sleeping together. That you both can jump into bed together without even seeing each other out of the house and then go for coffee weeks later like it's no big deal.'

'I'm sorry about Izzy and me.' I snorted another small laugh.

'No, you shouldn't be, though. If anything, I'm jealous. Of the fact you both felt free to go with it, and I've spent the last year in an open relationship being loyal to someone I'm not even sure I liked that much. I *loved* him. I think I do *still* love him, in fact. But, I don't know, I was pissed off at you because I was pissed off at him, so I'm sorry for always making it difficult between us.

I think I do still love him. Like with Vicky, it was bittersweet. I had said I wanted to be friends but I knew that was a distant second to what I really wanted. When I finished my champagne I put down the glass on the alleyway tarmac. I stood up and took a deep breath.

'I don't really fancy going dancing,' I grinned, as Katie also got up.

'Probably best. Me stopping off to throttle Izzy is going to put a dampener on the mood.'

Silently and slightly awkwardly we moved closer to embrace each other.

'I'll give you a call in a bit after I sort my head out. We can go for coffee or something?'

And that was all I knew it would be. All my cards had been played and Katie was far too bright to think anything otherwise. Christmas and that kiss under the mistletoe was embedded in my mind, though it all suddenly felt hollow as I fake smiled and turned to leave, hearing the loud, excitable voices of Lorenzo and his friends enter the alley from above. I gave Katie one more smile before turning on my heel and headed for the main road.

CHAPTER 32

AUNTIE PAM

It would be unfair to say that Auntie Pam had terrified us as children. Yes, we did dread those visits and joyless sleepovers at her house and, growing up on Disney, she was the wicked stepmother to mum's Snow White or Cinderella. Or perhaps she was the wicked witch, and Ellie and I were Hansel and Gretel. These are only analogies at the end of the day, and only a fool would try to realistically draw meaning.

Auntie Pam was Dad's only sibling. Mum's sisters had both married and emigrated to America and Australia when we were little, so she was effectively our only aunt. I think it was because I had stayed and Ellie had left that my relationship with her matured into something a little less dread-filled. I could see the kind side to her military-style organisation – how she would drop shopping off for us while Dad was coming to terms with his role as a single father, and check in on me when Dad was at a conference. We'd also have conversations over a cup of tea, initially while Ellie was still living with us, when some petty quarrel would result in Ellie slamming the door of her room. I remembered Auntie Pam's exhausted sigh and then how she would seem to pick herself up, smile at me, and ask if I wanted a biscuit.

She was strict, but I grew to like that about her. I never really associated Dad as being sad or the cliché of the jilted husband when Mum left, but he was definitely more preoccupied in that first year. Less jovial and chatty and spent a lot of time in his study. I think it was her influence that got Dad out of himself, maybe a little too late for Ellie to see, but she was the one who instigated those Sunday lunches and did become a steady presence in my life over a roast chicken and a few glasses of red wine.

But for Ellie, quality time with Auntie Pam seemed to remain very much consistent. She and Mike had collected her from Gatwick and her stay in Brighton was documented in WhatsApp messages every four and a half minutes.

We were searching for her for bloody ages! Why can't she buy a bloody pay-as-you-go FFS!!! She's been having coffee with a colleague. Who does that when they know someone is waiting for them?! We've had to give her our room so I'm in with the kids and she'd given the kids half a kilo of baklava so I'm now dealing with sugar rush comedowns and tantrums before bedtime!!!

And that was just a small sample. It did amuse me, receiving each update one after the other, but it also felt a pleasant distraction from thinking about Katie. Do not get me wrong, I had not returned to my duvet, nor was I moping – or at least I did not believe myself to be doing so, it is all relative, I guess. It just felt final. Terminal. Katie was starting out on a new journey and I didn't see an ex-flatmate having a place in it.

The small army of Ellie, Mike, Auntie Pam, and the kids arrived in the early afternoon, Millie bombing through the door fuelled on E-numbers. Ellie was next to enter the house, her eyes half-closed and teeth gritted. 'She went to meet a friend in

Worthing. That's why we're late. Her whole stay with us was just so she could get a door-to-door taxi service.'

'Scott, my boy!' called Auntie Pam over Ellie's hissed whisper, and joined us as Mike was last down the path with Ed and enough bags to last them a month.

'Uncle Scott, Uncle Scott!' cried Millie, back with us in the hallway after a lap of the house. 'Where's Auntie Katie? Can she play with me?'

Oh fuck, I thought, and what resilience I thought I had built up seemed to waiver.

'She's at her own little house,' Ellie interrupted crouching down to talk to Millie, whose face fell. 'Because today is about you and Eddie spending time with Daddy in Grandad's old house while Mummy and Uncle Scott have a nice cup of tea and a boring grown-ups chat with Auntie Pam.'

Auntie Pam wanted pretty much to get back to hers straight away and drop off her suitcase. 'There's a jolly new little café popped up in Alexandra Park. I have nothing for you in the house, so we might as well have a cake while we do this.'

She led us into the park which was blissfully sparsely populated on that gloomy February day. The grass looked damp underfoot and those few braving the conditions wrapped themselves in scarves and hats. Ellie and I were being led by a determined Auntie Pam, as if we were members of her expedition parties, to what looked like a glass conservatory just beyond a children's playground.

I volunteered to get the drinks and cakes while they took the only spare window table, giving us at least some privacy from accidental eavesdroppers. I was surprisingly less anxious than I thought I would be. Well, at least less anxious than Ellie. I think this sprang from anxiety fatigue. Seeing Orletta, the idea of her being in poor health instinctively didn't ring true. Instead, I was beginning to think Auntie Pam's mysteriousness was more a way to get Ellie and me running around after her – after all, we had neglected her since Dad's passing, enough to have her take up the travel bug and leave us for warmer climates.

When I arrived at the table, Ellie was already getting out our folder of documents from her bag.

'Auntie Pam, we found these invoices amongst Dad's things – '

'I know what they are, dear,' she replied, disregarding the papers Ellie was thrusting at her. Ellie gave her that wide-eyed glare she reserved for when she felt slighted, usually by Auntie Pam.

'Then perhaps you can tell us why we are here, why I've had to chase around the country after you, and we could not do this over the phone.'

Again, Auntie Pam looked completely unaffected as she poured each of us our tea from the communal pot.

'You have chased around the country because you are my only living family and I very much wanted to spend an evening in your company.'

I felt a jolt. The impressive comeback by Auntie Pam also felt a dig at me for those lack of visits.

'I take it you have not spoken to Orletta regarding this?'

I confirmed we had not while Auntie Pam sliced her cake into smaller pieces. Around us, people were warming themselves with their hot drinks as heavy coats lay over the backs of chairs. Prams and buggies were tucked into tables, and I faced the window overlooking the children's playground where cold-looking parents pushed wrapped-up toddlers on the swings and mini-roundabout.

'What you are asking of me is not straightforward,' she said, suddenly putting down her cup with an agitated sigh. 'I was asked to keep confidences, and now that George has passed away that should make these confidences more sacred, not less.'

It was all very solemn of Auntie Pam, I thought, and together Ellie and I gave each other a sideways look.

'We're not asking you to break a vow. We're just asking what the significance behind these pieces of paper is.' Ellie picked up and showed the invoices again, failing to hide the exasperation in her tone.

'But you are,' Auntie Pam said. I felt a coat brush my arm, and a tall woman with a buggy gave me an apologetic wave as she left her table. After chewing a mouthful of cake, Auntie Pam then set it aside looking somewhat more retrospective.

'I have to say firstly, I did respect – even admire – your mother but we did not gel at times as much as I would have hoped. Largely my fault, I have to admit. I can be a little set in my ways, so encountering a free spirit with all that glamour does not come readily. But your father loved her, and that was more than good enough for me.'

She took a quick refresh of tea and I huddled a bit closer, not wanting her to have to raise her voice.

'There were things you were not likely to have seen as children. To be honest, most of us adults selectively close our eyes to these things, significantly more then than we do now. But even now, you do tend to assume this is the way a person is.' Ellie and I both furrowed our brows again. We were not following her.

'Orletta was the life of the party amongst our social set. The room would light up when she would enter and she could bring a smile to even the most hardened sad-sack like myself. But when everyone had gone home, it would sometimes – not all the time – be a different story.

'There would be those long walks of hers, there would be those times she would retreat into her art and you would not hear a peep out of her for hours. And there were times when you both would be dropped off with me so she could have some peace and quiet. Lord,

I'm not saying you were a burden. No more than any other child or teenager – '

'Oh thanks a lot, Auntie Pam,' Ellie scowled.

'But there it was. She would take to her bed, with one of her heads, she would call them. She'd never call for a doctor and, to be frank, never did seem in enough pain for me ever to consider it more than an artist's temperament. And when the divorce came – or what should have been the divorce – well, I have to admit I thought she had acted selfishly and appallingly.'

Auntie Pam grimaced and made to top up her tea. Outside the window, children were happily chasing each other around the roundabout, looking thrilled, joyful and everything I remember being at that age. Auntie Pam stabbed her fork into another small piece of cake.

'Her career had taken off. She was invited to parties and asked to attend all these exhibitions, and George always made allowances for her exhaustion when something she found inconvenient came up.'

From revelling in Orletta's shortcomings, Auntie Pam suddenly sighed. As if someone had just turned a valve to let the air out of her vitriol.

'But what I have not said is that, despite all of this, she did cast a spell. Yes, we did not gel, but she was my sister-in-law and I loved her *as a sister*. She was kind and genuine, not false like I would have imagined her arty type to be. And I let her down.'

Ellie and I shot each other another look. I don't think Auntie Pam had ever said a nice word about our mother in all the time we had been alive, let alone said she had loved her. She just sat there nursing her teacup, temporarily lost in something. She then seemed to pull herself back to the present.

'Your father did try to win your mother back. There were trips to Devon and back in a single day, and each time he would return a bit more broken but still, infuriatingly, with never a harsh word to say about her. I accused him of allowing his blind spot for her to overlook all those cancelled visits, and how she expected you to be dumped at the doorstep of some gallery. That was meant to be quality time with her children. And do not let me start on those months abroad. And then, one day, she vanished. Just like that.'

Now the look Ellie and I shared was one of panic. I think we both assumed we were here to receive something trivial. There was then a clatter behind us. Something had dropped to the floor, but I blocked it out, just focusing on my aunt.

'She stopped calling. She and your father had arranged check-ins, and suddenly, no phone calls, no letters, no postcards to either of you. She was meant to have been abroad that summer taking *Orletta Roberts* on tour – drinking champagne standing alongside a painting of hers being told how wonderful she was. But she had not gone. Your father called mutual acquaintances, found hotel numbers, and she had never turned up. That Conrad fellow was just as elusive. He was off the grid as well, however as he ran a multimillion-pound business did mean your father was eventually able to get in touch with his secretary and be assured neither were missing persons.

'George had to travel to Devon to that retreat of hers. They had shut it up for the summer, and George told me there was not a soul. He received no answer at the house and had to wander empty cattle sheds or whatever they were meant to be until he found her in a barn, sitting on a stool, easel in front of her and staring at a blank canvas. She had paints but no paintbrush and just sat blankly staring, not responding as he called her name. That man of hers told George later that she had been like that for weeks.'

'She was catatonic?' said Ellie, eyes alert in alarm.

'George said she did eventually acknowledge him. As he tried talking to her she ultimately said 'do shut up, George' and returned to her staring. Apparently, it had begun at the start of that grand trip. Well, not begun exactly – there were warning signs – but as she led some circle of artists painting at some chapel, she got drawn to another's work and was suddenly preoccupied. From what that Conrad told your father, that evening she just flipped out. Paints thrown across the room, brushes in bits, and she took to her canvases destroying any work she had completed that week, crying what an embarrassment it was.

'They came back to England, mothballed their retreat thingy and tried to ride out the storm, as Conrad had put it.'

I was trying to visualise it. My mother sitting alone in the same barn that the redheaded Sylvia had walked out of, or slashing up paintings in some French château. But neither was in keeping with the woman I had either known or seen recently. Ellie was leaning forward, her mouth open, looking very much like she needed to ask questions, but Auntie Pam carried on.

'That man of hers thought it would blow over. Or hoped it would. So George intervened. He knew too well the mood swings – her *me-time* – and how when a painting was not quite right she would apparently go into her shell and get so dispirited she could not bear to see a soul. Even the two of you. Your father would ship you off to me for a night or so and that would usually be all it took to get your mother back on her feet again. But I guess the highs and lows of fame do come with quite the emotional burden.'

Auntie Pam let out a big exhalation of breath, allowing an increasingly agitated Ellie to jump in.

'Sorry, but this is ludicrous. You're saying Mum had some kind of breakdown, which no one told us about? It's not possible. We lived with her, for Christ sake. We would have noticed if she was suffering from depression.'

'You probably did, dear.'

Ellie scowled at our aunt, like it was one personal insult too many.

'She was a fabulous woman. A success. A fucking success!'

Auntie Pam took no notice of Ellie's deliberate swear and went back to focusing on refilling her cup with tea. I had hardly touched any of my own and wished I had bought a bottle of water instead – my mouth was dry and I felt uncomfortably warm in that greenhouse-like room.

'She was the life of the party. Any party! She occasionally would get a migraine and need some peace and quiet, but I would hardly call it depression.'

Again I was a passenger in the conversation, as I stared out of the glass. The playground was now deserted as the light grew dimmer. The image I had of Orletta was this vain abandoner of a woman. Strong and ruthless. The confidence, the flow, the hangers-on, and the glamour.

Auntie Pam told us that together Dad and Conrad had found Mum a clinic. I could vaguely recall an afternoon at sixth form when I had come home to find Auntie Pam in the house telling me Dad had been called to some urgent writers' conference or something which, in hindsight, was hardly plausible. 'He said it was more a hotel than, God forbid, an asylum. A country house with large grounds and woods and a doctor chap explained to them about individual sessions, group sessions, and even horse riding! He said it was the break she needed and though that man of hers could pay for it many times over, George was adamant he contributed half. She was still his wife, and despite the papers all being drawn up, they were unsigned, and he had no intention to do so until she was well again.'

There it was. At least, there was something. The reason why Auntie Pam had uncharacteristically kept her opinions to herself this last year.

'And did she?' I asked, finally finding my voice. 'Get well again?'

'I'm not sure if it is ever that simple, dear,' said Auntie Pam, a little the wearier. 'I have to say, I did not ask. I'm ashamed of that. Your father told me about each visit, and each time he would convince that man of hers to get her down to that fancy clinic as an outpatient, so she didn't keep bottling things up. But to answer your question, she was always Orletta, just sometimes she would get the occasional bad day, so said George.'

The light outside was quickly fading. Around us, there was less chatter or rattling of crockery. My tea was stone cold and I had not touched my cake. Neither had Ellie, who had turned her head to the side staring down at some patch of floor.

'She was okay,' mumbled Ellie in a low voice, her hand obscuring her mouth. 'I visited, and she was okay. She would have told us.'

'Eleanor, dear.' Auntie Pam then surprisingly reached for both our hands. 'I didn't want to be the one to tell you. George promised Orletta he would allow her to do so in her own time – she apparently got quite distressed and made him swear to it – and by that, I was sworn to the same vow. Back then, none of us were well versed in all this mental health. All I knew was that Orletta needed time to get back on her feet which, yes, she did. But all this is not my story to tell. All I can say is that I had held a grudge because of how she had left your father, and I'm ashamed to say that I never once made a telephone call to her to tell her she was loved.'

We walked Auntie Pam back home as dusk descended on the park. Ellie called Mike to tell him to feed the kids as we were to do some shopping for Auntie Pam so she would not have to leave the house again. Inside her sitting room, the grand space which was so intimidating and forbidden to play in as children, she looked thoroughly exhausted. I took it for granted that she had more energy than the rest of us combined, but today had drained her, and for the first time I saw a frailty that suddenly scared me. I did not have much family left, and I very much did not want to lose her.

Ellie too made no sighs of exasperation, but instead heated up some soup for her on the stove while I stocked the fridge. We had asked her if she had wanted to join us for some Chinese food, but she just wanted her chair and a night in front of the television, the two things she missed most about home. We sat with her into the evening watching Saturday night telly, and when we returned to Dad's, Mike had long since put the kids to bed, and Ellie and I were ready just to crash out on the sofa.

Ellie said they would make an early start back to Brighton in the morning as we ate in the living room, the TV on and cartons of Chinese food laid out on the coffee table.

'Do you want to do it, or should I?' I eventually said.

'I'll do it. It's better coming from me.'

We did not need to discuss it further.

CHAPTER 33

DEVON – AGAIN

'You know there are these things called dating apps? Apparently you get sent someone you might like and just press yes or no. Not exactly the height of romance, but definitely sounds an upgrade from your current love life.'

I was on the back seat of Mike's Volvo and he and Ellie were in the front. Mike was driving and Ellie had duped me into handing her my phone and was scanning through web pages and available apps.

'How do you know?' grinned Mike, as we travelled on an A-road through the heart of the Devon countryside.

'Hey, I'm just saying. This is beginning to look like some kind of complex. A compulsive attraction to the messed up and unattainable. That's all.'

'Err, thank you, Dr Eleanor?'

It was to be the three of us and just Orletta this time. Perhaps Conrad, but Ellie relayed that he would most likely be working in his study. She had brokered the meeting with our mother over text messages as we looped out Maxwell and solicitors and told her we only wanted to talk. We were not there to discuss the house, settlements, or legal notices. We would not be staying overnight, either at her house, which did seem a very unlikely offer, or in the village, and there were to be no stunts or gimmicks like last time's coincidental meeting of the Board. Not even lunch had been mentioned.

'Please tell me you didn't do the whole 'I'll wait for you, take as much time as you need' thing. Because that always works.'

'I'm glad someone finds it funny.'

'Well it's difficult not to,' she smirked and then spun around, slapping my knee with a big childlike smile. 'Oh, cheer up, sadsack!'

I had had a week to dwell on both what Auntie Pam had revealed about our mother, and what had happened with Katie, and I still had no idea how I was meant to feel. Part of me felt I should be moping about Katie, as I had done, and revert to type. But part of me was also still a little mesmerised by that bittersweet final kiss and needed to accept it for what it was – closure.

We had reached a wooden sign saying we were a mile away from the Colony. The journey seemed to have gone far quicker that Saturday morning, and there seemed a lot more energy about us than was probably appropriate. 'Well, I actually feel relieved,' Ellie had told me when we were arranging the trip. 'I know I should be angry that we were kept in the dark for so many years, but I thought she... Well, I thought I had done something wrong or disappointed her. Don't get me wrong, I'm still fucking pissed off and confused, but I've got so much shit on with the kids and everything I'm too tired to be angry or self-reflective.'

I could not have summed it up better. For me, it felt a little bit strange. There was something in how she looked at me when she had called me handsome that afternoon at the Colony. And when we stood together in front of the Turner at the gallery. Had she known? Could she see that sadness in me? Was it something she recognised in herself? I knew Ellie was both angry and shocked at finding out about Mum. But with me, I just felt I kind of got it. I understood why she wouldn't say anything, and it wasn't about a stigma. It was because it was part of her. If the modern world was now telling her that she should not feel ashamed about it, why should she even acknowledge it? With mental illness, I think we automatically feel we need to get overly understanding and bring out the kid gloves, emphasising the importance of talking about it and telling people how normal it is. Obviously, I am a walking example of the benefits of therapy, but I would also go as far as saying we need to start recognising that mental illness is an everyday part of life FOR EVERYONE. We will all have it, and we should anticipate it in others much like we would anticipate seasonal flu, and stop being so English about it.

Taking the correct route this time and risking neither the wrath nor flirtations of Sylvia De Vale, the Volvo was back on the cream-gritted driveway. This time only a silver BMW four-by-four and a sleek racing green Jaguar sat outside our mother's home. No fighting for space like last time, or chaotic fanfare with Orletta greeting us the moment we stepped out of the car. Instead, the three of us heard the crunch of our footsteps on the gravel as Mike gave us both an encouraging double thumbs-up as we made our way to ring the doorbell.

Conrad greeted us with firm handshakes and escorted us through their grand foyer and into the conservatory, exactly like we had done on our first visit. However, this time it was not holding a social event. Instead four chairs sat around a large circular glass coffee table, one of which was already occupied.

'Mike,' smiled our mother, looking up from the newspaper she was reading. 'What a surprise.' She rose gracefully to her feet and gave Mike a warm embrace, followed by the same with Ellie before lastly coming to me. As she said my name and again looked at me with those calm, forgiving eyes, I felt part of me crumbling. But I did not know which part. We had not embraced at the gallery. Our conversation was that of two strangers observing the same artwork. Now there were witnesses to my coldness. My brokenness. My inability to know what I should be feeling.

The embrace lasted just a second, but instantly a dozen or so memories came rushing back. I saw the numerous galleries I had been dropped off at over the years, and I saw a teenage boy waiting alone in the corridors, his mother otherwise occupied. I then saw a railway station in the middle of nowhere where that same boy, now approaching thirty, sat in the steady drizzle waiting for the train back to London.

'It is good to see you,' she whispered in my ear.

'You too,' I mumbled just as softly.

'Please, sit down. And help yourselves.' Coffee was laid out on the table in a silver pot with accompanying cups, saucers, and mini-milk jugs as if we were in the lounge of a fancy hotel. 'We also have biscuits baked in our local village. Fudge and toffee too – I remember how you both would love buying a little selection with your pocket money from those Natural Trust gift shops.'

'Scott spent all his on those stupid rocks we could have got for free down at the beach.'

Our mother glanced up as if playing the memory out for herself on that glass ceiling above us, a faraway smile on her face. She then grinned and began pouring coffee for the four of us.

'Maxwell tells me that you have been working very hard putting George's affairs in order.'

I tried not to groan. Maxwell's helpfulness did seem too good to be true. I wondered how much our mother's spy had divulged.

'I'm very impressed. When you were both little it was a chore to get you to be diligent about just about anything. Scott, you were always playing with those toy soldiers of yours, and, Eleanor, we would have wars even getting you to sit on that piano stool of yours.'

'Orcs,' I replied to three puzzled faces. 'They were orcs and warriors. And druids.'

Orletta smiled politely.

'I assume this visit is about the estate? My solicitor informs me that you would like to proceed with adjudication. You will have no objection from me. It does seem silly to drag this all out and perhaps we might even become friends if somebody else takes the wheel.'

It was like a micro-aggression bundled with a naïve thumping address to the elephant in the room. Did she think Ellie and I would jump up like a character in Mary Poppins and say 'yes, let us all become friends and never have another silly twenty years of hostilities ever again'?

'It's not about Dad's estate,' I said. I held my coffee cup and saucer at my lap. 'We wanted to ask you some questions about Dad. About you and Dad and why you never got divorced.'

'Oh,' she said, sounding a little surprised, a little intrigued. 'Please go on.'

Her formality and genuine composure stopped me. Who was I talking to? The artist, Orletta Roberts, or my mother from twenty years ago? Ellie also was surprisingly hesitant, so it was Mike who got us on our way.

'Ellie and Scott have been sorting through George's old paper-work, deciding what's important and needs to be kept, and there are a few questions that keep coming up about the divorce papers and why they were drawn up but never signed. I guess you can see their point.' Mike sat forward, both businesslike and amiable, casually gesturing to both of us. 'Everyone assumed you were divorced, even your family lawyer. This may have been a question for some time back, but I think they both would like to know what happened.'

The silent Ellie seemed to fold herself within her chair, all limbs crossed. I sat forward, mimicking Mike, and gave a small nod.

'For two people with a lot of questions, you both are remaining remarkably quiet.' She said it with a smile – a warm smile, contrary to the words actually said. However, it might have been the final straw for Ellie.

'Perhaps we shouldn't have to ask the questions?' She had one of the looks she reserved for Auntie Pam when she was beyond exasperated. 'Perhaps we kind of expected our sole surviving parent to reach out to us to explain what was going on and not just send solicitors or Conrad or anyone rather than have a fucking conversation.'

She'd never sworn at our mother before. No matter how angry or hurt she might have been. Orletta placed her coffee and saucer back down on the glass table.

'I guess it did not matter at the time. Everyone seemed happy with the arrangements. What did one piece of paper signify? Only that something had failed, which it had not. Those were wonderful years with your father – I have two wonderful children. I guess neither of us wanted to diminish that.'

'That's not what we're asking. Why didn't Dad sign the papers? He went to the effort to have them drawn up, but something stopped him signing – please stop treating us like children!'

Ellie's hand went to cover her eyes and pinch the bridge of her nose. Mike reached over to grab her other hand. Orletta gently adjusted her seat and took a breath.

'I loved your father. Every bit as much as he loved me. The only thing that changed was that I needed to start writing the new chapter of my life. There was always tomorrow to sign those papers. Until... well, we always think we have more time than we do.'

'But the house,' I said, quickly so we would not get lost in another reflection. 'If the papers *were* signed then you would have no claim on the house, so why not just act like he did sign the papers? Why benefit but make out it was just a paperwork error?'

'Because, Scott, it was *my* house.' Her voice had changed. It was sharper, not as flowery. 'It was your father's and mine. We bought that house together, we made so many plans in it, and I have now made promises regarding that house that, to be completely frank, keeping it as a mausoleum does him no credit and neither does it help either of you.'

The sharpness was still there, but so was the smile, like she had also finally realised the softly-softly approach – like the great American poet once said – *ain't getting us nowhere.*

'I am not stealing your inheritance. You and your children will be more than provided for when I depart this world. But there are things you would not understand about your father's and my relationship after our separation, and believe me, as unlikely as it would seem, he would want this.'

'But that's the thing,' I said, leaning forward, feeling more animated. 'We would. We would understand.'

Above us, a thick cloud rolled over the conservatory casting a shadow. *Orletta Roberts?* She was certainly speaking with the confidence of a renowned artist who chaired board meetings of famous galleries. But there were still those non-judgemental eyes that, as sappy as it was to say, did hold a mother's love and were staring at me calmly, allowing me to finish what I meant.

'Ell, could you give me and Mum a moment, please?'

My sister scowled at me like leaving me alone for negotiations would be the last thing she would even contemplate. 'It's about *Watership Down,*' I said.

· · ·

Mike had led Ellie outside through the conservatory doors, both with coffee cup in hand, leaving only two of the wicker armchairs still occupied. I stretched over the coffee table to refill my cup and then did the same for my mother. I shuffled in my chair, feeling for the best position from which to speak. My mother just waited, a small intrigued smile upon her face, not even asking why I had needed the room cleared.

'I was ill last year,' I began. 'I can't pinpoint when it started, a couple of months after Dad died perhaps. I had a brief friendship with a girl that got a little confusing, and suddenly I was unable to think straight. And it would not stop.'

My mother looked back at me, her poker-face relentless. There was not even a twitch to betray her.

'It got worse. I didn't do anything about it. And then I felt like something broke, and I could not function anymore. I was no longer me. So I started talking to someone. Every week. Month after month, and I still don't feel ready to stop. I'm still not...'

I shrugged. I blew out my cheeks and frowned, not sure where to go next. My mother was still giving me her undivided attention and still giving nothing away.

'What made me start seeing someone about – what was going on that I could not explain – was this one night where everything in my head was so loud I needed to get it all out. I was at Dad's, breaking our agreement and staying there over Easter. I was in his study, at his desk, I took out his writing paper and wrote him a letter about everything. All that I had not told him while he was alive. Everything I was ashamed about. And I put it in an old copy of *Watership Down*.'

I felt I was rambling. My monologue was falling on someone with deaf ears. Orletta neither nodded along nor gave me a hint that she understood what I was saying. Just that poker-faced stare while I tried to untangle my words.

'Ellie knows. She found the letter a few months later. But her knowing was this massive wave of panic like I couldn't cope with another person finding out that was how I felt. Like the shame would cripple me. But it didn't.'

I looked out through the glass doors, watching Ellie and Mike side by side standing over the vines below.

'If anything, it actually got us talking for the first time in our lives. We seem not to be so... *resentful* of each other. We tell each other things. We've started acting like brother and sister and not like two strangers who were forced to spend their childhoods together, and from my perspective it is a whole lot easier not having this constant guard up.'

Light was breaking through the clouds above us. I knew it was still not warm outside and I should tell Ellie and Mike it was safe to come back in. My mother still sat there watching me, listening. But then she leaned slowly forward and fixed her eyes on the coffee table picking up a plate of biscuits. She offered me one.

'They are awfully good.'

I took one and we both sat crunching through them.

'I guess you do take after me more than you had realised.' Orletta smiled. This time not looking at me but like a flicker of memory had come to her and she was temporary elsewhere.

'If you wouldn't mind calling your sister back inside, there is somewhere I should show you.'

Mum asked Conrad to show Mike the gardens leaving Ellie, me and her alone in the house. She led us back to the foyer and up the stairs. We followed her along the hall and past a number of spacious, immaculate bedrooms. At the end was another less grandiose set of stairs leading to another floor.

'No need for alarm. It is just my studio.'

We were in an attic room far more spacious than mine at Loughborough Road. A large skylight allowed a lot of light to flow in, giving the pale wooden beams and white walls a glow even on that grey February day. A solitary easel and chair sat at the centre, and all along the perimeter of the room were canvas upon canvas, the majority unfinished.

'I say this is my studio, but most of the time I only sit here to admire the view.'

My mother glided to the chair, resting her hands on its back while gazing through the skylight. As though we were alone with a cornered tiger, Ellie and I kept to the outside of the room, treading gently and silently in opposite directions past her paintings, careful not to invade what felt a private space.

'Your grandmother taught me to paint. She had me wielding a brush since I was not much older than a toddler. I suppose I did have those aspirations of becoming that unearthed talent and doing one thing of artistic note, but I progressed in life very much like every other friend of mine at art school – dream the big dream and then slowly replace it with more down-to-earth pursuits. When you have children, you realize how truly blessed you are and those old dreams fade in comparison.'

She momentarily turned to each of us and smiled politely. Ellie had made her way around to the other side of the room and was looking at another unfinished canvas.

'But painting was always part of me. An outlet, or more precisely, something I had to get out. When I began exhibiting, and the Italian suits and French shawls began to take notice and pay compliments, it was like a fire igniting in me. It seemed to erode everything else. And I'm not talking about the recognition itself. More, the recognition that I could do it.'

Ellie seemed determined to find something worth looking at in the canvases as she stared at her feet rather than our mother, who in turn was talking to the skylight. I found I had gravitated back to the doorway.

'I *could* be the one to paint that great work. The piece that would hang in the Royal Society. That I had a purpose. For once all those voices in my head chastising me for not being good enough ebbed away and suddenly, poof! There I was, Orletta Roberts.'

She gave us both this little ironic smile. I couldn't help wonder what Ellie was thinking as she had stopped staring at every half-finished canvas in her vicinity and was now just staring down at the floor.

'We call it *the Dip*. The feeling just before you paint your final stroke when you question whether what you are about to complete has been a waste of time. If anything you have done or will do will ever demonstrate any originality or amount to anything at all. You see nothing but flaws. The faker, pretending to be something you will never be.

'I believed my so-called success,' she then spun to her left and wandered closer to Ellie, 'would win over *the Dip*. After all, those fancy suits and shawls could surely not be wrong. All I had to do was devote myself fully and completely to my work, but alas,' I saw her put her hand on Ellie's arm, 'it does not work like that.'

She picked up the canvas upon which Ellie had her eyes fixed and held it up. It was a Van Gogh-style cornfield somewhere sunny and picturesque. 'I would meet fellow artists on my tours of Italy and France who said my work inspired them, and I would sit being guest of honour at these workshops where we would paint together. Oh, the hubris! My benevolence on the world. This is from Burgundy. My unfinished *masterpiece*.' There was a snarl to her voice as they continued to stare. 'Everything I despise about my work on one canvas. Derivative. To have thought I was there to inspire others.'

She scoffed again, putting it down.

'It wasn't just that particular day in Burgundy – everywhere there were artists with real talent who made you feel with their use of light and colour, and could truly capture grief in the face of a passer-by. So I abandoned my tour determined not to be one of those who lived off undeserved prestige, and we came back here, to this room, so I could find what I was missing.'

Orletta put down the painting. She turned, looked at me, and smiled.

'This became my private space.' She gestured around the room. 'Like with our conservatory. Here, I locked myself away, hoping to drive away those demons and let my talent shine through. Though this time it didn't. I would shut myself up here for days. Days then suddenly became months.'

She again glided across that smooth wooden floor, back to her chair and the skylight.

'When did it start?' I asked. My voice sounded strange. Too loud, compared to what had only been my mother's.

'Who knows. It either materialised or was there all the time, and I did not give it the respect it deserved.'

'How did you make it stop – '

'Is this going to be your excuse now?' muttered Ellie. 'Why you left and stopped picking up the phone?'

'For fuck's sake, Ell.'

'Oh you're allowed to wish her dead, but I can't say I'm a little bit pissed off that no one in this family tells me anything and thinks their problems are so important they can just go off and leave me...' Ellie's voice cracked. Her lip didn't even have a chance to wobble. It was just a deluge as our mother ran to embrace her.

It was like being taken out of the rain and huddled under a large towel. We were in a small sitting room, perhaps another private space of our mother's. Orletta lit a fire in the fireplace and we sat on armchairs surrounding it.

'People were less open about those things back then, even in the 90s.' Orletta sat down, her chair opposite mine and Ellie's. 'The terms mental health and psychotherapy were not ones we bandied about. It was all very much a legacy from our parents' generation of keeping calm and carrying on. Very English.'

She had brought with her into the room the biscuits from the conservatory and offered us the plate.

'I did not choose art over you both. It was not why I left, and God knows I have wanted to tell you so many times over the years. I left because I was afraid. Very much afraid of being a failure. As a wife, a mother, a person. I would be terrified that someone would look into my life and see the real me – an empty space. An imitation. I would have these bouts of sadness I would not be able to explain, and my only form of escapism was my painting, so I did the easy thing and chose escapism over reality. And because I did that, I was ashamed.'

The fire crackled and I could feel its warmth at my shin. Ellie still looked shell-shocked and was staring into another mug of coffee our mother had made her. Mine sat on a little side table between our chairs as Orletta calmly relayed her story.

'I threw myself into my work. And any talent I did have began to dwindle. All I could think of was what I had given up. That shame would grow until... well, I'm sure I do not have to repeat what you have already surmised, but I was very lucky to have some wonderful people around me, most notably your father.'

She exhaled and glanced into the fire. I followed her eyes, almost expecting to see Dad's image appear in the flames as a hint of a smile drew across her face.

'I was adamant I did not need help, and when I received it, I did not want a soul to know, especially you both. I had already let you down. I couldn't have you see me at what I deemed my worst.'

'You didn't let us down,' a croaky voice said from Ellie's chair.

'Yes. Yes, I did. Not for the illness. For hiding. I told myself I would tell you when I had invited you to the Colony for our little gathering. Then with you, Scott, I thought if we stood together long enough at the gallery some words would find their way out. But it was not the case.'

'Why wait till now?' Again, my voice came out a little strange. Too soft this time. Ellie looked very much like she did as a child, emotionally spent, curled up in that chair.

'Why go off-grid completely with us? Why go through Maxwell this last year and not just let us know you'd spoken to Dad? Why let us lose a year of our lives trying to sort all this out?'

'Are you bringing up the fucking house?' Ellie barked at me. I could not help the bubbling resentment I was feeling.

'It's not the house. It's that we *did* need you, and we would have been there for you. We should have been there for you. And you should have let us.'

My mother again smiled knowingly into the fire.

'Because I could not face you.' There was a warmth to her eyes in that glowing light as it began to darken outside. 'I would ask George about you. We'd speak most weeks. Strangely we spoke more after it all than we ever did when we were married. He would tell me about your travels, Scott. And, Eleanor, he would tell me all about your life in Brighton and those beautiful children of yours. I am so proud of both of you, and with George, I had still had a dear friend and routine where at least I knew everyone I loved was happy. But then, the worst happened.'

The smile faltered. Her face seemed to sink and to look weary.

'I do not expect you to believe me, but I have missed him enormously. He would visit, especially at the start of my illness. This all

– the Colony – it was my vanity project. Where I could bestow my benevolence at home. When I became unwell, we shut it down for the summer and retreated to my studio. But we reopened, if only to save face and quash any rumours. And on my return from the fancy clinic the second time, it was George who suggested I leave the house and walk with him around the barn and just watch the students at work. He remarked how he would watch me like that, in peace, lost in what I was doing.

'He then had me do something I had never done before. Sit with them – as a participant rather than mentor. George began asking the other artists about their work and their backgrounds. I just listened, realising it was the first time I had done so. Everyone had a story and a reason for being in that barn. I was not the only one trying to escape. We soon stopped painting and we all just talked. And laughed. It felt like the first time I had laughed in years.'

Orletta sat up and reached for another biscuit, looking at Ellie and me to see if we wanted one. I tried to smile politely, wondering how she managed to stay so calm, so many more questions running through my head. Ellie again was quiet, looking so much younger without her sarcastic fierceness.

'My art changed that day. I painted less aspirational master-pieces and more of the everyday. Depictions of our little colony. My circle of fellow painters. In fact I stopped being an artist and reverted back to a painter, one who would share their stories with those around them and listen in return to life stories of hardship and courage that left me awestruck, not just at their heroism, but the fact I had known some of these people years and had never bothered to ask. We have survivors of domestic abuse, I have friends who have fought addiction, and there are people like me who get a little sad from time to time.'

My mind started to wander back to when I was a boy and

would literally run into my mother's arms. I remembered when she would have those heads of hers. I would sneak into her room and curl up next to her, hoping a cuddle could soothe her pain, much like it would my knocks and scrapes.

I did not know how to process what was, after all, a story I had gone there somewhat expecting to hear. Twenty years was a long time not to forgive someone. Still, I felt this underlying animosity towards the older woman sitting in the chair opposite me, with the kind eyes and subtle patient smile, for taking away the younger one. I wanted to blame someone for losing my mother, and the only person I could blame was that shadowy spectre who hid in the dark corners taunting me, who didn't actually exist. All I had was the familiar-looking stranger sitting opposite me with my mother's eyes.

'And Dad knew all this?' I said. My mother smiled. She placed her hand on the arms of the chair and gently rose.

'I have something of his for you.'

'We'd better get going,' Ellie suddenly said, quickly but still a little apologetically. 'Mrs Rawlins has the kids and it's super late already.'

'Then I shall meet you at the door with it.'

She again smiled and left Ellie and me to silently steady ourselves.

'Mike must want to be getting back too,' she said as we got to our feet, both of us looking like it took considerable effort. But no sooner than we had stood, than Orletta had returned.

'But you both must be starving. And Mike too. Please let me at least feed you a sandwich before you go. We are very good at ploughman's in these parts.'

When I worked at the bank, we would have an away-day once a year where we were sent to a forest somewhere in Hampshire to be put through our paces by former SAS survival experts. Drill sergeants had us clambering through obstacle courses, over walls and through tunnels on our bellies, all under the pretext of team building, but really just a yearly form of humiliation to put us in our place and have us appreciate the fact we did a tedious desk job. Needless to say, at the end of it all, when we washed away the layers of mud and convened in the bar, we met each other with a smile of enormous relief. And that was exactly how I felt when I saw Mike outside the conservatory overlooking the vines.

'Let you out for good behaviour?' he grinned.

'Time already served.'

I joined him at the top of the slope and let out a breath overlooking the green and yellow stretching as far as the eye could see.

'You must be in your element out here.'

'You'd be surprised what we get in Brixton.'

Mike jumped down the hill to one of the vines and examined it, much like I had done on my first visit.

'You must know all the technical names and that? *Circumstantia Von Aliolis?*'

'I think it's called a grape, mate.'

'Here.' He threw me one. We both pulled faces at the intense rancid sourness.

'Maybe they taste better in liquid form.'

'I can assure you they do.' Conrad emerged from the house with a glass of wine in one hand and a tall drink in the other.

'Can't have you come all this way and not sample our vintage. Perhaps, Mike, you can permit yourself a sip?'

We were handed drinks, and I passed mine to Mike to try. Conrad was right. It tasted heavenly. Perhaps because I needed alcohol.

'Mike tells me you're a dab hand at all this.' Conrad nodded to his vines and crops.

'Kitchen gardens mainly. And not so grand a scale.'

'They're grapes, mate,' grinned Mike. 'Surely not too different from that plantation you worked on back in Burundi?'

'Yes, Scott, it's rare to meet someone over here, or even outside the vineyards of France, who has that kind of experience.'

'Why do I feel I'm late to the party here?' I said, looking at them both suspiciously and then looking back down at the tall plants winding themselves around their sticks. They were now both grinning.

'Conrad was just giving me the tour. Telling me he was expanding.'

'Thinking about it. A neighbour is considering selling some land with a similar slope. I was telling Mike that when we first put down roots here I was a younger man. I've had some offers of support from friends in Burgundy who know their onions, but I'd need a hand. There would be a lot of work – technical work – I won't be able to bring in anyone just to dig the odd trench – '

'You'll need to measure each out, depending on the slope, and run your irrigation channels,' I found myself quietly adding. 'I can let you know how busy I get with the landscaping, but, yeah I could give you a hand for a week or so if you decide you want to do it.'

'I think we're talking a bit longer than a week.'

Conrad then ushered us back towards the house, where he said our sandwiches were waiting. When we returned, Ellie was having a conversation with our mother about Millie and whether she was too young to start learning to play the piano. We joined them around the coffee table and, for an hour, forgot ourselves. Ellie told stories of the kids, my mother asked me about my gardening business, and we just *chatted* for an hour about everything that was not houses, wills, or settlements.

Perhaps it was tiredness after what had been an emotional day, but we began the car journey in pretty much silence, until Mike tried to start a conversation.

'It was a pretty good ploughman's.'

'Hmm,' mumbled Ellie. 'And it only cost us around two hundred and fifty grand each.'

CHAPTER 34

NORMAL

'It's not easy,' said Camille as we were back in the more normal surroundings of her office. 'I know a lot of people say that, but what they don't say is that it also does not come naturally either.' After so many months of therapy and having heartfelt discussions with flatmates, sisters, mothers, I was pretty much exactly where I had started – in a soft fabric armchair opposite Camille in the safe space of therapy.

'We build these walls throughout our lives to keep residual trauma at bay and get through the everyday, so when it comes to grief, there are no rules of how long it should take to process or even *when*.'

I had had a solitary few weeks since the trip to Devon. Not solitary in that I hid myself away under my duvet again. More like everything had simply gone quiet. Or, that everything for everyone else had gone back to normal. Ellie and Mike were getting on with the all-consuming job of raising two small children. My mother and Conrad had travelled to France and we agreed everything would be put on hold until they returned. As for my friends, well, we did live in London at the end of the day so radio silence for the entire gloomy, damp and dark month of February was not unexpected. I had my work at least. I even had a new garden – just some light work a street away from Mrs Elsop's but additional work none-theless. In truth, there was only one aspect of my life that did stretch beyond the mundane. That was a series of WhatsApp conversations with Izzy, who had not only taken me up on my offer of friendship but also seemed to be utilising me as a dating consultant.

Dullard again tonight. He's been very kind and patient espe-cially considering my No Sex Until Date Six dogma. If he only knew how desperately in need I am of some form of shag. Positively bursting! ;-)

While that was at least entertaining, the woman whose name I had hoped to see pop up on my phone remained unsurprisingly quiet. I did message, and she did reply, but the interaction was polite and far too enthusiastic and considerate to be anything more than superficial. *All good over here! Hope north London is treating you well. Thanks and have a good week!*

In a way, it hurt more than when she told me to go fuck myself.

But what came unexpectedly in that month of quiet reflec-tion was just how much I missed my dad. I was no stranger to staying at the house during the year after his death, so living there full-time should not have triggered this overwhelming sense of loss that had me having to take a seat and wait for the wave to pass.

'I was very close to my grandmother,' said Camille, holding the warm cup of coffee between her palms. 'When she passed away it wasn't her death which hit me hard. Or the funeral. It was the day after. When we were supposed to carry on.'

It was late afternoon at the end of the week. I could see the sun already falling in the sky. Camille crossed her legs and flicked her blonde hair to the side as she stared up at the ceiling as if trying to bring down that memory.

'Previously, I had to arrange flights, comfort my mum, greet distant cousins and help with the service. There wasn't any space to sit with nothing else on my mind. And then there it was. All that time. All that space. And I found it hard to breathe.'

I pressed my hands around my mug, feeling the chill now the sun was setting. For a moment, I questioned whether another coffee that late in the day was a good idea. Then I remembered the reason why I had asked Camille to have our session on that day, at that time.

'After we came back from Devon, I would have these dreams – none that I can remember but vivid ones featuring ex-girlfriends like Vicky and Sarah and us being happy before it all melted away and I realised I was alone. And then I would think of Dad and wonder what he would say. And I'd go down to his study and expect him to be there.'

'That is normal,' she smiled. 'Even years later. Grief is not a simple thing that can be modelled by that so-called five stages approach. Each does play their part, but loving someone does come with a lot of pain and heartache, and if it didn't, it probably would not be as wonderful as it is.'

Camille smiled again. This time it was that big encouraging smile of hers.

'And let's not forget that positive side of love. Scott, you have made huge strides this last year. And a lot of that is due to letting people in despite the cost it comes with. You've learned to deal with situations. Sure, each of us needs time to hunker down when a storm comes in, but you've come out of those moments. You've been honest about your feelings with Katie, you have a friend in Izzy, you have what seems a strong relationship now with your sister, and you're talking to your mother. That's a lot! You should not be discouraged by a little bit of quiet time where you can now mourn your father in your own way.'

On the way home, or I should say back to Dad's, I collected a few more storage boxes and arrived back at Wood Green after dusk, ready for the evening task. Entering the front door, I received a message from Izzy.

Fancy a girls' night out? You're pretty much one of us, considering our strange comradery. You might even have fun.

I smirked. Our friendship had not yet stretched to an evening out together, especially as part of a group. It did sound kind of fun. Unless Katie was going to be there. But then, obviously, they would never have a night out separately. Either this was another poorly conceived setup that would embarrass and annoy Katie, or perhaps it was Izzy's way of telling us to get our heads out of our arses again and go back to being friends. Either way, if one of the above was going to happen it probably would have by now, and, besides, I was unable to take her up on the offer anyway.

I actually really would but I'm packing up the whole of my Dad's house. Have family coming over tomorrow so it does need to be done by then.

So boring. But fair. By the way, things with dullard are going okay. My No-Sex pact is still intact but he was so very sweet and gentlemanly last night so... let's just say I gave him something your moral compass denied. From his reaction it was very much your loss ;-) I quite enjoyed it too actually. Nice to have someone appreciate my benevolence.

I almost dropped my phone, which I am sure was the reaction Izzy knew she would get. I also laughed, knowing I had gone slightly pink. We did have a strange friendship – it was so inappropriate it felt appropriate. But then I had a sudden flashback to our first night out together. I saw Katie sitting on a barstool at Joan's birthday years ago when we first met. How stunning she looked in her black dress, her legs crossed, smiling. Well, smiling initially. Luckily the home movies in my mind decided to replay no more of that night and instead shifted to where I was standing with my packing boxes. I saw Katie and me in the doorway to the living room kissing under the mistletoe. I let myself have that moment as after almost a whole year of therapy, I didn't see the point of either denying it had happened or that I had feelings for her. But I did need to accept those feelings were not reciprocated. I needed to break the habit of a lifetime and stop dwelling on what might have been.

'So I guess the only thing left for us to do is sort our own lives out,' Ellie had said after we had come back from Devon, not quite echoing this specific philosophy but that we had finally made our decision regarding Dad's house and will.

We were letting go. We both knew we would that afternoon with Auntie Pam. And we confirmed this to each other after spending the day with Orletta and Conrad. No need for Notices, no need for solicitors, just one word to Maxwell and it would be over. And that word would take place the following afternoon as we planned what would be an impromptu goodbye party of sorts. We had asked Orletta and Conrad to meet again, this time at Dad's, and they were travelling directly to meet us from the airport after they arrived back in the country. We had not yet told them what our plan was. 'Is it sketchy?' Ellie had said. 'To see if we could guilt her into upping that settlement offer? Perhaps if we asked her to meet us at the shithole you were living in or to come round to my shoebox-house, she'd pity the mess we've made with our lives.'

Ellie was joking. Kind of. Yes, neither of us were in a position to turn down money but nor had we remotely made a mess of our lives, despite my self-pitying to the contrary. After all, we still had so much of them to go. But we did have a slightly sneaky plan to get first dibs on Dad's worldly goods and prevent anything entering an auction house or going to the highest bidder. When our mother arrived, everything would be in boxes which would be divided between not just Ellie and me, but also Auntie Pam, Jane and Maxwell – whom we conveniently forget was Dad's best friend – all according to sentiment and who would appreciate what most. And how could Mum argue against that, especially if it was all done prior to telling her she could have the house? Even if some of the sentimental items were first edition novels worth a couple of thousand pounds each.

I assembled half a dozen of the storage boxes in Dad's study and acclimatised myself to the enormity of the task. So many books, and I was the decision-maker as to who received what. Ellie also asked me to assemble boxes in the living room for all the photo frames and ornaments. Finally, as Ellie put it, my biggest task was to pack away and dispose of all my *Games Workshop crap*.

By early evening each room had a box containing one item. Not the quickest of progress. It was not the most systematic approach. I roamed from room to room, hoping the living room might be easier than the study, and then my bedroom might be an easy win compared to the living room. In the end, I reverted to the study and soon decided the best course of action was to treat myself to fish and chips.

In a plastic carrier bag I had not only a piece of cod the size of my stomach and a mountainous portion of chips I knew I would never finish, but also a bottle of merlot from the newsagents, hoping that wine might offer me greater inspiration. As I walked back to the house my mind wandered to the following day and my mum being in our house for the first time since before I left for university. *Her house*, I should say. We would be putting it on the market soon, I assumed, and then an array of strangers would be trampling through it, seeing none of the memories that flooded back to me when I step into each room. But as I reached halfway down the street, the prospect of strangers trying to seek entry seemed to be taking place sooner than I expected.

I was two houses away when I saw the shadow in the front garden. It seemed to be peering through the windows. By force of habit I had switched the lights off, so the house did appear unoccupied. It was far too late for it to be Jane or any post, so there was only one likely possibility. Automatically I clutched the merlot and walked slower, eyes fixed on my burglar.

'Hello?' I called out. Was it like the films? Did intruders scarper at the first sign of detection, or did things instead turn into a violent mugging? My burglar didn't scarper. Instead, they moved out of the shadows. They were smaller than I expected. They were holding a phone to their ear and had a stylish canvas bag over their shoulder, and looked remarkably like my ex-flatmate.

'I was just calling you,' beamed Katie.

'What are you doing here?' I might have said this more severely than I intended as her smile faded.

'Oh, I just heard you were having to sort through your dad's things tonight. I thought I'd pop by and see if you needed a hand.'

'But you live almost an hour away?'

The fading smile then began to look surly.

'I can go if you like?'

'No!' I backtracked. 'I'm just surprised. I didn't think you wanted... I mean, I thought you were busy, and I wouldn't see you for a while.'

'Well, you know, you were there on my moving day, so I thought it was only fair I act like a friend and return the favour.'

She gave me this little quarter smile. I took out my keys and tried to give her a proper smile back.

'I've got more chips than I know what to do with.' I held up the package of faux newspaper in which the chip shop had wrapped my dinner. She reached into her bag.

'Well, I've brought wine.' Katie grinned and brought out a bottle with a fancy embossed label.

I opened Katie's wine and showed her into the study.

'Oh, you weren't kidding,' she said, staring gobsmacked at the mess. However, this was the woman who had turned Loughborough Road from a derelict squat into somewhere I referred to as home.

'Tell you what, why don't we have the chips in here? We can sort through things a little more... *systematically* with a bit of sustenance and some wine.'

Returning with a plate and two glasses, I had a flashback to Loughborough Road, seeing Katie sitting on the floor wearing the same pink hoodie and jeans she would do when cross-legged on her bed.

'You changed your hair back.'

'The new look wasn't really for me. When the roots started to show I just asked them to colour it back like it was. Not quite the same and not a lot I can do about the length.' She frowned and pulled a handful. It was a little longer than it was but not quite beyond shoulder-length.

'Scott, can we talk for a sec?' She looked a little more serious – well, more anxious.

'Last time, that whole kiss and secluded storeroom, that was out of order. I keep saying I want us to be friends and then I practically *Mrs Robinson* you. It was a weird time. A weird, *weird* time.'

'Weird seems to be our thing.'

'Yes!' she laughed. 'Definitely sums us up.' She reached for a chip looking a little more relaxed. 'And to make things probably more weird I just wanted to say you don't have to worry about any more of the same. On my best behaviour.'

She bit into her chip and then smiled at me, probably the first normal smile I had seen from her in months.

'And besides, Izzy's told me about that chastity belt of yours,' she winked.

At last, we were getting somewhere. It was easier with two, or perhaps it was simply easier with Katie. She was more systematic than me and she took to sorting Dad's books between the boxes much like the curator she was. She asked me about Jane and Auntie Pam's tastes and their relationship with Dad, and about what Ellie might have been expecting. She arranged neat piles alongside each box while I felt confident enough to take each of the one thousand or so books down from the shelves lining the four walls.

'Oh wow, we've finished the bottle,' she said, picking it up as she stood carefully looking through an old copy of *Down and Out in Paris and London*. The wine had given me the delusion that I was lithe enough to balance one foot on Dad's desk chair and the other on a shelf so I could reach the dusty top shelf.

'You can throw that in my pile, most apt and that,' I said.

'You're doing fine. Besides, you've not done Paris yet.' She gave me a wink and then bent down to pick up her wine glass, draining the last few drops. 'Are you going to think me a lush if I suggest opening up another bottle?'

It felt like the old days of Loughborough Road. Actually, not the old days – those would have seen Katie and me politely avoiding each other's company. The middle days of Loughborough Road, then. Us, opening bottles of wine, and sitting at our little square dining table, talking well into the night.

'Here you go.' She came back with the bottle and refilled our glasses. I had jumped back to the relative safety of the floor.

I took a sip, noting the quality difference between the wine Katie had brought and my cheap merlot. While I did, Katie took a far larger sip. Like she was trying to drain a quarter of the rougher tasting wine in one gulp.

'Do you mind if we sit down for a sec? There's something I wanted to talk to you about.'

We sat on the floor opposite each other. A pile of cold chips to our side and books and boxes lining the wall.

'It's about you and Izzy,' she said. I automatically sighed. It was beginning to become a drag that my past sins with Izzy would dictate every conversation I was to have with Katie.

'Nothing is going on with me and – '

'No, it's not about that – well, kind of about that. Oh, this is *not* easy.'

She put her glass down, covered her face with her hands, and took a deep breath.

'I am so pissed off with you.' Contrary to her words she had a big smile across what were suddenly very pink cheeks.

'And I don't want to be friends.' Again, the big smile making me feel highly confused.

'And I don't think you want to be just friends either?'

'*Just* friends?' I said, staring at her carefully as she smiled.

'It hurt, you sleeping together. And I didn't want to be around you when it happened again, even though I had Ethan. It's not fair. It's not that nice of me. But I was pissed off that you would have a relationship or sleep with someone else while being friends with me. There, that's it. That's me being honest.'

My eyes nervously flicked to the bottle of wine and then to her glass. I had no idea what she was saying. She seemed sober when we were standing up, now she was telling me she didn't want to be my friend if I slept with another person?

'Katie, I really don't understand what you're asking me here. You only want to be friends with me if I stop seeing other people?'

She rolled her eyes. She picked up her wine and took another sip before stretching behind her and placing the glass at the wall. She then rose to her knees, leaned toward me and placed a kiss on my lips. With her face close, she looked at me. She then looked down at my mouth again and closed her eyes. This time I kissed her back. She then stopped, gave me a smile, and knelt back down.

'I'm saying *friends* don't snog each other *three* times.'

'At Ruskin though, you said – '

'Yes! I did. And it is weird! And at the gallery it completely wasn't the right time, and I wasn't in the right place. But I like you. And it still feels too soon after Ethan, but I also wanted something to happen with us while I was still with him.' She then gave a big shrug and began laughing.

'I am not selling this well, am I? I would completely understand if you wanted me to go.'

'No, I'd like you to stay.' I reached for her hand, more as a test than a romantic gesture. She beamed and took it.

'So,' she half-smiled and then looked around us. 'Should we try to get some more of these packed away, or...' She raised her eyebrows and bit her lip. I leaned over and kissed her.

We were entwined on the floor. My right arms cradled the small of her back, and my left lay just under her head. Her hands were running under my t-shirt and up my sides. Both Katie's legs were hooked around my waist, allowing us to press together. It was like we were teenagers – kissing and rolling around on the floor un-choreographed like it was both the first and last night of our lives.

'Scott,' Katie said and stopped kissing me. She took a breath. 'Do you think we could stop for a second?'

'Oh. Yes. I didn't mean to – '

'It's not that.' I climbed off her, and she sat up. 'I guess I want to be consistent, and when I say we should take it slow not just pick and choose the fun stuff.'

'Fun stuff?' I couldn't help but grin as a warm smile shone across her face. Trying to savour the moment, I sat back down and picked up my glass, as did Katie.

'And if something does happen between us, I don't know if your Dad's study with all his things piled around us is the best location.'

Again, I felt a bit of a schoolboy smile rising. I was not sure what we had done was classed as a drunken fumble or was us finally breaking the ice. I had no idea what we were supposed to do now or what taking it slow meant in practice. I just felt this bubbling of elation, like I was about to get everything I wanted, and then this sinking dread that surely I would miss out again. But then they both seemed to dampen down as I watched Katie. She looked so cute in her pink hoodie. It reminded me of her oversized dressing gown. I suddenly felt this huge sense of relief. I was not a competition winner. Katie was not a prize, and my happiness was not tied to whether or not she chose to have feelings for me. I had my friend back. Someone I cared about was now sitting opposite me, sipping a glass of bad merlot and helping me pick up old books to place into boxes. I should allow myself just to enjoy that moment. But before that, I did need to address one last elephant in the room.

'How are things between you and Ethan?'

Katie made a snorting noise and puffed out her cheeks.

'Is he being any more reasonable about the flat?'

'I'm kind of ignoring him, to be honest. With him living over in Berlin and not showing much interest in doing any of this face to face, it's actually been a relatively civilised breakup. But I'm not sure how much I like him as a person. Or me when I was with him. Does that make any sense?'

She scrunched her face up, perhaps trying to understand what she was saying as much as look for understanding.

'Do you still... have feelings for him?' It was not the question I wanted to ask, but I did anyway. Katie let out a sigh.

'I'm not going to lie to you, Scott. I'm not a sociopath. There is always going to be something there for someone I was with for seven years. But...' She paused to put down the books in her hands. 'But last time. If I'm being *completely* honest that kiss was because of Ethan. I wanted to feel sexy. Prove to myself I didn't need him and ended up making a total fool of myself.'

'And tonight?'

She shrugged. But with a small smile.

'Who knows. I'm surrounded by rare, amazing books, drinking wine and eating chips, and am in the company of someone with whom I enjoy spending time. Not much room in my head for much else.'

She then leaned over and planted another kiss on my mouth before grinning and getting to her feet.

'That's your lot, for now. We've still got a lot to do and it's not getting any earlier. Perhaps we should switch rooms, go for a quick win.'

The quick win was my army of Games Workshop models and figurines. I told Katie that was Ellie's main request and as long as those were not still upon every shelf and surface we could get away with the other rooms being works in progress. She seemed to find this new bolt of energy, and I followed her upstairs and stood in the doorway watching her survey my bedroom.

'Scott, you've not even started!'

'I was trying to get the study done!'

She rolled her eyes and found herself again picking up my model of Estella, Warrior Queen.

'Really? Nothing to do with not wanting to say goodbye to this young lady? Or her little girlfriends? Says a lot for female empowerment that women can serve in battle just as long as they have slender figures, large breasts, and only fight in their underwear.'

'They have *some* armour,' I said a little defensively.

'We'll do these first. There's a half-empty box with your name I just started downstairs, we'll add Queen Whatshername and her – I assume – *bi-sexual* minions to that.'

I smirked at the newfound bossiness and did what I was told. I left the room and went back downstairs to the study. Collecting said box, I returned, expecting to either see Katie still making fun of my collection or decluttering all my comics and graphic novels.

'Okay, I've got it. Now, where would you – '

Bizarrely, the first thing I noticed was the little pile of neatly folded clothes on my bed. A pair of jeans way smaller than any I owned, a pink hoodie, and two purple tiny socks. Then standing at the end of my bed was Katie, dressed just in a black bra and underwear, still holding Queen Estella.

'What do you think?' she said, as I very much stood open-mouthed, staring at every inch of her, like I was in a dream.

'I saw this at a store while shopping with the girls.' So casually, she gestured to her smooth black bra and matching pants. 'Made me think of our little friend here. Am I appropriately attired to wage wars and join the Sisterhood of the Not-Wearing-Much?'

She smiled and put Estella down. I felt a little light-headed as my blood was rushing somewhere else.

As I cautiously walked over to her, she bit her lip in a completely seductive way and put her arms around my shoulders.

'I thought you wanted to take it slowly?'

She nodded and put on an innocent pouty face.

'Yes, but maybe starting tomorrow?'

I was about to kiss her, hoping my jeans which were positively choking me could quickly join hers on the bed, but she swung her head back.

'Scott, no one else has been here, right? You've still not done anything here with anyone?'

'You mean Izzy?' I smiled.

'That's exactly who I mean.'

'No, then.'

'Good,' she smiled and kissed me.

CHAPTER 35

MESH

Light was coming through the window when I opened my eyes. It was not a dream. A mesh of wavy brown and gold hair rested on the neighbouring pillow and a bare shoulder had crept out from under the duvet. I yawned, and as I did, she rolled and looked at me.

'Morning,' I said. My mouth felt dry from the wine. 'Have you been awake long?'

'Just a couple of minutes. Your phone went off. I think you've got a message.'

I looked down the bed. Our clothes must have fallen to the floor and with them my phone. Katie rolled onto her back and tucked the duvet up to her chin. It felt appropriate I then lay face up too.

We didn't say anything. Or more precisely, she didn't say anything and I wasn't sure if the silence was comfortable or awkward.

'That was – '

'Oh please don't, Scott. Let's not, can we?' She looked at me pleadingly and then hid her face under the duvet.'

'I was going to say lovely.'

'Ha!' came a muffled laugh. 'No it wasn't. It was embarrassing.

Very nice from my side, but well, it's not normally the woman who has to begin the pillow talk with, *that normally never happens.*'

I couldn't help laughing. She looked so attractive lying in my bed, her head on my pillow, covered under my duvet. I had no idea how to tell her I honestly didn't mind.

'You were just tired.'

'I can't believe I fell asleep! While you were essentially in... mid-act.' Katie let out a large groan, and I saw her hands rush to her mouth. From under the duvet a muffled voice again said, 'I just want to say I didn't expect you to do that. You know. *The first bit.* I don't want to bring up any names considering where we are and what we've been doing but let's just say *no one* has done that to me for a while. And with the wine on top... Don't laugh!'

She flung herself forward, keeping the duvet tight to her chest as she sat up and hit me with a pillow.

'You should have woken me.'

'You looked so peaceful.'

'Oh, you're such a gentleman.' Scowling, she lowered herself back down.

'For complete transparency, I almost called you Ethan. While I was, you know.'

'No problem, I almost called you Izzy.'

She kicked me in the shin, still not seeing the funny side of the situation.

'Seriously, if she ever hears about this. I'm picturing her smug face right now as it happens. How's this for a perfectly normal morning after.'

I lifted my arm and brushed back some strands of hair that had fallen across her face. She flicked her eyes at me and then away again. I then turned over to kiss her. The feel of her lips still felt electrifying.

'I enjoyed spending the night with you.'

She laughed. 'Thanks, Prince Charming.' She rolled away onto her side but took my hand with her, placing it on her stomach. I then felt her wriggle. Only just so slightly. And then again.

'It's still early,' she said. 'Let's just go back to sleep, shall we?'

So we both fell back asleep. But not quite at first.

This time it was my phone ringing that woke us. As we stirred the caller seemed determined not to hang up.

'God, is that the time?' Katie picked up her watch from off my bedside table, trying both to quickly shuffle out of bed and keep herself covered with the duvet. I clambered naked out of bed and retrieved my phone while looking for my briefs.

'Where have you been? Why haven't you answered any of my bloody... any of my messages?'

'Sorry, just been asleep,' I told my sister.

'For Christ's sake, we're almost there. Seriously, Scott, if you've ended up getting pissed again and the house is in a state I'm totally going to lose it.'

'It's okay, we've done some.' I turned and looked at Katie. Bizarrely, she was covering her eyes with her hand. I literally could hear Ellie's eyes roll as she hung up.

'Are you okay?' I said to Katie. Her cheeks had gone pink, and she was smiling.

'Yes. But perhaps we should put on some clothes? It's just a bit weird suddenly seeing you so... *naked*.'

I reached down for my briefs. Katie lowered her hand, grinning, and asked if I could pass her clothes.

'Oh, God, I should have left ages ago.' Her cheeks had gone bright red.

'How long do we have before they arrive?'

'Ten minutes or so.'

'Shit.' She swung back into bed and began the cumbersome task of dressing under a blanket. 'Actually, do you mind if I quickly use your shower?'

As I went downstairs, I expected two things. First, the elation to kick in and feel the need to jump around at how happy I was. And second, those little monsters telling me that it would be short-lived. But neither materialised. Instead, I looked from the living room to the kitchen to the study, seeing the number of still unmade boxes and the number of things left unpacked. Ellie was going to kill me.

I then heard the lock of the front door rattle and it push open.

'Uncle Scott!' Millie had managed to burst through the house and into the kitchen in the split second it took me to look up from the kettle.

'You look funny,' she grinned. I assumed she was referring to my bed-hair and crumpled t-shirt. Millie raised her arms for me to pick her up and I obliged.

'You've got to be kidding me,' came my sister's voice from the next room. 'Seriously?' it said coming closer, and I quickly held Millie in front of me as a shield. Ellie entered the room carrying what looked like an entire supermarket of bags and glaring at me.

'It was a bit of a late one last night.'

'No shit. You had one bloody job.' She flung the bags on the kitchen table and seeing the empty first bottle of wine, thrust it up accusingly. 'It's not like we've been up at the crack of dawn or anything getting kids ready and putting all this in the car.'

Her voice tailed away as she left the room, not waiting for me to offer an excuse.

'Alright, mate,' said Mike, bringing in a large cool bag and what looked like a sack filled with the kids' stuff while shepherding a waddling Ed. 'You look like how I feel.'

He noticed my eyes fall on the bags.

'Two hours in Morrison's yesterday. Family outing and a chunk of my life I will never get back.'

'Why?' I scratched my head with the hand not holding Millie.

'Apparently we're making lunch, dinner, afternoon tea, whatever meal is most appropriate and when – '

'FOR FUCK'S SAKE!' came a bellowing roar from the study.

'Mummy said a bad word!' I put Millie down who ran towards the danger while I remained glued to the spot. Mike smirked and then raised his eyebrows like he was saying, *good luck!* I did, however, have to face the music.

'You complete...,' Ellie glared as I joined her in the study. 'It absolutely reeks in here. Vinegar and old fish. Oh and more wine I see.' She began trying to force the window open. I had forgotten that the stale chips had remained in paper on the rug while the bottle of wine sat incriminatingly next to it.

'You had one day not to be a prick.'

'Mummy, what's a *pwick*?'

'Ask Uncle Scott.'

'Auntie Katie!' Millie shouted and ran. I turned around to see Katie nervously emerging through the hallway, now fully dressed and with damp hair. Unsurprisingly she looked hesitant on whether to join us. If I had been her, I would have thrown me a glare about the lack of opportunity she had to make a discreet exit and then ran to the door. But she didn't.

'Hello again,' she said to Ellie and then stumbled back as the juggernaut that was Millie collided into her hip. 'Sorry, I'll clean that up – '

'Mummy, can Auntie Katie play with me?'

Chaos ensued as Millie began jumping up and down on the spot grabbing Katie's hand. I looked over at Ellie who was now staring at me, less furious.

'Maybe later, sweetie, Auntie Katie is going to help Mummy go to the shop and buy some air freshener. You get to be in charge of Uncle Scott.'

'It's fine. I want to help,' Katie whispered to me as I finally got her alone. Well, not quite alone. We were supervising Millie drawing in the living room while Ellie and Mike took over the kitchen.

'No one would have blamed you if you didn't come back after Ellie tried to corner you.'

'Oh she's fine. Great, in fact. We had a really nice chat. She really gets it.'

Gets what? I wanted to ask. They had been gone a lot longer than it takes to buy one can of air freshener from the newsagents.

'She asked me how I was after Christmas. A bit awkward considering the circumstances, but super kind of her.'

Katie was drawing a cartoon cat while Millie was apparently focused on creating a piece of modern art. With the amount of crayons she was using, the end result was sure to rival that of Jackson Pollock.

'Unless you want me to go? I should before your mum gets here. It would be weird if I stayed.'

'Weird is our thing though,' I smiled and said I should check if Ellie needed a hand.

The kitchen was like the behind-the-scenes at a restaurant during peak service, with Ed's occasional screeches a surprisingly accurate impression of a celebrity head chef.

'What did you think I was going to say to her?' Ellie laughed, a little scornfully. 'Scott, for once you've done something not entirely stupid and brought us a babysitter while we get all this done and then sit down with Mum.'

It was refreshing to see my sister return to her cynical self.

· · ·

They were early. We all convened in the hallway with Millie both excitedly and shyly gluing herself to Ellie's leg, and Ed held by Mike. Katie waited behind us.

'*How was the trip? How was the drive? Was there much traffic?*' There were a lot of polite questions and then some manoeuvring as the hallway was not designed for gatherings of eight or more. Ellie and I tried to do hugs, we tried to pick up a now very shy Millie who understandably seemed a little daunted meeting her grandmother for the first time, and when Conrad and Mike formed a bridge over the rest of us to shake hands it was time to move everyone into the living room.

'And what's your name, young lady?' said Orletta to Millie as the crowd dispersed, crouching down to look her in the eye. I had never seen Millie that shy, still hiding behind Ellie's legs. 'You are very beautiful.'

'Millie, this is your grandmother,' Ellie said in a gentle voice.

'Yes I am! And I'm very proud of you. You look just like your mummy.' She said the first part in the traditional baby voice but her last comment was more in awe. She gently reached to hold Millie's hand and could not stop staring at her granddaughter.

'I've been waiting a very long time to meet you.'

Orletta remained transfixed by both Millie and Ed as we sat everyone down and laid out the tea and finger sandwiches that Ellie and Mike had prepared. The kids were doing more drawings as we all took refreshments and continued to ask polite questions about Orletta and Conrad's holiday.

'More like a busman's holiday. Conrad had us touring vineyards and speaking to old colleagues who are also producing their own crop.'

Then, at what seemed to be a prearranged signal from Ellie, Katie asked Millie and Ed if they wanted to play outside.

'You don't have to do this,' I whispered to Katie, rushing to intercept her.

'I want to,' she said and squeezed my hand. It felt strange her doing that, like it was something we didn't do. But it was also intensely reassuring.

I watched Millie running in circles on the lawn while Ed tried to catch her at a much slower pace, and then made my way back to the living room to join negotiations.

Orletta and Conrad had the sofa, and Mike and Ellie had squeezed themselves into one armchair. I, therefore, took the vacant armchair.

'She is beautiful,' said Orletta. 'And Edward, of course too, but I can't believe just how grown up she is.'

Our mother closed her eyes, rubbed them, and when she reopened them they were slightly watery.

'Apologies, I'm a little overwhelmed, to be completely honest.'

Ellie and I exchanged nervous glances. We had indeed planned to use the family reunion to emotionally blackmail our mother into a slightly more generous settlement, but now it seemed morally repugnant.

'We don't have to do this today,' I said leaning forward.

'Listen, Mum, there's a better way to have done this. Let's just bring the kids back in and we can talk over the phone or something another day.'

'And what if there's not another day, Eleanor?' smiled our mother, giving her eyes a dab with a tissue. 'Heaven knows we've lost so much time already. You have been busy.' She nodded at the boxes on the dining table.

'And Katie seems lovely, Scott.' She sounded almost as surprised as I was.

'Oh, don't bring that up. He'll only say they're just friends,' Ellie interrupted.

'Mum, we'd like to keep a lot of Dad's things. We don't want to let them go to auction. If you're happy to let us, we'll call off the lawyers and adjudication.'

I don't know what we were expecting but the response was very civil. Orletta gave a small quarter smile and then placed her tea cup on the coffee table.

'Eleanor, when I asked the auction house to catalogue your father's possessions, I did not intend to sell them off to the highest bidders. I called them because it had been a difficult time, and they have experience in dealing with the more painful aspects of an estate. They can sort through each item without memory after memory overwhelming the process. It was not my intention to hurt either of you.'

It seemed a long time ago now that I found Ellie upstairs in the house after our falling out about the *Watership Down* letter. There had been a lot of fences to mend that year and bridges to rebuild. We could have spoken to our mother rather than go straight to solicitors, but then we assumed she had stopped caring, and as ridiculous as it would sound, we were too scared to speak to her in case it was true.

'You still want to sell?' I asked quietly, breaking the silence.

My mother caught my gaze and gave me a small, sad nod.

'It holds too many memories for me. And we can do so much good at the Colony with the funds.'

Again came that glowing warm smile. The smile that made me feel twelve again. Reassured and safe.

'We had so many happy years as a family. It seems only right that another family take it on and start their own story.'

Ellie and I looked at each other again. She gave me a quick defeated smile and raised her eyebrows. We might have reached the end of the road.

'I assume, if you do not want to challenge probate anymore, perhaps we should talk about the settlement?'

Again Ellie and I glanced over to each other. She gave me a half frown and a small shake of the head.

'Actually, no,' I said. 'If you're happy that Ellie has the piano and we split up Dad's books, I think he would have wanted you to have the house for your...' The anti-hippy in me could not bring myself to say the word *Colony*, '... for your *project*. Your expansion. We think Dad would have liked what you have planned.'

And there ended the mystery of the will. Not that we would truly know Dad's intentions – the man who filed and kept track of everything so meticulously does not sign his divorce papers or leave a will – but we no longer needed to ask. If t*he Colony* did make a difference to one life and ward off those dark thoughts lurking in the shadows, perhaps Ellie and I could find our own peace.

'There will be something for you,' said Conrad. 'And something for your children – Orletta's grandchildren.'

'No need,' mumbled Ellie. 'Things will work themselves out. They always do.' I have to say, my sister did not have the greatest poker face. We had discussed this all, but now that push came to shove, she wasn't exactly masking a lack of enthusiasm. 'Scott and I both need to get on with things. After all, if Dad was still here we wouldn't be going to him cap in hand asking him to bail out our life choices. Best leave that to the Generation Zs.'

It seemed to break the tension. Ellie was probably the only one not to at least smirk as Mike then took her hand and placed it in his. Our mother, the artist Orletta Roberts, then slid forward on the sofa and just stared at us, her head tilted to the side. Like we were the Turner on the gallery wall.

'Your father was so proud of you. Of *both* of you.'

I think it was the mention of Dad and *proud* in the past tense that started Ellie and me off. This time it was not a deluge, rather just a rogue leakage. We both tried to wipe away the tears without them being noticeable, and I felt myself put on a smile to detract from that strange sadness I suddenly felt. It was over. Dad was gone. I had to let go – of him and of the past – and I still did not feel ready to do that. As Ellie went to call the kids back in, my mind landed on the image of Dad in his study leaning back in his leather chair, his record player spinning and a 1950s jazz singer serenading him while he read Fitzgerald for the umpteenth time.

It is fair to recognise that our pasts play a defining role in the person we become, but it is also worth acknowledging that it is always a selected version of the past. Or perhaps that's just me. My memory would isolate those solitary moments when I was an awkward teenager spending Saturday nights at home to explain why depression would stalk me in shadowy corners at the age of thirty-five. The disappearance of a mother would underpin a pining for female companionship and sense of unworthiness. But then, what about those joy-filled moments as a child aged six or seven, playing games with my sister, running in circles chasing each other, carefree? What about those basement bars aged twenty-one to twenty-five, dancing with no inhibitions, jumping about with my friends around me like I was that young child again?

There were times in my life when I was introverted. There were times when I was weird and wonderful. And there were probably many times in my life – undocumented and I do not have the data to back this up – when I was the same as everyone else. Introverts, extroverts, what does it matter as long as we step out of ourselves now and again and forget about the people we once were, take a deep breath and do something that makes the person we are now happy.

'What do we do now?' I asked Ellie as everyone allowed us both a few moments alone outside, not even pretending to smoke.

'Call the estate agents? Get the For Sale sign. Clear out the rest of Dad's stuff.'

We both leaned back against the conservatory doors listening to the wind rustle through the bushes and trees lining our garden.

'After that? With our lives, I mean.'

'You mean our pact? Who can make their life less shit first?'

Ellie took out a crumpled packet of cigarettes from her back pocket. She had a look at the contents and then deftly threw it into a small metal bin we had out there next to our old brick barbecue.

'Carry on, I guess. Stop whinging about Ji-Qei being a better pianist than me or Emily Brunswick having a perfect arse when she's also had two kids.' Ellie sighed and crossed her arms and I found myself mimicking her – little brother copying his older sister – as we stood resting against the glass doors waxing lyrical, neither of us used to being that emotionally spent. Ellie then gave a small, ironic-sounding laugh.

'Or I could actually do something about it and take up Perky Tits' offer of coffee and a chat despite me resenting everything she stands for. And that I know full well it won't lead anywhere. I should also take some solace in the fact I have two lovely children who aren't complete monsters like Alice Horton's, who also has ten grand spare for a boob job and her tits are *still* smaller than mine.'

I smiled, thinking what Camille would say. Probably, something about there being a critical side in each of us, judging how we are not achieving enough compared to whoever is next door. 'Hey, standards can be a good thing, they stop us hibernating on our couch all day eating Cheerios from the box in our PJs,' I think she once said. 'But they can be unrelenting. Uncontrolled. Insatiable. Being happy and overachieving are not necessarily the same thing. You're allowed to spend a weekend watching a whole series of

Breaking Bad. Very few of us need to become Prime Minister of Norway by the age of thirty-four.'

Letting my head voice spring into a West Coast American accent left me with an inane grin, and it took me a moment to realise that Ellie and I were no longer alone.

'Hey,' said Katie, this awkward smile on her face, her canvas bag over her shoulder. 'I should be making a move.'

Clumsily, I asked to walk her to the station. She said it was fine, that she didn't want to interrupt the family time, and we continued our exchange in complete awkwardness until Ellie briefly said, 'For fuck's sake, just let him walk you to the station. And, Scott, try not to screw this up.'

Ellie also suggested we leave via the back and forgo the chaos of Millie demanding Auntie Katie stay forever. However, sneaking out of the house in total silence did have the unintended consequence that neither of us said a word until we were almost at the end of the street.

Listen, about last night... were the words I was dreading, yet anticipating being her first.

'We used to talk about you,' she then said, taking me off guard. 'The girls – me, Izzy, Tara and Sophie.'

'About anything... in particular?' We were on the road leading up to the high street. It was still quiet and suburban, and I glanced suspiciously at Katie.

'Your arms, mainly,' she smiled, this pink glow colouring her cheeks. 'And you're aloofness. How you would come back from gardening or whatever in sweat-soaked t-shirts, muscles bulging and acting all indifferent. Sophie and Tara giggling and asking you plant-based questions as you tried to run away.'

'I thought you were taking the piss out of me.'

'Oh, we were. We still thought you were a creep. Though a cute creep. With nice arms.'

Katie then stopped and looked at me. I needed to get in there first, be less passive for once in my life, stop her from saying it had all been a mistake.

'Listen, Katie, I know it's difficult right now – '

'Scott?' she smiled. 'I'm trying to say I like you. That it's not just since from last night.'

'Oh.'

'And today was nice. Surreal. But nice.'

It *was* awkward, but in a different way than I had imagined. We were standing opposite each other on a quiet street, just about to reach the main road, Katie's face now completely red, and I still stared at her waiting for her to say *but*...

'I like you too. But I think you might already know that,' I smiled, looking back at those beautiful eyes and Katie's smiling mouth. 'So, what should we do from here?'

'Honestly?' Katie scrunched up her face, looking a little uncertain. 'This maybe a bit prudish and traditional, but I'd quite like it if you ask me out. On a first date.'

I laughed. This rush of relief almost knocked me off my feet as we stood together, and I stepped forward to hold her hands.

'Would you go on a date with me? Thursday next week, perhaps?'

Katie stared back into my eyes and then, after a moment, frowned.

'Next week's not great. I'm meant to be cleaning the flat on Thursday and, oh, don't get me started on how busy work is. Maybe next month? Actually, July might be more doable – '

Before she could say any more I leaned forward and kissed her.

THREE MONTHS LATER

It was a peculiar journey. Not one I would have envisioned myself making a few months before either out of need or in that company – me, Katie, Jane, and Auntie Pam on the 8.47 from Paddington. Katie and I had met them both at the station and we spent three hours on the train together with a table to ourselves having a 'packed breakfast' and antiquities review.

'Tuck in, I'm loath to waste money on the buffet carriage. Complete rubbish! All at exorbitant prices. In Addis Ababa we would make sausage and bacon rolls out of injera and have it with shiro first thing at the dig site.'

Auntie Pam gave us the traditional tour around world heritage sites as our train made its way through the southwest on what looked a perfect summer's day. I was not sure if Katie was genuinely as interested in Auntie Pam's stories as she kept letting on with her open-mouthed gasps and infinite questions. Instead, I traded wry smiles with Jane, who put her glasses on and brought out a novel.

'It does feel a waste, spending money on a full train journey when my Freedom Pass could have got me virtually to Gatwick, and your sister could have picked me up from there. I was quite happy to sit in the back with the children but I guess this makes more sense since Jane is joining us.'

Not to discredit Jane, but I had initially been surprised when Ellie had announced she had invited her to our mother's do. However, it all began to make sense when the travel arrangements – or moreover, the alternative travel arrangements – were laid out.

Instead, we were picked up by the familiar Volvo at a pretty village station. I felt the still unfamiliar feeling of a hand sliding into mine as the girl in the summer dress waved to Mike, and we loaded everyone and our respective overnight bags into the station wagon.

'The kids are having a field day. Literally. We have to keep an eye out Millie doesn't make a break for it and sprint into the next county.'

This time we were pre-warned of the day's events. We would have the afternoon to recuperate and change, and the other guests would start arriving in the early evening. Still, it did feel surreal attending my recently reconciled mother's wedding. Especially considering it was taking place on the same day I had been born.

Ellie had travelled down the day before as, probably even more surreal for her, she was asked to be my mother's bridesmaid. Despite it being her second wedding, our mother had kept with tradition and had arranged a night for them both away from *the Colony* so that her groom would not see her before the wedding. Arriving at the house, back on that cream gravel, it felt strange not to see either Ellie or my mother as we walked in. However, more worrying was seeing a pretty girl in a waitress outfit give me a big smile and a small wave while the rest of the catering staff laid out tables in the conservatory and on the patio. Luckily, at the same time, we were bombarded by the squeals of Millie and Ed, misdirecting Katie's attention. They were followed by Conrad and the ever-present Maxwell, who shepherded us all into the dining room for a glass of champagne.

And then there were just the two of us. Katie and I were staying in one of our mother's guest rooms and we laid our things out on the bed in preparation for getting changed. I then felt her arms around me.

'Nervous?' she said.

'Nothing to be nervous about. We just sit back and neck the free champagne.'

'About the whole your-mother-getting-married-again thing, I mean. Izzy had a fit when her dad got engaged. That wasn't pretty.'

I saw her smile slightly which made me laugh.

'Who would have thought Conrad would pop the question after twenty years. It's fine. We're coping. It does feel a bit weird with Dad not being here and the whole situation.'

As we stood at the end of the bed, she then kissed me as if passing on courage.

'Happy birthday, by the way.'

She kissed me again.

'Thanks,' I sighed.

'One thing though,' she said, her arms around my neck looking up at me. 'Who was that girl downstairs? The one who waved to you.'

Surprisingly, Katie and I had only had one falling out in the months that we had been dating – I say surprising considering the number of arguments we had when we were not dating. I had received a message while we were having dinner and must have gone slightly coy as she teased me whether I had another woman. She then playfully snatched away my phone, laughing, about to tease me with what she probably expected was another elderly lady asking if I could do some weeding for her. Instead, a girl called Lydia was telling me she and her friend Etta would be in London at the weekend and asked if I wanted to *chill with them – no strings*.

This wasn't the full argument. After trying to explain the situation, I did also say it would be a bit awkward not to reply at all as Lydia did, at times, work for my mother, so in my infinite wisdom while Katie was sitting in front of me, I replied telling Lydia it was not a good idea as I was spending the weekend with my girlfriend. Unfortunately, I had not anticipated Lydia's response.

Bring her xx You know I'm not averse to a bit of a group thing ;-)

The ceremony began with fifty or so of us all sitting outside on folding chairs. My first glimpse of my mum and Ellie was when they walked up the gangway to meet Conrad at the front overlooking the vineyard. She looked beautiful. Majestic. She wore silver and had a bouquet of red and white roses. Ellie also looked unrecognisable. She was not wearing jeans or casuals, but had her hair and makeup done and wore a purple satin dress. The only thing that could distract me from that moment was Katie, next to me, hand in my hand.

'There you are,' said Ellie, finding me after the formalities were over. I was looking out over the vines and fields. The sun was finally setting on the late summer's day, and I had escaped my dinner table to take a moment by myself.

'Well, aren't you going to compliment me on my speech?'

'I don't need to,' I smiled. 'People were practically wetting themselves. Dangerous considering the average age.' She punched me on the arm. I still had my glass of topped-up champagne from the toasts and took another sip.

'It was lovely. What you said about Mum. What you said about Dad. What you said about Conrad, well, what you said about everyone really. In fact I couldn't believe it was you talking.'

Another punch, and then she sipped from her own glass.

'They're looking for you. There's going to be dancing before the happy couple make a move – they're staying at some fancy five-star, which is good for Mike and me as we can haul up with the kids in their room. And good for you too as they'll be no parentals under the same roof when you and Katie start going at it.'

'There's Auntie Pam still. And Jane. And, Katie's... well...'

'*Blotto*?'

'I was going to say we're still taking it slow.'

'Yeah, right. This is the girl who has literally just been talking my ear off for half an hour about if you had started to find her boring and what she could do to make you more interested.'

I literally spurted my champagne all over the vines.

'She's said that? How on earth – '

'Don't be a prick. And stop dancing around her like you're both teenagers. You're a couple. Knowing you, you probably love the pretty little weirdo, and if so, you're very much suited to each other. But right now that girl is practically crying into her champagne because she thinks you fancy a slutty waitress called Lydia.'

I made to go back into the party, but Ellie grabbed my arm and pulled me back.

'But that's not why I wanted to talk to you. I've got good news. Guess who is writing the score for a drama?'

Ellie beamed, probably the biggest smile I had ever seen her give, and I firmly broke our family tradition and hugged her.

'It's only for some random channel nobody watches, but Perky Tits got me the gig, so I should really say some nice things about her. That with Mike's new job at Guildhall starting in September, we're quite the Bohemian household. Still broke. But musicians, through and through.'

I felt delighted. And relieved. *The Musician* would not only remain *the Musician* but would become one of two. It was probably the one thing Dad did get wrong, giving Mike his nickname. Perhaps, I like to think, it was because he knew Ellie was not just a musician but a prodigy, and music would always be part of her.

'Plus, on being broke, Auntie Pam's just announced she's considering selling up and joining her retired *chums* down in Worthing.'

Ellie took another sip of champagne, but this time a much larger one.

'And?'

'And nothing. She's offered us a bit of a hand if we want to buy somewhere bigger with her profits. London property, eh? But to be honest, it might not be too bad having her close. Keep your friends close, your enemies... You know the drill.'

She finished the remaining drops from her glass and we walked back toward the house. However, this time we were intercepted by the groom holding a thick-looking envelope. 'Scott, a quick word?'

Ellie went back inside as he steered me to the edge of the patio while the catering staff put away the outside chairs from the ceremony.

'Sorry to bring this up. Today of all days. But how is business going? Your gardening business?'

It seemed a strange question considering it was his wedding day, but I tried to answer the best I could.

'Alright. Got a few more jobs on now it's summer. Enough to pay the rent anyway.'

He looked down at the paving stones like he was taking careful consideration of what I was saying.

'Well, this may throw a spanner in the works.'

He handed me the envelope. It looked like some legal document and for a moment I thought he was suing me for rent arrears from my months staying at Dad's.

'I've bought that patch of land I told you about. To expand the vineyard. Well, Orletta's expanding her project so I thought I might as well mine.'

There were countless pages, but then Conrad had placed a large cross where a set of signatures were. There was his name and his signature, and then there was my name.

'I can't do it by myself. Not at my age anyway. Like I said, this isn't the best time but your mother and I will be away for a month. I need a partner. Someone who can put in the hard yards while I put in the capital. It will be a lot of work, but who knows, more land will come up, we could turn this into quite the venture. My contacts in Burgundy have offered to train you up – that would mean you taking some time off from your own business...'

Just at that moment music began to play, and Conrad looked at his watch.

'Listen, I must dash, but at least give it some thought. I can call you from Pisa to discuss it further and I've put in there some of the *relevants* regarding my fellows in Burgundy. Now seriously, your mother will have my guts for garters if I miss the first dance for my own wedding.'

Conrad left me, and I remained glued to the spot, shell-shocked, repeatedly turning over the papers and then glancing out at the vines. What did I know about wine? I was a lager man and my farming experience was largely vegetable crops. And I couldn't just up and leave my fledgling gardening business especially for a venture that would most likely take a few years to turn a profit. In a way, it seemed more like a way for Conrad to rope in some free labour just by putting my name on a piece of paper. A piece of paper that named me as a partner in an actual vineyard. Practicalities be damned, I could not help feeling a huge burst of excitement. As excited as Millie would be if you mentioned a visit from Auntie Katie. I put the documents back in the envelope and slotted it into my suit pocket, realising I too was meant to join the dancing.

As I reached the entrance, I saw that they had quickly trans-formed the conservatory into a full disco with cheesy lighting and everything. My mother and Conrad were already on the dancefloor and more surprisingly, jiving – yes, *jiving* – around the room to what I recognised as Sam Cooke's *'Twistin' the Night Away'*. Ellie and Mike, and another couple joined them and I suddenly remem-bered what Ellie said about Katie. I needed to find her and tell her that I was the boring one and the last thing I wanted to do with her was keep taking it slow. But then I saw her on the other side of the dancefloor.

She seemed to be having another heart to heart, her hand on the arm of a woman wearing a white blouse whose back was turned to me, talking earnestly and looking at her intently. I knew I needed to go up to her to tell her what was in my head, but I found myself just enjoying looking at her. I smiled at that kind-hearted manner and how much she loved engaging with people. She gave me more confidence in myself, and in every way, I knew I loved her. She then saw me. Her companion also turned around. I instantly felt a burst of panic as Lydia stared over at me, this amused smile on her face. What on earth were they talking about? But then the panic and the misplaced guilt faded. All I wanted to do was march across the dancefloor, take Katie in my arms and twist the night away with her. So I did. And she did not object.

Before they left for their luxury hotel – in what looked like a Bentley that awaited them on the gravel – my mother gathered Ellie and me and pulled us away from the remaining crowd who had come to wave them off. 'Thank you both so much, this has meant the world.' Both Ellie and I typically responded with a mumbling, 'we didn't do anything, it's been your day' and so on.

'Scott,' she took my hands. 'Do something about that girl. Don't you dare let her slip through your fingers or, for a second, not make her feel appreciated.' Again, I bashfully told her that I would not.

'And please tell Pamela it was lovely of her to make it. Her letter meant a great deal to me, and it was wonderful having a long chat. And the same with Jane, I was glad she accepted our invitation.'

'Us too,' I said. 'Dad and Jane being such close friends, it feels like part of him was here too.' I felt another welling about to develop in my eyes, and Mum put her hand on my cheek.

'Oh, sweetie,' she said just like she did when I was little. 'I think we all know they were more than just friends.'

With that revelation, Mum returned to the Bentley and acknowledged her public, bouquet in hand. But rather than throwing it, Mum walked it over to the onlookers and handed it to a very surprised Katie who went typically bright pink. And with a lot of cheering and raised champagne flutes we then waved them off and watched the Bentley roll away.

'Oh my God, you're an actual landowner,' beamed Katie sitting cross-legged on the bed as I told her the story of Conrad and the vineyard.

'Hardly, it's probably not practical.'

'Oh Scott! It sounds like everything you want to do. Who cares if it's not practical!'

We were sitting with mugs of coffee, and the only people left downstairs were the catering crew who had practically turned Mum's house into an extension of the local bed and breakfast. All the rooms were occupied by fellow wedding guests, and we were told that the team would stay at *the Colony* to provide breakfast in the morning and make sure everyone was settled overnight. We were even given a number to order room service, which did feel one step too far.

'And how are you feeling?' I asked my smiling girlfriend. 'Ellie told me a bit about your chat.'

'Oh, please don't remind me!' Katie through her head into her arms. 'That was so embarrassing,' she said through a nest of hair and then sat back up, again looking quite pink.

'Too much champagne on an empty stomach. Hence I stopped drinking after dinner and went to town on the cakes and sandwiches. One hundred percent sober now.' She sat up straight, demonstrating her sobriety, and then reached over and grabbed my hands.

'It's just weddings. They bring out a few insecurities and it's nothing to do with you. You're great!' I felt this jolt of pride and just looked at how radiant she was in her beautiful red dress with her hair and makeup still perfect.

'I wanted to tell you,' I began. 'I think you are the most amazing – '

'Seriously, Scott, you don't have to,' she laughed. 'It's more how I've been feeling. Not just recently, but for years in a way. It does kind of stem from your nights of passion with Izzy, but I do get a little fed up with everyone seeing me as *Katie the nice girl, Katie Little Miss Perfect.*'

'You really have to stop listening to anything Izzy says about that. She's actually a bit all-talk, if you must know.'

'Scott, are you really about to tell me how sex with my best friend was?'

She just gave me a look, and I knew we needed to change the subject sharpish as an awkward silence crept in.

'And speaking of your conquests, I had a chat with that Lydia girl...'

'Katie, seriously, nothing – '

'Oh, relax.' Katie placed her mug on the bedside table and stretched her legs out. 'I'm teasing. She told me what a gentleman you were. Which is a bit of a shame as I actually found her quite sweet.' She winked at me, still teasing. 'But anyway, it's not about her or Izzy or anyone. Just because I don't go around making innuendos or alluding to nights of passion with half the rugby club or girls' volleyball team doesn't make me prudish.' She frowned and looked at me hard as if making sure I was following her. 'Perhaps I just think what goes on behind closed doors should stay there and not relay the details to a best friend who, as much as I love her, I know will broadcast the details around my friendship group within a week. Perhaps I'm not as averse to having a wild side as people think. Who knows. Maybe. One day.'

She then smiled and let out a deep breath, flinging herself back onto the pillows.

I wanted to tell her that I found each moment with her wild and exhilarating, but I didn't need to. She looked happy. Content, and a little bit tired, lying on the bed. She reached to the other side of the bed and picked up her pyjamas. As long as she was happy, I was happy, and nothing could have pleased me more than just lying with her and holding her through the night.

She glanced at her watch and swung her legs off the bed, pyjamas in hand.

'I'll just get ready for bed,' she said and walked to our little ensuite. I was still in my shirt and suit trousers and walked around the bed to take my cufflinks off, thinking back to the events of the day. There was a knock at the door.

'Do you mind getting that?' said Katie sticking her head around the ensuite's door. 'This is a bit cheeky, but I asked the guys down-stairs if they could send up a bottle of champagne once they were done. I really fancied one more glass but didn't want to get tipsy again in front of everyone.'

She returned to the bathroom and I went to the door.

'Champagne, sir?' Lydia was outside our room holding a bottle and glasses.

'Ask her to bring it to the bed,' came Katie's voice. Lydia smiled at me. I didn't know if I was just uncomfortable that it was she who brought us the champagne, but I felt her smile slightly on the mischievous side.

'You heard the lady,' she said and handed me the champagne bottle, walking past me into the room. I stood at the door glancing between the empty hallway and the bottle, wondering why I was holding it, and then suddenly felt another surge of panic. Lydia was now in our bedroom while Katie was getting ready for bed.

I spun around. She was sitting on the end of the bed leaning back, glasses in one hand and still smiling.

'Lydia, sorry, but I think you better leave – '

I heard the door to the ensuite open and shot a terrified look to Katie. She wasn't wearing her pyjamas. Instead, just the expensive-looking underwear she had been wearing under her dress. Lydia grinned at her and handed her a champagne flute.

'Scott, you're doing a pretty rubbish job of hosting. Lydia's glass is still empty.'

I stared between the two trying not to let my imagination get the better of me as Katie sat next to our guest.

'I hope you don't mind. Lydia's shift finished a while back, so I asked her to join us.' Katie stared up at me.

'I only brought two glasses,' said Lydia, still grinning but now staring very intently at Katie. They were very close to each other. Their faces only a few inches apart.

'It's okay. I don't mind sharing. At least just this one-off. What goes on behind closed doors and that.'

ACKNOWLEDGMENTS

I'd like to thank Christopher Harris, Jon Bradley, Robert Murphy and David Smallbone for their support, sanctuary and inspiration during the real Exmouth Market and Loughborough Road days. Also Arlene Mosley and Leona Perumal for their love, advice and encouragement.

I am grateful to Curtis Brown Creative and the Faber Academy for their support during the writing process and to Julia Gibbs for an outstanding job editing this novel. Any errors are all mine.

I'd like to thank all the team at Indie Novella for the hard work and hours that went into bringing this novel to life. A truly inspirational publisher! Also the team at Become Psychology London and would recommend anyone who occasionally feels the same as Scott, Ellie or Katie visit www.become-psychology-london.co.uk.

The National's *Sleep Well Beast* was both soothing and an inspiration and I ask leniency and forgiveness for my interpretation and ramblings.

Finally, love and gratitude to the woman who changed my life, Jessica Garvey Birch, for her love, encouragement and inspiration.

|i
n

Indie Novella

www.indienovella.co.uk

EXMOUTH MARKET

RUSKIN PARK

LOUGHBOROUGH ROAD

WOOD GREEN

BLOOMSBURY

BARBICAN

GREEN PARK

BRIGHTON

DEVON